Scandalous Secrets

MARION LENNOX
MICHELLE DOUGLAS
NINA MILNE

MILLS & BOON

First Published in Great Britain 2019
by Mills & Boon, an imprint of HarperCollins*Publishers*
1 London Bridge Street, London, SE1 9GF

SCANDALOUS SECRETS © 2019 Harlequin Books S. A.

Stranded With The Secret Billionaire © 2017 Marion Lennox
Sarah And The Secret Sheikh © 2017 Michelle Douglas
Claiming His Secret Royal Heir Nina Milne © 2017 Nina Milne

This work includes words based on 'THE SERENITY PRAYER' by Reinhold Niebuhr.

ISBN: 978-0-263-27482-0

0319

MIX
Paper from
responsible sources
FSC® C007454

This book is produced from independently certified FSC™ paper to ensure responsible forest management.

For more information visit: www.harpercollins.co.uk/green

Printed and bound in Spain
by CPI, Barcelona

STRANDED WITH
THE SECRET
BILLIONAIRE

MARION LENNOX

This book is dedicated to the memory of Grace,
the warmest, most generous mother-in-law a woman
could wish for—and the baker of the world's best
ginger fluff sponge!

CHAPTER ONE

THE IMPECCABLE ENGLISH ACCENT had directed Penelope Hindmarsh-Firth twelve hundred kilometres across two states without a problem. From 'Take the third exit after the Harbour Tunnel', as Penny had navigated her way out of Sydney, to 'Continue for two hundred kilometres until you reach the next turn', as she'd crossed South Australia's vast inland farming country, the cultured voice hadn't faltered.

True, the last turn had made Penny uneasy. The accent had told her to proceed for thirty kilometres along the Innawarra Track, but it had hesitated over the pronunciation of Innawarra. Penny had hesitated too. The country around them was beautiful, lush and green from recent rains and dotted with vast stands of river red gums. The road she'd been on had been narrow, but solid and well used.

In contrast, the Innawarra Track looked hardly used. It was rough and deeply rutted.

Penny's car wasn't built for rough. She was driving her gorgeous little sports car. Pink. The car had been her father's engagement gift to her, a joyful signal to the world that Penny had done something he approved of.

That hadn't lasted. Of course not—when had pleasing her father lasted? Right now she seemed to be doing a whole lot wrong.

She was facing a creek crossing. It had been raining hard up north. She'd heard reports of it on the radio but hadn't taken much notice. Now, what looked to be a usually dry creek bed was running. She got out of the car, took off her pink sandals and walked across, testing the depth.

Samson was doing no testing. Her little white poodle stood in the back seat and whined, and Penny felt a bit like whining too.

'It's okay,' she told Samson. 'Look, it only comes up to my ankles, and the nice lady on the satnav says this is the quickest way to Malley's Corner.'

Samson still whined, but Penny climbed back behind the wheel and steered her little car determinedly through the water. There were stones underneath. It felt solid and the water barely reached the centre of her tyres. So far so good.

Her qualms were growing by the minute.

She'd estimated it'd take her two hours tops to reach Malley's, but it was already four in the afternoon and the road ahead looked like an obstacle course.

'If worst comes to worst we can sleep in the car,' she told Samson. 'And we're getting used to worst, right?'

Samson whined again but Penny didn't. The time for whining was over.

'Malley's Corner, here I come,' she muttered. 'Floods or not, I'm never turning back.'

Matt Fraser was a man in control. He didn't depend on luck. Early in life, luck had played him a sour hand and he hadn't trusted in it since.

When he was twelve, Matt's mother had taken a job as a farmer's housekeeper. For Matt, who'd spent his young life tugged from one emotional disaster to another, the farm had seemed heaven and farming had been his life ever since. With only one—admittedly major—hiccup to impede his progress he'd done spectacularly well, but here was another hiccup and it was a big one. He was staring out from his veranda at his massive shearing shed. It was set up for a five a.m. start. His team of crack shearers was ready but his planning had let him down.

He needed to break the news soon, and it wouldn't be pretty.

Hiring gun shearers was half the trick to success in this business. Over the years Matt had worked hard to make sure he had everything in place to attract the best, and he'd succeeded.

But this afternoon's phone call had floored him.

'Sorry, Matt, can't do. The water's already cut the Innawarra Track to your north and they're saying the floodwaters will cut you off from the south by tomorrow. You want to hire me a helicopter? It's the only alternative.'

A helicopter would cut into his profits from the wool clip but that wouldn't bother him. It was keeping his shearers happy that was the problem. No matter whose fault it was, an unhappy shed meant he'd slip down the shearers' roster next year. He'd be stuck with a winter shear rather than the spring shears that kept his flocks in such great shape.

So he needed a chopper, but there were none for hire. The flooding up north had all available helicopters either hauling idiots out of floodwater or, more mundanely, dropping feed to stranded stock.

He should go and tell them now, he thought.

He'd cop a riot.

He had to tell them some time.

Dinner was easy. They had to provide their own. It was only at first smoko tomorrow that the proverbial would hit the fan.

'They might as well sleep in ignorance,' he muttered and headed out the back of the sheds to find his horse. Nugget didn't care about shearing and shearing shed politics. His two kelpies, Reg and Bluey, flew out from under the house the moment they heard the clink of his riding gear. They didn't care either.

And, for the moment, neither did Matt.

'Courage to change the things that can be changed, strength to accept those things that can't be changed and the wisdom to know the difference…' It was a good mantra. He couldn't hire a chopper. Shearing would be a surly, ill-tempered disaster but it was tomorrow's worry.

For now he led Nugget out of the home paddock and whistled the dogs to follow.

He might be in trouble but for now he had every intention of forgetting about it.

She was in so much trouble.

'You'd think if there were stones at the bottom of one creek there'd be stones at the bottom of every creek.' She was standing on the far side of the second creek crossing. Samson was still in the car.

Her car was in the middle of the creek.

It wasn't deep. She'd checked. Once more she'd climbed out of the car and waded through, and it was no deeper than the last.

What she hadn't figured was that the bottom of this section of the creek was soft, loose sand. Sand that sucked a girl's tyres down.

Was it her imagination or was the water rising?

She'd checked the important things a girl should know before coming out here—like telephone reception. It was lousy so she'd spent serious money fitting herself out with a satellite phone, but who could she ring? Her father? *Dad, come and get me out of a river.* He'd swear at her, tell her she was useless and tell his assistant to organize a chopper to bring her home.

That assistant would probably be Brett.

She'd rather burn in hell.

So who? Her friends?

They'd think it was a blast, a joke to be bruited all over the Internet. Penelope Hindmarsh-Firth, indulged daughter of a billionaire, stuck in the outback in her new pink car. A broken engagement. A scandal. Her first ever decision to revolt.

There wasn't one she would trust not to sell the story to the media.

Her new employer?

She'd tried to sound competent in her phone interview. Maybe it would come to that, but he'd need to come by truck and no truck could reach her by dark.

Aargh.

Samson was watching from the car, whimpering as the water definitely rose.

'Okay,' she said wearily. 'I didn't much like this car anyway. We have lots of supplies. I have half a kitchen worth of cooking gear and specialist ingredients in those boxes. Let's get everything unloaded, including you. If no one comes before the car goes under I guess we're camping here while my father's engagement gift floats down the river.'

There was a car in the middle of the creek.

A pink car. A tiny sports car. Cute.

Wet. Getting closer to being swept away by the minute. *Of all the dumb...*

There was a woman heaving boxes from some sort of luggage rack she'd rigged onto the back. She was hauling them to safety.

A little dog was watching from the riverbank, yapping with anxiety.

Matt reined to a halt and stared incredulously. Reg and Bluey stopped too, quivering with shock, and then hurled themselves down towards what Matt thought must surely be a hallucination. A poodle? They'd never seen such a thing.

The woman in the water turned and saw the two dogs, then ran, trying to launch herself between the killer dogs and her pooch.

She was little and blonde, and her curls twisted to her shoulders. She was wearing a short denim skirt, a bright pink blouse and oversized pink earrings. She was nicely curved—very nicely curved.

Her sunglasses were propped on her head. She looked as if she was dressed for sipping Chardonnay at some beachside café.

She reached the bank, slipped in the soft sand and her crate fell out of her hands.

A teapot fell out and rolled into the water.

'Samson!' She hauled herself to her feet, yelling to her poodle, but Reg and Bluey had reached their target.

Matt was too stunned to call them off, but there was no need. His dogs weren't vicious. This small mutt must look like a lone sheep, needing to be returned to the flock. Rounding up stray sheep was what his dogs did best.

But Matt could almost see what they were thinking as they reached the white bit of fluff, skidded to a halt and started the universal sniffing of both ends. *It looks like a sheep but...what...?*

He grinned. The troubles of the day took a back seat for the moment and he nudged Nugget forward.

There wasn't a thing he could do about his shearing problems. What he needed was distraction, and this looked just what the doctor ordered.

She needed a knight on a white charger. This was no white charger, though. The horse was huge and black as night. And the guy on it?

Instead of armour, he wore the almost universal uniform of the farmer. Moleskin pants. A khaki shirt, open at the throat, sleeves rolled to the elbows. A wide Akubra hat. As he edged his horse carefully down the embankment she had the impression of a weathered face, lean, dark, strong. Not so old. In his thirties?

His mouth was curving into a smile. He was laughing? At her?

'In a spot of bother, ma'am?'

What she would have given to be able to say: *No bother—everything's under control, thank you.*

But her car was sinking and Samson was somewhere under his dogs.

'Yeah,' she said grimly. 'I tried to cross but the creek doesn't have stones in it.'

His lips twitched. 'How inconsiderate.'

'The last creek did.'

He put his hands up, as if in surrender. 'I cannot tell a lie,' he told her. 'I dropped stones in the first crossing but not this one. The first floods all the time. This one not so much. There's a lot of water coming down. I doubt you'd get back over the first crossing now.'

'You put the stones in…'

'Yes, ma'am.'

She stood and thought about it. She had bare feet—a pair of bright pink sandals had been tossed onto the bank on this side. Obviously she'd waded through first, which was intelligent. Driving into a flooded creek with a sandy base was the opposite.

But now wasn't the time for judging. The water was rising by the minute. 'Would you like me to help you get your car out?'

And any hint of belligerence died. 'Could you? Do you know how?'

'You have cushions on your passenger seat,' he said. He'd been checking out the car while they talked. A big car might be a problem but this looked small enough to push, and with the traction of cushions… 'We could use those.'

'They're Samson's.'

'Samson?'

'My poodle.'

'I see.' He was still having trouble keeping a straight face. 'Is he likely to bite my arm off if I use his cushions?'

She glanced to where Reg and Bluey were still warily circling Samson. Samson was wisely standing still. Very still.

'Your dogs…'

'Are meeting a poodle for the very first time. They won't take a piece out of him, if that's what you're worried about. So Samson won't take a piece out of me if I borrow his cushion?'

'No. Please… If you could…'

'My pleasure, ma'am. I haven't pushed a pink car out of floodwaters for a very long time.'

And then he got bossy.

He swung himself down from his horse. He didn't bother tying it up—the assumption, she guessed, was that it'd stay where he left it and the assumption seemed correct. Then he strode out into the water to her car. He removed the cushions, then stooped and wedged them underwater, in front of the back wheels.

'Rear-wheel drive is useful,' he told her. 'Four-wheel drive is better—it's pretty much essential out here. You didn't think to borrow something a little more useful before driving off-road?'

'This *is* a road.'

'This is a track,' he told her.

He was standing almost thigh-deep in water and he was soaked from pushing the cushions into place.

'I should push,' she offered.

The lips twitched again. 'I'm thinking I might just have a bit more muscle. Could you hop in and switch on the ignition? When I tell you to accelerate, go for it. Straight forward, and as soon as you feel the car get a grip, keep going.'

She thought about it for a moment and saw a problem. A big one. 'Um…'

He paused. 'Um?'

'Are there any more creeks?' she asked, her voice filled with trepidation.

'Any more creeks where?'

'Between here and Malley's Corner.'

'You're headed for Malley's Corner?'

'Yes.' She tilted her chin at the note of incredulity in his voice. It was the same incredulity she'd heard from every one of her family and friends.

He paused for a moment. The water level rose an inch.

'We'll talk about it later,' he said curtly. 'We have minutes to get your car clear before she's properly swamped. Get in and turn it on.'

'But are there more creeks?'

'A dozen or so.'

'Then I can't get to Malley's Corner,' she wailed. 'I need to go back the way I came. Can you push me back to the other side?'

'You want to do a U-turn in the middle of the creek?'

'No, but I don't want to be trapped.'

'I have news for you, lady,' he told her. 'You're already trapped. The only hope we have of getting your car out of this water is to go straight forward and do it now. Get in your car and I'll push or it'll be washed away. Move!'

She gave a yelp of fright—and moved.

She was in such a mess.

Actually, if she was honest, she wasn't in a mess at all.

She was perfectly dry. Her little car was on dry land, still drivable. Samson had jumped back up into the passenger seat and was looking around for his cushions. It looked as if she could drive happily away. There were more creeks but for now she was safe.

But she had a cowboy to thank, the guy who'd saved her car—and he was the mess.

Though actually… She *should* be able to describe him as a mess, she thought. He'd shoved the cushions under her back wheels to get traction and then, as she'd touched the accelerator, he'd put his hands under the back of her car and pushed.

She'd felt the strength of him, the sheer muscle. With the acceleration behind him he'd practically heaved the little car free.

She'd stopped and looked back, and her cowboy—her rescuer—was sprawled full length in the water.

When he stood up he almost looked scary. He was seriously big, he was soaked and he was spitting sand. He did not look happy.

When he reached the bank she backed off a little.

'Th…thank you,' she ventured. 'That was very good of you.'

'My pleasure, ma'am,' he said with obvious sarcasm and she winced.

'I'm sorry.'

'All in a day's work. I've heaved stock from bogs before this. Your car's not much bigger than a decent bull.' He wiped away some sand and she had a clearer view of his face. He had deep brown eyes set in a strongly boned face. Strength and capability and toughness was written on every inch of him. This wasn't the sort of guy she ever met in her city life.

'Do you live round here?' she managed and he nodded.

'Over the rise.'

'Then… I guess that means at least you can go home and have a shower. Look, I really am sorry…'

'So what will you do?'

'Go on until I reach the next creek,' she said in a small voice. 'Samson and I can sleep in the car if the water doesn't go down before nightfall. We'll go on tomorrow.'

'Tomorrow…'

'I start work on Tuesday. I guess it's just lucky I left myself a day's leeway.'

Something seemed to be happening on her rescuer's face. There was a tic right next to his jaw. It was sort of… twitching.

Laughter? No. Exasperation?

Maybe.

'You'd better follow me,' he said at last and she blinked.

'Why? I'm sorry; that doesn't sound gracious but you've done enough. Samson and I will be fine.'

'For a fortnight?'

'A fortnight?'

'That's how long they're saying before the floodwaters subside.' He sighed. 'There's been rain all over central New South Wales. It's been dry here, which is why you've been lulled into thinking it's safe to drive, but it's been raining up north like it hasn't for years. The water's pouring into the Murray catchment and all that water's making its way downstream. Creeks that haven't seen water for years are starting to fill. If you'd followed the main road you might have made it…'

'The satnav lady said this way was much shorter,' she said in a small voice.

'Then the satnav lady's a moron,' he said bluntly. 'There's no way you'll get this little car through to Malley's Corner and there's no way you can get back. You're stuck right here and you're stuck for a while.'

She stood and stared at him and he gazed right back.

He was looking at her as if she were some sort of strange species.

An idiot.

All her careful plans. All her defiance…

This was just what her father expected—Penelope being stupid once again.

She thought of the last appalling tabloid article she'd read before she'd packed and left—her father explaining to the media why the man who'd intended to marry Penny was now marrying Penny's older half-sister, the gorgeous, clever, talented Felicity.

'They're a much more suitable match,' George had told the journalist. *'Brett is one in a million. He's an employee who's going places and he needs a woman of class to support that. My younger daughter means well, but she's much more interested in her cakes than in taking care of her man. I'm not sure why we all didn't see this was a more sensible match to begin with.'*

Sensible. Right.

She shook herself, shoving painful memories harshly behind her. No, she wouldn't be calling her father for help.

'Is there somewhere I can stay?' she asked in a small voice.

'You're on my land,' he told her. 'From here until the next two creek crossings there's nowhere but Jindalee.'

'Jindalee?'

'My home.'

'Oh.'

She looked at his horse and her mind was twisting so much she even thought of offering to buy the thing and ride off into the sunset. Fording rivers on horseback with Samson riding up front.

Um…not. Even if she could ride a horse. Even if she was game to go near it.

'Do you…do you have a four-wheel drive?' she asked. 'Is it possible that a truck or something could get through?'

'It might,' he said grudgingly.

She'd been trying to figure a way out, but she thought she saw one. 'Could you take me on to Malley's? If you have a truck that can get through we could make it. I could leave my car here and get someone to bring me back to collect it when the water goes down.'

And this is my last chance, she thought desperately, looking into his impassive face. *Please.*

He gazed at her and she forced herself to meet his gaze calmly, as if her request was totally reasonable—as if asking him to drive for at least four hours over flooded creeks was as minor as hiring a cab.

'I can pay,' she added. 'I mean… I can pay well. Like a good day's wages…'

'You have no idea,' he said and then there was even more silence. Was he considering it?

But finally he shook his head.

'It's impossible,' he told her. 'I can't leave the property. I have a team ready to start shearing at dawn and two thousand sheep to be shorn. Nothing's messing with that.'

'You could…maybe come back tonight?'

'In your dreams. The water's coming up. I could end up trapped at Malley's Corner with you. I can't risk sending a couple of my men because I need everyone. So I don't seem to have a choice and neither do you.' He sighed. 'We might as well make the best of it. I'm inviting you home. You and your dog. As long as you don't get in the way of my shearing team, you're welcome to stay at Jindalee for as long as the floodwater takes to recede.'

CHAPTER TWO

PENNY DROVE, slowly and carefully, along the rutted track. He followed behind on his horse, his dogs trotting beside him, and she was aware of him every inch of the way.

He could be an axe murderer. He was sodden and filthy. His jet-black hair was still dripping and his dark face looked grim.

He'd laughed when he first saw her but now he looked as if he'd just been handed a problem and he didn't like it.

She didn't even know his name.

He didn't know hers, she reminded herself. He was opening his house to her, and all he knew about her was that she was dumb enough to get herself stranded in the middle of nowhere. She could be the axe murderer.

She had knives. She thought fleetingly of her precious set, wrapped carefully in one of her crates. They were always super sharp.

What sort of knives did axe murderers use?

'They use axes, idiot,' she said aloud and that was a mistake. The guy on the horse swivelled and stared.

'Axes?' he said cautiously, and she thought, *He'll be thinking he has a real fruitcake here.*

That was what she felt like. A fruitcake.

'Sorry. Um…just thinking of what I'd need if… I mean, if I was stuck camping and needed something like wood to light a fire. I'd need an axe.'

'Right,' he said, still more cautiously. 'But you don't have one?'

'No.'

'You seem to have everything else.'

'I'm going to Malley's to work. I need stuff.'

'You're working at Malley's?' He sounded incredulous. 'That place is a dump.'

'The owner has plans,' she said with as much dignity as she could muster. 'I'm employed to help.'

'It could use a bit of interior decorating,' he agreed. 'From the ground up.' His lips suddenly twitched again. 'And you always carry a teapot?'

'They might only use tea bags.'

'You don't like tea bags?'

'I drink lapsang souchong and it doesn't work in tea bags. I love its smoky flavour. Don't you?'

'Doesn't everyone?' he asked and suddenly he grinned. 'I'm Matt,' he told her. 'Matt Fraser. I'm the owner of Jindalee but I hope you brought your own lapsang souchong with you. Sadly I seem to be short on essentials.'

'I have a year's supply,' she told him and his grin widened.

'Of course you do. And you are?'

'Penelope Hindmarsh-Firth.' He was laughing at her but she could take it, she decided. She should be used to people laughing at her by now. 'And I'm the owner of one pink car and one white poodle.'

'And a teapot,' he reminded her.

'Thank you. Yes.' She concentrated on negotiating an extra deep rut in the road.

'Penelope...' Matt said as the road levelled again.

'Penny.'

'Penny,' he repeated. 'Did you say Hindmarsh-Firth?'

And her heart sank. He knows, she thought, but there was no sense denying it.

'Yes.'

'Of the Hindmarsh-Firth Corporation?'

'I don't work for them.' Not any more. She said it almost defiantly.

'But you're connected.'

'I might be.'

'The way I heard it,' he said slowly, seemingly thinking as he spoke, 'is that George Hindmarsh, up-and-coming investment banker, married Louise Firth, only daughter of a mining magnate worth billions. Hindmarsh-Firth is now a financial empire that has tentacles worldwide. You're part of that Hindmarsh-Firth family?'

'They could be my parents,' she muttered. 'But I'm still not part of it.'

'I see.'

He didn't, she thought. He couldn't. He'd have no idea of what it was like growing up in that goldfish bowl, with her father's ego. He'd have no idea why she'd finally had to run.

'So if I rang up the newspapers now and said I've just pulled a woman called Penelope Hindmarsh-Firth out of a creek, they wouldn't be interested?'

No! 'Please don't,' she whispered and then repeated it, louder, so she was sure he could hear. She was suddenly very close to tears.

'I won't,' he told her, his voice suddenly softening. 'Believe me, I have no wish for media choppers to be circling. Though...'

'Though what?'

'There's someone I need to get here,' he told her. 'It'd almost be worth it—I could tell them they could find you here as long as they brought Pete with them.'

'Pete?'

She hit a bump. The car jolted and the teapot bounced and clanged against the pots underneath it.

'It doesn't matter,' he said roughly. 'I won't do it. I can understand your situation might well cause humiliation. I assume you're heading to Malley's to get out of the spotlight?'

'Yes,' she said and could have wept with gratitude.

'Then you've come to the right place,' he told her. 'And this is a lot cleaner than Malley's. Jindalee has plenty of spare bedrooms, though most are in desperate need of a good dust. As long as you and Samson keep out of my way, you're welcome to hunker down for as long as the flood lasts.'

And then they topped the last rise before the house and Penny was so astounded she stalled the car.

The rain clouds up north must have visited here a while back because the pastures were lush and green. The property was vast and undulating. There were low hills rolling away as far as the eye could see. The land was dotted with stands of magnificent gums. She could see the occasional flock of sheep in the distance, white against green.

But the house… It took her breath away.

It was a real homestead, built a hundred or more years ago. It sat on a slight rise, huge, long and low, built of whitewashed stone. French windows opened to the vast verandas and soft white curtains fluttered out into the warm afternoon breeze. Grapevines massed under the veranda and massive old settees sat under their shade. An ancient dog lay on the top step by the front door as if he was guarding the garden.

And what a garden. It looked almost like an oasis in the middle of this vast grazing property. Even from here she could see the work, the care…

Wisteria hung from massive beamed walkways. She could see rockwork, the same sandstone that lined the creeks, used to merge levels into each other. Bougainvillea, salvia, honeysuckle… Massive trees that looked hundreds of years old. A rock pool with a waterfall that looked almost natural. Roses, roses and more roses.

And birds. As they approached the house a flock of crimson rosellas rose screeching from the gums, wheeling above their heads as if to get a better look, and then settled again.

For why wouldn't they settle? This place looked like paradise.

'Oh, my…' She slowed to a halt. She needed to stop and take it all in.

And Matt pulled his horse to a halt as well. He sat watching her.

'This is… Oh…' She could hardly speak.

'Home,' Matt said and she could feel the love in his voice. And suddenly every doubt about staying here went out of the window.

He loved this place. He loved this garden and surely no one who loved as much as this could be an axe murderer?

'Who does this?' she stammered. She'd tried gardening in the past. It had been a thankless task as her parents moved from prestige property to prestige property, but she knew enough to know that such a seemingly casual, natural garden represented more hard work than she could imagine. 'Your wife?' she asked. 'Or…'

'I don't have a wife,' he said, suddenly curt, and she thought instinctively that there was a story there. 'But I do have someone helping me in the garden. Donald loves it as much as I do. He's in his eighties now but he won't slow down.'

'Your dad? Grandpa?'

'No.' Once more his reply was curt and she knew suddenly that she needed to back off. This guy wasn't into personal interrogation. 'Donald owned this place before I bought it. He's stayed on because of the garden.'

'That's lovely,' she breathed.

'It is,' he said and he wasn't talking of Donald. His eyes

skimmed the house, the garden, the country around them and she saw his face soften. 'There's nowhere I'd rather be.'

She gazed around her, at the low lying hills, at the rich pasture, at the massive gum trees, at the sheer age and beauty of the homestead which seemed to nestle into its surroundings as if it had grown there. 'How much of this do you own?' she breathed.

'As far as you can see and more.' It was impossible for him to hide the pride in his voice.

'Oh, wow!' The property must be vast. She sat and soaked it in, and something in her settled. Who could be fearful or even heartbroken in a place like this?

Okay, she was still heartbroken but maybe she could put it aside.

'What's the building over there?' A low shed built of ancient handmade bricks sat under the gum trees in the distance. It looked so old it practically disappeared into the landscape.

'That's the shearing shed. The shearers' quarters are behind that.'

And suddenly she was diverted from the farm's beauty.

'There's a dozen trucks. At least.'

'They belong to the shearing team. We start at dawn. You'll need to keep out of the way.'

'Oh, but...' Surely with so many...

'No,' he said, seeing where she was heading and cutting her off before she got started. 'No one's driving you anywhere. You'll find an empty garage around the back. I need to take care of Nugget and talk to the men before I come in for the night, but the back door's open. Put the kettle on and make yourself a cup of...what was it? Lapsang souchong. I'll see you in an hour or so. Meanwhile, welcome to Jindalee, Miss Hindmarsh-Firth. Welcome to my home.'

* * *

Matt led Nugget into the stables, unstrapped his gear and started brushing. Nugget looked vaguely surprised. Knowing shearing was about to start, knowing life was about to get crazy, he'd given him a decent brush this morning. But two brushes in one day wouldn't hurt and it might help get his head together.

In one sense the worsening flood was a blessing. The shearing team hadn't listened to the weather forecast. They'd come straight from a property south of here this morning, and there'd been no hint of the flooding to come. That meant when they woke tomorrow and found he had no shearers' cook they couldn't leave in disgust. At least his sheep would be shorn.

But he was facing two weeks of disgruntled shearers. Plus two weeks of a society princess who asked questions.

Penelope Hindmarsh-Firth…

He took his phone from the waterproof protector he always used—thank heaven he'd had it today—and hit the Internet. Thank heaven for satellites too, he thought, glancing at the dish on the top of the house. If he'd used the Internet to good effect he could have tracked the speed of the flooding. He could have let the shearers know not to come, but he'd gambled. He'd known the water was on its way but he'd thought they'd be able to get through this morning. They had. He had two weeks' work for them and a decent amount of supplies.

He'd also thought his cook could get through, but he'd been coming from another property in a different direction. And that had spelled disaster.

First World problem—shearers having to cook their own tucker? Maybe it was, but from time immemorial shearers had counted the quality of food and accommodation as a major enticement. This was a crack team and they expected the best. They couldn't blame him but it would be a sullen two weeks.

'So what are the odds of Miss Hindmarsh-Firth being able to cook?' he asked Nugget and thought of the teapot and grimaced. He needed to know more about the blonde and her white poodle. He leaned back on his horse's hindquarters and Nugget nibbled his ear while he searched *Penelope Hindmarsh-Firth* in his Internet browser.

And what sprang up were gossip columns—a list of them, longer than his screen. Current gossip.

'*Is one Hindmarsh-Firth as good as another?*' '*Sister Swap!*' '*Taggart's gamble pays off...*'

Bemused, he hit the first and read.

Brett Taggart, chief accountant to investment banker George Hindmarsh and heiress Louise Firth, has played a risky hand and won. He wooed the pair's daughter, company PR assistant Penelope, with what we hope were honourable intentions... Familiarity, however, meant a change of direction for our dubiously intentioned Brett. As he was welcomed into the golden world of the Hindmarsh-Firth family, his attention was obviously caught by his fiancée's older half-sister, glamorous social butterfly Felicity. Never let a promise get in the way of a good time, seems to be Brett's philosophy, and rumour has it that he and Felicity might be expecting a Happy Event in the next few months.

Such a ruckus in the family might have some parents casting children out. 'Never darken our door again!' would have been this columnist's reaction to such a back-stabbing sibling, but George and Louise seem to have taken the situation in their stride. In a recent tabloid interview George even insinuated he understands why Brett would choose the gorgeous

Felicity over her dumpy, media-shy sister, and Louise refuses to comment. So one wedding has been swapped for another.

Ugh, Matt thought, feeling a wave of sympathy for the 'dumpy, media-shy' Penny.

And then he thought…*dumpy?* What a description for those curves.

Um…let's not go there. He didn't need distraction.

He did not need anyone—except a shearer's cook.

'At least she can make her own tea,' he muttered to Nugget. 'There's a bonus. I wonder if she can make her own toast?'

Penny ventured in through the back door and was met by silence. Samson sniffed forward so she cautiously opened a few doors. The house was a beautiful…mausoleum?

It looked like a magnificent homestead built for a family of a dozen or so, with entertaining on a lavish scale. But it also looked like it hadn't been used for years. The massive sitting room off the main entrance was covered in dust sheets, as were the two other rooms she ventured into. She peeked under the dust sheets and saw furniture that'd look at home in an antique store. An expensive antique store.

There was a small sun-drenched den that looked well used. It was crammed with farming journals, books, a computer, dog beds. Matt's study? A wide passage led to what must be the bedroom wing but she wasn't game to go there.

Feeling more and more like an intruder, she retreated to the kitchen.

Which was…spectacular.

Windows opened to the veranda, to the shearing shed in the distance and to the hills beyond. Sunbeams were dancing on the floor, the ancient timbers worn by years of use. A battered wooden table ran almost the full length of the room, with scattered mismatched chairs that looked incredibly inviting. A small, slow combustion stove stood to one side of an old hearth, as if a far bigger wood stove had been removed. Beside it was a vast industrial oven and cooktop. It looked as if it could feed a small army.

How many people lived here? Hardly anyone by the look of the closed-up rooms, but these ovens... *Wow!*

She glanced again at the firestove. It was lit and emitting a gentle warmth. She'd never used one. Could she make bread?

What was she thinking of? Baking?

This situation was a mess. She didn't want to be here and Matt Fraser didn't want her here. Her job at Malley's Corner was in doubt. She'd ring them now but would they still want her when she arrived two weeks late?

She was stuck here for two weeks, with a man she didn't know.

But she was suddenly thinking: did he have decent flour?

There was a door to the side which looked like it could lead to a pantry. She shouldn't pry. The very stillness of the house was making her nervous, but he'd said she could make herself a cup of tea.

She did have tea but it was packed at the bottom of one of her crates. So she needed to check the pantry...

She opened the pantry door and gasped.

This pantry was huge, and it was stocked as if Matt was expecting to feed an army.

There were flour bins, big ones, topped to overflowing. There were bins of rice, of sugar. There were mountains of cans, stacks of packs of pasta. There was every dried herb and sauce she could imagine.

There were two vast refrigerators and freezers, and another door led to a coolroom. She saw vegetables, fruit, every perishable a cook could need. There were whole sides of beef and lamb. Who could eat this much meat?

The shearing team? She'd read descriptions of life on the big sheep stations. Gun shearers, working twelve-hour days, pushing themselves to the limits, while the farmer's wife pushed herself to the limit feeding them.

Matt had no wife. There was no evidence of a house-keeper.

Was he planning to cook, or did one of those trucks out there belong to a cook?

She closed the lid of the freezer and saw an enormous list pinned to the wall. It was an inventory of everything she'd just seen.

It was printed out as an email. She flicked through to the end.

Can you get all this in stock and have it waiting? I'll be there on the seventh by mid-afternoon, but my first cook will be smoko on the eighth. See you then.

So he did have a cook. He'd probably be over with the men now, she thought. Maybe Matt was there too. Maybe they were sitting round drinking beer while Matt told them about the dopey blonde he'd pulled out of the water.

And suddenly all the fears of the past few weeks crowded back.

She was stuck in the middle of nowhere, where no one wanted her. She was stuck for two weeks.

A shearer's cook would be taking over this kitchen from tomorrow morning. Maybe she could help, she thought, but she'd worked in enough kitchens to know how posses-sive cooks could be.

'I might be allowed to wash dishes,' she told Samson morosely.

She found a tea bag—actually, she found about a thousand tea bags. They weren't generic, but they weren't lapsang souchong either.

'We'll have to slum it,' she told her dog, and made her tea and headed out to the veranda.

The big, old collie she'd seen earlier was still snoozing on the step. He raised his head and gave his tail a faint wag, then settled back down to the serious business of sleeping.

An old man was dead-heading roses. He was stooped and weathered with age, almost a part of the land around him. He glanced up from his roses as she emerged from the back door, and startled as if he'd just seen a ghost.

'Hi,' Penny called. 'I'm Penny.'

He didn't answer. Instead he dropped the canvas bag he'd been carrying and backed away. Ghosts, it seemed, were scary.

Penny sighed. She plonked herself down on the edge of the veranda and gazed out over the garden to the rolling plains beyond. Samson eyed the old dog warily, and then plonked down beside her.

'This is a beautiful view,' she told Samson. 'But I might just get sick of it after two weeks.'

Samson put his nose into the crook of her arm and whined. Samson, it seemed, was in complete agreement.

To say the men were unhappy would be an understatement.

'So who's going to cook?' Bert, self-proclaimed shearers' foreman, sounded incredulous.

'Me,' Matt told him. 'It means I can't spend much time in the shed, but Ron and Harv will have things under control.' Ron was his right-hand man, Harv his jackeroo. They were both capable sheep men.

Leaving the shed in their hands was still a risk. Half the trick of a smooth shear was the owner being hands-on. Men worked at full capacity, day after day, pushing themselves to the limit because the sooner they finished the sooner they'd be paid, and that was a recipe for problems. Tensions escalated fast. Ron and Harv were both men who disliked conflict and backed away from it—there was a reason they both worked on such an isolated property. Matt didn't like conflict either, but he could deal. He had the authority to dock wages, to kick a drunk shearer off the team or, worse, to recommend to other station owners which teams not to employ.

But Ron and Harv couldn't cook to save their lives. They lived on a diet of corned beef, beer and the occasional apple to prevent scurvy. At least Matt could do a decent spag. bol.

He had no choice. The kitchen was his.

'So we'll be eating pasta and boiled beef for two weeks?' Bert demanded and Matt shrugged.

'I'll do my best. Sorry, guys. I'm as unhappy about this as you are.'

'So what about the sheila we just saw you drive in with?' Bert demanded. 'Have you replaced Pete with a bit of fluff?'

'I haven't. She was stuck in the creek and I pulled her out. She's stuck here too and, before you ask, I suspect she might be able to brew a decent tea but not much else.'

'Great,' Bert growled. 'That's just great.'

'Sorry,' Matt told him. 'But that's the situation and we're stuck with it.'

And also a cute blonde with curves?

Do not go there. What was wrong with him? That was the second time he'd thought it.

Two weeks...

Stay well clear, he told himself. The last thing he needed was yet another woman complicating his life.

CHAPTER THREE

MATT RETURNED TO FIND Penny on the veranda, trying to make friends with Donald's dog. He greeted her curtly. There was a lot to be done before he could sleep. If she was expecting to be entertained he might as well make things clear now.

He showed her which bedroom she could use. It was big, it overlooked the garden and it had the extra advantage of being as far away from his as possible. Plus it had its own bathroom. For a Hindmarsh-Firth it might still be slumming it, he thought, but it'd be a thousand times better than the accommodation she'd get at Malley's Corner.

What on earth was she intending to do at Malley's? He'd ask some time, he thought, but he had to be up before dawn to make sure the first mob was ready to go, he had to check the sheep again tonight and he needed to eat.

But he should offer to feed her, he decided. From tomorrow he was faced with feeding the multitude. He might as well start now.

'Dinner's in half an hour,' he told her as he dumped her gear in her bedroom—how much stuff could one woman use? 'At seven.'

'I can help.' She hesitated. 'I'd like to.'

'I'll do it.' He wanted to eat and run, not sit while she fussed over something fancy. 'Thirty minutes. Kitchen. Oh, and there's dog food...'

'Samson has his own dog food.'

'Of course he does,' he said shortly and left her to her unpacking.

Showered, clean of the river sand, he felt better but not much. He tossed bacon and tomatoes into a frying pan, put bread in the toaster and set plates on the table.

Right on seven she walked in the door. She'd changed too. She'd obviously showered as well, for her curls were still damp. She was wearing jeans and a T-shirt and she'd caught her curls back in a ponytail.

He glanced around as she came into the room and had to force himself to turn back to the frying pan.

She looked fresh and clean and…cute? More than cute. Curvy? Bouncy?

Sexy.

Cut it out, he told himself and concentrated on the bacon.

'The house is lovely,' she told him. 'Thank you for taking me in.'

'It's not like I had a choice.' He thought about that for a moment and decided he sounded a bore. 'Sorry. You're welcome. And yes, it's lovely. Eggs?' Then he figured as a conversational gambit it needed a little extra. 'How many?'

'Two, please.' Her feet were bare. She padded over to the bench beside the firestove and hauled herself up so her legs were swinging. 'You can fry on this? I've never used a slow combustion stove.'

'It's a skill,' he said, deciding to sound modest.

'What else can you do on it?'

Uh oh. She'd called him out. He grinned and cracked an egg into the pan. 'Sausages,' he told her. 'And I can boil stuff.'

'So you use the big oven?'

'Not usually. The firestove suits me. If it's a cold morning I put my boots in the oven. Oh, and the occasional live lamb.'

'You put lambs in the oven?'

'It's the best place for a lamb that's been caught in the frost,' he told her. 'I can fit a lamb and boots in there all at once. Lamb and boots come out warm and ready to go. It's a win-win for everyone. Who needs an oven for baking?'

'But you can still bake in it?'

'I could try,' he told her. 'But anything I put in there might come out smelling of wet wool and boot leather.'

'Yum,' she said and then looked down at his frying eggs. 'Don't let them get hard.'

'What?' He stared down at the five eggs he'd cracked. He picked up the egg slice to flip them but Penny put her hand out and held his. Stopping him mid-flip.

'You want runny yolks?'

'I don't mind.'

'Runny's nicer.'

'Yeah, but…'

'Just spoon a little hot fat over them. It's much less likely to burst the yolks.'

'I don't have time for nice.'

'Then let me,' she told him and jumped down, grabbed a spoon and edged him out of the way.

Her body hit his and all of a sudden they were close. Too close.

He felt… He didn't know what he felt. How long since he'd stood beside a woman in a kitchen?

This was not a sensation he needed to be feeling tonight.

He edged away fast, and stood and watched while she carefully spooned hot fat over the yolks.

'Done,' she said.

She flicked bacon and tomatoes he'd fried earlier onto the toast and then carefully slid the eggs on top.

How had she done that? It was weird but somehow she'd made it look…sort of gourmet? When he piled eggs and bacon onto a plate they looked like eggs and bacon. She'd sort of set the tomatoes at one side and then made a round of bacon. The eggs slid on top and it looked…great.

He'd been hungry. Now he was even hungrier.

And so, it seemed, was she. She sat down and tackled her eggs and bacon as if she hadn't seen food in a week. She was enjoying every mouthful of this very plain meal.

He thought of the few women he knew and the way they ate. Not like this. This was almost sensual.

'Wow,' she breathed as she finished her first egg and tackled her bacon. 'Yum!'

'It's all in the cooking,' he said and she grinned. It was a great grin, he decided. Kind of endearing.

'Yeah, great fat scooping.' She shook her head. 'Nope. These eggs… This bacon…'

'Home grown,' he told her. 'They're Donald's projects.'

'Donald?'

'I told you about him. He used to own this property. He got too old to run it; he sold it but the thought of leaving broke his heart. I offered him one of the shearers' cottages in return for keeping up the garden. He's been with me for ten years now, running a few of his precious pigs, caring for his hens and keeping my garden magnificent. Win-win for everyone.'

'Are the eggs free range too?' she asked.

'We lock 'em up at night. Which reminds me…' He headed for the sink, dumping his dishes. 'I need to go. Sleep well. Anything you need in the morning, help yourself. I'll be gone before dawn.'

'You start shearing before dawn?'

'The pens are already full for the dawn start but I'll run the south mob into the home paddock to refill the pens as the men work. But I'll be back here by about nine to make sandwiches.'

'*You're* making sandwiches?'

'Yeah.' He grimaced. 'That's all they're getting. But it

doesn't affect you. Just stay away from the sheds, that's all I ask. I don't like distractions.'

'I'm a distraction?'

He turned and looked at her. *Cute*, he thought again. *Definitely cute.*

Her poodle was at her feet. Most of the shearers had dogs.

Penny and Samson in the shearers' shed? No and no and no.

'Definitely a distraction. Stay away,' he growled, possibly more gruffly than he intended.

But she looked distracted now. She was frowning. 'You're making sandwiches?' she said again.

'Yes.'

'And you just said all you can do is sausages and boiling stuff.'

'I'll boil a couple of slabs of beef for lunch.'

The thought of it was almost overwhelming but who else would do it? Ron and Harv could be depended on to keep the sheep coming in and clear the pens but their cooking skills were zero. Donald was eighty-seven. That was his pool of workers.

He could imagine the reaction of the shearers if he went over there now and said: *Hey, do any of you cook? Care to swap jobs?*

But he was eyeing the woman at the table with caution. She'd known how to cook an egg. That was about twenty per cent of his cooking skill. Maybe…

But she drove a pink car. She had a poodle. She came from one of the richest families in Australia.

Ask.

'I employ a shearers' cook,' he told her. 'The best. Pete sent me lists. I have everything I need—except Pete. He's stuck on the far side of the floodwater.' He hesitated. 'So I'm stuck with cooking. But any help you could give me…'

'I'll cook.'

Silence.

I'll cook.

Two magic words.

'You can cook?'

'Don't sound so shocked. Why do you think I was heading for Malley's Corner?'

'You were going to Malley's to *cook*?' He couldn't keep the incredulity from his voice.

'What's wrong with that?' She glared. 'Just because my family's…'

'The richest family in Australia?'

'We're not. There are mining magnates richer than us.'

'Of course there are.'

'Don't be sarcastic. Besides, this has nothing to do with money. Though…' she considered '… I'm stuck here so I might as well make myself useful. Consider it payment for board.'

'Do you have any idea how hard it is to cook for a shearers' team?'

'You were going to do it.'

'Now you sound sarcastic.'

And she grinned. 'I do,' she conceded. 'But I can do better than sandwiches.'

'We have a team of twenty shearers, classers and roustabouts. Do you have any idea how much they eat?'

'I've cooked for hundreds.'

'*You…*'

'You say that like I'm some sort of amoebic slug,' she said carefully. 'Why shouldn't I cook? Why do you think Malley hired me?'

'Malley would employ anyone with a pulse. Come to think of it, rumour was that his last cook didn't have one.'

'Then he's about to be surprised. I even have qualifications.'

'You're kidding.'

'Only a basic apprenticeship,' she admitted. 'But I've done lots of cooking classes in amazing places. Mum and Dad approved of those.'

'I just read an article online,' he told her. A man had to be careful but he might as well say it. Not that he had a recruitment pool of hundreds but he needed to know what he was getting into. 'It described you as a PR assistant in your family corporation. It also said you were nursing a bruised ego and a broken heart.'

She froze. 'You checked up on me.'

'I did. About the broken heart bit. Your sister… I'm sorry…'

And all of a sudden the apologetic, polite blonde was transformed by temper.

'Don't you dare go there,' she snapped. 'I don't want sorry. Every one of my so-called friends are sorry, but not sorry enough to refuse an invitation to the massive wedding my parents are organizing right now. My father says a big function's important to show there's no family rift. So there's no family rift. Business as usual.'

He winced. 'That must hurt. Every major tabloid…'

'Is enjoying it very much.' She cut him off bitterly. 'But that's important how? Right now I'm offering to cook for you. Isn't there a Discrimination Act somewhere that says asking employees about their past appalling taste in men is illegal?'

'Are you applying for a job?'

'I might be,' she snapped. 'As long as you don't rake up my family. I've left them in Sydney and that's where they're staying. I like the fact that half of Australia is flooding between here and there. Do you like the fact that I can cook?'

There was no arguing with that. 'Yes.'

'So let's move on. Your shearers like sandwiches? Are you any better at making them than frying eggs?'

'Mine would be pretty basic sandwiches,' he admitted.

The grandfather clock in the hallway chimed eight. He should be gone, he thought. There was so much to do before dark.

But he had the offer of a cook.

She intrigued him. She was half perky, half defensive.

It sounded as if her family had cut her a raw deal and he'd seen enough of the tabloids to realize how widely her humiliation must have spread. She must be hurting a lot under her pink bravado.

What he wanted was to probe deeper into what was behind her blind run to Malley's. But then…this was personal and hadn't he learned a long time ago not to get personal with women? The last thing he needed was a wealthy blonde socialite sobbing on his chest while she spilt all.

And she was right. Her past had no bearing on her ability to cook.

She could probably only do fancy, he thought. Soufflés and caviar and truffles. But she *had* cooked a mean egg, which was more than he could do. And how could her cooking be worse than his efforts?

'If you really could…'

'I could try,' she told him, her glare fading. She looked as if she was sensing his train of thought. 'You can sack me if it doesn't work.' She smiled suddenly, and he thought she had a great smile. It lit her face.

It lit the room.

'Tell me what you need,' she said and he had to force himself to focus on something that wasn't that smile.

'Morning smoko, dinner and arvo tea. The shearers make their own breakfast and evening meal, but our dinner's midday, when we need a full, hot meal to keep going.

You have no idea how many calories a gun shearer burns. Are you really serious about helping?'

'I'm serious.'

'Okay.' He took a deep breath, seeing clear air where from the time he'd had the call from Pete he'd only seen fog. 'At ten you'd provide smoko—morning tea. You'd bring the food over to the shed. I'll come and help you carry it. Then at twelve-thirty they all come here for a buffet dinner and take it onto the veranda to eat. At three it's time for arvo tea and you take that to the shed as well. It saves time. You'd be expected to cook a couple of extra roasts and leave them in the shearer's quarters so they can use that as a base for their evening meal.'

'Wow,' she said and looked at the big stove. 'No wonder you have three ovens. Is there an instruction manual?'

'On the Internet.'

'You have Internet?'

'Yep. Satellite. I'll give you the password.'

She stood up and her smile widened until the defensiveness of moments ago disappeared entirely.

'You have no idea how good that makes me feel,' she told him. 'Half an hour ago I was trapped in the middle of nowhere feeling useless. Now I have a job and Internet and there's nothing more I need in the world. Right. You'd better put those chooks to bed and gather those sheep or whatever you have to do. Leave me be, Matt. I'm about to get busy.'

He'd been dismissed.

She was needed! She stood in the great kitchen and, for the first time since that appalling night when Brett and Felicity had appeared at the family dinner table hand in hand and smugly announced the new order of things, she felt as if she was standing on firm ground again.

A shearing team of twenty. Two weeks' hard work, she

thought with satisfaction. Two weeks when she could put her head down and forget that every tabloid in the country was running articles pitying her.

She'd be working for Matt.

Matt…

And suddenly her thoughts went off at a tangent. Matt. The way he'd said he was sorry. He'd said it…as if he understood. How was that possible? It had been a throwaway line, a platitude, something that had been said to her over and over before her family and her friends had moved on to the new normal.

But his eyes were kind.

And the rest of him…

Wow.

And that was enough to make her give herself a fast mental slap to the side of the head. What was she thinking? He was her new boss. He was the owner of this place, a guy who lived and breathed the land, a guy who'd practically lifted her car and heaved it out of the water.

She'd been brought up with suits. She'd never met anyone even vaguely like Matt.

He made her feel…breathless.

Oh, for heaven's sake. It had been less than a month since she'd been unceremoniously dumped by Brett. She'd thought she was in love, and look how that had turned out.

'I have no sense at all,' she told Samson. 'Okay, he might be good-looking enough to make my toes curl but my toes are not a good indicator. My father thinks I'm an idiot, and where men are concerned I've just proved him spectacularly right. I need to ignore Matt Fraser and get on with my job.'

She opened the pantry again and gazed at the contents in delight.

This place was like a miniature supermarket. Filled with hope, she headed out the back. A vegetable garden! Herbs!

Her head was spinning in all directions. What first?

She could make cupcakes for morning tea. No. She pulled herself up short. Cupcakes might seem girly and the last thing she needed was guys thinking her food was girly. Okay, lamingtons. Better. She could whip up a couple of sponges now and coat them first thing in the morning. Then maybe a couple of big frittatas for lunch, with salads from the gorgeous stuff in the garden and fresh crusty bread. She had an overnight bread recipe. She could start it now so it'd rise magnificently overnight.

She looked at the sacks of flour and realized that Matt had supplies for an army. This must be provisioning for the rest of the year.

She wasn't complaining.

Next? What had Matt called it…arvo tea? If they'd eaten a big lunch they wouldn't want much. Chocolate brownies?

'Let's go,' she told Samson and he wiggled his tail at the joy in her voice.

There hadn't been much joy lately but she was feeling it now.

And she had to ask herself—was it just a little bit because a guy called Matt Fraser would be sharing a house with her for the next two weeks?

Was it just a little bit because a guy called Matt Fraser had caused a tingle of something she couldn't put a name to?

'It has nothing to do with Matt,' she told Samson severely. 'It's only the fact that I'm a world away from ghastly Brett and smug Felicity, and I'm needed.'

And the fact that Matt was sexy as…

Surely that had nothing to do with anything at all?

He'd met her only hours before. She was a society princess in a pink car and she had nothing to do with his world.

So why was he still feeling her hand on his, the way her

body had seemed to melt into his as she'd edged him aside to stop him doing the unthinkable—flipping his eggs!

Why did it suddenly feel as if his world was tilting?

There was no reason at all, he told himself and headed out to make sure the hens were locked up for the night.

'Who is she?' It was Donald—caring for the chooks was his job. But increasingly Donald forgot. Age was beginning to fuddle him, but he didn't seem to notice that Matt double-checked on most things he did.

Donald had run this property alone for fifty years. He was a confirmed bachelor and to say he treated women as aliens would be an understatement. Penny's presence, it seemed, had shocked him to the core.

'I pulled her out of the creek,' Matt told him. 'She was taking a dumb shortcut. She's stuck here until the water goes down.'

'Stuck. Here.' Donald said the two words as if they might explode and Matt almost laughed. He thought of the ditzy little blonde in his kitchen and wondered if there was anything less scary.

Although there were scary elements. Like the way his body reacted to her.

Um...let's not go there.

'She can cook,' he told Donald as he shooed the last hen into the pen and started collecting the eggs. 'The shearers' cook is stuck on the far side of the floodwater. If she can keep the team happy...'

'She can cook!' Donald's mother had run off with a wool-buyer when Donald was seven. His opinion of women had been set in stone since.

He grinned. 'I hear some women can.'

Donald thought about it. 'Rufus seems to like her,' he conceded at last. 'I watched her scratch his ear so she can't be all bad. What's that bit of fluff she's got with her?'

'A poodle.'

'A poodle at Jindalee! What next?'

'I'm thinking of getting him to help drafting the mobs in the morning,' Matt said and Donald gave a crack of laughter.

'He might end up getting shorn himself. I wonder what the classer'd make of that fleece?' He grinned. 'So you've got a woman and a poodle in the homestead. Want to kip in my place for the duration?'

'That'd be a bit of overkill. I've put her in your old bedroom and you know I sleep at the other end of the house. I think we can manage.'

'Women reel you in.'

'That's eighty years of experience speaking?'

'Eighty years of keeping out of their way. Mark my words, boy, it's like a disease.'

'I've been married, had a kid and have the scars to prove it,' Matt said, his grin fading. 'I'm immune.'

'No one's immune.' Donald shook his head and gestured to the house with a grimy thumb. 'Don't you go in till she's safely in bed and leave before she wakes up. Have your cornflakes at my place.'

'I'll be careful,' Matt promised him and smiled, although suddenly for some reason he didn't feel like smiling.

He thought of Penny—maybe Donald's advice was wise.

Lifting eggs from the nesting boxes, he enjoyed, as he always did, the warmth, the miracle of their production. He'd never quite got over the miracle of owning this place. Of never being told to move on.

He found himself thinking of his mother, going from one disastrous love affair to another, dragging her son with her. He'd learned early that when his mother fell in love it meant disaster.

She'd left and finally he'd figured he didn't need her.

After that…his first farm, financial security, finally feeling he could look forward.

And then deciding he could love.

Darrilyn.

And there it was again—disaster. Because Darrilyn didn't want him. She wanted the things his money represented. Two minutes after they were married she was pushing him to leave the farm he loved, and when he didn't…

Yeah, well, that was old history now. He didn't need Darrilyn. He didn't need anyone. But Donald was right.

He needed to be careful.

CHAPTER FOUR

THEY LOOKED BEAUTIFUL.

Penny gazed at the table in satisfaction. She had two plates of lamingtons ready to go. She'd rolled her cakes in rich chocolate sauce, coated them in coconut and filled them with cream. She'd thought of the difficulties of plates and spoons over in the yard so she'd gone small, but she'd made two each to compensate.

She'd piled them in beautifully stacked pyramids. They looked exquisite.

But this wasn't a social event, she reminded herself. Two lamingtons might not be enough, so she made a few rounds of club sandwiches, bite-sized beauties. She cut them into four-point serves and set them on a plate in the lamingtons' midst. They looked great.

She glanced at the clock and felt a little swell of pride. She had the ovens hot for the frittatas for lunch. They were almost ready to pop in. She had fifteen minutes before smoko and she was totally in control.

Matt would walk in any minute.

And here he was. He looked filthy, his pants and open neck shirt coated in dust, his boots caked in…whatever, she didn't want to think about it. His face was smeared with dust and his hair plastered down with sweat. 'Hey. Nearly ready?'

She lifted her lamingtons for inspection. 'We can take them over now if you like.'

He glanced at the table and his gaze moved on. 'Where's the rest?'

'The rest?'

There was a pregnant pause. And then… 'This is all there is?'

'Two lamingtons, two points of sandwiches each. How much more…'

He swore and headed for the pantry, leaving a trail of filthy footsteps over her nice, clean kitchen floor.

Her kitchen. That was how she felt when she worked. This was her domain.

Um…not. Matt had flung open the pantry door and was foraging behind the flour sacks. He emerged with three boxes.

Charity sale Christmas cakes. Big ones.

'They hate them but they'll have to do,' he snapped. 'Help me chop them up. They'll stop work in half an hour and if this is all you have…'

'But there's plenty,' she stammered and he gave her a look that resembled—eerily—the one her father gave her all the time. Like: *You've been an idiot but what else could I expect?*

'This isn't your society morning tea,' he snapped, ripping cartons open. 'It's fuel. Grab a knife and help me.'

She was having trouble moving. This was supposed to be her domain, the kitchen, her food—and he was treating her like an idiot. She felt sick.

A memory came flooding back of the dinner a month ago. She and her parents in the family home, the mansion overlooking Sydney Harbour. It had been her birthday. She'd like a family dinner, she'd told them. Just her parents, her half-sister and her fiancé.

And she'd cooked, because that was what she loved to do. She'd cooked what Brett loved to eat—stylish, with expensive ingredients, the sort of meal her father would enjoy paying a lot of money for in a society restaurant. She'd worked hard but she thought she'd got it right.

She'd even made time to get her hair done and she was wearing a new dress. Flushed with success, she'd only been a little disconcerted when Brett was late. And Felicity... Well, her sister was always late.

And then they'd walked in, hand in hand. *'We're so sorry, Penny, but we have something to tell you...'*

Matt was already slicing the first cake but at her silence he glanced up. Maybe the colour had drained from her face. Maybe she looked how she felt—as if she was about to be sick. For whatever reason, he put the knife down.

'What?'

'I...'

'It's okay,' he told her, obviously making an effort to sound calm. 'They're very nice lamingtons but this isn't a society fund-raiser where everyone's spent the last three hours thinking about what to wear. Some of these guys have shorn forty sheep since they last ate, and they intend to do forty more before their next meal. Calories first, niceties second. Help me, Penny.' And then, as she still didn't move, he added, 'Please.'

And finally her stunned brain shifted back into gear. She shoved away the sour taste of failure that followed her everywhere.

Fuel. Hungry workers who'd been head down since dawn.

Cute little lamingtons? She must have been nuts.

What then? Hot. Filling. Fast.

She had it.

'Ramp the ovens up,' she snapped and headed for the freezer. 'All of them. High as you can go. And then wash your hands. I need help and you're not touching my food with those hands.'

'We don't have time...'

'We'll be ten minutes late. They have a choice of a late smoko or eating your disgusting cake. You choose.'

He could order her aside and chop up the fruitcake the team despised—or he could trust her.

He went for the second. He cranked up the ovens and headed for the wash house. Two minutes later he was back, clean at least to the elbows.

By the time he returned, Penny had hauled sheets of frozen pastry from the freezer and was separating them onto baking trays.

'Three ovens, six trays,' she muttered. 'Surely that'll feed them.' She indicated jars of pasta sauce on the bench. 'Open them and start spreading,' she told him. 'Not too thick. Go.'

Hang on. He was the boss. This was his house, his kitchen, his shearing team waiting to be fed. The sensible thing was to keep chopping fruitcake but Penny had suddenly transformed from a cute little blonde into a cook with power. With Matt as an underling.

Fascinated, he snagged the first jar and started spreading.

Penny was diving into the coolroom, hauling out mushrooms, salami, mozzarella. She didn't so much as glance at him. She headed to the sink, dumped the mushrooms under the tap and then started ripping open the salami.

'Aren't you supposed to wipe mushrooms?' he managed. To say he was bemused would be an understatement.

'In what universe do we have time to wipe mushrooms?' She hauled out a vast chopping board and, while the tap washed the mushrooms for her, she started on the salami. Her hands were moving so fast the knife was a blur. 'I could leave them unwashed but I have an aversion to dirt.' She gave herself half a second to glance with disgust at his boots. 'Even if you don't. You finished?'

'Almost.' He poured the last jar over the pastry and spread it to the edges. 'Done.'

'Then I want this salami all over them. Rough and thick—we have no time for thin and fancy.' She hauled the mushrooms out of the sink and dumped them on a couple of tea towels, flipping them over with the fabric to get most of the water out. World's fastest wash. 'Back in two seconds. I'm getting herbs.'

And she was gone, only to appear a moment later with a vast bunch of basil. 'Great garden,' she told him, grabbing another chopping board.

He was too stunned to answer.

They chopped side by side. There was no time, no need to talk.

And suddenly Matt found himself thinking this was just like the shearing shed. When things worked, it was like a well-oiled machine. There was a common purpose. There was urgency.

His knife skills weren't up to hers. In fact they were about ten per cent of hers. He didn't mind. This woman had skills he hadn't even begun to appreciate.

Wow, she was fast.

It was the strangest feeling. To have a woman in his kitchen. To have *this* woman in his kitchen.

She was a society princess with a pink car and a poodle and knife skills that'd do any master chef proud.

Her body brushed his as she turned to fetch more mushrooms and he felt...

Concentrate on salami, he told himself and it was a hard ask.

But three minutes later they had six trays of 'pizza' in the oven.

'The herbs go on when it comes out,' she told him.

'We won't have time to garnish...'

'Nothing goes out of my kitchen unless it's perfect,' she

snapped. She glanced at the clock. 'Right, it's nine minutes before ten. This'll take fifteen minutes to cook so I'll be exactly ten minutes late. I hope that's acceptable. Come back at eight minutes past and help me carry it over.'

He almost grinned. He thought of his shearing team. Craig was the expert there, and Matt was wise enough to follow orders. Did he have just such an expert in his kitchen?

'How can it be ready by then?' He must have sounded incredulous because she smiled.

'Are you kidding? I might even have time to powder my nose before I help you take it out there.'

Taking the food over to the shed was an eye-opener.

A campfire had been lit on the side of the shed. There were a couple of trestle tables and a heap of logs serving as seats. Three billies hung from a rod across the fire.

The fire was surrounded by men and women who looked as filthy as Matt—or worse.

One of the men looked up as Penny and Matt approached and gave a shrill, two-fingers-in-the-mouth whistle. 'Ducks on the pond,' he called and everyone stopped what they were doing and stared.

'Hey.' It was hard to tell the women from the men but it was a female voice. 'You idiot, Harry. Ducks on the pond's a stupid way of saying women are near the shed. What about Marg and me?'

'You don't count,' one of the shearers retorted. 'You gotta have t… I mean you gotta have boobs and legs to count. You and Margie might have 'em but they're hidden under sheep dung. Put you in a bikini, we'll give you the respect you deserve.'

'Yeah, classifying us as ducks. Very respectful.' One of the women came forward and took plates from Penny. 'Take no notice of them, sweetheart. I'm Greta, this is

Margie and the rest of this lot don't matter. If they had one more neuron between them, it'd be lonely.' She glanced down at the steaming piles of pizza. 'Wow! Great tucker.'

And then there was no more talk at all.

The food disappeared in moments. Penny stood and watched and thought of the two frittatas she had ready to go in the oven.

How long before the next meal?

But Matt had guessed her thoughts. He'd obviously seen the pathetically small frittatas.

'There are a couple of massive hams in the cool room,' he told her. 'We can use your pretty pies as a side dish for cold ham and peas and potatoes. Penny, you saved my butt and I'm grateful, but from now on it doesn't matter if it's not pretty. At this stage we're in survival mode.'

And she glanced up at him and saw…sympathy!

The team had demolished the food and were heading back to the shed. Matt was clearly needing to head back too, but he'd stopped because he needed to reassure her.

He wanted to tell her it was okay to serve cold ham and peas and potatoes.

She thought again of that dinner with her parents, the joy, the certainty that all was right with her world, and then the crashing deflation.

This morning's pizza had been a massive effort. To serve quality food for every single meal would see her exhausted beyond belief.

She *could* serve his horrid cold ham, she thought, but that would be the equivalent of running away, as she'd run away from Sydney. But there was nowhere to run now.

She braced her shoulders and took a deep breath, hauling herself up to her whole five feet three. Where were stilettoes when a girl needed them?

'I'll have lun…dinner ready for you at twelve-thirty,' she told him. 'And there won't be a bit of cold ham in sight.'

* * *

He should be back in the shed. These guys were fast—they didn't have the reputation of being the best shearing team in South Australia for nothing. The mob of sheep waiting in the pens outside was being thinned by the minute. He needed to get more in.

Instead he took a moment to watch her go.

She was stalking back to the house. He could sense indignation in the very way she held her shoulders.

And humiliation.

She'd been proud of her lamingtons.

They were great lamingtons, he conceded. He'd only just managed to snaffle one before they were gone. There was no doubt she could cook.

She'd pulled out a miracle.

He watched as she stopped to greet Donald's dog. She bent and fondled his ears and said something, and for some reason he wanted badly to know what it was.

She was wearing shorts and a T-shirt. Her bouncy curls were caught in a ponytail. The media thing he'd read yesterday said she was twenty-seven but she looked about seventeen.

'Hey, Matt…' It was Harv, yelling from the shed. 'You want to get the next mob in or will I?'

He shook himself. It didn't matter what Penny did or didn't look like. He needed to get to work. He'd have to knock off early to go and make sure she'd sliced enough ham. Could she guess how many spuds she had to cook?

He glanced at her again. She was heading up the veranda. She looked great in those shorts. Totally inappropriate for this setting but great. She'd squared her shoulders and she was walking with a bounce again. Rufus was following and for a weird moment he wouldn't mind doing the same.

* * *

Food. Fast. Right.

She stared at her two quiches and three sticks of bread dough doing their final rise in a sunbeam on the window ledge—an entrée for that mob, she thought. A snack.

The reason that pantry was packed... Yeah, she got it.

There were sides of lamb, pork and beef hung on great hooks in the coolroom. Whole sides.

She usually bought lamb boned out and butterflied, pork belly trimmed to perfection.

But she had done a butchering course. Once upon a time a two star chef who'd agreed to have her help in his kitchen had yelled it at her. 'You want to understand meat, you need to understand the basics.' He hadn't made her kill her own cow but she had handled slabs of meat almost as big as this.

But to cut it into roasts, marinade it, get it into an oven she didn't know...

'Not going to happen,' she muttered. 'But I reckon I could get chops cut and cooked in time. First, let's get the bread divided and pies baked, and then I'm going to tackle me a sheep.'

Matt didn't leave the shed until ten minutes before the team was due to head to the kitchen.

He was running late. With Penny's knife skills though, and now she knew how much they ate, surely she'd have plated enough?

He opened the kitchen door—and the smell literally stopped him in his tracks. He could smell cooked lamb, rich sauces, apple pies redolent with cinnamon and cloves. Fried onions, fried chicken? His senses couldn't take it all in.

He gazed around the kitchen in stupefaction. The warming plate and the top of the damped-down firestove were piled high with loaded dishes, keeping warm. There were rounds of crumbed lamb cutlets, fried chicken, slices of some sort of vegetable quiche that looked amazing. Jugs of steaming sauces. Plates of crusty rolls. A vast bowl of tiny potatoes with butter and parsley. Two—no, make that three—casseroles full of mixed vegetables. Was that a ratatouille?

And to the side there were steaming fruit pies, with great bowls of whipped cream.

'Do you think we still need the ham?' Penny asked demurely and he blinked.

This wasn't the same clean Penny. She was almost as filthy as he was, but in a different way. Flour seemed to be smudged everywhere. A great apricot-coloured smear was splashed down her front. The curls from her ponytail had wisped out of their band and were clinging to her face.

And once again came that thought… She looked adorable.

'I'm a mess,' she told him when he couldn't find the words to speak. 'The team'll be here in five minutes, right? If you want me to serve, I'll go get changed. Everything's ready.'

And it was. The team would think they'd died and gone to heaven.

'Or do you want me to disappear?' Penny added. 'Ducks on the pond, hey?'

'Ducks is a sexist label,' he told her. 'Harry's old school—Margie and Greta have spent the last couple of hours lecturing him on respect.' He grinned. 'But, speaking of respect… You, Penelope Hindmarsh-Firth, are a proper shearer's cook and there's no greater accolade. Don't get changed. What you're wearing is the uniform of hard work and the team will love you just the way you are.'

CHAPTER FIVE

THE TEAM KNOCKED off at five but Matt didn't. Matt owned the place. No one gave him a knock-off time. He and Nugget headed out round the paddocks, making sure all was well. Thankfully, the night was warm and still, so even the just-shorn sheep seemed settled. He returned to the homestead, checked the sheep in the pens for the morning and headed for the house.

Then he remembered the chooks; Donald hadn't fed them for a week now. He went round the back of the house and almost walked into Penny.

'All present and correct,' she told him. 'At least I think so. Fourteen girls, all safely roosted.'

'How did you know?'

'I saw you do it last night. I took a plate of leftovers down to Donald and saw they were still out. I don't know how you're coping with everything. You must be exhausted.'

'It's shearing time,' he told her simply. 'Every sheep farmer in the country feels like this. It only lasts two weeks.'

She eyed him sideways in the fading light. He waited for a comment but none came.

She'd changed again, into jeans and a windcheater. She looked extraordinarily young. Vulnerable.

Kind of like she needed protecting?

'Thank you for thinking of Donald.'

'He wouldn't come in with the shearers so I saved some

for him. I think he was embarrassed but he took it.' She hesitated a moment but then decided to forge on. 'Matt… he told me he had to put Jindalee on the market but it broke his heart. And then you came. You renovated the cottage for him, even extending it so he could fit in everything he loved. And he can stay here for ever. I think that's lovely, Matt Fraser.'

'It's a two-way deal,' Matt growled, embarrassed. 'Don knows every inch of this land. I'm still learning from him. And I bet he appreciated the food. How you had the time to make those slices…'

'For arvo tea?' She grinned. 'I even have the jargon right. There'll be cakes tomorrow, now I'm more organized.'

'I'll pay you.'

'I don't need…'

'I'd have paid Pete. A lot. You'll get what he was contracted for.'

'You're giving me board and lodging.'

'And you're feeding a small army. I know it's a mere speck in the ocean compared to the money your family has, but I need to pay you.'

'Why?'

'So I can yell at you?' He grinned. 'I haven't yet but you should hear the language in the sheds.'

'Margie and Greta don't mind?'

'They use it themselves. As an official shearers' cook, you're entitled as well.'

'Thank you. I think.'

He chuckled and they walked back to the house together. The night seemed to close in on them.

The moon was rising in the east. An owl was starting its plaintive call in the gums above their heads.

She was so close…

'There's a plate of food in the warming oven,' she said

prosaically and he gave himself a mental shake and tried to be prosaic back.

'There's no need. I could have cooked myself...'

'An egg?' She gave him a cheeky grin. 'After my lesson last night you might do better, but if you're hungry check what's in the oven first.'

'You're going to bed now?'

'If it's okay with you, I might sit on the veranda and soak up the night until I settle. It's been a crazy day and here's pretty nice,' she said diffidently.

'It is, isn't it?' He hesitated and then decided: *Why not?* 'Mind if I join you?'

'It's your house.'

'That's not what I asked.'

She stopped and looked up at him. Her gaze was suddenly serious. There was a long pause.

'No,' she said at last. 'I don't mind if you join me. I don't mind at all.'

She should go to bed. She shouldn't be sitting on the edge of the veranda listening to the owls—waiting for Matt.

Why did it seem dangerous?

It wasn't dangerous. He was her employer. Today had been a baptism of fire into the world of cooking for shearers and she needed downtime. He'd asked to join her—it was his veranda so how could she have said no?

She could change her mind even now and disappear.

So why wasn't she?

'Because I'm an idiot with men. The only guys I've ever dated have turned out to be focused on my family's money.' She said it out loud and Samson, curled up by her side, whined and looked up at her.

'But I do a great line in choosing dogs,' she told him, and tucked him onto her knee and fondled his ears. 'That's my forte. Dogs and cooking.'

He still looked worried—and, strangely, so was she. Because Matt Fraser was coming to join her on the veranda?

'He's my employer,' she told Samson. 'Nothing else. He could be a seventy-year-old grandpa with grandchildren at heel for all the difference it makes. I'm over men. Matt's my boss, and that's all.'

So why were warning signals flashing neon in her brain?

Leftovers? He stared at the plate incredulously. These were some leftovers!

The midday meal had been crazy. For the shearers it was a break, a time where they stopped and had a decent rest. They'd come in and seen Penny's food and basically fallen on it like ravenous wolves. Then they'd settled on the veranda to enjoy it.

Meanwhile, Matt had grabbed a couple of rolls and headed back to the shed. The shearers' break was his only chance to clear the place and get it ready for the next hard session.

Shearing was exhausting. He'd been supervising it since he was a teenager and he'd never become used to it. Even when Pete was here, the best shearers' cook in the district, Matt usually ended up kilos lighter by the end of the shear. He'd come in after dark and eat what he could find, which generally wasn't much. Shearers didn't leave much.

But Penny must have noticed, for in the warming drawer was a plate with all the best food from midday.

It hadn't been sitting in the oven all afternoon either. She must have guessed he'd come in at dark, or maybe she'd asked one of the men.

He poured himself a beer, grabbed his plate and headed out to the veranda. He settled himself on one of the big cane settees. Penny was in front of him, on the edge of the veranda, her legs swinging over the garden bed below.

'Thank you,' he said simply.

'You're welcome.'

Silence. It wasn't an uncomfortable silence though. Matt was concentrating on the truly excellent food and Penny seemed content just to sit and listen to the owl and swing her legs. She was idly petting her dog but Samson seemed deeply asleep.

Samson had spent the day investigating chooks, making friends with the farm dogs and checking out the myriad smells of the place. This afternoon he'd even attempted a bit of herding but some things were never going to work. Matt had plucked him from the mob, hosed him down and locked him in the kitchen with Penny.

There'd be worse places to be locked, Matt thought idly, and then thought *whoa*, Penny was his shearers' cook. It was appropriate to think of her only as that.

'So where did you learn to cook?' he asked as he finally, regretfully finished his last spoonful of pie.

'Not at my mother's knee,' she said and he thought about stopping there, not probing further. But there was something about the night, about this woman…

'I'd have guessed that,' he told her. 'The article I read… It doesn't suggest happy families.'

'You got it.'

'So…cooking?'

She sighed. 'My family's not exactly functional,' she told him. 'You read about Felicity? She's my half-sister. Her mother's an ex-supermodel, floating in and out of Felicity's life at whim. My mother was Dad's reaction to a messy divorce—and, I suspect, to his need for capital. Mum was an heiress, but she's a doormat and the marriage has been…troubled. To be honest, I don't think Dad even likes Mum any more but she won't leave him. And my sister… Even though Mum's been nothing but kind to Felicity, Felicity barely tolerates Mum, and she hates me.

My life's been overlaid with my mother's mantras—avoid Felicity's venom and keep my father happy at all costs. So my childhood wasn't exactly happy. The kitchen staff were my friends.'

'So cooking became your career?'

'It wasn't my first choice,' she admitted. 'I wanted to be a palaeontologist. How cool would that have been?'

'A…what?'

'Studier of dinosaurs. But of course my father didn't see a future in it.'

'I wonder why not?'

'Don't you laugh,' she said sharply. 'That's what he did. I was the dumpy one, the one who hated my mother's hairdresser spending an hour giving me ringlets, the one who'd rather be climbing trees than sitting in the drawing room being admired by my parents' friends. And then, of course, I was expelled from school…'

'Expelled?' He'd been feeling sleepy, lulled by the night, the great food, the fatigue—and this woman's presence. Now his eyes widened. 'Why?'

'Quite easy in the end,' she told him. 'I don't understand why I didn't think of it earlier. I didn't mind being expelled in the least. It was boarding school—of course—the most elite girls' school my father could find. But I wasn't very…elite.'

She kicked her legs up and wiggled her bare toes in front of her and he could see how she might not be described as elite.

She wasn't elite. She was fascinating.

'I hated it,' she told him bluntly. 'I was there to be turned into a young lady. We had a whole afternoon every week of deportment, for heaven's sake. We learned to climb in and out of a car so no one can catch a sight of knickers.'

'Really?'

'It sounds funny,' she told him. 'It wasn't. I learned to

wrangle a purse, a cocktail and an oyster at the same time, but it's a skill that's overrated.'

'I guess it could be.' She had him entranced. 'So…'

'So?'

'Expulsion? Explain.'

'Oh,' she said and grinned. 'That was our annual ball. Very posh. We invited the local Very Elite Boys' School. Deportment classes gave way to dancing lessons and everyone had Very Expensive new frocks. And hairstyles. It was the culmination of the school year.'

'So…'

'So you might have noticed I'm little,' she told him. 'And…well endowed?'

'I hadn't,' he told her and she choked.

'Liar. I'm a size D cup and it's the bane of my life. But my mother bought me a frock and she was so delighted by it I didn't have the heart to tell her I hated it. It was crimson and it was low-cut, with an underwire that pushed everything up.'

He had the vision now. He blinked. 'Wow.'

'My mother's willowy,' she said, with just a trace of sympathy for a woman who'd never understood her daughter's figure. 'It would have looked elegant on Mum, but on me? It just made me look like a tart, and it got attention.' She paused for breath. 'Rodney Gareth was a horrid little toad, but sadly he was also the son of Malcolm Gareth QC, who's a horrid big toad. Rodney asked me to dance. He held me so tight my boobs were crushed hard against him. He swaggered all over the dance floor with me and I could feel his…excitement. I could hear the other girls laughing. And then…'

She fell silent for a moment and he thought she was going to stop. 'And then?' It'd kill him if he didn't get any further, he thought, but she relented.

'We all had these dinky little dance programmes, with

pencils attached,' she said. 'And, before I could stop him, he pulled mine from my wrist and held it up, pretending to check for my next free dance. And then he deliberately dropped the pencil down my cleavage.'

'Uh oh,' he said.

'Uh oh is right,' she said bitterly. 'I was standing in the middle of the dance floor and suddenly he shoved his whole hand down there. And people started laughing...'

'Oh, Penny.'

'So I kneed him right where it hurt most,' she said. 'I used every bit of power I had. I still remember his scream. It was one of the more satisfying moments of my life but of course it didn't last. I felt sick and cheap and stained. I walked out of the ball, back to my dorm, ripped my stupid dress off and called a cab to take me home. And don't you dare laugh.'

'I never would.' He hesitated. 'Penny... Did your parents laugh?'

'They were appalled. Mum was horrified. She could see how upset I was. But Dad? The first thing he did was ring Rodney's parents to find out if he was okay. His father told Dad they weren't sure if I'd interfered with the Gareth family escutcheon. He said they were taking him to hospital to check—I hadn't, by the way—and they intended to sue. Then the headmistress rang and said I wasn't welcome back at the school. Dad was furious and Mum's never had the nerve to stand up to him.'

'So what happened?'

'So I was packed off to Switzerland to a finishing school. That pretty much knocked any idea of being a palaeontologist on the head but, on the other hand, they ran cooking classes because that was supposed to be seemly, and if I wanted to do five cooking classes a week that was okay by them. So we had Monsieur Fromichade who I promptly fell in love with, even though I was sixteen and he was sixty. We still exchange recipes.'

'So happy ever after?'

She grimaced. 'It worked for a while. I took every cooking course I could and that was okay. Dad approved of what he told his friends were my three star Michelin intentions. Finally I took a job as an apprentice in a London café. It was simple food, nothing epicure about it. But I loved it.'

She paused, seemingly reluctant to expose any more of her family's dirty linen, but then she shrugged and continued. 'But then things fell apart at home.' She sighed. 'My sister had been overseas for years. There were rumours circulating about her behaviour on the Riviera and somehow Dad made it all Mum's fault. He's always favoured Felicity and he blamed Mum for her leaving home. Then Grandma died and Mum…got sick. Depression. She started phoning every day, weeping, begging me to come home. Finally I caved. I came home and Mum was in such a state I was frightened. I even agreed to what my Dad wanted, for me to be a company PR assistant. I thought I'd do it for a while, just until Mum recovered.'

She shrugged again. 'And it worked for a while. With me around to stand up for her, Dad stopped being such a bully. That took the pressure off Mum and things looked better. For Mum, though, not for me. And then Brett decided to court me.'

'Brett?' He shouldn't ask but how could he help it?

'It seems every guy I've ever dated has turned out to be fascinated by my parents' money,' she said bluntly. 'So I should have known. But maybe I was vulnerable, too. Brett's yet another toad, but I was too dumb and, to be honest, I was too unhappy and caught up in family drama to see it. I hadn't realized until I got home how close to the edge Mum was, and I was scared. I was trying every way I knew to make her feel good. Brett's a financial guru, smart, savvy and he knows how to pander to Dad. He's also good-looking and oh, so charming. In those awful months Brett helped. He honestly did. You have no idea how charming he was. He made me feel…special, and when he asked me to marry him I was dumb enough to say yes.'

'So celebrations all round?'

'You think?' she said bitterly. 'You know, the moment I said yes I had my doubts but I'm my mother's daughter. Dad was happy. Mum was well. For a while it was happy families all round. But then Felicity returned and Brett realized Felicity was Dad's absolute favourite and he could be part of our family and not have to sacrifice himself with the dumpy one.'

'Humiliation piled on humiliation,' he said softly and she cast him a glance that was almost scared.

'Yeah. I was paying too big a price to keep people happy and I've realized it. I'm over it.'

'I'm sure you're not.'

And she managed a smile. 'Maybe not quite, but I will be after a year's cooking at Malley's.'

'You can't go there.'

'When the water goes down, of course I can.'

'You'll hate it. The last time Malley set a mouse trap… Well, I've never seen one. What I have seen are dead mice.'

'Ugh!'

'Everywhere. He baits them and doesn't bother to clean.

'I can clean,' she said in a small voice.

'I bet you can but you shouldn't have to. Don't Mummy and Daddy supply you with enough money to be fancy-free?'

'That's offensive.'

'True.'

'Okay,' she conceded. 'Dad holds the purse strings but a legacy from Grandma left me basically independent. Not rich, but okay. Eventually I might set up a catering company in Adelaide or in Brisbane, but for now I need time to get my head together. I need to be as far from Sydney as possible.'

'Which is why you headed into the outback in *that* car?'

Now she grinned. 'Isn't it fun? Dad probably wants it back, though. He gave it to me when Brett and I got engaged. With a huge pink ribbon on it. I was momentarily the golden girl.'

'Shall we take it back to the creek and launch it? Let it float ceremoniously a few hundred miles to the ocean?'

She stared. 'Pardon?'

'We could take pictures of it floating out of sight and send them to your father. Very symbolic.'

She choked. 'Dad'd have a stroke. To say he's careful is an understatement.'

'But not careful of his daughter,' Matt said, his voice softening.

'Don't.'

'Don't what?'

'Get sympathetic. I'm fine as long as no one minds.'

'So no one minds?'

'No,' she said fiercely. 'No one at all. That last awful dinner, when Brett and Felicity walked in hand in hand, Mr and Mrs Smug… I was too gobsmacked to yell and Mum didn't have the strength to stand up for me. But I guess that was my line in the sand. I can't help Mum and I won't keep trying to please my father. And in a way it's liberating. I've walked away. I'm free.'

Then she paused. The night stilled and he thought of what he should say next.

But she got there before him.

'So what about you?' she asked.

He'd finished his beer. He was tired beyond belief. He should pick up his dishes and head via the kitchen to bed.

'What do you mean, what about me?'

'Who minds?' she asked. 'That's what you asked me. Who cares, Matt Fraser? You live here by yourself. No girlfriend? Boyfriend? Whatever?'

'I have a...' he said slowly, and then he paused. He didn't want to talk about Lily.

But this woman had just opened herself to him. She might say she was free, she was over being hurt, but he knew vulnerable when he saw it.

She'd trusted him with her story. How mean would it be not to give the same to her?

He tried again. 'I have a daughter,' he told her. 'Lily's thirteen years old and lives in the States with my ex-wife.'

She'd been gazing out over the farmland but now she swivelled to stare at him. He hadn't turned the porch lights on, but the moonlight and the light filtering from inside the windows was enough for her to see.

Not that he wanted her to see. He wanted his face to be impassive.

Which was pretty much how he wanted to be when he thought of Lily.

'Thirteen! You must have been a baby when she was born,' she stammered and he thought: *Yep, that just about summed it up.*

'I was twenty-four.'

'Wow.' She was still staring. 'So your wife took Lily back to the States. Isn't that hard to do? I mean...did you consent?'

'Darrilyn met an investment banker, coming to investigate...a project I was working on. He was rich, he lived in New York, she was fascinated and he offered her a more exciting life than the one she had with me. She was also four months pregnant. When you leave Australia with your child, the child needs the permission of both parents. When you're pregnant no one asks.'

'Oh, Matt...'

'It's okay,' he said, even though it wasn't. 'I have the resources to see her a couple of times a year.'

'Does she look like you?'

And, for some reason, that shook him.

The guys on the farm knew he had a daughter—that was the reason he took off twice a year—but that was as far as it went. When had he ever talked about his daughter? Never.

'I guess she does,' he said slowly. 'She has my black hair. My brown eyes. There's no denying parentage, if that's what you mean.'

'I guess. I didn't mean anything,' she whispered. 'I'm just thinking how hard it would be to leave her there.' She gave herself a shake, a small physical act that said she was moving on from something that was clearly none of her business. But it seemed she did have more questions, just not about Lily.

'So you,' she said. 'I've told you all about my appalling family. Your mum and dad?'

'Just mum.' Why was he telling her this? He should excuse himself and go to bed. But he couldn't. She was like a puppy, he thought, impossible to kick.

Or was there more? The need to talk? He never talked but he did now.

'This farm,' she was saying. 'I assumed you'd inherited it.'

'Sort of.'

'So rich mum, hey?'

'The opposite.' He hated talking about it but he forced himself to go on. 'Mum had me when she was eighteen and she had no support. I was a latchkey kid from early on, but we coped.' He didn't say how they'd coped. What use describing a childhood where he'd been needed to cope with his mother's emotional messes?

'Give me a hug, sweetheart. Sorry, I can't stop crying. Can you go out and buy pies for tea? Can you go down to the welfare and say Mummy's not well, we need money for food? But say I've just got the flu... I don't want them sticking their noses in here...'

He shook himself, shoving back memories that needed to be buried. Penny was waiting for him to go on.

'When I was twelve Mum took a housekeeping job about five hundred miles inland from Perth,' he told her. 'Sam Harriday was an eighty-year-old bachelor. He'd worked his parents' farm on his own for years and was finally admitting he needed help. So off we went, to somewhere Mum hoped we'd be safe.'

'Safe?'

'Sorry.' He caught himself, but now he'd said it he had to explain. A bit. 'There were parts of Mum's life that weren't safe.'

She was silent at that, and he thought she'd probe. He didn't want her to but he'd asked for it. But when she spoke again she'd moved on. Maybe she'd sensed his need for barriers. 'Good for your mum,' she told him. 'But so far inland... You were twelve? How did you go to school?'

'School of the Air.' He shrugged and smiled at the memory of his not very scholastic self. 'Not that I studied much. I took one look at the farm and loved it. And Sam...' He hesitated. 'Well, Sam was a mate. He could see how hungry I was to learn and he taught me.'

'But—' she frowned, obviously trying to figure the whole story '—this isn't his farm?'

'It's not,' he told her. 'Cutting a long story short, when I was fifteen Mum fell for a biker who got lost and asked for a bed. She followed him to the city but Sam offered to let me stay. So I did. I kept up with School of the Air until I was seventeen but by then I was helping him with everything. And I loved it. I loved him. He died when I was twenty-two and he left me everything.' He shrugged. 'An inheritance seems great until you realize what comes with it. The death of someone you love.'

'I'm sorry...'

'It's a while back now and it was his time,' he said, but he paused, allowing a moment for the memories of the old man he'd loved. Allowing himself to remember again the pain that happened when he'd been needed so much, and suddenly there was no one.

'So the farm was mine,' he managed, shaking off memories of that time of grief. It was rough country, a farm you had to sweat to make a living from, but it did have one thing going for it that I hadn't realized. It was sitting on a whole lot of bauxite. That's the stuff used to make aluminium. Apparently geologists had approached Sam over the years but he'd always seen them off. After he died one of them got in touch with me. We tested and the rest is history.'

'You own a bauxite mine?' she said incredulously and he laughed.

'I own a great sheep property. This one. I own a couple more properties down river—economies of scale make it worthwhile—but this place is my love. I also own a decent share of a bauxite mine. That was what got me into trouble, though. It's why Darrilyn married me, though I was too dumb to see it. But I'm well over it. My current plan is to make this the best sheep station in the state, if not the country, and the fact that I seem to have hauled the best shearers' cook I can imagine out of the creek is a bonus.'

He smiled and rose, shaking off the ghosts that seemed to have descended. 'Enough. If I don't go to bed now I'll fall asleep on top of a pile of fleece tomorrow. Goodnight, Penny.'

She stood up too, but she was still frowning. 'The mine,'

she said. 'Bauxite… Sam Harriday… It's not Harriday Holdings?'

'That's the one.'

'Oh, my,' she gasped. 'Matt, my father tried to invest in that mine. He couldn't afford to.'

'The shares are tightly held.'

'By you?'

'Mostly.'

She stood back from him and she was suddenly glaring. 'That must make you a squillionaire.'

'I told you I'd pay you. Now you know I can afford to. And I doubt I'm a squillionaire.' He shrugged. 'I don't even know what one is. And, by the way, I'd appreciate it if you didn't broadcast it. The locals don't know and I have no idea why I told you.'

'Because it's our night for secrets?' She hesitated and then reached out to touch his hand. 'Matt?'

He looked down at her hand on his. It looked wrong, he thought. This was a gesture of comfort and he didn't need comfort. Or maybe she intended to ask a question that needed it.

'Yes?' That was brusque. He tried again and got it better. 'Yes?'

'Where's your mother now?'

How had she guessed? he thought incredulously. How had she seen straight through his story to the one thing that hurt the most?

'Dead.'

'I'm sorry. But something tells me…'

'Don't!'

She hesitated and then her hand came up and touched his cheek, a feather-touch, a fleeting gesture of warmth.

'I won't ask but I'm sorry,' she whispered. 'And I'm even more sorry because…you might be a squillionaire, but something tells me that all the whinging I've just done doesn't come close to the pain you're hiding. Thank you for rescuing me yesterday, Matt Fraser. I just wish I could rescue you right back.'

CHAPTER SIX

IF EVER THERE was a cure for humiliation piled on humiliation, it was ten days of cooking for shearers. Ten days of pure hard work.

'We've only two more mobs left,' Matt told her with satisfaction. 'That's four days shearing and we're done. We've had the best weather. The best food. The best shear I've ever organised. You're our good luck charm, Penny Hindmarsh-Firth. I've a good mind to keep you.'

Matt hadn't stopped for ten days, Penny thought. He'd worked until after midnight almost every night. He said he went to bed but she saw his light at the far end of the veranda.

She had his situation pretty much summed up by now. Five sheep properties. A bauxite mine worth heaven only knew how much. Responsibilities everywhere.

The drapes in his bedroom were often pulled back. She could see his shadow against the light, sitting at his desk, working into the night.

He had a massive desk in his study. He wasn't using that.

Because she was here? She knew it was, but he wasn't avoiding her.

They'd fallen into a routine. Matt left the house before dawn, she saw him only briefly at meals but at dusk she sat on the veranda and talked to the dogs and he'd finally fetch his plate of leftovers from the warming drawer and come out to join her.

He was always dead tired. She could hear it in his voice, in the slump of his shoulders. Sometimes he seemed almost too tired to talk and she respected that, but still he seemed to soak up her company. And for herself? She liked him being here too, and she didn't need to talk. She was content to sit and watch the moon rise over the horizon, to breathe in the night air and let go of her fast-paced day.

And it was fast-paced. She'd set herself a personal challenge. Each day's cooking had to be at least as good as the days' before. It was worth it. 'Great tucker,' a shearer growled as he headed back to work. Or, 'Strewth, Pen, that sponge's almost as good as my gran used to make.'

And Matt had nothing but praise. 'I'd have pulled a rhinoceros out of the creek to get cooking like this,' he'd told her after the first couple of days and she had no idea why that throwaway line had the capacity to make her feel as if her insides were glowing.

The way he ate her food at night was compliment enough. He was always past exhaustion but he sat and savoured her food as if every mouthful was gold. He was enjoying his dinner now, as she sat and watched the moon rise.

She thought about the way he'd smiled at her when she'd handed him his plate. Somehow he didn't feel like an employer. She wasn't sure what he felt like, but...

'Malley doesn't know what he's getting.' Matt's low growl from where he sat behind her made her jump. She'd been dreaming. Of a smile?

Idiot!

She didn't answer. There was nothing to say to such a compliment. There was no reason his comment should have her off balance.

Though, actually, there was.

There were four more days of shearing to go. The floodwaters were slowly going down. She could probably leave now, though it'd still be a risk. And Matt still needed her.

But in four days…

'You are still going to Malley's?' Matt asked and she tried to think of a way to say it, and couldn't.

But he guessed. Maybe her silence was answer enough. 'You've changed your mind?' Matt put his empty plate aside and came across to where she sat on the edge of the veranda. He slipped down beside her and the night seemed to close in around them, a warm and intimate space that held only them.

What was she thinking? *Intimate?* He was her boss!

He was a man and she didn't trust herself with men. Didn't they always want something? Something other than her? Even Matt. He needed her to cook. She was useful, nothing else.

So stop thinking of something else.

'Malley changed my mind,' she managed, and was disconcerted at the way her voice worked. Or didn't work. Why were emotions suddenly crowding in on her?

And it wasn't just how close Matt was sitting beside her, she thought. It was more. In four days she wouldn't be needed. Again.

Wasn't that what she wanted?

Oh, for heaven's sake, get over it, she told herself and swung her feet in an attempt at defiance.

As if sensing his mistress needed a bit of support, Samson edged sideways and crept up onto her knee. He was filthy but she didn't mind. Penny had given up on the bathing. Samson was now a farm dog.

If her mother could see her now she'd have kittens, Penny thought. She was filthy too, covered in the flour she'd used to prepare the bread dough for the morning. She was cradling a stinking poodle.

But Matt was sitting by her side and she thought, *I don't*

care. Mum has Felicity if she wants a beautiful daughter. I'm happy here.

It was a strange thought—a liberating thought. She tried to think of Brett. Or Felicity. Of the two of them hand in hand telling her they'd betrayed her.

They can have each other, she thought, and it was the first time she'd felt no bitterness.

Ten days of shearing had changed things. Ten days of sitting outside every night with Matt? But there were only four days to go.

'You going to tell me about Malley?' Matt asked. He'd given her time. He'd sensed there were things she was coming to terms with, but now he was asking again.

What had she told him? *Malley changed my mind.*

Yeah, he had, and she'd been upset and she should still be upset. But how hard was it to be angry when she was sitting with this man whose empathy twisted something inside her that she hadn't known existed.

'I phoned Malley the night I got here,' she admitted. 'He told me I was a…well, I won't say what he said but the gist of it was that I was a fool for taking the route I did and he was an idiot himself for thinking a citified b…a citified woman could do the job. He said he'd find someone else. He called me a whole lot of words I'd never heard of. I guess I was pretty upset so when he rang back and expected me to drop everything…'

And then she stopped. She hadn't meant to say any more. What was it about this man that messed with her head? That messed with the plan of action she knew was sensible?

'Drop everything?' he said slowly, and she thought *uh oh*. She went to get up but he put his hand on her arm and held her still. 'You mean abandon this place?' He was frowning. 'Is that what he meant?'

'He rang me back two days after I got here,' she admitted. 'But it's okay. I used a few of his words back at him. Not…not the worst ones. But maybe the ones about being an idiot for ever thinking I'd take the job.'

'But why did he ring?'

This was sort of embarrassing. She'd been dumb to say anything at all but Matt was watching her. He was frowning, obviously thinking through the words she'd let slip. She had no choice but to be honest.

'He ended up almost as trapped as we are, so finding another cook wasn't an option,' she told him. 'And it's costing him. Malley's hotel is the base for scores of stranded tourists. He has supplies but no one to cook. He's losing a fortune.'

'So?' Matt said slowly.

'So he knows one of the chopper pilots who's doing feed drops up north. I gather for two days he fumed at how useless I was and then he realized he didn't have a choice. So he bribed the chopper pilot to come and get me.'

There was a loaded silence.

'So why didn't you go?'

'You told me he had mice.'

'And you told me you could clean.'

'So I could,' she said with sudden asperity. 'But I didn't see why I should clean for someone with such a foul mouth. The tourists can cook for themselves if they need to. Why should I go?'

'But you came all the way here to take a permanent, full-time job.'

'I did.'

'And shearing finishes in four days.' He frowned. 'Why didn't you accept? I don't understand.'

And she didn't, either. Not totally. It had been a decision of the heart, not the head, but she wasn't about to tell him that.

She reverted to being practical. 'The chopper pilot was

supposed to be dropping food to stranded livestock, so what was he about, agreeing to pick me up? How could I live with myself knowing cows were hungry because of me? Besides, they couldn't fit my car into the chopper.'

'You were the one who suggested leaving your car here until after the floods.'

Drat, why did he have to have such a good memory?

'So why?' he asked again, more gently, and suddenly there seemed nothing left but the truth.

'You needed me,' she told him. 'And…'

'And?'

Her chin tilted. This was something her family never got. Her friends never got. She'd been mocked for this before but she might as well say it. 'I was having fun.'

'Fun?' He stared at her in amazement. 'You've worked harder than any shearer. You've planned, you've cooked, you've cleaned. You've gone to bed as exhausted as me every night and you've got up every morning and started all over again. You call that fun?'

'Yes.' She said it firmly. It was a stand she'd defended for years and she wasn't letting it go now. Cooking was her love, and cooking for people who appreciated it was heaven. 'But you needn't sound so amazed. Tell me why you're here. You own a bauxite mine, one of the richest in the country. You surely don't need to farm. You're working yourself into the ground too. For what?'

'Fun?' he said and she smiled.

'Gotcha.'

'Okay.' He sighed. 'I get it, though I'm imagining the work at Malley's would have been just as hard. So where do you go from here? You knocked back a permanent job to help me.'

'I knocked back a permanent job because I wanted this one. And, even without the mice, Malley sounds mean.'

'The man's an imbecile,' Matt said. 'To bad-mouth a

cook of your standard? He obviously has the brains of a newt. To lose you…'

And then he paused.

The atmosphere changed. That thing inside her twisted again. To have someone defend her…value her…

It's the cooking, she told herself. She was never valued for herself.

But suddenly his hand was covering hers, big and rough and warm. 'Thank you,' he told her and it sounded as if it came from the heart. 'Thank you indeed—and I think your wages just went up.'

Fun.

He thought of the massive amount of work she'd put in over the last ten days. He thought of the drudgery of planning, chopping, peeling, cooking and cleaning. He thought of the mounds of washing-up. How had he ever thought he could handle it himself? In the end he'd hardly had time to help her cart food across to the shed, but she hadn't complained once.

She was a pink princess, the daughter of one of the wealthiest families in Australia, yet she'd worked as hard as any shearer.

And in four days? Shearing would be over. The water was already dropping in the creeks. Cooking at Malley's was obviously out of the question. Penny's long-term plan to set up a catering company would take months. Meanwhile, what would she do?

She'd come a long way to be here, and she'd come for a reason. She'd exposed her pain to him. She'd exposed the hurt her family had heaped on her. She was here to escape humiliation—and now, because she'd decided to help him she had little choice but to head back and face that humiliation again. Even if she went to another city the media would find her. He had no doubt the media frenzy during her sister's wedding would be appalling.

'Stay for a bit,' he found himself saying. Until the words were out of his mouth he didn't know he'd intended to say them, but the words were said. He'd asked the pink princess to stay.

There was a moment's silence. Actually, it was more than a moment. It stretched on.

She was considering it from all angles, he thought, and suddenly he wondered if she was as aware as he was of the tension between them.

Tension? It was the wrong word but he didn't have one to replace it. It was simply the way she made him feel.

She was little and blonde and cute. She played Abba on her sound system while she worked and she sang along. This morning he'd come in to help her cart food over to the shed and found her spinning to *Dancing Queen* while balancing a tray of blueberry muffins. She'd had flour on her nose, her curls had escaped the piece of pink ribbon she'd used to tie them back and Samson was barking at her feet with enthusiasm.

He'd stopped at the door and watched, giving himself a moment before she realized he was there. He'd watched and listened and he'd felt…

It didn't matter how he'd felt. He didn't *do* women. His mother and then Darrilyn had taught him everything he needed to know about the pain of relationships and he wasn't going there again. Especially with an indulged society princess.

The label wasn't fair, he told himself, and he knew it was the truth. Penny had proved she was so much more. But past pain had built armour he had no desire to shed, and right now he felt his armour had to be reinforced. Yet here he was asking her to stay.

'Why would I stay?' Penny asked cautiously and he tried to think of an answer that was sensible.

'I… This place… I was thinking maybe I could open it up a bit. Get rid of a few dustcovers. There's a possibility my daughter might come and visit.' That was the truth, though he wasn't sure when. 'I wouldn't mind if it looked a bit more like a home when she came. Maybe you could help. I'd pay.'

'I don't need…'

'I know you don't need to be paid,' he said. 'But I pay for services rendered. The shearers will move on, but I'd need you for another two weeks in total—a few days' slack then getting the house in order. Of course—' he grinned suddenly '—cooking would be in there as well. Donald and Ron and Harv would kill me if I didn't say that. They've been in heaven for the last ten days.'

And then he paused and tried to think about why he shouldn't say what came next. There were reasons but they weren't strong enough to stop him. 'And so have I,' he added.

Heaven…

That was pretty much what she was feeling.

She was breathing in the scents from the garden, watching the moon rise over the distant hills, listening to the odd bleat of a sheep in the shearing pens and the sound of a bird in the gums at the garden's edge.

'What's the bird?' she asked. It was an inconsequential question, a question to give her space and time to think through what he was proposing. There was a part of her that said what he was suggesting was unwise, but she couldn't figure out why.

Or maybe she knew why; she just didn't want to admit it. The way he made her feel… The way his smile made her heart twist…

'It's a boobook owl,' Matt said, quietly now, as if there was no big question between them. 'It's a little brown owl, nocturnal. He and his mate are the reason we don't have mice and places like Malley's do. Malley's stupid enough to have cleared the trees around the hotel and he's probably even stupid enough to shoot them. They're great birds. Listen to their call. *Boobook*. Or sometimes people call them mopokes for the same reason. So there's a question for you. Do you side with mopoke or boobook?'

It was an ideal question. It gave her time to sit and listen, to settle.

'Mopoke,' she said at last. 'Definitely mopoke.'

'I'm a boobook man myself. Want to see?'

'You need to go to bed.'

'So do you, but life's too short to miss a boobook.'

'A mopoke.'

He grinned. 'That's insubordination,' he told her. 'I believe I've just offered you a job for the next two weeks. Therefore I demand you accept your boss's edict that it's a boobook.'

'I haven't agreed to take the job yet.'

'So you haven't,' he said equitably. 'But you are still employed for four more days. So it's boobook tonight.' He pushed himself to his feet and held out his hand to help her up. 'Come and see.'

She looked at his offered hand and thought… *I shouldn't.*

And then she thought: *Why not?* There were all sorts of reasons, but Matt was smiling down at her and his hand was just there.

She shouldn't take it—but she did.

What was he doing?

He was more than tired. By this stage in shearing he was operating on autopilot. He'd averaged about five hours of sleep a night for the past ten days and, apart from the tiny window of time on the veranda at night, every minute he was awake was crammed with imperatives. Most of those imperatives involved tough manual labour but he also had to be fine-tuned to the atmosphere in the shed. One flare-up could mess with a whole shear. Angry shearers usually meant sloppy shearing and the flock suffered.

So far the tension had been minimal. The shearers had worked through each run looking forward to Penny's next meal, bantering about the last. This shear was amazing and it was pretty much thanks to the woman beside him. So surely he could take a few minutes to show her a boobook?

Besides, he wanted to.

He had a torch in his pocket. It was strong but it was small, casting a narrow band of light in front of them as they walked. They needed to go into the stand of gums behind the house. The ground was thick with leaf litter and fallen twigs so it was natural—even essential—that he keep hold of her hand. After all, she was a vital cog in his business empire. He needed to take care of her.

Even though it made him feel... How did he feel?

Good. That was too small a word but his mind wasn't prepared to think of another. Her fingers were laced in his and her hand was half his size. His fingers were cal-loused and rough, too rough to be holding something as warm and...trusting?

That was what it felt like but that was dumb. He'd fig-ured enough of Penny by now to know that she could look after herself. One move that she didn't like would have her screeching the farm down, and an inkling of Penny in peril would have the entire shearing team out in force.

He grinned at the thought and Penny must have heard his smile. 'What's the joke?'

'I just thought...if I tried a bit of seduction you'd have the team out here ready to defend you. Shears at the ready. Ron was watching you go back to the house yesterday and said you had a nice rear end. Margie told him where he could put his sexist comments and suddenly we had the whole shearing shed coming down on Ron like a ton of bricks. The poor guy had to bury himself packing fleeces into the wool press for the rest of the afternoon. You have an army at your disposal, Penelope Hindmarsh-Firth.'

'Excellent,' she said and smiled and was it his imagination or did her hold on his hand tighten a little? She paused for a moment as if she was thinking of something important—or trying to find the courage to say something—and finally out it came.

'Do you think I have a nice…rear end?'

Whoa. 'You have a very nice rear end,' he admitted. Who could argue with the truth?

'Thank you,' she told him. 'Yours isn't so bad either.'

That set him back. A woman telling him he had a good butt?

'But don't let it go to your head,' she told him. 'And I'll try and swallow my conceit too. Where did you say these owls are?'

The calls had ceased. That was because they were standing right under the trees the birds were nesting in.

It took him a moment to collect himself and direct his torchlight up. She disconcerted him. She was so close. She still smelled faintly yeasty, from the bread she'd set to rise. From something citrusy in her hair. From…being Penny?

What was he here for? He was looking for owls. *Right.*

'There…' Penny breathed—she'd caught sight of the first bird before he had. Even though he was holding the torch. *Good one, Fraser*, he told himself. *Get a grip.*

'The other will be close,' he managed.

'The other?'

'This is a nesting pair. They've been using the same nest for years, very successfully. Their young populate half this valley. Look, there's the female. She's a bit bigger than the male. They're feeling a bit threatened now. See, they're sitting bolt upright, but they've seen me so often I can't imagine they think of me as a threat.'

He was concentrating on the birds rather than Penny.

'Would the shearing team leap to their defence too?' she asked mildly and he smiled.

'They might. No one likes their quarters overrun by mice. These guys do us a favour. But I don't think they'd come quite as fast as if you needed help. You've—deservedly—made some pretty fierce friends.'

'Matt?'

'Mmm?'

'Stop it with the compliments. They don't mean anything and I don't want them.'

And the way she said it made him pause. It made him stop thinking of how she smelled and, instead, think about where she'd come from.

He got it, he thought. She'd just been through one messy relationship. He didn't know this Brett guy who'd been such a toe-rag but he could imagine. Somehow, he had a pretty clear idea of her family dynamics by now. In some ways Penny was tough but in others…she was exposed, he thought, and Brett must have sensed that weakness. If he'd said great things to her she would have believed them. She'd believed them all the way to a calamitous engagement.

So now she thought compliments were a means of manipulation and he could understand why. He had to shut up. Except suddenly he couldn't.

'Right,' he told her. 'No more compliments. But there are a few truths—not compliments, truths, that I'm not taking back. Firstly, your cooking is awesome and I'm incredibly grateful. Second, I'd agree with Ron—you do have a nice rear end, even though it's an entirely inappropriate comment for a boss to make about his employee. And finally there's one more thing which I need to say and it'll make you blush because it's a ripper.'

'A ripper?' she said faintly. 'A ripper of a compliment?'

'Not a compliment,' he told her, throwing caution to the wind. He took her other hand and tugged so she was facing him. 'Just the truth. Penelope Hindmarsh-Firth, you smell of fresh baked bread and yeast and the aroma of a day spent in the kitchen, my kitchen, and if you think me telling you that you have a nice backside is an empty compliment then the world's upside down. This is a gorgeous night and I'm holding the hands of a woman who's saved my butt. She has a beautiful backside, not to mention the rest of her—and she smells and looks beautiful. Messy but beautiful. No more compliments, Penny. Just the truth. So...'

He paused then and took a deep breath and fought for the strength to say what had to be said. Because it was unwise and shouldn't be said at all but how could he not?

'So?' she whispered and somehow he found himself answering. Still telling it like it was.

'So we need to go in now because if we stay out here one moment longer I'll be forced to kiss you.'

And there it was, out in the open. This thing...

'And you don't want to?' It was a whisper, so low he thought he'd misheard. But he hadn't. Her whisper seemed to echo. Even the owls above their head seemed to pause to listen.

This was such a bad idea. This woman was his employee. She was trapped here for the next four days, or longer if she took him up on his offer to extend.

What was he doing? Standing in the dark, talking of kissing a woman? Did he want to?

'I do want to,' he said because there was nothing else to say.

'Then what's stopping you?'

'Penny…'

'Just shut up, Matt Fraser, and kiss me.'

And what could he say to that?

The night held its breath and Matt Fraser took Penny Hindmarsh-Firth into his arms and he kissed her.

Wow.

Um…

Wow?

This was wrong on so many levels. Firstly, she should still be in mourning for her broken engagement and the betrayal that went with it.

Second, this man was her boss.

Third, she was alone out here, under the gums and the starlight with a man she'd met less than two weeks ago.

The owls above their heads had decided they no longer needed to be wary and were swooping off, dark shadows against the moonlight as they continued their night's hunt.

Under her feet was a carpet of leaf litter that gave off the scent of eucalypts when she moved. But how could she move?

Matt was tugging her close. Her face was tilting up to his and his mouth met hers.

Matt hadn't shaved for a couple of days—when would he find time? His clothes were rough, heavy moleskin pants and a thick shirt open at the throat, sleeves rolled back to reveal arms of sheer brawn. His hands were scarred and weathered.

He smelled of the shearing shed. He'd washed and changed before he'd come out to the veranda but the lanolin from the fleeces seemed to have seeped into his pores. He smelled and felt what he was. He owned this land but he stood beside his men. He did the hard yards with them.

He was a man of steel.

He kissed her as if this was the first time for both of

them. As if he had all the time in the world. As if he wasn't sure what it was he'd be tasting but he wasn't about to rush it.

His hands moved to her hips but he didn't tug her into him, or if he did it wasn't hard, and maybe the fact that she was melting against him was an act of her own voli-tion. She could back away at any time.

But oh, the feel of him. The sensation of his lips brush-ing hers. For now it was just brushing, almost a feather-touch, but it was the most sensual thing she'd ever felt. His hands on the small of her back… The feel of his rough hair as she tentatively lifted her hand and let herself rake it…

Oh, Matt.

Oh, wow.

But he wasn't pressing. He wasn't pushing and suddenly she saw it from his point of view.

She was in his terrain, and she was all by herself. He was a man of honour. He was kissing her on terms that said the control was hers. She could pull back.

And with that thought came the most logical next thought.

If she was in control then bring it on. How could she not? This man was gorgeous. The night was gorgeous. She was a twenty-seven-year-old woman out under the stars with a man to die for.

And then, quite deliberately, she let her thoughts dis-solve. She raised her hands to his hair so she had his head and she tugged him closer. She stood on tiptoe to get closer still.

She opened her lips and she welcomed him in.

Penny was melting under his hands and there wasn't a thing he could do about it.

How could he want to do anything about it?

She'd stood on tiptoe and surrendered her mouth to him.

Her hands claimed him. Her body said she wanted this kiss as much or more than he did, and he'd better get on with it.

And so he did, and the sensation was enough to do his head in. The warmth, the heat, the fire… The night was dissolving in a mist of desire where nothing existed except this woman in his arms. This woman kissing him as fiercely as he kissed her. This woman whose body language said she wanted him as much as he wanted her.

A moment in time that was indescribable. Inevitable. World-changing?

The moment stretched on, a man and a woman in the moonlight, almost motionless, welded together by the heat from this kiss. From this need.

From this recognition that something was changing for both of them?

And with that thought…*trouble*.

It was as if his past had suddenly flown back, a cold chill of memory. Of love given and not returned. Of faith and trust blasted. Of the emptiness of loss. The grief…

He felt it almost as a physical jolt and, as if she'd felt it, she was suddenly tugging back. Maybe she'd had the same jolt of uncertainty, the same frisson that their worlds were both under threat by some new order.

And it almost killed him, but he let her go.

'W…wow,' she breathed and he thought: *Good description*. He couldn't think of a better word himself.

'You kiss good,' she managed. She looked dazed. A curl had escaped her ponytail and was coiling down across her eyes. He couldn't help himself—he lifted it and pushed it back.

But he didn't take her back into his arms.

'You're not so bad yourself,' he ventured, but the ghosts had been right to tug him back. He had no intention of getting involved with any woman. He would not face that kind of grief again.

But this wasn't any woman. This was Penny.

'We…we should be careful.' She couldn't quite disguise the quaver in her voice. 'If we go any further we'll shock the owls.'

'Probably not wise,' he managed.

'None of this is wise,' she whispered. 'But I'm not sure I care.'

It was up to him. And somehow he made the call. Somehow the ghosts prevailed.

'I need to be up before dawn,' he told her.

There was a long silence. Then, 'Of course you do.' There was still a tremble in her voice but she was fighting to get it under control.

Somehow he stayed silent. Somehow he managed not to gather her into his arms and take this to its inevitable conclusion.

It almost killed him.

But she had herself under control now. He could see her gathering herself together. This was a woman used to being rebuffed, he thought, and somehow that made it worse. But the ghosts were all around him, echoes of lessons long learned.

He didn't move.

'Then goodnight, Matt,' she whispered at last, and she reached out and touched his face in the most fleeting of farewell caresses. 'Sleep well. Sleep happy and sensible.'

And she turned and, without a torch, not even noticing the rough ground, she practically ran back to the relative sanctuary of the house.

It was done.

Sense had prevailed.

CHAPTER SEVEN

THEY WORKED SOLIDLY for the next four days. The timetable remained the same. They hardly saw each other during the day but at night Matt continued bringing his meal out to the veranda. Penny was always there, watching the moonlight, soaking up the stillness. Nothing had changed.

Except everything had.

There was a stillness between them. It was a kind of tension except it wasn't a tension. There was something happening that Matt couldn't figure.

He'd hurt her. He knew he had, he thought, as he sat on the veranda four nights later. He'd seen her face as he'd pulled away that night. She'd practically thrown herself at him. Now she was humiliated and he didn't know what to do about it.

Saying sorry wasn't going to cut it. Saying sorry would simply be saying she'd offered herself to him and he'd refused, but that wasn't how it had been. The tug between them was mutual.

But he'd had no choice. Penny had been honest enough to accept their desire was mutual, but the barriers he'd put up over the years had held. He wasn't going down that path again.

But what path? The path of grief he'd felt when his mother had left? When the old man who'd befriended him had died?

Or the path of betrayal both his mother and his wife had shown him?

He'd put Penny in the same bracket and she knew it. He'd humiliated her. He'd hurt her. He knew it but he didn't have a clue what to do about it.

And maybe Penny was used to such humiliation because she simply got on with it. She smiled at him, she used the same casual banter, she sat on the veranda now and shared the silence and it was as if nothing had happened.

Except the hurt was still there. How did he know? The sparkle of fun behind her eyes had changed, just a little. She was good at hiding hurt, he thought. If he didn't know her so well...

How did he know her so well? He didn't have a clue. He only knew that he did and he also knew that it had him retreating.

If he went one step further...

He couldn't. The next step would be a crashing down of those boundaries. A shattering of armour.

After all those years, how could he do that?

Penny rose. They'd been sitting on the veranda for only twenty minutes or so and they usually stayed an hour, but tomorrow was the last day of the shear. He had things to do and maybe she did too.

Or maybe this thing between them was too much.

'I'm making bulk choc chip cookies before I go to bed,' she told him. 'The team's heading on to McLarens' tomorrow and they're already whinging about the cooking they'll get there. I thought I'd send them with a goodbye kit.'

'They'll expect you back next year,' Matt told her and she paused and looked down at him in the dim light.

'I'll be well into organizing my catering company by then,' she said thoughtfully. 'But if you pay me enough I'll come.'

'Is that what you plan to do? Set up a catering company?'

'Yes,' she said, almost as if she was speaking to herself. 'I'll make it a success. I know it. Maybe I can find enough competent staff interested in outback experiences to let me offer catering for shearing.'

And he had to ask. 'So will you come, or will it be your competent staff?'

'Who knows?' She said it lightly but he still heard the pain.

'Penny?'

'Mmm?' She leaned down to lift his empty plate from the bench beside him but he reached out and took her wrist before she could lift it.

'Are you staying for the next two weeks?' he asked. 'You haven't said.'

She stilled. She looked down at her wrist.

He released it. No pressure.

What was he thinking, no pressure? There was pressure everywhere.

'Do you still want me to?'

And of course he should say no. He should say the thought had been a dumb one when he'd made the offer. His barricades needed reinforcing.

He'd hurt her and he had no intention of hurting her again. He needed to back off and let her go.

But the night was still and Penny didn't move. His grip on her wrist was light. She could pull away if she wanted.

She didn't.

And all at once he thought: *To hell with barricades. Let's just…see.*

'This thing between us…' he managed and she stayed silent. What happened next was obviously down to him. As it should be.

'Penny, the way I feel…it's been so long. And, to be honest…' He shook his head and finally released her wrist. 'Penny, you've been hurt. You know how it feels. But me?'

And then he stopped. How could he explain? How could he tell anyone the hurt of those long years?

But then he thought this was Penny and he'd hurt her. He couldn't let it stay like this. He needed to let down the barricades a little.

He needed to talk.

'If you don't want to tell me, you don't need to,' she said gently.

She was giving him an out. Her generosity almost took his breath away, and it tore away the last of his reservations.

She sat beside him, as if she understood he needed time. He couldn't look at her. For some reason it seemed impossible to say what had to be said when he was watching her.

But her body was touching his and the warmth of her, her closeness—her trust?—made it imperative to tell her what he'd told nobody. Ever.

And finally he did.

'Penny, my mother was a serial relationship disaster,' he said at last. 'She went from man to man to man. Every time she fell deeply, irrevocably in love, and every single relationship meant our lives were turned upside down. Romance for my mother inevitably ended in chaos and heartbreak. Moving houses, moving schools, debt collectors, sometimes even assault, hospitals, the courts. The best thing Mum ever did for me was run from a calamitous relationship and take the housekeeping job on Sam's farm. That was my salvation. If she hadn't done that, heaven knows where I'd have been. Sam's farm was my first and only taste of stability and I stayed there for ten years. Sam left me the farm and I thought I'd stay there for ever. And then I discovered the bauxite and Darrilyn discovered me.'

'More chaos?' Penny whispered. She was looking out at the moonlight too, giving him space. Giving him silence to work out what he needed to say.

'More chaos,' he said grimly. 'I was naïve, little more than an idiot kid, and I was besotted. I didn't put the discovery of bauxite and the sudden interest of the neighbouring farmer's gorgeous daughter together. I married her and when we found out she was pregnant I was over the moon. But marriage and pregnancy had been her only goals. Legally, they gave her the right to the money she wanted. She headed to the US with a guy who knew her worth and was probably in on her plan from the beginning. So that's it. I see Lily twice a year and it breaks my heart.'

'But now?' She sounded as if she was walking on eggshells. 'You said she might be coming home.'

'Home?' He gave a hollow laugh. 'Does she have such a thing? Her mother's relationships have broken down again and again. Lily's been given the same raw deal as me, but there's nothing I can do about it. Her mother's always refused to let her come to Australia. I leave the farm with the boys twice a year and spend as much time with her as I can, and every time I leave it rips me in two. But even if I moved there Darrilyn wouldn't give me more access. So that's it, Penny. That's where I've been with relationships. Burned. I don't need them.'

'So…' Penny took a deep breath '… Matt, what's that got to do with me?'

'I don't know.' And it was an honest answer. How could he explain what he didn't understand himself? 'Penny, how I feel…'

'Must be like I feel,' she ventured when he couldn't go on. 'Like I've been an idiot and how can I trust myself to try again? Only your ghosts must be harder on you than mine. My parents have their faults but they've given me stability.' Her gaze raked the moonlit landscape. 'You know, this is the most settled place I've ever been in. I'm imagining how you must have felt as a child when you finally made it to Sam's farm. And now. Here's your home and life is good. You wouldn't want to mess with that for anything.'

'You mean I wouldn't want to mess with that for you?'

'I'm not putting words into your mouth,' she said with sudden asperity. She rose, breaking the moment, and a tinge of anger entered her voice. 'I can't help you, Matt. I have my own demons to deal with and, believe me, the fact that I've been monumentally dumb is a huge thing to accept. I don't need a relationship either.' She took a deep breath as if she was having trouble forcing the words out, but finally she managed it.

'But you know what? Regardless of relationships, I'm moving on. Being here has kept my demons at bay, regardless of…of what's happening between us. And I still have the same problem—media interest in my appalling sister and her equally appalling fiancé. I like working here,' she confessed. 'It feels good and I suspect if I made a pile of meals and stocked the freezer, you guys would be grateful.'

'We would.' He definitely would.

'There you go, then. Maybe that's my bottom line. There's cooking to be done and organization in the house. I can put my head down and go for it.'

'I don't want you to work…'

'I'm staying to work, Matt,' she said, still with that trace of astringency. 'Anything else…who knows? As I said, we each have our own demons. But should they affect the next two weeks? Maybe not. So let's make this an employment contract only. Two more weeks of work—at shearers' cook rates.'

'Hey! You're not cooking for a team. Shearers' cook rates?' But he felt himself starting to smile.

She arched her brows and met his gaze head-on. 'I'm filling the freezer and that'll be like cooking for a team. Shearers' cook rates or nothing. That's my offer, Matt Fraser, and it's final. So…do you still want me to stay or do you not?'

She was looking up at him, resolute, courageous, firm.

When he'd first met her he'd thought she was ditzy. She wasn't. She had intelligence to spare.

She was beautiful.

Suddenly he wondered—was this the courage to try again?

And then there was no choice. The night righted itself. He rose and took her hands.

'Penny, I want you to stay.'

'Really?'

'Really.'

'Then I accept. I'm on a great wage. You have big freezers and I like a challenge. What's not to love?'

What's not to love?

It was all he could do not to kiss her. And then he thought: *Why not?*

So he did and, amazingly, wonderfully, she didn't object. She responded.

But this wasn't the kiss of passion they'd shared on the night of the owls. It was tentative—a question—and when they pulled apart the question was still in their eyes.

'You know, when you're around I have trouble being interested in how empty my freezers are,' he confessed.

'Well, you should be.' She was smiling as she stepped back. She seemed suddenly a woman in charge of her world, ready to move on. 'Because you're paying me heaps.' She tugged her hands back and he let her go. 'For the rest, let's just see. But for now… Matt, I need to go bake some cookies. Freezers, here I come.'

He headed out to check on the last pens of sheep, the last runs before the end of shearing.

Penny headed for the kitchen.

She'd promised the shearing team takeaway choc chip cookies. Right. She could do that.

Samson snoozed by the fire. The kitchen felt like a refuge.

She mixed her two flours and then stared at the mixture and stared at the flour sacks and wondered—had she just used half self-raising flour, half plain, or had she put in two lots of plain?

Uh oh.

She started again, this time trusting herself so little that she made a list of ingredients that were usually in her head and ticked them as she put them in.

But how could she think of ingredients?

Matt had kissed her. Twice. Matt wanted her to stay.

And she understood him. From that first day when she'd seen him on his gorgeous black horse she'd thought of him as a man in charge of his world, and little had happened to change that. The shearers looked up to him and it wasn't because he owned the place. She'd learned enough of human nature now to know bosses earned respect; they didn't buy it.

So Matt was a man of strength, intelligence and honour, but she'd just been allowed a glimpse of the building blocks that had made him. It felt like an enormous privilege.

She put both her hands in the bowl and started mixing. The feel of the cookie dough under her hands was a comfort. It was a task she'd loved doing for years.

The family cook had taught her to do this. Her parents hadn't been around much but they'd been in the background.

Who'd baked choc chip cookies for Matt?

No one. She knew it as surely as she knew what he'd told her was scarcely the tip of the iceberg that was the nightmare of his childhood.

'Bless you, Sam,' she told the old farmer who'd finally

taken the young Matt under his wing. 'I wish I could make you choc chip cookies.'

And suddenly her eyes filled with tears. Why? It hardly made sense. She sniffed and told herself she was a dope but the tears kept coming.

'So we're adding a little salty water into the mix,' she said out loud. 'My secret ingredient.'

Two weeks to cure a lifetime of hurt?

That wasn't the way it worked. Matt didn't see himself as someone who needed curing, and she was hardly qualified to help.

'But he might kiss me again...'

The tears disappeared. Hope was suddenly all around her, a bright, perky little voice that bounced with delight. Enough with the past. She had freezers to fill.

And demons to scatter?

'I hope he likes choc chip cookies,' she told the sleeping Samson. 'Because I'm about to fill his freezers with a ton.'

He'd hired her for two more weeks. He'd told her his past.

Was he nuts?

He checked the pens and then walked down the paddocks to check the newly shorn sheep. The weather was brilliant, as it had been for the whole shear. The starkly white sheep didn't even appear to notice that they'd lost their coats. They were relaxed, hardly edging away as he walked the boundaries of the holding paddocks. There were no problems with the flock that he could see. No problems on the horizon either.

He opened the gates of the house paddocks to the pastures beyond. To all intents and purposes, the sheep were free.

Like he intended to be.

Freedom. That was what he'd craved when he'd somehow hauled himself together after Darrilyn walked out.

His mother had moved from one hysterical mess to an-other. He'd spent his childhood dealing with her tears, her drama, her hopelessness, and his one foray into marriage had been more of the same.

Freedom had looked good. This place was his solace, his refuge, his love.

But now? Not only had he just opened himself up to Penny, exposing pain he'd never thought he'd reveal, but he'd pushed her to stay for two weeks.

And a question was starting to niggle.

Did he have the courage to try again? With a pink prin-cess with a past almost as troubled as his?

He walked on. In the distance he could still see the house. The lights were on at the south end, which meant the kitchen was still in use. Penny would be cooking.

He could go and join her. He could sit at the kitchen table and watch her hands create food to die for. He could watch the flour accumulate on her nose—she always seemed to have flour on her nose.

Maybe he could offer to help—he could wash while she wiped.

There was a romantic thought.

He stopped and closed his eyes. The silence was almost absolute. Even the owls were silent and he thought sud-denly: *It's as if something momentous is about to happen.*

Momentous? Like Matt Fraser breaks his own rule and lets his guard down with a woman?

How insulting was that? he thought, and swore silently to himself. What was he expecting, that Penny jump him? That he'd have to fight her off?

It was a dumb thought, but it had its merits. He found himself smiling as he walked on. He wouldn't mind.

He wouldn't fight her off.

'I won't hurt her.' There was another thought, almost a vow.

How serious was he getting, and how fast?

'Not serious at all,' he told himself as he finally turned for home. Surely she'd finished cooking by now? The house would be in darkness and he could slip in without seeing her.

Was that what he wanted? To avoid her for two weeks?

'You know it's not or you wouldn't have invited her,' he told himself and he found himself wishing his dogs were with him. His own company wasn't cutting it. But the dogs were exhausted after a full day in the yards.

So was he. He needed to go to sleep and stop worrying about what lay ahead.

And stop fancying what else might happen.

'When are you coming home?'

Penny's mother hadn't phoned her for two weeks. When she didn't phone, Penny knew she was in trouble. Depression dogged her mother, and silence was a symptom. But Louise's silence while Brett and Felicity outlined their marriage plans had made Penny decide enough was enough.

Penny's father was a bully and her half-sister was a self-serving shrew, but Louise didn't have the courage to stand up to either of them.

Tonight her mother's voice sounded thick with tears. Penny was willing herself not to care.

It didn't work. How could she stop caring?

'I told you, Mum, I'm working out here. It doesn't matter when I get home.'

'Where exactly are you working?'

'South Australia. Murray River country. I'm working as a cook, Mum. I'm safe, I'm doing a good job and I'm keeping…' She paused, but why not say it like it was? 'I'm keeping myself occupied so I don't need to think about Felicity and Brett.'

'They're both unhappy about hurting you.'

'You know, I'm very sure they're not.'

'No, they are.' And here she went again, Penny thought. Her mother spent her life pretending they were happy families. 'I'm sure Felicity would like you to be her bridesmaid.'

'I'm sure she'd hate it.'

'Well, she *should* have you.' The tears were unmistakable now. 'I don't like you unhappy. I want you to be her bridesmaid and I told her that.'

'It's not going to happen,' Penny said gently. 'I wish Felicity all the best but I'm not coming home for the wedding.'

'Not even coming?' Her mother sounded appalled.

'Mum, how can I?'

'Sweetheart, you must.' Her mother hiccupped on a sob. 'It's in three weeks. St Barnabas Chapel followed by a grand reception on the Harbour. For you not to be there...' Another sob. 'Felicity's mother will lord it over me. Your father won't care. Penny, I can't do it without you.'

How impossible was it to harden your heart? She tried. 'Mum, I'm happy here.'

There was a moment's pause. Maybe something in Penny's voice had got through. 'Really?'

'I am,' she told her. 'And Samson's turning into a sheepdog. You should see him.'

'I thought you were working at a hotel.'

'This is sheep country.'

'So you're meeting the locals?'

'I...some of them. But Mum, I can't come to the wedding. I'm so busy I'm even starting to forget what Felicity and Brett did to me.' She took a deep breath and decided to say it like it was. 'To be honest, I'm even starting to feel sorry for Felicity. And worried. You should tell Felicity there are a lot nicer men than Brett.'

'You wanted to marry him.'

'That was before I knew what a toerag he was. There are still some honourable men in the world.'

She shouldn't have said it. If there was one thing Louise was good at, it was sussing out gossip and, despite her distress, she could almost feel her mother's antennae quiver. '"Honourable men",' she said slowly. There was a loaded pause and then, 'Penny, have you met one?'

Shut up, Penny, she told herself. Get off the phone fast.

But she wouldn't lie. Had she met an honourable man? Yes, she had, and the thought was a good one.

'That's for me to know and you to guess,' she told her mother, forcing herself to sound breezy. 'Goodnight, Mum.'

'Penny, please come.'

'I can't.'

But she lay in bed that night and thought of her mother's tears. She thought of her mother, isolated at the wedding by her appalling husband and her even more appalling stepdaughter.

How did you rid yourself of the ties of loving?

She should ask Matt.

CHAPTER EIGHT

IN THE NEXT few days, while Matt coped with the tasks that had to be done before the wool was sent for sale, Penny attacked the house.

If anyone had ever told her she'd find joy in a mop and bucket, she'd have told them they were crazy. But cleaning took her mind off her mother's increasingly distressed phone calls, and this was a challenge worth tackling.

Ever since she'd walked into the house she'd thought of it as something out of a Charles Dickens novel. 'I feel like I might find Miss Havisham under one of these dust sheets,' she told Matt as they sat on the veranda that night. 'How long have they been here?'

'Donald's mother was a socialite,' Matt told her. 'She ran away when Donald was seven and his dad pretty much closed the house. When Donald sold me the house and contents I left it as it was. I use my bedroom, the den and the kitchen. I've no need for anything else.'

'You're two male versions of Miss Havisham,' she told him. 'Not that I mind. You can gloat over your wool clip while I clean. I'll even enjoy it.'

'I would be grateful,' Matt admitted. 'If Lily comes…'

'Is that likely to happen?'

'Maybe,' he said slowly. 'She's not getting on with Darrilyn's new partner. Darrilyn's talking about sending her to school in Australia so it's not impossible.' But he sounded like a man who was scarcely allowing himself to hope.

'Does she know anyone in Australia?'

'No, and that's why I'm telling Darrilyn she'd need to come here first. So she knows some sort of base.'

'Poor kid,' Penny said, and meant it. She knew all about being a teenage thorn in her socialite parents' lives and the thought of the unknown Lily was part of her driving force.

'The sofa in the main sitting room's so hard it feels like sitting on bricks,' she told him. 'Why not replace it with something squishy? Now the flood's receded you can get it delivered and, with the fire lit, that room would be lovely. It needs a big telly, though, and all the things that go with it. If Lily comes she won't feel welcome if she has to sit on a horsehair brick. And her bedroom... I'd suggest buying a four-poster bed. Not pink, unless you see her as a pink girl.'

'I don't,' he said faintly. 'Penny, she probably won't come.'

'You know,' she said diffidently, 'if I was thirteen and there was conflict at home, my dad sending pictures of the bedroom he'd prepared for me might well make me feel a whole lot better about myself, whether I was allowed to come or not.'

'Even if they're never used?'

'You can afford it,' she told him bluntly. 'And Lily sounds like she needs it.'

'How do you know?'

'I don't. I'm guessing. You want to go with my guess or with yours?'

He looked at her for a long moment and then raked his hair. 'You probably do know more about thirteen-year-old girls than I do.'

'Hey, I was one once,' she said cheerfully. 'If you agree, I'd suggest we go with a theme of antique white. The rooms are so old-fashioned, why don't we...'

'We?'

'Me then,' she said and grinned. 'Why don't I go for white on white? Broderie anglaise, heritage quilting, a deep rug on the floor, some old-fashioned sampler type pictures on the wall…'

'How do you know what she'd like?'

'I know what I'd like,' she told him. 'If my parents had done something like this for me…'

And then her voice cracked. She heard it but there wasn't a thing she could do about it.

'Still hurting, huh?' Matt said. They were sitting on the edge of the veranda and he reached out and touched her face. It was a fleeting gesture, but it said, in some deep way, that he understood the distress she still felt whenever she thought of her mother's pleas. The knowledge was enough to make her toes curl.

She concentrated fiercely on getting them uncurled.

'I can forget about it here,' she managed.

'But you can't stay here for ever?'

'No. And Malley's isn't an option any more. But neither is staying away, I guess. My sister's getting married on the seventeenth and Mum's organising a family dinner on the twelfth. On Dad's orders. To heal differences, he says, and he expects me to be there. He'll blame Mum if I'm not.'

'Surely you won't go?' He sounded appalled. That was how she felt but what choice did she have?

'You see, I love Mum,' she said simply.

She loved, therefore she did what was expected.

Matt was silent for a while. The night was closing in on them and somehow it felt…almost threatening? Why did this man make her feel so exposed?

'I guess that's why I don't love,' Matt said at last. 'I won't let myself need people and I won't be needed.'

'No?' She gave a hollow laugh. 'What about Lily?'

'Lily's different. She's my kid.'

'And this is my mum.'

'And your mum should be protecting you, as I'd protect Lily. Penny, your mum's an adult. She's had a lifetime to form her own armour and maybe that's what you need to do.'

'That's cruel.'

'It is,' he said gently. 'But your mother's made her own choices and maybe it's time for you to do the same. You only have one life. Will you spend it trying to please your family? Being a doormat?'

'What's the alternative? Carrying a bucketload of guilt for the rest of my life?' She tried to say it lightly but failed.

'So you'll go back to your mum.'

'I might.' But she knew she would.

'Maybe your mum could come to you?'

'What, here?'

'Maybe not. It'd be a bit of a culture shock—from Sydney to Jindalee.' She heard Matt's smile rather than saw it. They hadn't turned on the veranda lights and the darkness had crept up on their silence. 'But Penny, if you make yourself a life, set up your catering company, do what you want to do… If your mum wants, then maybe she could choose to help you? Maybe she could live near you, on her own rather than in an unhappy marriage? You could help her on your terms rather than hers.'

'She'll never leave.'

'Then that's her choice,' he said gently. 'But it doesn't have to be your choice. Attending the wedding should be your line in the sand. Maybe you should do something for yourself instead. Have a weekend in a fabulous resort. I'll arrange it for you if you like, as a thank you for getting me out of such trouble at shearing. But, no matter what, just say no.'

'Oh, Matt…'

'You can do it,' he growled and he rose and leant down and ran a finger lightly through her curls. The touch made her shiver. 'If you can keep a mob of shearers happy, you can do anything. I believe in you, Penny Hindmarsh-Firth, so maybe it's time for you to believe in yourself.'

And then there was another of those silences which fell between them so often. Mostly they felt natural. Mostly they felt good. But this one…

This one seemed loaded.

You can do it. That was what Matt had said.

Do what? What she really wanted?

If she really believed in herself, Penny thought, she'd get up from where she was sitting and she'd kiss this guy senseless. She might even demand he let go of his own ghosts and come to this luxury resort with her.

But she was Penny. Asking for love? She never had. She'd loved and loved and where had that got her?

You can do it.

Yeah, right. Not in a million years.

'Goodnight, Penny,' Matt said heavily then, as if he too acknowledged the impossibility of moving on.

'Goodnight,' she whispered.

She felt sad. No, she felt desolate, but still she went inside and rang her mother. She said no and she meant it—and, despite the weird feeling of desolation, it felt like a beginning.

Two days later, the year's wool clip was finally loaded for market. She saw the slump of Matt's shoulders as he watched the line of trucks roll off the property. She thought of the work he'd put in, the late nights he'd pulled, the light on in his study until almost dawn.

And suddenly she thought…picnic?

She walked out to meet him in the driveway.

'Well done,' she told him.

'The fleece is great. It feels a whole lot better than taking money from a bauxite mine.'

'I'll bet it does,' she said and then added diffidently, 'Want to come on a picnic?'

'What?' It was as if he hadn't heard the word before.

'You haven't stopped for weeks,' she told him. 'Ron and Harv are rested. They can take over anything that needs to be done. Is there anywhere we can go? Somewhere you can't see a single sheep? Honest, Matt, you must be seeing them in your sleep.'

'If I fell asleep every time I counted them I'd be in trouble,' he agreed, smiling faintly. 'But now I need to get onto drenching.'

'Matt. One day. Holiday. Picnic.'

And he turned and looked at her. 'You must be exhausted too.'

'If it'll make you agree to a picnic, yes, I am.'

She met his gaze, tilted her chin, almost daring him to refuse.

Finally he seemed to relent. 'There is somewhere…' he said doubtfully. 'But we'd have to take horses. The ground's undermined by rabbit warrens and the four-wheel drive won't get in there without damaging the ferns.'

'And we don't want that,' she said, not having a clue what he was talking about but prepared to encourage him. And then she thought about it a bit more and said, less enthusiastically, 'Horses?'

'Do you ride?'

'My mother bought me a pony when I was seven,' she said, feeling more and more dubious. 'It was fat and it didn't go any more than a dozen steps before it needed a nap. So I know which side to get on and I'm not too bad at sitting. Anything else is beyond me. Is there anywhere else we can go?'

'I have a horse who'll fit the bill,' he said cheerfully and her heart sank.

'Really?'

'Maisie's thirty. Sam bought her for me when I was

twelve, and I loved her. She and I ruled the land but she has become rather fat. And lazy. But she'll follow Nugget to the ends of the earth. It'll be like sitting on a rocking chair.'

But she'd been distracted from the horse.

'Why do I keep loving your Sam more and more?' she whispered. 'He bought the son of his housekeeper a horse?'

'Yeah, he did,' Matt told her and his voice softened too. 'He changed my life.'

'Would he tell you to go on a picnic?'

'I guess…maybe.'

'Then let's do it,' she told him. 'As long as I can borrow one of the living room cushions. How far is it?'

'It'll take about an hour.'

'Two hours there and back?' She took a deep breath and then looked up at Matt and thought…

'I'll take two cushions,' she told him. 'Let's do it.'

Maisie was a fat old mare, used to spending her days snoozing in the sun and her nights nestled on the straw in Matt's impressive stables. But she perked right up when Matt put the saddle on her, and when Penny tentatively— very tentatively—clambered aboard, she trotted out into the sunshine and sniffed the wind as if she was looking forward to the day as much as Penny.

Matt's two dogs raced furiously ahead, wild with excitement, as if they knew the day would be special. Samson, however, had been racing with them since dawn. He was one tired poodle and he now sat in front of Matt, like the figurehead on the bow of an ancient warship. He looked supremely content and, fifteen minutes into the ride, Penny decided she was too.

The old horse was steady and placid. The day was perfect. Matt rode ahead, looking splendid on his beautiful Nugget. There was little for Penny to think about, or do, for Maisie seemed totally content to follow Nugget. And Matt.

As was Penny. 'I'm with you,' she muttered to Maisie. 'Talk about eye candy. Wow…'

'Sorry?' Matt turned and waited for her to catch up. 'I didn't hear that.'

'You weren't meant to. Maisie and I were communing. I think we're twin souls.'

'I can see that,' he said and grinned and the eye candy meter zipped up into the stratosphere. Matt was wearing jeans and riding boots, and an ancient khaki shirt, open at the throat, sleeves rolled above the elbows. He'd raked his hair too often during shearing and the lanolin from the fleeces had made it look more controlled, coarser. Now, though, the last of the lanolin had been washed away. His hair was ruffled in the warm wind. His face looked relaxed. His deep-set eyes were permanently creased against the sun, but they were smiling. He looked a man at ease.

His horse was magnificent. He looked magnificent.

If I were a Regency heroine I'd be reaching for my smelling salts right now, she thought, and she wanted to tell Maisie because Maisie was watching Nugget with exactly the same look of adoration.

Wait, was she looking at Matt with adoration? She pulled herself up with a jolt.

'You be careful of those saddlebags,' she said, fighting for something prosaic to say. 'I don't want squashed cream puffs.'

'You packed cream puffs?' He'd loaded the cartons of food into his saddlebags without question.

'Why wouldn't I?' she asked with insouciance.

'Why indeed? I thought picnics were sandwiches and apples.'

'Not in my world. Where are we going?'

'We're heading for the hills,' he told her. 'After this rain I'm betting the place we're going will be amazing. I hope I'm right.'

* * *

This was his favourite place on the entire property. He'd seen it first the day he'd come to inspect the land. Donald had driven him over the paddocks, shown him the house, the shearing sheds, the outbuildings. He'd shown him the sheep and then he'd driven him here. Donald couldn't make it down the last steep climb. He'd driven him to the top and said, 'There's something down there that's worth a look, boy, if you have the energy to walk down.'

When he did, he'd known that not only would he buy Jindalee, but Jindalee would be his home.

This was his refuge. His quiet place. His place for just… being. Over the years, he and Nugget had forged a track through the undergrowth that was secure enough to get right down to the bottom. He led the way now, slowly and surely, with Maisie plodding behind. He glanced back to tell Penny to hold on tight but he didn't need to. Penny's knees were tight to the saddle. Her hands gripped the knee-pads even though her fingers were still light on the reins. She wouldn't take her fear out on Maisie. And now…fear or not, her face reflected pure awe.

The country on this section of the river was so rough, so undermined by underground waterways that no farmer had ever tried to clear it. Now the massive gum trees towered over their heads. The vast, shading canopy meant the understory was an undulating carpet of ferns, a wondrous mat of green that flowed down to the water.

They weren't going all the way to the river. The Murray here was wide and wild, a vast expanse of water where the banks would still be covered with debris from the recent floods. This place was better.

He remembered Donald describing it to him all those years ago.

'There's a place, boy, where one of the creeks flowing underground sneaks up and burbles up over the rocks,'

Donald had told him. 'Then it falls and forms a pool bigger'n most swimming pools. You can swim there if you can cope with a bit of cold. It's the cleanest water on God's earth, I swear. And then it slithers through a bed of tumbled rocks and disappears back underground. The ground around is covered with moss. A man can lie on that moss and look up through the gums and see the sky. It's like a slice of heaven.'

Matt had come and seen and fallen in love, and now, as their horses turned into the final clearing, he saw Penny's face and knew she saw it exactly the same way.

'Oh,' she breathed and then fell silent. Awed.

'Not bad, huh?' he said, trying to bite back pride and then he thought: *Why not say it like it is?* 'Best place in the world.'

'Oh, Matt.' She slipped off Maisie and the horse turned to nibble her ear. Her hand automatically went to scratch Maisie's nose. She was a natural horsewoman, Matt thought. He could buy another horse and...

What was he thinking?

The dogs were heading into the ferns, wild with excitement at the smell of rabbits, of something other than sheep, maybe simply at the day itself.

Matt pretty much felt the same—although he surely wasn't thinking of rabbits.

'Can we swim?' she breathed.

'It's icy.'

'But there aren't any... I don't know...crocodiles?'

He grinned. 'No crocodiles.'

'Then I'm in.'

'Did you bring your swimmers?'

'No,' she said and suddenly she was glaring. 'I did not because no one told me that swimming was an option.' She looked again at the waterhole and he saw the moment she made a decision. 'Well,' she said, 'you didn't tell me so you need to face the consequences. My knickers and bra are respectable. You're sure there isn't a posse of photographers behind these trees?'

What sort of world did she live in? 'I'm sure.'

'Don't sound so cocky. They'd be onto you if you didn't have such an ordinary name. You must have kept deliberately under the radar. Matt Fraser? No headlines and I bet you've fought hard to keep it that way. As squillionaire owner of Harriday Holdings, you'd be every women's magazine's Bachelor of the Year, no sweat.'

'So you didn't fight?' he said curiously. 'To keep under the radar?'

'With my father? I was in front of a camera practically before they cut the cord. And with a name like Hindmarsh-Firth it's impossible to duck.'

'So change it.'

'Right,' she said grimly. 'By deed poll? I don't think so. I'd be splashed all over the dailies with *Family Feud* as the headline.' She shrugged. 'No matter. It's all a long way from here and this place is magic. Can I swim?'

'The water's coming straight up from underground. Cold doesn't begin to describe it.'

'You swim here?'

'Yes.'

'But you never bother to pack your bathers when you come here?' Her smile returned. 'I get it. Every respectable squillionaire has his own private swimming pool and this is yours. Can I share?'

'If you dare.'

And she chuckled and tugged her T-shirt off, revealing a sliver of a pink lace bra. 'Of course I dare,' she told him. 'But I'm not doing your naked thing. I happen to be wearing matching knickers and panties—isn't that lucky? Will you join me?'

'I...yes.'

'Then are your boxers respectable, because we Hindmarsh-Firths have our standards?'

He grinned. 'I believe they are—although they're not pink and they're not lace.'

'I don't know what squillionaires are coming to,' she said, mock serious. 'But I can slum it. Swimming with a guy in cotton boxers? If I must.'

And she turned her back on him, kicked off her shoes, tugged off her jeans—to reveal a pair of knickers that were just as scanty as her bra—and dived straight in.

He'd said it was cold, but this wasn't just cold. This was half a degree above ice. She reached for the rock ledge and gasped and gasped.

And Matt was beside her.

He must have dived in almost as soon as she had. She hadn't noticed him shedding his clothes. She'd been more than a bit embarrassed about the panty-bra thing and had turned her back but now he was beside her.

His arm came out to support her. Maybe he thought her heart might stop.

It felt as if it might stop.

'I told you it was cold,' he said, a trifle smugly, and the iciness of the water and the sudden sensation of his arm around the bare skin of her waist and the smugness in his tone made her want to retort—but how could a girl retort when she was gasping like a fish out of water?

'Oh… Oh…'

'You get used to it if you swim,' he told her. Dammit, his voice wasn't even quavering. Was the man immune?

'This is like those winter plunge ceremonies in the Antarctic,' she stammered and tried to tug herself up to the ledge.

'Penny?'

'Mmm?' She couldn't get a handhold.

'There's a ledge over there that makes it easy to get out, but if you can bear it then try swimming. The cold eases and there's something I want to show you.'

Every nerve ending in her body was screaming for her to get out. But something else was cutting in, overriding the cold of the water.

Matt's arm was around her waist. He'd stripped to his boxers. His body was big and tanned and strong and he was holding her against him.

Was it her imagination or was she warm where she was touching him?

The initial shock was wearing off now—a little. She could breathe again, enough to take in her surroundings.

The pool was magnificent. At one end was a waterfall, not high, maybe head height, but enough to send white water tumbling down over rocks to the pool below. The pool itself was clear and deep, but not so deep that she couldn't see the sandy bottom. Now that she had her breath back she could see tiny slivers of darting fish.

The canopy of trees had parted a little over the pool, so dappled sunlight was playing on the water. Moss covered the surrounding rocks, and beyond the moss the horses had started grazing. They were obviously appreciating the lush grass in the slice of land where the moss ended and the ferns began.

The scene was idyllic. Enough to make her forget the ice?

Or maybe that was because Matt was beside her. Holding her.

What was a little ice compared to Matt?

'Sh...show me,' she managed through chattering teeth and he grinned.

'Swim first,' he told her. 'Half a dozen fast laps to warm up. Can you do that?'

'Of course. Bossy.'

'I'm not bossy, I'm wise,' he told her. 'Swim or you'll have to get out. Believe me.'

So she swam. The pool was the length of the pool her parents had in their current mansion. She'd spent a lot of time in that pool since the night Brett and Felicity had made their announcement. Swimming was a way she could block out the world.

But she had no intention of blocking the world now, for Matt swam beside her, matching her stroke for stroke. Maybe he wasn't too sure of her ability, she thought. Maybe he thought she might drown if he didn't stick close enough to save her.

Saved by Matt... It was a silly thought but it did something to her insides. The water was still icy but she was warming up, and half of that warming process was Matt. Matt's body inches from hers. Matt's presence. Matt...

They turned in unison and then turned again. Four lengths, five...and then six. She reached the end and grasped the ledge. Matt's arm came around her and held again.

He couldn't think she was drowning now. He was holding her because...?

'Game for the next bit?' he asked and she thought: *With your arm around me I'm game for anything.*

'I...yes.' Her teeth weren't chattering any more. She couldn't say she was warm but the iciness had dropped a notch. The water felt amazing. You could drink this water, she thought, and took a tentative mouthful and it tasted wonderful.

'If the bauxite mine ever fails I can put a bottling factory here and make a mint,' Matt said smugly.

'Don't you dare.'

'Don't worry, I won't,' he told her and he smiled at her again. That smile... It was a caress all by itself.

But he was a man on a mission. He had something to show her.

'The waterfall,' he told her. 'We're going behind it.'

'We are?'

'You can't see anything from out here,' he told her. 'But if you aim to the left of centre, put your head down, hold your breath for thirty seconds and swim right through, you'll find there's a cave.'

'Really?' She stared at the innocent-looking waterfall. 'There's no way I can be trapped?'

He grinned at her note of suspicion. 'You guessed it. You'll find forty-seven skeletons in there, the remains of every single maiden I've ever enticed into my secret lair.'

And she thought suddenly: *How do I know he's not telling the truth?* She'd known him for less than three weeks.

She'd been a fool for Brett. How could she trust her judgement now?

Except this was Matt. And Matt was smiling just a little, teasing.

'I know you're lying,' she told him and he raised a quizzical brow.

'How?'

'Because you couldn't possibly have persuaded forty-seven maidens to jump into this ice.' And she turned towards the waterfall and swam.

It was a weird feeling, to think of swimming through the wall. Instinct told her to reach the tumbling water and stop. She did for a moment, pausing to tread water, feeling the spray of the falls splash on her face.

But Matt was beside her. She could scarcely see him through the mist but he touched her shoulder. 'Here,' he said. 'Straight ahead. Put your head down and swim. It's narrow—you'll feel rocks on either side—but you'll be through in seconds.'

'I...is it dark in there?'

'I promise it's not,' he told her. 'It's safe as houses.'
'Really?'

'Well, not a centrally heated house,' he admitted. 'But it's worth it. Penny, trust me?'

Did she trust him? She stared at him for a long moment. His face was blurred behind the mist of the waterfall but she could still see him. He'd ceased smiling. He was waiting for her to come to a decision—and suddenly it was about more than the trust required to swim through a waterfall.

It was about total trust.

It was about taking a step that felt momentous.

He put out a hand and touched her face, making the rivulets of water stream across his hand rather than across her eyes. Her vision cleared and she saw him as he was.

A loner. A man of strength and courage. Matt.

And something shifted inside her. Something she couldn't name. Something that had never been touched before.

She put out her hand and touched his face back.

'I trust you,' she whispered and he smiled but it was a different kind of smile. It was a smile that said he was in the same unchartered territory as she was.

'Then let's go,' he told her. 'Come on, Penelope Hindmarsh-Firth. Let's do it.'

And he put his hands on her shoulders and twisted her around so she was facing the waterfall and gave her a slight push forward.

'Through you go,' he told her. 'And know that I'm with you all the way.'

Okay, it was scary. The first bit did involve trust. The wash of tumbling water as she swam through was almost enough to push her under, and then she felt the rocks on either side.

Matt had said to swim through. Just keep on going.

She wasn't completely enclosed. She could still surface and breathe if she needed to, though the mist from the falls made that hard. It was a narrow channel through the rocks, and it was getting narrower.

But Matt was behind her. She held her breath and dived like a porpoise.

The rocks on both sides touched her shoulders. She used them to pull herself the last little way.

And emerged…to magic.

It was an underground pool that must feed out somehow into the pool they'd just been in, but at the same level. She could hear the rush of water over her head. The creek must branch, above and below. This pool was roofed, and yet not. There were fissures where the sunlight glimmered through, shafts of golden light making the surface of the underground water glimmer in light and shade.

She could see the canopy of the trees through the fissures, but only glimpses. In a couple of places the water course above was overflowing and spilling down, so rivulets of water splashed the surface of the water in the cavern. Some sort of tiny, pale green creeper was trailing downward, tendril after tendril of soft, lush vine.

And at the edges were flat rock ledges. It was, as Matt had said, totally safe.

It took her breath away.

She trod water and turned and Matt was right behind her. Watching her. And the expression on his face… He loved this place, she thought.

'Oh, Matt, it's beautiful,' she breathed, and he smiled, an odd little smile she'd never seen before.

'Beautiful,' he agreed, and the way he said it… It took her breath away all over again.

'I…do you come here often?' She sounded nervous, she thought, and maybe she was, but in a weird way. It was as if the world was holding its breath. Something seemed about to happen and she wasn't sure what.

'Just when I need to,' he told her. 'Even Donald doesn't know about this secret place. Isn't it great?'

'It is,' she breathed. 'So…your forty-seven maidens?'

'Okay, I made 'em up.' They were treading water. If they swam a couple of yards further on they could stand, but for some reason that seemed dangerous. 'The water above doesn't run except in times of flooding, so the waterfall's a rare thing. But this underground cavern's always here. You're the first person I've ever brought here.'

'That sounds…momentous.'

'I think it is,' he said seriously. 'Penny?'

'Mmm?' What else was a woman to say?

'I'd like to kiss you.'

And suddenly she wasn't cold at all. She was exceedingly warm.

Apart from her body.

'I'm all for it,' she told him. 'Except that I can't feel my toes and if I kiss you I might forget about them and I'll get frostbite from the toes up.'

'Ever the practical…'

'Someone has to be,' she told him and only she knew what a struggle it was to say it. 'But I have a suggestion.'

'Which is?'

'That we swim back through that waterfall, we get ourselves dry and then we think about kissing.'

There was a moment's pause. 'You mean we have an agenda?'

'I think it's more than an agenda,' she told him, and smiled and smiled. 'Agendas can be changed. The time for agendas is past. Consider the kiss a promise.'

'Then one for the road,' he told her and he tugged her forward and kissed her, as long and as deeply as two people treading ice-cold water could manage.

And then they turned to the sheen of white water that marked the entrance to their tiny piece of paradise and swam right through.

Back to where the horses were waiting. Back to where their picnic was waiting.

Back to the promise of a kiss and so much more.

Matt produced a towel and insisted on drying her. He rubbed her body until she could feel her toes again, until her body was glowing pink, until the feel of his hands rubbing her dry started sending messages to her brain she had no hope of fighting.

Who'd want to fight?

Then he gathered her to him and he kissed her as she'd never been kissed before.

His skin was still damp, but out of the water the sun did the drying for him. And who was worried about a little damp? He felt almost naked and her tiny wisps of lace hardly seemed to exist.

She melted into him. His mouth claimed hers, her body moulded to his and the kiss lasted an eternity.

But of course it couldn't.

'Dammit, I should have…' he said at last, putting her away from him with what seemed an almost superhuman effort.

'So should I,' she told him, knowing exactly what he was talking about. 'I packed sandwiches, cream puffs, wine, chocolate. I can't believe I forgot the After-Picnic essentials.'

'It wouldn't have been After-Picnic,' he told her and tugged her forward again. This kiss was even better. Longer. Deeper.

This was a kiss that had a language all its own. It was a kiss that promised a future.

It was a kiss that sent her senses into some sort of orbit.

But finally sense prevailed—as did hunger. They attacked the picnic basket as if there was no tomorrow—indeed, for now it seemed as if tomorrow wasn't on the horizon. And then they lay back on the moss and gazed up through the canopy at the sky above.

We might just as well have made love, Penny thought dreamily. She was held close in the crook of Matt's arm. They hadn't bothered dressing—with the warmth of the sun there was no need, and to put any barrier at all between them seemed wrong. She was warm, she was sated, the ride and the swim had made her sleepy...

'Penny?'

'Mmm?' It was hard to get her voice to work.

'How heartbroken are you about Brett?'

Brett. He seemed a million miles away. Part of another life.

If it hadn't been for Felicity, she'd be married by now, she thought, and it was enough to wake her up completely. She shuddered.

Matt tugged her tighter. The warmth of him was insulation against pain, but then she thought: *There's no pain.*

Humiliation, though, that was a different matter.

'There's no need to be jealous,' she told him.

'Hey, I'm not jealous.' She could hear the smile in his voice. 'I've got the girl. Whoever Brett's holding now, he's welcome. No one can match the woman I have in my arms.'

It took her breath away, even more than the icy water had. The statement was so immense...

And it was the truth. She heard it in his voice and part of her wanted to weep. Or sing. Or both.

Instead, she twisted herself up so she could kiss him again. He kissed her back but then tugged her close, held her tight and said again, 'Talk about Brett.'

'Why do you want to know?'

'Because he's important,' he told her. 'Because he made

you run. Because your family's important to you and I figure if they're important to you then maybe I need to know about them. So Brett seems a way in.'

And there was a statement to take her breath away all over again. He wanted... No, he hadn't said wanted... He needed to know about them.

He was talking of the future?

So tell him.

'It was dumb,' she told him. 'I was dumb. I'm a people pleaser. My family's nothing if not volatile and my father's a bully. My half-sister's an airhead but she also has a temper. My mum...' She hesitated. 'She might seem like an airhead too, but she's not. Maybe underneath she's like me. She tries to keep us all happy. But she won't stand up to Dad. She never has. She just tries to smooth things over, to present the perfect appearance to the outside world. And somewhere along the line I learned to go along with her. Keep the peace. Make them happy.'

'So... Brett?'

'I was cooking in London,' she told him. 'I seldom went home—to be honest, as little as possible because Dad hates what I do and he gives me a hard time. But Mum rang me every night. Things seemed okay. But then Grandma died—Mum's mother—and I hadn't realized how much Mum needed her. Like she needs me. It's weird but being needed seems to be hardwired into us. Grandma supported Mum any way she could, which gave Mum the strength to stay in an awful marriage. When Grandma died she fell apart.' Penny sighed.

'Anyway, I came home and Dad pushed and pushed me into the PR job and I was so scared for Mum that finally I said yes. And what a disaster. I must have been depressed too, or at least my radar for slimeballs was depressed because Brett found me easy pickings. I was the daughter of the man he wanted to schmooze. Only, of course, he misjudged. He hadn't figured the family dynamics until it was too late—that Felicity is Dad's favourite. But then Felicity came home and he figured it out and the rest is history.'

'He's an idiot.'

She thought about that for a while. It was odd, but lying here on the moss, held hard against such a man as Matt… her perspective changed. Somehow the fog of humiliation that had been with her since that appalling dinner suddenly cleared, vaporising into the filtered sunlight and the shadows of the gums above her head.

'He's not an idiot,' she said softly. 'He's a lying, scheming toad who thinks he can get near Dad's fortune by marrying into the family. And maybe he can, and yes, he now has the beautiful daughter, but what he hasn't reckoned on is Felicity's temper. Felicity's hysterics. He doesn't know what it's like to live with Felicity. I wish him joy.'

'Punishment enough?'

'You said it,' she said softly. 'And now… I'm here with you. I still worry about Mum but, as you said, there's no way I can fix her problems for her.'

'Not when there're cream puffs and waterholes and sheep…'

And there it was again. That suggestion of a future.

'No indeed,' she said and smiled, because how could she not? She kissed him again because there was no choice in that either. 'Brett and Felicity are no longer in my world. I think, right now, I could even face their wedding. But you're right, I won't.'

And then Samson, who'd been sleeping on the edge of the clearing in between Matt's two dogs, suddenly decided he needed a little of his mistress's attention. He edged forward to wiggle between them, and suddenly they were both laughing.

'Right now my world seems to smell of sheep,' she said happily, even joyfully. 'And eau de rabbit burrow and damp dog. And is there horse dung in the mixture as well? And you know what? I love it. Just for now, Matt Fraser, I am a very happy woman. Brett and Felicity can have my old world. For now I'm happy in this one.'

CHAPTER NINE

THE NEXT WEEK passed in a blur of hard work and happiness. Matt was pressuring her to slow down, to give herself a break after the exertion of shearing, but why would she?

She made the house pristine. The orders for the new furniture were coming in, to be admired, placed, enjoyed. She was still cooking but there were only four men to cook for. She could do it with her hands tied.

Matt was outside working, so she was too.

She was getting pretty good at riding Maisie now. She could round up the mobs of sheep with him, listening to his plans for building his bloodlines, or explaining how this ewe had triplets last lambing and all of them survived, or introducing her to Roger the Ram, whose bloodlines were suspect but who'd been having his way with the ladies for so long that he didn't have it in him to get rid of him.

His pride in his land and his flock was contagious. Penny found herself starting to decipher individual differences, knowing what to look for in the best breeding stock, looking at the signs of capeweed in the top paddock and frowning because Matt had told her the effort it was to keep the pasture lush and healthy.

Then they started drenching, and working in the house disappeared from her agenda. They lived on soup and sandwiches because Penny was out there, learning how to deal with a drenching gun to make sure the sheep would be pest-free, learning how to encourage the dogs and herd a mob of sheep into the yards, how to be a useful farmhand.

She came in at night tired and filthy—she smelled the same as Samson—and every night she fell into bed exhausted.

She fell into bed with Matt.

On the night of the picnic he'd taken her to his bed and she'd melted into his arms with joy. It felt right. It felt like home.

It was as if she hadn't lived until now. He smiled and her heart sang. He touched her and her body melted into his.

This wasn't forever. She was sensible enough to know those demons were still out there. She was still Matt's housekeeper, being paid the exorbitant wage she'd demanded. He was still her boss.

But he wasn't her boss at night and the nights were theirs. Their nights were a time for no promises, no thought of the future and no looking back on the past.

Here, in Matt's arms, she could pretend the rest of the world didn't exist. She could forget her father's scorn, Brett's betrayal, her mother's needs.

Here she could pretend she was loved and, for the moment, it was all she asked.

And as for Matt's demons? She wasn't asking questions and neither was he. For both of them the future seemed too far away, too hard. There was just the oasis of now.

Old resolutions were put aside. She knew they were still there—for both of them—but for now why ask questions? Right now was perfect.

If this was all there was, she'd take it.

So would Matt, but in the dawn light he was awake, staring at the ceiling, seeing trouble.

There'd been a couple of phone calls from Darrilyn, hysterical ones—calls that reminded him of times past.

'She's impossible!' Darrilyn had practically screeched it down the phone. 'She's a thirteen-year-old witch. Ray's starting to say he won't have her in the house. All she does is sulk and listen to her appalling music and throw insults at Ray. If it gets any worse… You'll have to cope.'

You'll have to cope.

His mother had used that line. He remembered her getting ready to go out for an evening with her latest boyfriend. He must have been about seven.

'You're a big boy now, Matt. There are cold sausages in the fridge and cola. If I'm not back by morning you know where your school uniform is. Make sure you brush your hair before you walk to school. And make sure you're not late or I'll have teachers asking questions.'

'I don't like being by myself.' He could still hear his childish plea.

'Nonsense,' she'd said. 'Don't be stupid, Matt. I'm entitled to have fun. You'll just have to cope.'

He did have to cope. Somehow.

But this woman in his arms? This woman who trusted absolutely? Penny, who wore her heart on her sleeve…

She was the best thing to happen to him, he thought. She was someone he'd never thought he could meet.

He was a loner. He'd learned not to need anyone. But he lay with her in his arms and he thought it'd be okay. He could love her.

His life was changing. His life right now was better than okay.

But Penny looked at him with love and a voice inside his head was telling him that love came with strings.

If she needed him… If he admitted he needed her…

What was wrong with that?

Nothing, he told himself as she woke and he held her close. As her body melted into his, as the dawn dissolved in a mist of love and desire, the problems of the past seemed far away.

What was wrong with needing this woman?

Nothing at all?

* * *

They were at the end of drenching—squirting stuff on the sheep's backs that'd protect them from internal parasites. Penny was having more fun than she'd ever had in her life.

There'd been a mishap. A tree had fallen over a fence. It meant one mob of sheep already drenched had surged through and mingled with the final mob. So Penny was now in charge of drafting.

The sheep were being herded into the yards by the dogs—with Samson helping a lot! Penny stood at the gate separating the runs.

She had to hold the gate, check the markings and direct the sheep either way by opening and shutting the gate.

Ron and Harv stood beyond her in the drenching run, and Matt stood beyond that, doing a fast visual check of each animal. It meant that not only were they drenched but any problems left from the shear, nicks and cuts that hadn't been picked up and hadn't healed, were picked up there and then.

She was part of a team. The sun was warm on her face. Samson was having the time of his life, and so was she.

In an hour or so the final drenching would be done. She and Matt would head to the house and clean up, and the evening would be theirs.

She felt like singing—though maybe not, she thought. Her nice, calm sheep might decide not to be so calm.

'What's funny?' Matt asked and she glanced along the run and saw him watching her. She smiled at him and he smiled back, and Harv groaned.

'Leave it off, you two. You're enough to curdle milk.' But he was grinning as he said it.

Matt and Penny. The men were starting to treat them like a couple.

It felt…okay.

'I was just considering a little singing to work by,'

Penny said with as much dignity as she could muster. 'Like sea shanties. Heave, ho, blow the sheep down.'

'You'd have the sheep scattering into the middle of next week,' Ron told her but he was grinning too, and Penny felt so happy that even a sea shanty wasn't going to cut it.

In deference to the sheep she was singing inside herself, but still she was singing.

She glanced back at Matt again and saw his smile which was a mixture of laughter and pride and something else.

Something that took her breath away.

And then his phone rang. The moment was broken.

Interruptions happened often enough to be mundane. The line slowed. Harv continued with the drenching and Ron moved to do the checking. Penny slowed letting the sheep through. The team worked on, but Matt disappeared behind the shed to talk in private.

And when he returned…he didn't say anything. Work continued, but Penny saw his face and knew that things had changed.

With the drenching finished, Matt excused himself and took Nugget up to the top paddocks to check the flocks. He did it every night, but tonight he took longer and went alone. 'I need some time to think,' he told Penny and she headed inside feeling worried.

She showered and changed, made dinner, waited and eventually ate hers and put Matt's in the warming drawer.

She sat on the veranda as she always did, but tonight she sat with a sense of foreboding.

She'd seen Matt's face when he'd returned from the call. She knew trouble when she saw it.

She knew this man by now.

Finally he came. He snagged himself a beer, brought his plate from the warming drawer and came out to join her.

'All's well,' he said briefly.

She didn't comment. She knew a lie when she heard one.

She hugged Samson while he ate. She'd washed him while she was waiting and he was fluffy and clean on her knee. He looked almost normal, a little white poodle instead of a sheepdog.

And with that word *normal* came another thought. What was normal?

Her life before, where Samson was clean all the time?

Life before Matt.

'That was great,' Matt said, and Penny looked at his empty plate and knew something was seriously wrong.

'Sausages and chips that have been in the warming drawer for over an hour? I don't think so.'

'Your cooking's always great.' He shrugged and tried to smile. 'You're great.'

'What's wrong?'

He didn't answer. He hadn't come to the edge of the veranda to join her as he usually did. He was sitting on the cane sofa, back in the shadows.

The silence stretched. It felt as if something was hovering above their heads, Penny thought.

Something fearful?

'Matt?' she said again, and it was a question.

He rose and walked to the edge of the veranda. For a couple of moments he stayed silent, staring out into the night. Finally he spoke.

'Penny, Lily's coming.'

Lily? His daughter.

'That's good? Isn't it?'

'The timing's appalling, but it is.'

'Why is the timing appalling?'

'I never thought she'd come so soon.' He hesitated. 'To be honest, I never thought she'd come at all.'

'So why now?'

'The phone call this afternoon was from Darrilyn. It

seems there was a fight last night between Lily and Darrilyn's boyfriend. Apparently Ray's a hunter. He has trophies
all over the house. He's just been to Africa and brought
home stuffed heads from his latest kill, and it seems Lily
hit the roof. According to Darrilyn, she said some unforgivable things and Ray hit her. They went out and left Lily
at home, and Lily took scissors and Ray's razor and shaved
every single stuffed head in the house.'

'Oh…' Penny almost laughed. So the kid had spunk.
'Oh, my…'

'So Ray wants her gone, now. She's been in boarding
school, but it's vacation and Ray says she's not even staying with him until school starts. And Darrilyn… To be
honest, I don't think she ever really wanted her. Having
Lily's simply been a way of accessing my money and now
it's all too hard. So Darrilyn's organizing a school here but,
until she can start, she's sending her to me. She's putting
her on a plane as we speak. I'll pick her up in Adelaide and
bring her here. Not for long, though. Darrilyn's currently
researching schools, probably finding the most expensive
one she can make me pay for.'

'I…see.' She felt vaguely ill for the unknown and unwanted Lily. Maybe she could help, she thought.

And then she thought: *No—really no.*

Because suddenly she saw exactly what the problem
was and, looking at Matt's shadowed face, she knew that
he'd got there too. She understood the heaviness.

She was suddenly imagining the thoughts of the unknown Lily. The kid was being thrown out of the only
home she knew and was heading halfway across the world
to meet a father she saw twice a year.

She'd be terrified.

But Matt would have told his daughter about this farm.
All her life she'd have heard stories of Jindalee, of Ron and
Harv and Donald, and the dogs and the sheep. Maybe she

knew about Maisie as well. Being here… Riding Maisie… Exploring the farm with her father…finally they might bond.

But, to do that, to have any chance at all, they couldn't have an outsider, a pink princess tagging along with them.

She saw the whole situation now, and it made her feel… hollow? Lily would arrive traumatised—Penny knew enough of troubled teenagers to realise that. She'd need all Matt's attention and more.

But, as for Penny? As for Penny and Matt? Well, that was never going to work out.

Relationships and Penny? *Ha.*

And reality flooded back. For these last few nights, lying with Matt's body curved protectively against hers, she'd allowed herself to dream, but that was all it was. A dream. Matt had needed her over shearing, and he'd enjoyed her in his bed. But now he no longer needed her and it was time to move on.

Matt knew it. They both did. So say it.

'I need to go.'

'No.' Matt's response was a savage growl, but she met his gaze and she knew he saw the situation as clearly as she did.

He should be joyful that his daughter was finally arriving. Instead he was heavy-hearted because an embryonic relationship was getting in the way of what had to happen.

Matt Fraser was a good man. An honourable man. She knew he'd do the right thing, but for now the right thing was to put his daughter first.

So if he couldn't—maybe she had to be cruel for him.

'It's been fun,' she managed and she set Samson down and pulled herself to her feet. 'But you don't need me here when Lily arrives. She'll need your sole attention.'

'I want you to stay.'

'Do you really?' She put her hands on her hips, feeling a surge of anger. She'd faced enough harsh reality in relationships to be used to confronting the truth, and he needed to see it, too. Coating it with sugar, with regrets, with apologies, didn't help at all. 'Matt, I came uninvited. I've had a wonderful time and, what's more, you've paid me brilliantly. It's been the job of a lifetime and you and I have had fun. But it's time for Samson and me to move on.'

'Penny, I need you to stay.'

But the anger was still with her. She knew impossibility when she saw it.

'Why?'

'Because I think I might love you.'

And the night stopped, just like that.

Love.

It was a tiny word. It was a word that was terrifying.

Normal people understood the love thing, she thought bleakly. Normal parents picked their kids up when they fell over, kissed scraped knees, told them they were loved and set them down to toddle off to the next scrape.

For Penny, though… *'Penny, how can you expect us to love you if you look a disgrace? Why aren't you more like your sister? For heaven's sake, lose a few pounds—that a daughter of mine looks pudgy… If you love us, girl, you'll do what I tell you…'*

It was always her father's voice, with her mother in the background, looking distressed but saying nothing.

And then Brett… *'Penny, I love you and all I want is to make you happy.'*

Love. It should make her heart sing and yet all it did was make her mistrust.

'No,' she said, more harshly than she intended. She hauled her dignity around her like a cloak, and maybe only she could see how tattered that cloak was. 'Love. It doesn't mean anything. We've known each other for how long? To talk of love is crazy. We need to face reality. These last weeks have been great but you don't need me any more. If and when Lily settles into school and you'd like to catch up then maybe we can meet, but let's leave it with no promises. Don't make your life any more complicated than it already is. Samson and I will leave in the morning.'

'What will you do?' And he'd accepted it, she thought. He knew there was no choice.

He really did love his daughter and he was an honourable man.

'I'll go back to Sydney,' she told him. 'I'll get myself together and decide on a serious career path rather than head back to the outback on a whim. I might even help my mother face this wedding down.'

'Penny, don't!'

'I think I must,' she said, striving for lightness. 'Because I love my mum. Like you love Lily. We shouldn't fight these things even if we want to. You know your first commitment needs to be to Lily?'

'Yes,' he growled. 'But I don't have to like it.'

But she smiled and shook her head. 'This is your daughter and I'm very sure you do. Love between you and me? Well, that's something we can control. It's something we can back away from because we both know it won't work. But the way you love Lily, and the way I love my mum, well, that's non-negotiable.'

And then she couldn't help herself. She stood on tiptoe and kissed him lightly on the lips, but retreated before he had the chance to respond.

'You're a wonderful man, Matt Fraser,' she told him. 'I've had an amazing time. You've rescued me really well, but now it's time for your rescued maiden to move on.'

Matt stayed on the veranda for a long time.

She was desperately hurt. He could see it in the way her face had closed, in the way she'd tucked herself into herself, in the dignity she'd summoned as she'd said good-night.

All he wanted to do was follow her, fold her into his arms and tell her how loved she was. How she was the best thing to happen to him…ever? Love was something they could control? *Ha!*

But he'd known her for less than a month. Maybe she had it right.

He thought of his mother, bursting in the door after a night out. '*Darling, I've met the most wonderful man.*' Then there'd be weeks, even months, of glowing happiness while she ignored everything else but the new love in her life. In the end Matt had learned to ignore it, put his head down, battle through as best he could until his mother finally surfaced. Even when he was tiny, she'd wanted him to pick up the pieces.

'*Oh, darling, give your mummy a hug. Hug her until she feels better. Is there anything in the fridge? Oh, sweetheart, is that all? You need to come with me to the Welfare. They'll give me more if I take you with me.*'

This wasn't anything like that, he thought savagely. It didn't come close.

But his daughter? Lily had been brought up with Darrilyn's version of the same scenario. Darrilyn had moved from one disastrous situation to another as she'd searched for the next socially desirable catch. If he'd thought there was any way he could help he'd have moved to the States, but Darrilyn had sole custody, granted by the US courts. His visits had been formally arranged and necessarily brief. But now, finally, Lily was coming home.

He'd always told her she was welcome here. 'If ever your mother agrees, you have a home in Australia,' he'd told her. 'A farm, your own horse, stability. And a dad who loves you and only you.'

Okay, it had been a promise that in retrospect was

stupid, but he'd never believed he could fall for another woman.

He had fallen, but what he had with Penny was only weeks old. Even his mother's relationships had looked rosy after less than a month.

'Leave it,' he told himself heavily and he knew he couldn't do anything else. He'd try and talk to Penny again at breakfast. Try and explain.

Except she understood. He knew she did.

She got it.

She was one amazing woman. When Lily was settled, he could find her...

'Yeah? You think she'll hang around and wait?'

There was no answer. She'd gone to bed. Even the dogs had gone to bed.

He was alone, as he'd promised his daughter he would be.

'And that's the way it has to be.' He knew it but he didn't have to like it.

He'd hurt Penny but how could he fix it?

'Maybe in time...'

Or not. *Leave it,* he told himself. For now he had this one chance with his daughter and he couldn't blow it.

Even if the hurt in Penny's eyes was like a stab to his own heart.

CHAPTER TEN

MALLEY'S DIDN'T WANT HER, or if they did she didn't stick around to find out. Malley's was too close to Jindalee. Too close to Matt.

She headed back to Sydney because her mother's pleas were still ringing in her ears. She no longer had an excuse not to attend her sister's wedding and, for some strange reason, she now felt she had the strength to be there.

She wasn't sure where it had come from but this new strength was with her. The new, improved Penny... She could have cried all the way home, but she refused. Instead she lowered the sunroof, put every powerful woman singer she knew on her sound system and let them rip. *I am woman...* She surely was. She arrived back in Sydney sunburned and with no voice but she didn't care.

Anger helped. And a new-found determination.

She'd put her career aside once because she loved her mother. What a disaster. Then she'd thought she'd loved Brett and where had that got her?

Now...she'd exposed her heart even more, and all she felt was pain.

'So no one needs me and I refuse to need anyone,' she told Samson. 'Who needs love?' It didn't quite work but it was worth a try.

Her mother was overjoyed to see her but Penny didn't stay at home except to sleep. She had things to do. Moping gave her time to think and the last thing she wanted was thinking time.

In some strange way things had changed inside her. She thought of the times she'd pleaded with her father to do what she wanted, and had passively accepted dismissal and scorn. But this time…

'I'm setting up my own catering company,' she told her parents. 'My plan is to do proper meals—family meals. If a young mum has a baby, I'll come in with a full week's worth of nutritious comfort food. If someone's ill, I'll supply what the family needs. I'll start small, but I'm thinking in the end I'll have staff and a fleet of delivery vans and caterers who can move into people's homes. And I'll be hands-on. Any time there's a need for a good feed, I'm your girl.'

'I won't have the media saying my daughter's a servant,' her father snapped but she'd had enough.

'I'm not a servant, and the only time I've ever felt like one was when I tried to please you. Look where that got me. So this time I'm pleasing myself and don't you dare put pressure on Mum to make me change my mind. And I won't be staying in Sydney. I'll be moving to Adelaide or Melbourne. It depends where I can get decent premises and that'll take time but I'll do it right. And Mum, I won't let Dad blackmail me into doing what he wants by using your sadness, so you might as well get used to the new order.'

She left them speechless. To say her father was unused to the women in his family standing up to him would be an understatement but she'd done it. She'd stay for a few weeks. She'd get her mother through this wedding, she'd get her own head together and then move on.

Matt would be proud, she thought, but that was a concept that hurt. So, instead of thinking about Matt, she forced herself to focus on work.

She put out feelers for long-term premises in Melbourne and Adelaide but she was sensible enough to accept that long-term plans should be put on hold until she was emotionally level-headed again.

She found a decent commercial kitchen and took a short-term lease, then contacted a local refuge for the homeless. The homeless were delighted, and cooking was a balm.

She needed someone to help her if she was going to do the deliveries as well so she advertised for an assistant. A young woman applied who was from Adelaide. Was that a sign? Maybe her new life could be in Adelaide.

It was too soon to decide. For now she was busy. She was doing what she wanted.

So why did she feel so empty?

At least Matt had banished the humiliation Felicity and Brett had caused, she conceded. That was the one good thing, so when her mother asked again—very tentatively—about the family pre-wedding dinner, she agreed.

Do it and move on, she told herself. *I am woman...*

'That's lovely, dear,' Louise said. 'It'll be just the five of us.'

Just like last time, Penny thought, and was proud of herself for not saying it.

So, two weeks after she'd left Jindalee, five days before her sister's wedding, she found herself dressing up and heading downstairs for a formal pre-wedding dinner.

Not a dinner cooked by her, though. Her parents had hired a trendy caterer for the occasion.

'It'll be something with kale in it,' she muttered to herself. 'With accents of Japanese on the side. Seaweed maybe.'

She thought suddenly of her shearers being given kale and seaweed and found herself grinning.

'Hold that thought,' she muttered and headed for the dining room. She was halfway down the grand staircase when the doorbell rang.

Felicity and Brett had arrived together ten minutes earlier. She could hear Brett pontificating with her father in the dining room. They weren't expecting anyone else.

Her parents' butler swung the door wide. The porch was well lit.

It was Matt.

She was halfway down the stairs and she was dressed as he'd never seen her—in a sky-blue cocktail dress that accentuated her curves to perfection. It had a mandarin collar, slit deep to reveal the beautiful curves of her breasts. It had tiny capped sleeves, a cinched waist and a skirt that swirled softly to below her knees. She was wearing high silver stilettoes and loopy silver earrings. Her hair was caught up in a soft knot of tumbled curls.

She looked elegant and poised and about a million miles from the Penny he knew. She looked as if she belonged here.

What was he doing? He felt like he should cut and run.

But it had cost him considerable trouble to get this far. There were security gates at the start of the mansion's long drive but by coincidence they'd been left open. That coincidence had taken research, an extensive phone call to the family butler, an explanation he was hardly ready to give and an eye-watering bank transfer.

So now he was where he needed to be, but did Penny want him? This house was all marble stucco, Grecian columns—grand, grand and more grand. And Penny looked... amazing.

Was this the Penny he knew?

He'd spent the last two weeks fighting an internal battle, which he'd lost. He was in Sydney, Penny was close and he knew her appalling family dinner was tonight. Letting her face it by herself seemed the act of a coward.

That was what he'd told himself, but he knew it was more than that. He'd spent two weeks without her and those two weeks had left him feeling gutted.

It was too late to back out now. Penny had seen him. She paused on the stairway, looking stunned. 'Matt,' she breathed and he felt his world settle a little. Just to hear her voice made him feel better.

'Hi.' He smiled, but the butler moved imperceptibly, blocking the path between them. Refusing him entry.

Fair enough. The man had agreed to let him as far as the door. He now had to resume his role.

'I had no right to come,' he managed, talking up towards Penny. 'But I don't have your phone details. I've brought Lily to Sydney to her new school and I wanted…well, I hoped for your advice.' He took a deep breath and looked again at the vision in blue. *Wow.*

'I'd hoped to talk to you,' he managed. 'But if it's a bad time…'

'What's happening?'

A woman emerged from double doors leading from the hall. She was slim and elegant, immaculately groomed, looking worried. Penny's mother?

'Brian, who is it?' she demanded of the butler. 'You know George said no interruptions. Felicity says Brett must have failed to hit the remote and left the gate open. George is already angry.'

Matt glanced again at Penny. Penny's initial smile had faded. She was standing like stone.

Okay, back to the plan. He turned to her mother. 'I'm sorry to interrupt,' he said. 'I met Penny when she was working in South Australia. I've brought my daughter to school in Sydney but I didn't have Penny's contact details. Your number's not listed but I knew where you live. I'd like to talk to her for a moment, but if I'm intruding …'

'Are you her friend?' The woman's gaze flashed to her daughter, interest quickening. 'I *knew* she'd met someone.'

'Mum, no…'

But welcoming good-looking men into her orbit was one of Louise's principal skills, coming to the fore no matter what personal turmoil surrounded her. 'Come in. Brian, let the man in. Penny, introduce us.'

'This…this is Matt,' Penny stammered. 'He's a farmer… from where I worked. Matt, this is my mother, Louise.'

'A farmer?' Louise's smile hit high beam. 'How lovely. Come and have dinner with us.'

And this was exactly what he'd hoped for. Plan B was to sweep her up and take her out to dinner somewhere else. Or leave.

But a third option seemed most likely. 'He can't stay,' Penny said in a haunted voice and her mother looked at her again. Harder.

'Really? You don't want him to?'

He'd accept it. His plan had been simply to give her an escape route, or support, or both, but only if she wanted it. If she didn't then he'd walk away.

But Louise was looking exasperated. She turned back to him. 'Dear, if you know Penny then you'll know this is an awkward night for her,' she confided. 'She's agreed to have dinner with her sister and her ex-fiancé. Has she told you about it?'

'I…yes.'

'Then what we want,' she said with asperity, 'is a stranger to leaven the occasion.' She eyed him up and down. It'd have been too obvious to arrive dressed for a dinner party, but he was wearing new chinos, a decent shirt and a tie. His jacket was aged leather but it was decent quality. He could see Louise assessing and deciding to approve.

'Please, come on in,' she told him. 'Penny, you want him to stay? Don't you?'

* * *

Did she want him to stay?

Yes! part of her was yelling, but this was a new Penny. Okay, she'd only had two weeks of wearing her new skin but it had been a long drive back to Sydney and she'd had that radio up loud.

I am woman...

She was not her mother. She was not a doormat.

Did Matt want something? Didn't they all? She was suddenly feeling unbearably tired.

But her mother was letting her guard slip. Her social façade had disappeared and she was addressing her daughter with a degree of desperation. 'Penny, agree,' she told her. 'What your father is asking of you is impossible.' She turned back to Matt. 'Penny's ex-fiancé and her pregnant sister are here, and her father's expecting her to act as if everything's normal. I know she can do it—my daughter can do anything—but your presence...' She turned back to Penny again. 'Sweetheart, it would help. You know it would.'

It was the first time her mother had acknowledged her pain, and her words pierced a chink into the armour she'd so carefully built.

And then Matt looked up and met her gaze. He didn't smile. His gaze was serious, steady—loving?

And the chink grew wider.

'I won't be where I'm not wanted,' he said simply. 'Penny, if you'd like me to stay, then of course I will. You helped me and of course I'd like to help you. But I didn't come to intrude.'

Of course I'd like to help you. How could she believe that?

And then she thought: *I told him the date of this dinner.* Was it possible he'd planned this?

The thought that he'd do that for her... It was like a lightning bolt.

He'd come...for her.

'Stay.' She couldn't believe she'd said it, but it was out there.

His gaze didn't leave hers.

'You're sure?'

'Yes.' And she was sure. He'd planned it. It would be too big a coincidence. She gazed at Brian, who was looking blandly at nothing. Matt. Brian.

This was a plot!

For her.

'Then thank you, I will,' he said but still he didn't smile.

Her mother did, though. This was what she was all about—trying to please everyone, keeping her family happy. And Penny had a man! Penny could almost hear her think it, and the fact that he looked...well, he looked a hunk, did him no disservice in her mother's eyes.

Her father, though... And Brett and Felicity? A complicated night had suddenly become a whole lot more complicated.

But he'd planned it. For her.

Introductions all around.

George was urbane enough to be polite, even though he clearly didn't like his family dinner being gate-crashed.

'Sherry?' he asked Matt. 'It's a magnificent one my people have sourced from Almacenista. Or would you prefer a red? We have an aged...'

'I'd like a beer, if you have one,' Matt told him. 'Otherwise, water's fine.'

'As you wish,' George said stiffly, glancing at Penny as if she was responsible for allowing the cat to drag something in. And, as Brian poured a designer beer, he homed right in. 'So... Matthew, is it? What do you do?'

'I run sheep on the Murray,' Matt told him.

'You're a farmer?'

'Yes, sir.'

'That's where my daughter met you?'

'It is.'

'Her mother tells me it's flood country. How long have you been there?'

'Ten years.'

'It's a family farm?'

'No, sir, I bought it.'

'Well, that's a risk I wouldn't have taken. Small holdings take a lot to make them pay and if they're on flood plains…' Matt had clearly been pigeonholed and dismissed. 'I wish you well making a success of it.'

'Thank you,' Matt said. He took a swig of his beer and Penny almost smiled. Matt was drinking from the finest crystal but he drank like he was swigging from a can. She saw the exact moment when he stopped holding himself erect, when his voice took on the country drawl he used among the men—when he decided that if George had him down as a small time farmer then that was what he'd be.

And he'd also decided to be jovial.

'So Brett,' Matt said to Penny's ex-fiancé as he finished his beer and Brian poured him another. 'What do you do?'

'I'm a financial controller for the Hindmarsh-Firth Corporation,' Brett told him. 'If you understand what that is. Imagine the day-to-day cash flow problems you have on the farm and multiply them by thousands. Possibly millions.' Brett was smirking a little. He hadn't realised yet, Penny thought, that Matt's arrival had made him look small.

And then she thought, why hadn't *she* realised how small Brett was? Or maybe the word shouldn't be small. Maybe the word should be *insignificant*.

'Well, that must be fascinating,' Matt was saying, his

voice full of awareness of the huge responsibility Brett faced. 'All that adding up. So...you work for your fiancée's father?'

'He works *with* my father,' Felicity snapped.

'Of course. And you, Felicity?' His attention was suddenly switched to high beam on Penny's half-sister. 'Penny tells me you've been overseas. Working or pleasure?'

Felicity was not in a great mood. She was twelve weeks pregnant and she was nauseous. She was drinking soda, which she hated. What was worse, the new dress she'd bought specifically for this event only ten days ago would no longer fit, but she wasn't pregnant enough for the sexy maternity clothes she'd been admiring when she'd decided to try for a baby. She'd had to revert to last year's fashion.

And now her half-sister was sitting opposite her with a guy who might well be a small time farmer but wow...

'It's nice that Penny's found herself a friend,' Felicity said waspishly, ignoring Matt's question. 'Even if she had to go halfway across Australia to do it.'

'And wasn't I lucky that she did?' Matt said, and he smiled at Penny, and that smile...it even made her mother gasp. 'I hear you found your man much closer to home. Not that I'd describe myself as Penny's man, but I hope I'm her friend. That's such a privilege I can't begin to tell you.' He glanced at Brett. 'The local men obviously don't know what they're missing. Penny's one in a million.'

And suddenly, despite her discomfiture, Penny started enjoying herself. Matt could hold his own. Her mother was beaming. But the rest...

Her father and Brett were reacting like two roosters with a much larger and more impressive rooster invading their patch. Both were assured of their own superiority but Matt's calm acceptance of snide criticism had unnerved them.

And Felicity was jealous. Again.

Penny watched Matt smile at something her mother said. She witnessed his skill in deflecting Brett's barbs, and she watched him flirt mildly with the bristling Felicity. He was placating her with compliments. He was also exposing her shallowness and making Brett angry, but she knew instinctively that he was doing it only because he was angry on her behalf.

He'd come tonight, to this dinner, because he'd thought she needed him. She did need him.

No! Had she learned nothing? She did not need him! *I am woman...*

I'm no longer the poor relation at this table, she thought. She had her embryo catering company. She'd stood up to her father. She'd baked—successfully—for a full mob of shearers, and she had a friend. And such a friend.

She looked across the table at Matt and found him watching her, and suddenly she was smiling and smiling.

'How long are you in Sydney?'

'I've been here for a week and I may stay longer,' he told her. 'I need to wait until I'm sure Lily's settled.'

'What school's she going to?'

Matt told her—and that pretty much brought the conversation to a standstill.

'Why...that's the one Penelope and Felicity attended,' Louise gasped.

'How can you afford that?' George demanded and Penny thought a lesser man might have got up and punched her father's lights out for the offensiveness in the way he'd barked it.

But Matt merely shrugged. 'I'm divorced,' he said neutrally. 'My ex-wife has money.'

'Lucky for some,' Brett sneered but Penny wasn't listening. She was side-tracked.

'Matt, I hated that school.'

'It's the one Darrilyn's chosen.'

'Then un-choose it.'

'I'd like to talk to you about it, if I could,' he confessed. 'But now's not the time.'

And then the main course arrived, with all the theatre the hired, trendy catering staff could muster. Penny fell silent.

The choice of Matt's daughter's school was nothing to do with her, she told herself. It was none of her business.

But Matt wanted her advice.

He wanted her to be his friend.

He'd come tonight to help her.

The talk went on around her. She was aware that Matt was watching her but she wouldn't meet his gaze.

He chatted on easily, ignoring the undercurrents, making the gathering seem almost civil, but Penny's mother also fell silent. She looked as if cogs were whirring unseen. Comments to Louise went unanswered, and then, halfway through the dessert, she looked up from her peach flambé and beamed.

Penny knew that beam. *Uh oh.*

'Matthew?' Louise asked and Penny thought *uh oh, uh, oh, uh oh.*

'Ma'am?'

'What are you doing on Saturday?'

'I'm not sure,' he told her, glancing at a bemused Penny. 'It depends on my daughter.'

'Bring her to Felicity and Brett's wedding,' Louise said, with what was, for her, a defiant look at her husband. 'We seem to have invited half of Australian's *Who's Who* to this wedding so two more won't make a spot of difference. Do you have a suit?'

'I do,' he said gravely.

'Then I'd like to invite you. Please,' she added. 'If you're a friend of Penny's then you'll know that there are things about this wedding that make her...uncomfortable. You'll be doing us all a favour if you come. We'd love it if you could bring your daughter, but for the night...' She cast an uncertain glance at Penny but decided to forge right on. 'Come as Penny's partner. Like a little family. It'll take the media attention off Penny and I'm sure we'd all be very grateful.'

There was a deathly silence.

George and Brett and Felicity all looked as if Matt would be doing them the very opposite of a favour.

Louise smiled defiantly on.

And Matt looked at Penny.

'Penny?'

Matt, as her partner, at a wedding she didn't wish to go near?

But this was her half-sister's wedding and, hate it as she did, she'd made the decision to support her mother. The media fuss if she didn't go would be worse than if she did.

And, besides, there were parts of tonight's dinner she'd actually enjoyed.

Matt.

In a suit.

With his daughter?

His daughter was being sent to a school she'd surely hate.

Okay, she didn't want to be involved but she was. Like it or not. But she wouldn't be a doormat.

'I'm setting up a catering company,' she told him. 'I have temporary premises in Darling Harbour and I'll be there all day tomorrow. If you'd like to come around we can discuss it then.' And she could tell him exactly what she thought of his choice of school.

'I'd appreciate that,' he said gravely.

'So you will come to the wedding?' Louise demanded.

'Only if Penny wants me to,' Matt told her. 'I'd never pressure her.'

But it was too much for Felicity. She'd been growing angrier and angrier.

'Penny doesn't choose the guests,' she said in a voice that dripped ice. 'This is my wedding. I decide.'

'It's my wedding too,' Brett corrected her. '*Our* wedding, sweetheart. But he's certainly not on my list.'

But Felicity didn't take rebukes well. From anyone. She cast her fiancé a look loaded with such acid it could have cleaned warts off toads, and of course she changed her mind. 'Oh, for heaven's sake,' she muttered. 'If it'll make Penny feel better then of course she can bring a friend.' And she sent Penny such a condescending smile that she thought she might throw up.

'I don't need your sympathy,' she managed.

'But you have it,' Felicity said and smirked. 'Brett's in love with me.'

'Of course he is.' But then Penny hesitated. She cast a look at Matt. He was just…here. Big and strong and solid. She had backup, she thought. He'd come to support her— why not use it? Why not say what she'd been wanting to say to a big sister she'd once looked up to? 'But Felicity, have you any idea what you're getting into?' she asked gently. 'Brett went behind my back to get you pregnant. Do you think he'll stay loyal to you? You'll have family support, no matter what you do. It's not too late to pull out of a wedding you're not committed to.'

And that was too much for her father.

'Keep out of what's not your business,' George snarled. 'The wedding's happening in five days.'

'And this man's not coming,' Brett snapped.

'I agree,' George snapped back. 'My wife's in charge of the invitation list for this side of the family, and this man's not on it.'

So that was it.

Except Matt was looking at Louise.

Just looking.

And suddenly Penny wasn't sure what was happening.

Matt had charisma. Or something? She wasn't sure what. She only knew that Matt was looking directly at her mother and whatever was passing between them had the power to make the rest of the table shut up.

Even her father seemed momentarily baffled. Stymied by silence.

When finally Matt spoke his voice was low, reasonable and total mesmerizing.

'It seems to me,' he said softly, speaking directly to Louise and no one else, 'that Penny's been treated appallingly by those who love her. It seems to me that no one's spoken up for her. She's attending her sister's wedding—to support you, I suspect—and in the circumstances that leaves me stunned. If she needs me to lend her even more dignity and honour—two virtues that Penny already has in spades—then it would be my very real pleasure to be there for her. But, ma'am, I suspect that decision is up to you. And maybe it's time we all showed Penny how much she means to us. Especially, maybe, it's time her mother did.'

And he smiled at Louise, a smile that took Penny's breath away. A smile she'd never seen before.

'Maybe it's the right time now,' he said gently. 'To show Penny how much she's loved by us all.'

Silence. Deathly silence.

George was staring at Matt as if he were something from another planet.

Felicity and Brett were sitting with their mouths open, obviously struggling to find the words to retaliate.

But Penny's mother stared at Matt and he kept smiling at her. She stared…and then she turned to Penny.

'Penny,' she whispered and Penny gave her a wobbly smile.

'It's okay, Mum.'

'But it's not,' Louise whispered and she looked again at Matt.

And then, suddenly, Louise was standing. Her eyes were over-bright. She'd had one, possibly two more wines than was wise, but her speech was clear. 'Matt's right,' she quavered, speaking to Felicity. 'I've done every scrap of organization for this wedding, and you and your father haven't lifted a finger. And after the way you've treated *my* daughter... I could make one phone call to the caterers tomorrow, and with the demand for their services you'd find yourself without a wedding. Even if you did manage to salvage it, the ensuing media fuss would cause a riot.'

'You wouldn't,' George barked. 'Felicity's your daughter. We agreed when we married that you'd...'

'Look after her as if she were my own? Yes, I did.' She glanced again at Matt and what she saw there seemed to give her courage. 'I've loved Felicity even though she has a perfectly good mother of her own. But I've had enough. Felicity's not acting like my daughter. She and Brett have hurt Penny deeply, so deeply that all deals are off.'

And she turned again and looked at Matt.

Penny thought, *It's as if Matt's giving her strength.* She'd never known her mother to stand up for herself. Or stand up for her.

What was it about Matt?

'I've shut up for years,' Louise went on, enunciating every syllable with care. 'But now... Felicity, Penny's right to question what you're doing. You took Brett because Penny was marrying him and you were jealous of the attention. Amazing bridal gowns and maternity clothes are the latest fashion. Penny was getting what you don't have, and you've always thought like that. So now you're having your wedding and you're having your baby and you have Brett. And if you don't let Penny have Matt...'

'I don't want Matt,' Penny managed and the look Louise cast her was wild.

'It doesn't matter,' she told her. 'He's lovely—even I can see that. But it's *your* choice. Matt said it himself.'

'It is your choice,' Matt said. The corners of his mouth were twitching. The table seemed in total shock. 'But Penny, we're talking about a partner for a wedding, not a choice of life partner. Louise, thank you for your kind invitation. I may well take you up on it, if Penny thinks it's appropriate.' He smiled at Penny, a reassuring smile that held warmth and strength and promise but then he rose. 'I need to go,' he told her apologetically. 'I'm expecting a call from New York in half an hour. But are you okay by yourself here?' He cast a glance at the almost apoplectic George. 'There's room at the Caledonian. You can come back with me if you like.' And then he looked at Louise. 'Your mum too, if she'd like.'

If she'd like, Penny thought wildly. To get up from this table and run…

No.

I am woman?

Her world was quaking, but running away wasn't an answer. And running to Matt? For protection? For sympathy?

She had no need of either, she thought, and she looked at her father.

How had he grown to be such an ogre when he was just a puffed-up bully?

She looked at her mum and she grinned.

'We can look after ourselves, can't we, Mum?'

Louise was wavering a little on her feet—she really had had too much wine—but once again she looked at Matt and what she saw there seemed to reassure her.

'I…yes. I believe we can.'

'Excellent,' Penny said. She smiled at Matt and only she knew how much of an effort it cost her to stay perky.

'We're fine,' she told Matt. 'Obviously, I'm not sure about the wedding—for all sorts of reasons. But I'll tell you where my catering premises are and if you're still interested then we'll talk about it tomorrow.'

'Tomorrow,' Matt said and smiled at her and her heart twisted in such a way...

Tomorrow.

It was enough.

CHAPTER ELEVEN

PENNY'S NEW ASSISTANT arrived at ten the next morning. Noreen was a shy nineteen-year-old who was practically shaking in her boots. During the phone interview she'd seemed confident and perky, but it had obviously been an act. The only way to settle her and see what she could do was to cook.

And the promise from the interview was more than fulfilled. By late afternoon the kitchen was filled with the smells of tantalizing food.

Penny was covered in flour, elbows deep in baking, trying to focus on what Noreen was doing—and trying very hard not to wonder why Matt hadn't come.

If Noreen hadn't been here she might have gone crazy, she thought, but then she thought she was going a little crazy anyway.

And then the outside bell rang and her heart seemed to stop.

'Do those pies need to come out of the oven?' Noreen asked and her world settled a little. Pies. Cooking. That was the important stuff.

Not Matt?

She wiped her hands on her apron, which made no difference to her general level of messiness. She ran a floury hand through her curls—*gee, that helped*—and then she tugged the door open.

Matt was right in front of her—and so was his daughter. He was holding her hand.

She looked young for thirteen, but there was no mistaking who she was. She was thin and dark like her father. Too thin. Her hair was shaped into an elfin cut. Her eyes looked too big for her face, and they were shadowed.

She looked like a nervous colt, needing to escape but not sure where to run.

She was wearing the school uniform Penny had loathed and she looked so scared it was all Penny could do not to gather her into her arms. But she'd been thirteen once, and she knew such a thing was unthinkable.

She stood back and smiled a welcome. 'Hi,' she managed. 'I'd started to think you weren't coming.'

'I've been at Lily's school.' He looked almost as nervous as his daughter. 'Penny, this is my daughter, Lily. You don't mind that we came together?'

'Of course not.' She stepped back to let them in. 'Noreen and I are in the middle of baking. We have fifty homeless men to feed tonight. We've just finished apple pies. We're now making gingerbread men, as a post dinner snack.'

'Gingerbread men?' Matt said faintly and Penny fixed him with a look.

'Shearers need calories and so do the homeless, but the homeless have more time than shearers. So we'll feed them calories and then have fun. We thought we'd ice them with little backpacks and swags. Our aim is to make everyone smile.'

She cast a glance at Lily and saw her gaze around the messy, warm kitchen. She had the same starved look she remembered from her own childhood, when the kitchen was a refuge.

She thought of Matt's story, of this girl standing up to her stepfather, with his appalling stuffed animals, and the chord of recognition grew louder. 'Do you like cooking?'

'I haven't done much,' Lily whispered. She gazed at the

bowls of coloured icing and piping bags. 'It looks fun but I wouldn't know what to do.'

But Noreen, herself a gangly adolescent, saw a kindred spirit and beamed.

'It's easy,' she scoffed. 'I'll show you.' So, two minutes later, Noreen and Lily were piping multicoloured skirts on gingerbread ladies and Penny and Matt were free to talk.

Matt couldn't believe the transformation in his daughter. Lily was intent on her piping. Noreen said something to her and she giggled.

Matt felt as if he might cry.

He felt the strain lift from his face as his daughter relaxed.

'So what's happening?' Penny asked him. 'I can't tell you how grateful I am for last night, but now... You look more tired than when you were facing thousands of sheep and no cook.'

He gave a tired smile. 'Maybe I am,' he said. 'I've had one heck of a day.'

'Want to tell me about it?'

She led him over to the table at the end of the room. Sun was streaming in through the clerestory windows overhead. The room was full of the smells of new baking.

It felt like home, Matt thought, and then he realized he didn't really know what home was. And neither did Lily.

Suddenly there was a mug of tea in front of him and Penny was sitting opposite him. Waiting.

The last thing he wanted was to offload his problems onto her. The last thing he wanted was to need her.

'Tell me,' she said simply.

Penny had driven away from him because he'd put his daughter first. How could he do it again? But he glanced across at Lily and he knew that once again there was no choice.

'I knew there'd be settling in problems with a new school,' he started. 'But I hoped it'd work. But this morning she rang and she couldn't stop crying.'

'Because?'

His gaze was still on Lily. She seemed so young. Thirteen... He'd hoped she'd be old enough to fend for herself.

She wasn't.

'She's been there for a week,' he told her. 'And she's been put into a shared dorm with three other girls. But it seems they had to give up a settee so they could fit her bed into the room and they resent it. They complained to the school and to their parents, and then they stopped speaking to her. But they still didn't get what they wanted. Lily had to stay. Finally this morning they woke her with iced water tossed in her face. And they gave her a note.'

'A note?'

'It seems they're the school bullies,' he told her. 'Girls with rich families, used to getting their own way. The note told her that she should leave. It said no girl in the school will talk to her and if they do then they'll get the same treatment she does.'

'Oh, Matt...'

'So of course I fronted the headmistress,' he told her. 'I showed her the note and was expecting horror. But instead I heard pretty much what Lily did. "Friendships have been formed, Mr Fraser," she said. "It's difficult to make the girls accept an outsider, especially when she's arriving mid-term."

'Then I asked if Lily could be moved into a friendlier dorm and I had my head bitten off. She can't be bothered with what she terms "childish squabbles". She says if that dorm's unsuitable then the school's unsuitable.'

'So?'

'So we grabbed Lily's gear and moved out,' Matt told her.

'Oh, Matt.' And then she smiled. 'Good for you.'

'Yeah,' he said morosely, still watching his daughter. 'But now... Darrilyn's decreed that's the school she'll attend, and I don't want her taking her back to the States.'

'Does Darrilyn want her?'

He raked his hair. 'I don't know. No, I suppose not.'

'You could always call her bluff,' Penny told him. 'Choosing another school is hardly cause for her to change her mind.'

Matt fell into silence, feeling the weight of the world on his shoulders. How to cope with a kid he hardly knew— but a kid he loved.

The silence stretched on. Penny watched Lily. The girl was carefully piping, laughing shyly at something Noreen said. She was gangly, awkward, tentative. Even her smile was scared.

She looked like Matt.

She knew how Lily felt. She'd been given everything money could buy but no foundations.

'You can't keep her on the farm with you?'

'She's great there,' Matt told her. 'She was only there for a week, but already she loves the animals and I think she feels safe.' He hesitated. 'Penny, I'm sorry, but it was the right call...that you left. Thank you,' he said simply and her heart gave that twist again. The twist that was all about Matt.

He'd come last night because she needed him.

'Moving on,' she managed hurriedly, because emotions were threatening to derail her. 'There's no school she can attend as a day kid?'

'Are you kidding? You know how isolated Jindalee is. I'd need to move back to the city.'

'Yeah, and you'd hate that. Making one person happy at the expense of another sucks.' She stared into the dregs of her mug and then looked again at the two girls, who were now giggling over designs for clothes for their homeless gingerbread. Lily... Matt's daughter...

And suddenly—where it came from she could never afterwards figure—she had such a surge of bonding that she couldn't explain.

Maybe she could help.

'Adelaide's a lot closer to Jindalee than Sydney,' she said slowly. 'And Noreen's from Adelaide. She came to Sydney following a boy. It didn't work out.'

'Yeah?' He obviously wasn't following.

'There's nothing holding me here either,' she said.

He'd been watching the girls. Now he turned and stared. 'Penny, what are you suggesting?'

'I know a good boarding school in Adelaide. One of the Aussie girls at finishing school in Switzerland told me about it. They run a decent academic programme but they also have their own farm. There's an emphasis on things other than academia. Lots of camping, hands-on stuff, fun. Alice told me it was the only time in her life she'd felt she belonged.'

'I need the details.'

'Yeah, but it won't be enough,' she told him. 'Lily needs a base in Adelaide. She'll know no one outside school.'

'I can get an apartment and be there whenever I'm needed. Or I'll stay if I must.'

'And leave the farm completely? That'd suck.'

'I'll do it if I need to.'

Of course he would, because this was Matt.

But maybe... Maybe she could help. *I am woman.*

Matt was a friend. Women helped their friends. And didn't this fit into her plans anyway?

'It's early days yet, but if she likes the school... Matt, if you think it might work, maybe I could set myself up in Adelaide?' And then, as his face creased into a frown, she rushed on.

'I've decided not to stay in Sydney,' she told him. 'This place is temporary while I sort things out, apply for finance, put a business plan together. My hope is to set up a catering company in a city other than this one. Noreen would love to go home to Adelaide with her pride intact and I'm thinking we could search for premises near Lily's school. It would mean she doesn't feel so alone. With your permission, she could drop in after classes. She'd have you coming back and forth, and my place as a backup when you're not there.'

'Why would you do that?' he asked at last. 'Penny, what are you offering?'

'Not much,' she said diffidently. 'Lily might not need or want me but it doesn't matter. And it might end up working for us both.'

'To move your whole life…'

'Hey, it's better than cooking at Malley's,' she said and grinned. 'And I need to move somewhere.' She took a deep breath. 'Where Mum got the courage from I don't know, but we've talked and she's decided to leave Dad. She should have done it years ago. Dad's had mistress after mistress but she's tried to keep everyone happy. It'll take decent lawyers to extricate her money from Dad's clutches, but now… You saw the way she pulled you into dinner last night. She's a born hostess. I see her as the front man for my company.'

'But… Adelaide? For Lily?'

She hesitated, still watching Lily. It was a good way not to look at Matt.

'Matt, this isn't a sacrifice,' she told him. 'Who knows if Lily will even need somewhere like my kitchen after she's settled? Who knows whether my mum will like Adelaide, and who knows if Adelaide likes my kind of catering?'

'But you'll do it for Lily.'

'Lily could be a deciding factor,' she confessed. 'But

it's no big deal. Helping your daughter seems right. We are friends, are we not?'

'No,' he said forcibly, and he said it so loudly that Lily and Noreen stopped what they were doing and turned and stared.

'No, Penny, we're not friends. Or not *just* friends. Penny Hindmarsh-Firth, I said it before and I hardly believed that I'd said it. But I believe it now. I believe that I love you.'

In a romance movie she might have fallen into his arms right then. Hero declares his love. Heroine swoons with joy.

She wasn't having a bar of it.

I am woman...

In an hour a van would arrive from the homeless refuge and she'd promised a meal for fifty. She didn't have time to sit around and listen to declarations of love.

Because she had qualms and she wasn't falling for a line she'd heard before.

She'd been nice to his daughter and he'd told her he loved her. But she had no intention of being loved because she was needed. Of being loved because she'd done the right thing.

Not any more.

There was a part of her that would have allowed Matt to sweep her up in his arms and carry her off into the sunset with violins playing in the background.

She wanted him—but not on those terms.

So... *Get thee back*, she told the insidious voice in her head that would have welcomed being carried off on whatever terms Matt offered. But she'd been burned too often. She'd spent her life trying to please her father, learning from her mother that love meant sacrifice. Heaven, she'd almost married the despicable Brett because of it.

And then she'd fallen heart over head in love with Matt and broken her heart when she'd had to leave. And yes, leaving had made sense on all sorts of levels, but Matt had let her go. Two weeks ago she'd stood on his veranda and part of her had felt like dying.

She'd been burned too often. How could she believe?

'Why don't you kiss him?' Noreen asked. Both girls were watching, fascinated, but Penny turned away from Matt with a disbelieving snort and headed back to her pies.

'Because it's cupboard love,' she said, fighting to keep her voice light. To keep the whole thing light. 'It's like giving a kid a cookie. Will you love me if I give you this cookie?'

'Hey, Dad.' Lily picked up one of her luridly dressed gingerbread ladies. 'Will you love me if I give you this cookie?'

And Matt looked at Penny for a long, long moment while emotion went zinging back and forth between them. But finally he nodded gravely, as if acceding to an unspoken request.

He turned to his daughter.

'I surely will,' he said and headed over to eat the proffered cookie.

Good. That was the way she wanted it—wasn't it?

How else can I have it? she thought. *How can I trust?*

And then she thought, maybe it had just been a throwaway line after all.

Penny... I love you.

Easily said.

Prove it, she whispered under her breath. But why should he prove it?

'Am I still invited to your sister's wedding?' he asked and she blinked. Felicity's wedding. Okay, life had to go on.

'My mother invited you.' She was fiddling with the oven. She didn't turn round to face him. She daren't.

'So that's a yes?'

'If it's still on. I told Felicity…'

'She won't cancel a wedding,' Matt told her. 'Besides, they suit. Will you be leaving from your parents' house?'

'I…yes. Mum and I have decided to stay until after the wedding. We don't dislike Felicity enough to cause a media furore beforehand.'

'So what time would you like me to meet you?'

She turned to face him. 'Matt…'

'Penny.' He smiled that gorgeous, heart-warming smile that had her totally befuddled. 'I still want to come. Your mum says you need me.'

'I don't want to need you.'

His smile faded. 'Really?'

'Really.'

'Even if it's a two-way deal?'

'I don't know what you're talking about,' she said shortly, breathlessly. And then, more seriously, 'Matt, I need time. I know you can hurt me and I don't like that I'm exposed. I'm trying to get myself back together. To find who I really am. Falling for you complicates things.'

'It might simplify things.'

Noreen and Lily were watching with fascination but it couldn't matter. What needed to be said was too important.

'How?' she demanded. 'Matt, I've just come from a very messy relationship. I've spent my life watching my mother ruin her life trying to please everyone. I won't do the same.'

'If I swore to spend my life making you happy…'

'Matt, don't,' she said breathlessly. The memory of that moment on the veranda was still so raw it made her cringe. It made her block her heart from what was happening. 'I can't,' she said. 'It's too soon. I can't get my head around it. I can't…'

'Trust?'

'Exactly.' She shook her head. 'I'm sorry.'

'No, I'm sorry,' he said gently. 'Maybe if I hadn't met your family I wouldn't have understood, but I do. Penny, let's give this time.'

'I won't...'

'You might,' he told her and he came back to take her hands. He tugged her forward and kissed her. It was a light kiss, a fleeting touch of lips, but it was enough for her to know she was in serious trouble. But then he put her away and the smile he gave her was rueful.

'Saturday,' he told her. 'Wedding. What time?'

'Four. But...'

'I'll pick you up,' he told her. 'If I see you sweep out in one of the bridal limousines I'll know you don't want me to come but if you decide you want me then I'll be there. But no pressure, Penny, love. Lily and I will fly to Adelaide and check out this new school but we won't make any decisions and you shouldn't either. We'll see you Saturday—or not.'

'Matt...'

'No decisions,' he said again and he turned to Lily. 'Ready to go?' he asked her. 'Penny's suggested a new school you might like. Are you ready to try again?'

'I don't know whether I'm brave enough,' Lily whispered.

'That makes all of us,' Matt told her. 'Where can we buy courage?'

CHAPTER TWELVE

It's a happy bride the sun shines on...

Felicity should be gloriously happy, Penny decided, as she fiddled with a recalcitrant wrap and gave her reflection one last glance before heading downstairs. The sun had been shining all day.

She doubted Felicity had noticed. Felicity's six perfectly matched and beautiful bridesmaids had filled the house since morning and the place had been chaotic.

Penny had snuck out at dawn and taken a long walk around the harbour front. She'd come back an hour before they had to leave.

Even that was too early. She'd taken half an hour to dress and now she was pacing.

Matt had said he'd come, but why would he? He'd gone to Adelaide with Lily. Why would he come all the way back?

There was a faint tap on her door. Her mother was there, looking magnificent. And anxious.

'Is he coming?'

'I don't know,' Penny said shortly. She glanced at her watch. 'But we should go. It'd be nice to sneak into place before the media gets its hype together.'

'There won't be hype over me. I'm not exactly mother of the bride,' Louise told her. Felicity's mother would be sitting in the front pew with George. Penny suspected she and her mother would be relegated to a pew quite a way back.

But, even now, Louise was still trying to keep her family happy, Penny thought. She'd made the decision to leave George but she wouldn't do it until after the wedding. Instead she'd stay in the background and try and smooth things over.

'You're a very nice woman,' Penny told her and kissed her and Louise blushed and gave her a tentative hug back. But she still looked worried.

'I was sure Matt would be here.'

'It doesn't matter that he's not.'

'But Penny...'

'We can manage on our own, Mum,' she told her. 'Who needs men?'

'Yes, but Matt...'

'He's just another guy,' Penny said airily and swallowed her pride as best she could and hooked her arm into her mother's. 'Let's go slink into our back pew. You want to ride in my little pink car? Come on, Mum, let's get this thing over and done with and then we can get on with the rest of our lives.'

And she propelled her mother out of the room, down the stairs, out of the front door—where Matt was waiting.

He took her breath away.

He was standing in front of probably the world's most beautiful—and expensive—four-door sports car.

The gleaming white car looked as breathtaking as the guy leaning nonchalantly beside it. Or almost.

Because this was Matt.

He was wearing a deep black dinner suit, a suit that seemed to have been moulded onto him. It screamed Italian designer, bespoke quality. His crisp white shirt accentuated his gorgeous tanned skin, his hair seemed even darker than usual and his shoes gleamed almost as much as the car.

And his face... It was strong, angular and weathered. His crinkly eyes were smiling straight at her.

'Good afternoon,' he said formally to both of them but

oh, his eyes were only for her. 'You're a little earlier than we expected but we came prepared.'

She managed to tear her eyes from Matt and saw Lily in the back seat. The window was down. 'H…hi,' Lily managed and emerged to join her father. Matt took her hand and led her forward.

The girl was wearing a pale blue frock, deceptively simple. Strappy white sandals. A single pearl necklet and earrings.

She looked very young and very lovely and also very nervous.

'Louise, this is my daughter, Lily,' Matt told her and there was no disguising his pride. 'Lily, this is Mrs Hindmarsh-Firth.'

'Lily, call me Louise. Oh, my dear, you look perfectly beautiful. And how brave of you to let your father drag you to a wedding where you know no one.' And Lily was embraced in a cloud of expensive perfume.

Matt gave Penny a grin and a thumbs up that said a grandma-type figure was what he'd hoped for. And Penny thought this was just what her mother needed, too. Someone to mother. And then she thought—they'd arrive at the wedding *en famille*.

This was a day she'd been dreading, and her mother must have been dreading it just as much.

Louise would have walked up the aisle as a second wife, the odd one out. Penny would have walked up the aisle as a jilted bride. Now, they'd arrive at the church in this car. With this man. Together.

'Ready to go?' he asked and she managed to smile back. 'Oh, Matt…'

'Don't say a word,' he told her and he kissed his fingers and then put them gently on her lips. 'Let's just soak up our first family wedding.'

And that was breathtaking all over again.

* * *

Penny had expected to walk down the aisle as the ugly duckling. The sister who'd been dumped for the more beautiful model. She'd thought people would be looking at her with sympathy.

But as she walked down the aisle with Matt beside her she felt as if she were floating, and who cared who was looking at her?

She almost felt like a bride herself.

Louise was right behind them, holding Lily's hand. Somehow it had seemed natural to do it this way. Matt and Penny. Louise and Lily.

They slid into the pew reserved for Stepmother. As Penny had predicted, it was well back. Felicity's mother had decreed the seating arrangements for the bride's side and it was a slap to Louise. Louise was used to such slaps, as was Penny, but now it didn't affect them.

It made it harder for all the necks craning to see who they were, but Penny didn't care about that either.

Penny and Matt and Lily and Louise.

Mum and Dad and Daughter and Grandma?

She peeked a look at Louise and her mother was beaming. *Oh, Matt...* Of all the ways to dispel sympathy. They'd have the church agog as to this new order.

Had Matt known?

She dared to look up at him and found him smiling.

'You knew,' she breathed. 'The car.' She looked at him again. 'The suit.'

'I figured it might help,' he admitted. 'A bit of bling.'

'I can't begin to tell you...'

'Then don't,' he told her and grinned and held her hand tighter.

And turned to watch the wedding.

* * *

It was the perfect wedding. It was orchestrated to the last minute detail.

It was faintly…boring?

'I'm sure we can think of a better way to do this,' Matt whispered as the groom kissed the bride and six perfect bridesmaids and six beautiful groomsmen lined up to march out of the church—and Penny almost stopped breathing.

'Matt…'

'I know. It's far too soon,' he told her cheerfully and went back to watching the truly impressive bridal procession. And Penny tried really hard to start breathing again.

And then they were outside, still in a tight family group. Louise was clutching Lily's hand as if she were in danger of drowning, and Penny thought how inspired had Matt been to organise it this way.

For Lily was intelligent enough to know she was needed. The memories of her week at her horrid school had obviously been put aside. She looked lovely and she knew it. She was even beaming at the cameras.

And there were plenty of cameras. Media attention should have been on the bride and groom but it wasn't.

For, as the crowd clustered round in the sunshine, someone twigged.

'Isn't that…? Surely it's not… No, I'm certain…'

It started as a ripple, a rumour, but in seconds it was a wave of certainty.

'Matthew Fraser! Owner of Harriday Holdings!'

'Surely not!'

'I'm sure. My dear, he's possibly the richest man in the country. But he's intensely private. Oh, my heaven… Didn't they say it was Brett who dumped Penelope? Goodness, maybe it was the other way around.'

Penny could see the wave of amazement, the wash of speculation—and the absolute switch of attention.

The media was suddenly all over them.

But it still didn't matter. Matt's hold on her hand tightened. He kept Louise and Lily in his circle.

The feeling of family deepened.

She'd dreaded this wedding but the dread had gone.

This wedding felt like her own.

The reception was on the Harbour, in a restaurant with a view to die for. But of course they were seated right at the back, on a table with others Felicity's mother had deemed insignificant. They were placed with the vicar who'd conducted the marriage service and his lively wife and three great-aunts.

For someone who lived alone, Matt did an extraordinary job of pulling people together, and Louise helped. She hadn't been meant to sit with them—that would have been too big an insult to seat her so far back—but she insisted on staying. She and Matt were determined to make their table lively. The great-aunts rose to the occasion. The vicar's wife announced that she'd attended Lily's new school in Adelaide and proceeded to tell scandalous stories of the teachers.

Lily visibly relaxed and so did Penny. She sat back and watched Matt weave his magic, and the feelings she had for him grew stronger and stronger.

Who was he doing this for? His daughter? He'd turned her into a princess for the night.

Penny's mother? Louise was charmed and charming. This day had turned out to be so different to the one she'd dreaded.

The great-aunts? These were three spinsters, insignificant aunts of Louise, but Penny and Louise both loved them. And they loved Matt.

They were having fun.

They had people at the other tables staring, and Penny was starting to see an almost universal wish. Theirs was suddenly the party table.

The dancing started. Bride and groom. Then the groom's parents—and Felicity's mother with George.

This was the moment when it would have truly sucked to be Louise, but suddenly Matt was on his feet, propelling Louise to the dance floor to be the fourth couple, and if Penny hadn't been in love with him already she fell right then.

Her mother wasn't the insignificant other. Matt was heart-meltingly handsome, and he swirled her mother round the dance floor as if she were a queen.

As other couples poured onto the floor she tugged Lily up and they had fun. The vicar and his wife came out to join them and then they swept down on the great-aunts.

'We can't dance if we don't have partners,' the great-aunts said in horror, but Lily put them straight.

'That's so last century,' Matt's daughter pronounced. 'Waiting for a guy to ask you is sexist and dumb. Get with it.'

So then they were all on the floor, and the great-aunts were teaching Lily to jive and Matt and Louise joined them—and then somehow Matt had hold of Penny, steering her effortlessly away from the giggling jivers—and somehow everything around them seemed to slide into oblivion.

The music changed to a rhumba and Matt was good. Very good. Penny could dance a mean rhumba herself and it felt as if she was almost part of him.

His hand held hers, tight, strong, warm. He tugged her in and out again, swung her, danced effortlessly, held her gaze the entire time.

She felt like Cinderella at the ball, she thought wildly, and then she wondered: *Is there a midnight?*

Surely there had to be a catch.

'Where did you learn to dance?' she managed as they swung. She was breathless, laughing, stunned.

'My mum,' he said simply. 'I think she had me dancing before I could walk.'

'You do still love her then?' She said it wonderingly.

His smile faded a little but the warmth was still there. 'She was an appalling mother, but I couldn't stop loving her.' The dance had him tugging her into him, and he brushed her hair with a fleeting kiss before the moves pushed them apart again.

'It seems once I give my heart, it breaks me apart to get it back,' he said simply. 'Loving seems to be forever. Is that scary? Yes, it is. Is it contagious? I hope so.'

Out she swung and then in again, but this time his arm didn't propel her out again.

Instead he held her close, closer, and closer still.

He kissed her.

It was her sister's wedding day. The focus of the entire day should be on Felicity.

Penny stood in the middle of the dance floor and melted into Matt's arms and let him kiss her.

For how could she pull away from Matt?

The kiss was plundering, deep, hot, a public declaration but a private vow. The music faded to nothing. There was only each other.

And half Australia's polite society.

She didn't care. She kissed him back, with all the love in her heart, and she thought: *If this night is all I have, then I'm Cinderella.*

And finally, when the kiss stopped, as all kisses eventually must, when she finally stood at arm's length, when he smiled down at her, just smiled and smiled, she knew where her heart was. She knew there'd be no midnight.

As the dancers around them erupted into laughing applause she blushed, but Matt held her hand and she held his hand back.

'Hey, Penelope.' It was a reporter from the biggest society tabloid in the country, calling from the side of the room as Matt led her back to the table. 'How's it feel to be the jilted bride?'

And there was only one word to say to that.

'Perfect.'

Because it was.

Lily wilted. Matt needed to take her home and the entire table decided to follow.

'I know you're supposed to wait for the bride to leave,' one great-aunt grumbled. 'But these days they stay until three in the morning and if *you* leave, young man, there's not a person in this room who can criticise us.'

'And you don't know your way around this part of town,' Louise declared. She wasn't about to let the night end on a whimper. 'Let's make the grand exit.'

So they said their goodbyes—politely, but *en masse*—and departed and Matt thought the bride and groom would be pleased to see them go. Brett had been sending him dark looks all night. Felicity had been carefully avoiding looking at her half-sister.

They'd have much more fun without them.

'But drop in tomorrow,' Penny's father said to Matt, clapping him on the shoulder. He'd learned by now who he'd patronized five days ago.

'Thank, you, sir, but I'm heading back to Adelaide tomorrow,' Matt told him. 'I have a daughter to settle into school.'

He smiled and held Lily by one hand and Penny with the other and led them out. It was a defiant little team and it felt great.

And then they were outside, breathing in the warm night

air of Sydney Harbour, and he felt Penny almost slump beside him.

'Done?' he said gently. 'Not so bad at all, really.'

'Thanks to you,' she whispered. 'Matt, if you knew what you've done… For Mum… For me…'

'Sort of like charging in and cooking for a shearing team of twenty,' he told her. 'But with far less work.'

'Are you really heading back to Adelaide tomorrow?'

'Um…no,' he told her. The great-aunts and Louise were at his back and Lily was beside him. He needed to choose his words with care. 'I thought I might head back tonight, if it's okay with you.'

'Tonight?' Her face became still and he thought, he hoped, it was disappointment. But the expression was fleeting. Penny had herself under control.

She'd been verbally slapped too many times, he thought. He wouldn't mess with this woman again.

Ever.

'Of course it's okay with me,' she was saying but he shook his head.

'Don't say that until you hear my plan.'

'What plan?'

'I thought I'd take you with me.'

There was a gasp from the great-aunts and from Louise. Not from Lily, though. His daughter was grinning.

She'd been in on this plan and was loving it.

'What…why?'

'I have things I need to show you,' he told her. 'Important things. Lily and I have been busy.'

'I thought you were looking at schools.'

'We have been,' he told her. 'Lily's planning to try out the school you recommended as a day kid, before deciding to try boarding. Boarding there looks fun but we're taking this slowly. Meanwhile, we have a master plan and I want to share it with you.'

'So...you'll both fly back tonight.'

'Not Lily,' he told her. 'Lily's exhausted, aren't you, Lily?'

And Lily looked at him and grinned. She'd made an excellent show of wilting inside the wedding venue, but now she was all smiles.

'I'm so tired,' she said meekly.

'So we're taking her back to the hotel on the way to the airport,' Matt told Penny.

'You can't leave her alone!'

'Who said anything about leaving her alone? Noreen's booked in with her. It took a bit of trouble to track her down but we managed it. Staying in the Caledonian, all expenses paid—Noreen thinks it will be awesome. Tomorrow they're taking the ferry over to Manly to check out the beach. They'll have two nights together while Lily recovers from her very exhausting night tonight...'

'I'm so exhausted,' Lily added, her smile widening. She looked so like her father!

'And they'll both fly over to Adelaide on Monday,' Matt told the speechless Penny. 'How about that for a plan?'

'Hey,' Louise said. 'What about me?'

'Hey, yourself,' Matt told her and grinned. He was no longer holding Penny's hand. He'd tugged her in so she was hugged against him. 'You're included anywhere you want to be included.' But then he reconsidered. 'Though not tonight. Not with us. But the girls would love a chaperone tomorrow.'

'I could take them to my very favourite restaurant for lunch,' Louise told him and smiled at Lily. 'My friend Beth has a son who's a lifeguard at Manly. Do you think you and Noreen would like surfing lessons?'

'Wow,' Lily breathed. 'Wow!'

Louise hesitated. 'I might stay at the Caledonian too. If that's okay with you.'

'Come over to Adelaide on Monday with the girls,' Matt told her. 'I think Penny would love it.'

'Hey, what about us?' one of the great-aunts demanded. 'This sounds fun.'

'Any and all of you are welcome,' Matt said, hugging Penny tighter. 'As of Monday, but not before if you don't mind.' He glanced at his watch. 'Apologies, folk, but I have a private jet chartered in an hour. My plan includes sweeping Penny away...'

'Sweeping?' Penny gasped.

'Sweeping.' He smiled broadly. 'But not without a plan. I'm sweeping you up in my jet and taking you off to places unknown and I'm keeping you only unto me until Monday. And, before you start with the practicalities, I had a conversation with your father's esteemed butler and it turns out he's a romantic at heart. He has a bag packed and one dog, brushed and fed and ready to go. A confirmation phone call from you, and they'll be on the tarmac waiting for us.' And then he couldn't help himself. He swept her up into his arms and held her close. His dark eyes gleamed. 'If that's okay with you, darling Penny.'

She thought suddenly of her lonely drive across outback Australia in her little pink car. Woman and dog.

I am woman...

She'd thought she was strong. She'd thought she'd cope alone.

And she was, she thought mistily. Except right now she was woman in the middle of...love.

Her family. Her mum, her great-aunts. Lily.

Her man.

'*I am woman*,' she whispered to Matt as he held her close. 'I can do anything I want.'

'I'm sure you can,' he told her. 'So what do you want?'

'I want to be with you.'

CHAPTER THIRTEEN

PENTHOUSE SUITE. Adelaide's most prestigious hotel. Gorgeous, gorgeous, gorgeous.

They'd arrived at two in the morning and Penny had hardly noticed her surroundings.

She didn't notice them now. She was spooned in the great wide bed, her body moulded, skin to skin, with the man she loved with all her heart.

She had no idea where this was going. She had no idea how their lives could mesh, but for now all she cared about was that she was with Matt. And somehow things had been taken out of her hands. The great swell of loneliness she'd felt practically all her life had suddenly been lifted.

Last night had been fun, she thought dreamily. Her sister's wedding, an event she'd been dreading, had turned out to be an event where she'd felt she'd belonged for the first time in her life.

Because of the man who held her in his arms right now.

A sunbeam was playing on her face. She felt warm, loved. She had no intention of stirring, but somehow Matt must have sensed her wakefulness.

He opened his eyes, tugged her closer and she felt him smile.

She wriggled around so she faced him, looping her arms around his neck and she thought: *If I could hold this moment... This is where I want to be for the rest of my life.*

But there was a whimper from the floor beside them and the outside world broke in, in the form of one small dog.

'I need to…' she started but Matt tugged her tight with one hand and reached for the phone with the other.

'You don't need to do anything,' he told her, and a minute later a discreet hotel employee arrived. Matt donned a bathrobe, and Samson and his leash—and a discreet bank note—were handed over. Matt returned to bed, his dark eyes gleaming.

'Now, where were we?'

It took them a while to surface. Samson was obviously being taken for a very long walk.

'He's having breakfast downstairs,' Matt told her when she managed to ask. 'Speaking of breakfast, we need room service. Can I interest you in croissants? An omelette? Champagne? Okay, maybe not champagne. We have things to do, you and me.'

'Really?'

'Or things to see,' he told her. 'Though how can I look at anything else when you're right here?' He kissed her and croissants were put on the back burner for a while.

An hour later, dressed in her very favourite jeans and sweater—*how had Brian managed that?*—they were in an open-topped roadster heading for the hills. Literally.

'It's where Lily's school is,' he told her and that was where she thought he was taking her. But instead he pulled up outside an eclectic, fashionable village-type shopping centre, lined with trees, full of enticing cafés and Sunday morning visitors.

He helped her out of the car, tucked Samson under one arm, took her hand and led her to the end of the street. Then he paused.

He stopped in front of a building that looked like an old warehouse. It was built of clinker brick, weathered with age, long and low and looking as if it was part of the land around them. It had only one storey, but the roof rose in the middle to form a rectangle of clerestory windows.

Huge barn-like doors looked as if they were built of solid oak. A smaller entrance door was built within, so one person could go in, or twenty.

It was beautiful.

There was a 'For Sale' sign out the front. A notice had been plastered over it: 'Contract Pending'.

'Want to see?' Matt asked and Penny turned her attention from the gorgeous old brick building and looked up at Matt. He looked anxious.

'Matt…'

'Nothing's final,' he said hurriedly. 'This is your decision. But come inside.'

And he opened the small door and ushered her in.

Outside it was lovely. Inside it was perfect.

It took her breath away.

It was already set up as a commercial kitchen. Great wooden benches ran along the middle of the hall. Sinks were inserted at regular intervals. More benches lined the walls with a bank of commercial ovens. There were massive dishwashers, heating banks, storage…

There was a loading ramp at the back so vans could back in. A rear door could be opened and food loaded.

'There's parking for six trucks at the rear,' Matt told her and he still sounded anxious.

'It's perfect,' Penny breathed. Samson was down on the floor, investigating smells left from a hundred years of baking. 'Wow.'

'It's an old bakery,' Matt told her. 'The original ovens are still out the back.'

'So I could make wood-fired bread. I could…'

He put a finger on her lips. 'Wait until you see the rest,' he told her. 'It's a package deal.'

And he led her out the back, across the car park and through a small garden. There were two small cottages, side by side. Built as a pigeon pair.

He opened the door of the first and she saw perfection. Two bedrooms. An open fire. Sunlight streaming through the windows.

Modern touches, subtly adding every comfort.

'It's a package deal,' Matt repeated as she prowled in wonder. 'Two cottages or nothing. Penny, it's only five minutes' walk from Lily's school.' Suddenly he sounded almost apologetic. 'I thought… I hoped…'

And then he stopped, as if what he was about to say was too big to put into words.

She turned and held his hands and smiled up at him, and she thought her heart might burst. But she waited for what he might say.

'I thought…for the first few months, until she's settled, I could stay here,' he told her. 'Well, I'll stay in Adelaide anyway. I'll pay someone to manage Jindalee but I'll go home at weekends. I can organize a chopper to go back and forth, daily if needed. If Lily's a day kid she can come back and forth at weekends too. I thought…you could have one cottage and Lily and I could have the other. Unless…'

'Unless?' She could scarcely breathe.

And then she stopped breathing entirely, because he had both her hands in his and his smile was uncertain, tremulous, but filled with such hope…

'It's too soon to ask you,' he told her. 'I know that. It's unfair to put pressure on you. But Penny, my feelings won't change. I've figured that out about myself. My heart seems to have a will of its own. I figured I'd be alone for ever but I was wrong. Penny, if you allow me to buy this…'

'I…allow…!'

'This is your place,' he told her. 'Lily and I both knew it the moment we saw it. I have no doubt you could raise the capital to buy it yourself, but it would be my very great honour to buy it for you. With no strings attached.'

'No strings?'

'Except…maybe once a month for the next six months, you allow me to ask you to marry me. No pressure to accept. Just listen to my proposal. And every month I'll think of more reasons why you should. At the end of those six months, if you're still unsure, I'll walk away. I promise. So it's a small string. One question, once a month.'

'And that's the cost of my lease?' She could scarcely make her voice work.

'Not a lease. A sale. My weekly proposal doesn't make a difference as to whether you'll own it or not.' The hold on her hands grew tighter. 'So, my love, what will it be? Do we have a deal?'

She shook her head. Somehow she made herself smile although she could feel tears welling behind her eyes.

'The cost being six proposals?'

'Yes.'

'Then how can that work?' she whispered. 'How can that possibly work when I'm answering your proposal right now. The building is sold. Of course I'll marry you, Matt Fraser. With all of my heart.'

It was a wedding with a difference. A Jindalee wedding.

Matt Fraser had been a recluse for most of his life. He wasn't a recluse any more but this was no huge wedding. This was a wedding for the closest of their family and friends and no one else.

The reception was to be held back at the homestead because the caterers—Penny's team, led by the now indomitable Noreen—couldn't cart the food all the way to the river. But the ceremony itself was held at the billabong Matt had shown Penny after shearing.

Expecting guests to arrive on horseback was too big an ask, but they'd had time to build a carefully concealed track. The wedding was twelve months in the planning.

Which wasn't quite true, Penny thought as she rode

steadily to the place where she and Matt were to be married. They hadn't spent twelve months planning a wedding. They'd spent twelve months building a life together.

For the first few months Matt had commuted back and forth between Jindalee and Adelaide. He now had his pilot's licence—and his own chopper. He'd built up his flying hours fast as he flew back and forth a couple of times a week.

He could have made his home in Adelaide but neither Penny nor Lily wanted it.

Lily boarded at her new school and loved it.

Penny had established a catering firm that was already inundated with more orders than she could handle.

And at weekends they all went home.

Home. Jindalee.

The farm looked magnificent, Penny thought, as Maisie plodded steadily on, with Ron and Harv riding side by side as her proud escorts. Matt would have bought her a younger mare, as he'd bought a lovely bay mare for Lily, but Penny and Maisie had developed a bond she had no intention of breaking. Maisie went so slowly she had time to admire the scenery, the rolling hills, the lush pasture, the contentedly grazing sheep.

This year's shearing had been the time when she'd finally handed the day-to-day running of her company over to Noreen. Shearing had been when she'd come home.

It felt good. No, it felt great.

Lily was still coming home most weekends, although Louise was now living permanently in Adelaide. The two were as close to grandmother-grandchild as made no difference. A cottage behind the old brick bakery was home for Louise and a second home for all of them.

'We're late already,' Ron warned her. 'You want to get that nag to hurry up?'

'Maisie doesn't do hurry,' she said contentedly and it

was just as well. She'd decided to do the full bridal bit, which meant she felt like a cloud of white lace, riding side-saddle with an immaculately groomed Samson up before her. She couldn't hurry.

Nor did she want to. This was a ride to be savoured.

And suddenly Lily was thinking of a wedding twelve months ago... The wedding Felicity had stolen.

How lucky am I? she thought, wonderingly. *How blessed?*

And then they reached the ridge down to the water. The newly made track made it easy. The guests were there and waiting, on chairs set up on the mossy grasses by the waterfall.

Lily was waiting to help her down, in full bridesmaid splendour. And Louise. They fussed about her dress, clucking that it had crushed a little during the ride. Smoothing it down. Her mother was smiling through tears and Lily was handing her her bouquet.

Penny hardly noticed.

All she saw was Matt.

He too had ridden to the wedding—on Penny's instructions. 'Because it's how I first saw you,' she'd told him. 'My knight in shining armour, on a horse to match.'

'I seem to remember I was a pretty soggy knight,' he'd told her and she'd chuckled but she'd stayed firm.

So his big black horse was calmly grazing behind the makeshift altar and Matt was standing waiting. He smiled and the world stood still.

He looked stunning. 'I'm damned if I'll wear a dinner suit if I'm riding a horse,' he'd told Penny and she'd agreed—the Matt she loved wasn't a dinner suit kind of person. But he'd compromised.

He was wearing the breeches of a true horseman, buff, moulded to his legs. He wore glossy riding boots reaching to his knees, a deep black dressage jacket and a cravat, white silk, intricate, splendid. He'd do a Regency hero proud.

He'd do anyone proud, she thought mistily. He looked spectacular. Drop dead gorgeous. Toe-curlingly handsome.

Her Matt.

Music swelled in the background. She'd thought they'd have recorded music but, amazingly, Matt seemed to have organized a grand piano. *How the...?* But now wasn't the time to ask. The pianist and a cellist were playing *A Thousand Years*, a song to take her breath away. To make all eyes well.

But she was no longer hearing the music.

Matt was smiling and smiling. Their guests were on their feet, smiling almost as much as Matt.

'Are you ready, my love?' Louise asked, groping for her lace handkerchief and then giving up and sniffing.

'Of course I'm ready,' Penny told her. 'How could I not be? This is my Matt. This is the rest of my life.'

He thought of the first time he'd seen her—little, blonde, hot and cross. Bare toes covered with sand.

He'd thought she was beautiful then. How much more so now?

The dress she'd chosen—ignoring her mother's questionable advice—was perfect for her. It was mermaid style, white silk, the bodice perfectly cupping her breasts. Tiny slivers of shoulder straps made it safe for the ride. It was figure-hugging to her hips, then flared out to her feet in a gorgeous rustle of silk and taffeta.

Shoulder straps or not, how had she ridden in that?

How could he ask? There was nothing this woman couldn't do.

Her hair was caught up loosely, curls cascading from a fragile spray of jasmine and tiny white rosebuds.

How could he look at her hair?

All he saw was her smile. And her eyes. She was smiling and smiling—just for him.

And, at that moment, something in him settled. Something strong and sure.

They hadn't hurried this wedding because it hadn't seemed important but now, here, suddenly it was.

Will you take this woman...

The words had been spoken thousands, millions of times, but they'd never been spoken as they would be today.

And now she was beside him. Lily was taking her bouquet and stepping back, and Penny was smiling up at him.

'I'm sorry I'm late,' she whispered and it was all he could do to make his voice work.

'What kept you?'

'Ron found a lamb,' she told him. 'It got through the fence down the back paddock and spent the night separated from its mum. You know we had a frost? Ron brought it in just before we left, so Noreen and I had to take the meringues out of the oven and replace them with lamb. But no drama. We have mum waiting impatiently in the home paddock, baby warming up nicely and the meringues doing their final dry in the sun on the veranda.'

And she took his breath away all over again.

'Don't tell me,' he said faintly. 'You coped with a lamb in that dress.'

'I only got it a little bit smudgy,' she told him, lifting an arm so he could see a tiny smudge of mud on her waist. 'And somehow I already had a little smear of lemon icing on the hip. But it's okay. It's pretty perfect.'

And he couldn't help himself. He chuckled and then thought: *To heck with convention.* He gathered her to him and hugged her and swept her round and round until she squealed.

And then he set her on her feet again and they both stopped laughing.

Pretty perfect? She was absolutely perfect.

Life was perfect.

They turned together, hand in hand, to be made man and wife.

* * * * *

SARAH AND THE SECRET SHEIKH

MICHELLE DOUGLAS

To my Auntie Ellen and Uncle Reg
for letting me run wild on their Mount Vincent
property when I was a wee, small thing…and for
trusting that I'd neither inadvertently drown myself
in the dam or be eaten alive by the wildlife.

CHAPTER ONE

SARAH SLID ONTO a stool and held her hand up for a high five as Majed passed on the other side of the bar. The palm-on-palm contact from the sexy barman sent heat ricocheting up her arm.

His raised eyebrow told her he was intrigued and she had to tamp down a laugh of pure, ridiculous exhilaration. His briefly raised finger told her to give him a moment while he served someone down the other end of the bar.

She settled onto the stool. She'd happily wait a hundred moments to share her news with him.

A hundred moments?

She rolled her shoulders and shook out her arms and legs. Maybe not a *hundred* moments. It wasn't as though she thought of Majed in *that* way. Even if he was sexy as all-get-out, with his dark hair, tawny skin, and eyes as dark as a desert at midnight. She bit back a dreamy sigh. Eyes that were edged with long, dark lashes that should be wasted on a man but weren't in this case as they only made him look more exotic.

But no. It wasn't because Majed was hot with a capital H that she'd quite happily wait until closing time to tell him her news but because she knew he'd *understand*. An easy-going friendship had sprung up between them over the past year when she'd barely been paying attention and she gave thanks for it now.

He prepared the order for the three women at the far end of the bar—mojitos—with a casual elegance Sarah envied. The women all flirted with him—flashing smiles and cleavage with a good-natured abandon that had Sarah biting back a grin. He said something that made them laugh, looking for all intents and purposes completely at ease, yet she sensed he held some part of himself back.

Majed: man of mystery, man of contrasts. He managed this bar but he didn't drink. He attracted women in droves—and some men—and was equally pleasant and courteous to all. He could have his pick from the beautiful people who frequented this inner-city Melbourne bar but she'd never seen him go home with anyone.

Mike, her best friend's older brother and the owner of the bar, had asked her to keep an eye on Majed, to give him a hand if need be. As he was letting her crash at his swanky inner-city apartment for the six months of his current overseas sabbatical, it had seemed little enough to promise in return. Mike called her his house-sitter but, as he had no cat to feed or houseplants to water, Sarah had secretly dubbed herself his charity case. Mike had simply taken pity on her.

Pity or not, she'd jumped at the chance to cut forty-five minutes each way from her daily commute.

And keeping an eye on Majed had proved no hardship at all.

Mike had mentioned that he and Majed had gone to university together. She knew where Mike had gone to university. Majed should be a banker or a businessman or some hotshot lawyer. Like Mike, he should have a whole chain of bars, restaurants and resorts across the world—or at least be working towards it. What he shouldn't be doing was twiddling his thumbs behind some bar in Melbourne.

Oh, right, and you think you're qualified to be dispensing vocational advice, right?

She winced.

Good point.

She knew all about treading water in a job that was going nowhere. She knew all about not living up to her potential. She ought to. Her mother reminded her of it every single time they spoke.

Majed moved back down the bar towards her and she resolutely shoved her mother's voice out of her head.

'Your usual?'

Her usual was a glass of house white. She straightened and rubbed her hands together. 'I'll have bubbles, please.'

That eyebrow rose higher. 'Celebrating something?'

She laughed because she couldn't help it. 'I can't drink alone tonight. Let me buy you a drink.' He opened his mouth but she cut him off. 'Be a devil and have a lemon squash on me.'

Shaking his head, he did as she bid, and she noticed that at her end of the bar his smile was more relaxed and his shoulders swung a little freer. The fact he relaxed around her loosened the hard knots that the working day had wound up tight inside her.

He slid a glass of bubbles in front of her and she promptly clinked it to his glass of squash. 'To the fact that I am now officially a single woman again.'

Stunned midnight eyes met hers and his smile, when it came, was low and long and sent a spiral of heat circling through her belly.

He leaned towards her. 'You did it? You broke up with Superior Sebastian?'

Ah...not exactly. Sebastian had been the one to dump her. But it came to the same thing—she was single and rid of the awful boyfriend. And Majed looked so happy for her...he looked *proud* of her. It had been an age since anyone had looked at her like that, so she didn't have it in her to correct him.

She pointed to herself. 'Free woman.' That, after all, was

the material point. She then waved her hand through the air, assuming supreme indifference. 'I've kicked his sorry ass to the kerb. Never again, I tell you.' And she meant it. She was having no more of Sebastian's on-again, off-again mind games. She couldn't even remember why she'd put up with it all in the first place.

Majed took a long pull on his drink and she couldn't help but notice the lean, tanned column of his throat and the implicit strength in the broad expanse of his shoulders. He set his glass down. 'Never again?'

She shook her head. 'Never.'

'Cross your heart?'

She crossed her heart. In one smooth movement Majed leaned across the bar, cupped her face in big, warm hands and then his lips slammed down on hers in a brief but blistering kiss.

When he eased back all she could do was stare.

He frowned. 'I shouldn't have done that.'

She tried to marshal her scattered wits, tried to corral her racing pulse. 'Oh, yes, you should.' She found herself nodding vigorously. 'You *really* should've done that.'

Whatever he saw in her face chased his shadows away. He shrugged, and she swore it was the sexiest thing she'd ever seen. 'I couldn't kiss you when you were going out with another man.'

Majed had wanted to kiss her? If she'd known that, she might've broken up with Sebastian sooner.

Her heart pounded. 'I was an idiot to put up with Sebastian and his so-called *"this is for your own good"* sermons for so long. It's just…' It was just that sometimes she was *hopeless*.

Majed folded himself down on the bar until he was eye-level with her. 'You will get his voice out of your head right now and you won't let it back in. You hear me? You do *not* need to lose weight. You do *not* need to wear more make-up. You do *not* need to do your hair differently. And there is absolutely nothing wrong with ordering a fluffy duck rather than a martini, because you *don't* have to be too cool for school, Sarah Collins. You're perfect just the way you are.'

She stared at that mouth uttering those delicious words—words she sorely wanted to believe—and her chest coiled up tight and her mouth dried. She glanced up and moistened her lips. He watched the action and midnight eyes glittered and sparked. Her blood pounded so hard it made her thighs soften. 'Now I want to kiss you,' she whispered.

'That wouldn't be wise.'

But he was staring at her lips with unadorned hunger and he didn't move away.

'Perhaps not, but it'd be fun.'

He gave the tiniest of nods in acknowledgement.

She lifted her chin. Mike *had* asked her to keep an eye on him. 'When was the last time you had fun, Majed?'

His pupils momentarily dilated. 'A long time.'

In those eyes she saw unexplained pain before heavy lids lowered to block it from her sight.

She sat back and surveyed him. He'd been counselling her for months now, telling her she deserved something better than a constantly critical boyfriend. And he'd been right—she did deserve better. And so did he. The way he was going, he'd work himself into an early grave.

She pursed her lips. That might be an exaggeration. She was rubbish at the work side of things but she could make up for it on the play side of the equation. 'Do you ever drink?' she asked.

He straightened. 'I'll be back.'

He moved away to serve a customer. When he returned he folded himself down into the same eye-level position. Did he know how sexy that was? Did he know she'd only have to close the space with a small forward movement to kiss him? If she did...

'You have very speaking eyes.'

His grin was full of temptation. It was all she could do not to swoon—or kiss him. She settled for grinning back at him instead. 'I'm feeling happy, free…and in the mood for some fun.'

She'd never been this bold before, but she couldn't find it in herself to regret it. She'd made a fool of herself over far less worthy things.

She shrugged but she doubted it was one of those confident, nonchalant gestures all the cool girls managed. Something in the gesture, though, made Majed's face soften. 'What can I say, Majed? I like you.'

He was quiet for a long moment and just when she'd started readying herself for a hot squirm of embarrassment, and the shame of a kindly worded rejection, he said, 'Brandy. Sometimes, late at night when I'm home alone, I'll indulge in a small glass of brandy.'

Her heart grew so big it blocked her throat, leaving her temporarily unable to speak. Finally she swallowed. Air flooded her lungs and her blood danced. 'Maybe you'd like to have a brandy with me tonight? When you're done here?'

He reached out to wind his finger around a lock of her hair. 'There's no maybe about it. I'd like it very much.'

Ooh! Ooh! She found it impossible to form a coherent thought.

He gestured towards the far end of the bar to the waiting customers. 'Don't go anywhere.'

'I'm not going anywhere.' She couldn't believe how strongly her voice emerged when the rest of her felt as weak and shapeless as smoke. Well…it felt weak until his smile sent her floating up towards the ceiling.

Sarah stretched and encountered a warm male body.

She opened one eye to find Majed sending her a low, sexy smile that warmed her blood. Her other eye flew open as the events of the previous night flooded her. Their love-making had... Wow! She gulped She hadn't known it could be like that.

'Good morning.'

She couldn't contain a grin. 'From where I'm lying, it's a *very* good morning.'

She lifted a hand to trace the firm contours of his bare chest. Majed sucked in a breath. And then three loud knocks pounded on her front door. Her hand stilled. Majed raised an eyebrow.

She lifted a finger to her lips. 'If we're quiet they might go away.'

The knocking started up again.

And again.

Majed's lips twitched. 'They don't seem to want to give up.'

She bit back a sigh before pointing a finger at him. 'Don't go anywhere.'

He brought her finger to his lips and kissed it. 'I'm not going anywhere.'

She slipped on a robe and belted it at her waist. 'I'll be back. *Very* soon.' She'd get rid of whoever it was in double-quick time.

And then maybe they could resume last night's...de-lights.

Majed shucked up the bed, resting his hands behind his head. The sheet threatened to slip beyond his waist. All she had to do was grab the sheet in one hand, tug, and...

If it were possible, Majed's smile grew wider and sexier. 'Answer the door, Sarah.'

Oh, yes! The sooner she got rid of her unwelcome visitor the sooner she could get back to bed...and Majed.

It was all she could do to contain a shimmy when she flung open the door.

'What the hell took you so long?' Sebastian barrelled into the room.

Her jaw dropped and then she pointed back the way he'd come. 'Leave, Sebastian. Right this moment. We've nothing to say. We're done, so just please go.'

'Hey, baby, don't be so hasty.'

He tried to take her in his arms, but she side-stepped him. Majed had been *so* right about Sebastian. Why hadn't she realised that sooner?

Because you wanted to annoy your mother.

'Aw, Cuddles…'

'Don't call me baby and do *not* call me Cuddles!' God, how she loathed that nickname. It made her sound like an over-fed cat. A neutered over-fed cat. 'We have nothing—'

'I'm sorry, baby. I know I was awful yesterday. I'd had a terrible day at work. I didn't mean what I said, and I don't want to break up with you.'

Had she honestly fallen for this tripe in the past? 'I don't want you to want me back, Sebastian. What I want is for you to leave. *Now.*'

He frowned evidently baffled. Shame, hot and queasy, made her stomach churn. When had she let herself become such a pushover? When had she decided to settle for so little?

He straightened and moved towards her, determination glinting in the hard twist of his mouth. Good God, did he mean to kiss her into submission? If he tried it he'd find himself on the floor clutching his groin. Her mother had taught her about men like him.

'If you touch the lady, I'll be forced to take action.'

Majed leaned against the doorway to the bedroom, wearing nothing but a pair of snug cotton trunks—royal blue—that did nothing to hide his…impressiveness. Her mouth dried at the sheer magnificence of six feet of honed muscle lounging in the doorway, waiting for *her* to come back to bed. A sigh of pure appreciation rose through her.

Sebastian stared from Majed to Sarah and back again. It would've been almost comical if his surprise hadn't been so darned offensive. Finally he swung around and called her a one-word name that made her flinch.

With the casual elegance she envied, Majed strode across and landed a right hook to Sebastian's jaw. Hauling him off the floor, he dragged him to the door and flung him out into the hallway before closing the door on him.

He did it efficiently. Like a trained warrior. And Sarah had no hope of getting her pulse back under control. 'Um… thank you.'

'You're welcome.'

Her heart thundered in her ears. Would it be really poor form to push Majed back into the bedroom and have her wicked way with him? Or should she offer him coffee first? Actually, she had no intention of doing anything without his signal consent because…

She swallowed. Because at the moment he looked seriously forbidding.

She gripped her hands in front of her and prayed for her fantasy lover—the Majed of last night—to come back.

'You lied to me.'

She blinked. 'When?'

'You told me you'd dumped him.'

She swallowed, her hands twisting together. 'I told you I was a free woman.'

'But you deliberately let me believe the break-up was at your instigation, yes?'

Her heart sank. She had. He'd been so proud of her… and she'd wanted to revel in the sensation. She refused to compound the lie with another one. She couldn't speak, so she nodded instead. She wished he'd smile. She tried for levity. 'Are you going to punch me on the nose now?'

He did smile, but it was the kind of smile that made her heart ache. 'I would never do anything to hurt you, Sarah.' He strode over and lifted her wrist to his lips. 'I've had a wonderful night.'

She did what she could to swallow the lump that tried to lodge in her throat. 'So did I,' she whispered. 'But from the look on your face, I'm guessing this is goodbye.'

'Yes.'

He let go of her hand and it felt as if she'd been cast adrift on an endless grey sea. 'Goodbye…for good?'

He nodded.

'Even though I didn't instigate the break-up, I wanted it just as much as Sebastian did. I was relieved that it was over.'

'So why do I now feel as if you were searching for a distraction last night to take your mind off your hurt?'

That wasn't true! But she could see he wouldn't believe her. She'd ruined it—ruined the chance at something amazing—with one careless lie. She tamped down on the sob that rose in her chest. 'I messed up.' *Again.* 'I'm sorry.'

'Ah, Sarah.' For a moment regret stretched through his eyes. 'You're on the rebound, and I'm in an impossible situation. There really wasn't anything to mess up.'

He kissed her cheek and then strode back into the bedroom to dress. Sarah stumbled into the kitchen to make coffee and try to formulate a plan to salvage something from the situation. The click of the front door told her not to bother.

She walked back into the living room and stared at the closed door. With an effort, she straightened and pushed her shoulders back. Majed was right. Great sex didn't automatically make for a great relationship.

For heaven's sake, she didn't need a boyfriend. What she needed was some time alone to get her head straight—work out what she really wanted. It might be for the best if she didn't drop into the bar quite so regularly this week. Maybe not drop in at all for a couple of weeks.

But the thought of not seeing Majed at all caught at her in a way that made her ache. Not to have the chance to chat with him or share a joke…

She dragged both hands back through her hair. 'No, Majed, you're wrong. I did mess up. I messed up bad.'

Majed sensed the exact moment Sarah walked into the bar.

Even though he had his back to the door.

Even though it was a Wednesday night and she hardly ever came into the bar on a Wednesday night.

Not that she'd shown her face in here all that often in the last six weeks.

He set a Scotch and soda in front of the customer he was serving, took their money and gave change, all the while readying himself for the jolt of seeing her. He glanced towards the door. She'd stopped to chat to a table of her friends—other regulars—and he did what he could to ignore the clutch low down in his gut. She'd had this effect on him from the very first moment he'd met her. In all likelihood she'd have it on him till the day he died. Some things were just like that—desert sunsets, palm fronds moving in a breeze, the scent of spices on the air…and the sight of Sarah.

It didn't excuse the fact he'd been an idiot to go home with her. He should've resisted the temptation. After all, he'd managed to avoid desert sunsets, date palms and spice markets with remarkable ease.

He pushed the memories away—memories of home. They might haunt his sleeping hours, but he refused to dwell on them when he was awake.

He pinched the bridge of his nose. He still couldn't believe he'd relaxed his guard so much.

It was just…

He grabbed a cloth and vigorously wiped down the bar. She'd made him feel like he could be someone different—that he *was* someone different. When she spotlighted him with those pretty blue eyes of hers, she made him feel worthy. And, God forgive him, but he'd been too weak not to revel in it.

The man at the far end of the bar tapped his empty beer glass. Majed got him another. He bent down to check the stock in the fridge. But, rather than rows of wine bottles and mixers, all he could see was fragments from the night he'd spent with Sarah. They replayed through his mind on an endless loop—the curvaceous length of her leg, the way her body had arched to meet his, the taste of her. They drew him so tight, his muscles started to ache. That night had been spectacular—unforgettable.

But the morning after…

He straightened in time to see her laugh at something one of her friends said. Her stupid lie—it hadn't even been a big lie—had reminded him of the mistakes that lay in his past. His hands clenched. Mistakes he had no intention of repeating.

And it had reminded him of all that he owed his family. He forced his hands to unclench. Where on earth did he think a romance with an Australian woman could go? He grabbed a tray of dirty glasses and stacked them in readiness for the dishwasher. If he wanted to redeem himself in the eyes of his family he'd have to submit to a traditional marriage—a marriage made for political purposes that would cement democracy in his beloved Keddah Jaleel and ensure peace for future generations.

Love for his homeland welled inside him. He missed the desert night sky. He missed walking beneath the date palms on the banks of the Bay'al River. He missed the bustle of the undercover markets, the air heavy with the scent of clove and nutmeg. He missed…

His throat started to ache. When he returned—*if* he returned, *if* his father ever countenanced it—Ahmed wouldn't be there to greet him, and he didn't know how he could bear to live there without his brother. He didn't know how he could meet his father's bitter disappointment every single day, or how to assuage his mother's heartbreak. He missed his homeland but he didn't know how he could ever return.

And yet for one night Sarah had made him forget all of that. He hungered now for the respite she represented— the respite she would probably still offer to him freely if he asked for it—but he had no right to such respite. And the thought of making love to a woman who was in love with another man was anathema to him. Pride forbade it.

He lifted his chin and didn't pretend not to see her as she made her way towards the bar…and him. 'Good evening.' The words growled out of him and she stopped a pace short of the bar. He could've bitten his tongue off for sounding so damned forbidding. He tried to inject a note of friendliness as he flipped a coaster onto the bar in front of the nearest stool and said, 'Your usual?'

She eyed him warily as she slid onto the stool. 'Just a lemonade, please.'

It might be a work night but that had never stopped her drinking before. Not that she ever got rollicking drunk. She'd once told him she drank in an effort to anaesthetise herself to the mind-numbing mundanity of her life. It had made all the sore places inside him ache.

Fellow feeling—that was what he and Sarah had shared from the first.

And attraction. At least on his part. It had been instant. And insistent. And it had had nothing to do with his covert—and not so covert—scheme to rid her of Superior Sebastian.

He set her lemonade in front of her. 'Has Sebastian been giving you any trouble?' Was she seeing him again?

She paused in the act of reaching for her drink. 'Good God, no. Not since...'

Not since Majed had thrown him out of her apartment?

'And good riddance to him.' She drank deeply and then shot him a mischievous, if half-hearted, grin. 'Sebastian who?'

He wished he could believe her. She deserved better than the likes of the Sebastians of this world. He took in her pallor, the dark circles under her eyes, and wondered how long it would take her to get over him. 'You're better off without him.' Sebastian had never been worthy of her, had never appreciated her the way she ought to be appreciated.

'I know.'

He could almost believe her...

'Look, Majed, I didn't come here to talk about Sebastian. I—'

She broke off to bite her lip. Something in Majed's gut coiled at the way her gaze slid away, at the way she compulsively jiggled her straw in her drink. 'What have you come here to talk about?'

She glanced around the room. It was a quiet night but there were still a dozen people in the bar. 'It's not the time or place. I was hoping to talk to you once you'd closed. Or...some other time when you're free.'

He didn't want to be alone with her. He folded his arms. His right foot started to tap. 'Can't you just tell me now?'

She stopped jiggling her straw to fix him with a glare. 'No. You deserve more respect than that. And so do I.'

Her gaze slid away. Again. She had a lock of hair that always fell forward onto her face. She'd push it back behind her ear, but it would always work its way free again. Majed held his breath and waited... He didn't release it until it had fallen forward to brush across her cheek. That silly, defiant, joyful lock of hair could always make him smile.

Stop it!

He continued to gaze at her. She didn't look like other women. At least, not to him. Which made no sense at all because, of course, she looked like a woman. And while she wasn't stunningly beautiful, she drew his gaze again and again. He found her...lovely.

Her hair was neither gold nor brown, her skin was neither fair nor olive, and it had taken him a while before he'd realised her eyes were a clear brilliant blue, but once he had he couldn't forget them. Her features were regular, though some might claim her mouth was too wide, but nothing about Sarah immediately stood out. Not physically. Except... She exuded warmth, as if she housed her own internal sun, and everything about her made his fingers ache to reach out and touch her. He had to fight the urge now, and the effort made his muscles burn.

But... There was something in the set of her shoulders.

It hit him then, why she was here, and his hands slammed to his hips. Her eyes caught the movement...followed it... The pink of her tongue snaked out to moisten her full bottom lip and he went hot all over. He cleared his throat. 'You've lost another job.'

His rasped accusation had her gaze spearing back to his but the heat continued to circle in his blood. Her cheeks went pink but, whether at the accuracy of his accusation or the fact he'd caught her staring, he didn't know.

'Well, yes.' One shoulder lifted. 'But that's not what I came to talk about either.'

No?

She stared down her nose at him. 'Mike told you to keep an eye on me, didn't he? He told you to give me a job if I needed one.'

He had, but Majed had no intention of admitting as much.

'Don't worry, Majed, I haven't come to beg you for a job.'

He gave thanks for that mercy. If he had to work with

her day in and day out, he didn't know how he'd manage to keep from touching her.

'Mike asked me to look out for you too, you know?'

He jerked upright. 'I don't need looking out for.'

A smile hovered at the corners of her lips. 'Oh, that's right. I forgot. You're an island unto yourself.'

That was *exactly* what he had to become if he was to ever return to Keddah Jaleel, and the fact she found the idea so nonsensical irked him. Sarah was more than happy to tell anyone who'd listen that she was a complete flake, but she had a perspicacity that was remarkable in its accuracy.

'I don't need looking after either, despite appearances to the contrary. I might be a flake...'

There she went, putting herself down.

'But I'm an independent flake.'

'I don't consider you a flake at all.'

She gave a short laugh. 'I'm going to ask you to hold that thought in the forefront of your mind when we have our conversation.'

What on earth had she come here to discuss?

He stiffened. Was she leaving Melbourne? Had he somehow left her feeling that she had to leave?

Damn it all to hell!

He strode into the middle of the room and clapped his hands together. 'Excuse me, everyone, but something has come up and I need to close early. Can I ask you all to finish your drinks and leave?'

When he'd locked the door behind the last customer he spun to face Sarah. 'What did you want to talk to me about?'

She stood and wiped her hands down the sides of her trousers. 'I think you should come and take a seat and—'

'Stop fudging! Don't delay any longer, Sarah. Out with it.'

'Fine!' She folded her arms and stuck out a hip. She swallowed but lifted her chin. 'I'm pregnant.'

For a moment her words made no sense. He even momentarily revelled in the relief that she wasn't planning to leave Melbourne. 'You're—' he rubbed his nape '—pregnant?'

She nodded. 'That's right.'

'And…?'

She flopped down to her stool. She lifted her arms and then let them drop back into her lap. Her mouth trembled and her eyes were full of fear, sadness, tears and, strangely, some laughter. Her eyes contained the entire world. 'And the baby is yours, Majed.'

CHAPTER TWO

THE SHOCK OF brandy hitting the back of his throat had
Majed jolting back to himself. It was only then he realised
Sarah had pushed him into a chair, had poured him a snif-
ter of brandy and was urging him to drink it.

He did what she demanded because he was at a loss to
know what else to do. *She was having his child!*

'I know it's a shock.' Sarah moved to the chair opposite.
'And I didn't mean to blurt it out quite so baldly.'

But he'd ordered her to.

Heat scored through him, followed by a wave of ice. He
stared at her. Was she okay? It didn't matter what kind of
shock he might be experiencing, it had to be far worse for
her. Physically he was exactly the same as he'd been before she'd told him the news. But, regardless of what decision she made, Sarah would never be the same again. He
had to focus on what she needed from him—and do his
best to provide it.

She was pregnant with his child!

He opened his mouth but before he could speak she said,
'I understand your reservations concerning the baby's paternity.'

She thought his silence indicated that he didn't believe
her?

*She'd lied about instigating the break-up with Supe-
rior Sebastian.*

She wouldn't lie about something as big as this.

'Sarah—'

'Please, just let me explain. It's taken me this long to screw up my courage and now that I've started I'd…I'd rather just keep going.'

He gave a terse nod, hating the thought that she'd been afraid to tell him her news.

'So, the thing is…' She drew a loop of circles in the condensation of her glass. 'Sebastian had mumps when he was fifteen, which means the likelihood of him being able to father children is pretty slim. But, besides that—'

She broke off to stare at her hands. He reached out and wrapped one of his hands around both of hers. She had such small hands, and every protective instinct he had surged to the fore. 'Don't be frightened of me, Sarah. I'm not angry. Just stunned.' He made his voice as gentle as he could. 'I want to help in any way I can.'

Her lips trembled. 'That's lovely of you.'

'You've had a lot to bear on your own. I want you to know you're not alone now.' *She was having his child!* He forced himself to swallow. 'What were you saying about Sebastian?'

'Oh.' Her lips twisted. 'Before we broke up…for the two months before we broke up… Sebastian and I…'

'Yes?'

She disengaged her hand from his to rub her nape. 'We hadn't been intimate.'

He'd always known the man had rocks in his head. This simply confirmed it.

'I don't doubt your word.'

The little moue she made informed him she didn't entirely believe him. 'We'll have a paternity test done to put your mind at rest. If I decide to keep the baby.'

If. His heart clenched at the word, though he wasn't sure

why. A child was the last thing he'd expected at this point in his life. It should be the last thing he wanted.

But the ultimate decision rested with Sarah. It was her body and he'd support her whatever she decided to do.

'Are you and the baby healthy?'

'The doctor says so.'

'You've been to see a doctor? That's good.'

She frowned. 'You're taking this very calmly.'

Inside he was a mass of conflicting emotions but he refused to reveal them. 'We're in this together. I want you to know you're not alone. Between us we'll sort it out.'

Her mouth opened but no words emerged.

'Have you eaten this evening?'

She wrinkled her nose. 'I haven't had much of an appetite.'

He rose and took her hand. 'Come, I'll make you an omelette.'

He switched off the lights to the bar and led her upstairs to the flat above.

'You can cook?' she asked when he'd seated her at the breakfast bar of his open-plan kitchen-dining-living room.

'I make omelettes that are out of this world.'

She glanced around and he wondered what she made of his bachelor pad. 'An omelette sounds kinda nice.'

It wasn't until Majed pulled the eggs from the fridge that he remembered pregnant women were supposed to avoid certain foods. What about eggs? He swung back. 'Will you excuse me for a moment?'

He sped into the bathroom and pulled his phone from his pocket to open his web browser. He typed in his query and then read down the list of foods that pregnant women shouldn't eat. Right—the eggs shouldn't be runny. Okay, he'd cook the omelette a little longer than usual... Actually, he might cook it a lot longer than usual, just to be on the safe side. Hard cheeses like cheddar were fine too.

Right. He snapped his phone shut. He'd keep it simple with a plain cheese omelette. Well cooked.

Sarah tried to find some trace of Majed in his flat—in his furniture and in the décor—but… Well, it was all very comfortable and commendably tidy, but something was missing, though she couldn't put her finger on what it was.

'What do you think of the place?'

She glanced around from the window that overlooked the busy inner-city Melbourne street to find Majed surveying her from the doorway. And just like that her heart started to jackhammer. 'It's nice.' She ignored his raised eyebrow to add, 'I've always been curious to see up here.'

He stared at her for a bit longer. 'The bathroom is just down the hall on the left.' He pointed back behind him. 'And the bedroom is at the end of the hall. Feel free to take a look.'

'Oh, no, I'm all good.' She couldn't invade his privacy that much.

She slid onto her stool again when he started clattering pots and pans and whisking eggs. She knew they were skirting around the main topic of conversation but…dear Lord…the shock on his face when he'd finally realised what she'd been trying to tell him. It made her stomach churn just remembering it. She wanted to give him a chance to get a little more used to the idea before they launched into a discussion about what they would do.

Frankly, she had no idea what that might be.

He moved with easy grace in his compact kitchen and it was no hardship to watch him rather than make small talk…or think. He started to slide her omelette onto a plate, and then jerked, as if he'd burned himself. His gaze speared hers before he seemed to recall himself and finished serving her food.

She stared at the plate he pushed in front of her and

had to fight a frown. This did *not* look like an out-of-this-world omelette—it looked flat and rubbery. And brown. Her stomach gave a sick little squeeze but she gamely forked in a mouthful. He *had* gone to all the trouble of making it for her.

His hands went to his hips as he watched her eat. It only made her stomach churn harder. She set her fork down. 'What?'

'Did you lose your job because you're pregnant? They *cannot* fire you for being pregnant.'

She picked up her fork again. 'True. But apparently they can fire me for calling the manager a weasel of a bully who's nothing more than a boil on the backside of the universe that's in dire need of lancing.'

He choked. 'You didn't?'

'I did. And I can't begin to tell you how utterly satisfying it was.' But now she had no job. And she had a baby on the way. Could her timing have been any worse? Talk about irresponsible!

She blew out a breath. She was such a screw-up.

Just ask Sebastian.

Just ask her mother!

'Eat your omelette,' Majed ordered.

She didn't know if it was her self-recriminations, or if the eggs hadn't agreed with her, but she only just made it to the bathroom before losing the contents of her stomach. Majed held her hair back from her face while she was sick. He pressed a cool, damp cloth to her forehead, and through it all she wished she felt well enough to feel even a modicum of embarrassment.

Eventually she closed the lid of the toilet and sat on top of it. The concern in Majed's face caught at her. She tried to find a smile. 'Did you know that *morning* sickness is a misnomer? Apparently it can happen at any time of the day.'

'It's...*wrong*!'

'It's certainly unpleasant.' But her legs finally felt steady enough to hold her so she rose and rinsed out her mouth. 'Majed, I know we have a lot to talk about, but I'm feeling beat and—'

The rest of her words stuttered to a halt when he lifted her off her feet and into his arms. 'You need to rest, *habibi*. It's been a difficult day for you. Sharing with me your news has been nerve-racking, yes? We have time yet to talk and make decisions.' As he spoke, he carried her down the short hallway to his bedroom. Very gently, he lowered her to the bed. She had an impression of vast luxury and comfort and had to bite her lip to prevent a sigh of pure bliss escaping as softness enveloped her.

'I shouldn't—'

'Of course you should.' He pulled off her shoes.

'Maybe just a little rest,' she murmured as he pulled the covers over her.

'Rest for as long as you like,' he murmured back.

'Majed?'

'Yes.'

'What did that word mean—*"habibi"*?'

'It's a term of endearment…like "sweetheart".'

A sigh fluttered out of her. She suspected it would be rather lovely to be his sweetheart for real.

Sarah woke as the first fingers of dawn filtered through the curtains of Majed's bedroom windows. She lay still and listened intently but couldn't sense any signs of movement throughout the rest of the flat. Very quietly, she pushed back the bedclothes and tiptoed into the living room to find Majed sprawled across the sofa that barely contained his bulk, fast asleep.

Most people when they slept looked unguarded, younger… vulnerable. Not Majed. If anything he looked slightly forbidding and stern. It suddenly struck her that the easy-going façade he assumed every day at the bar might be exactly that—a front.

Or maybe your news has given him unpleasant dreams.

She scratched her hands through her hair. How long had he sat up last night, churning over her news? She'd had a few extra days to get used to the idea. Yesterday evening her sleepless nights had finally caught up with her. She felt rested and well now, though, and she didn't have the heart to wake him.

A shiver shook through her. When she got right down to it, how well did she *know* Majed? Barely at all. She had no idea if he wanted a child. She gripped her hands together. For all she knew, he might welcome a child with unbridled enthusiasm. Or the idea of fatherhood might be a total anathema to him. Surely one should know these things about a man before becoming pregnant by him?

Your mother didn't.

Perhaps not, but she didn't intend to take her parents as role models. They'd spent her entire childhood using her as a pawn in their war to score points off each other. That was the only thing she was certain of—that she wouldn't do that to any child of hers. If she had this baby she'd do her best to ensure its childhood was happy and carefree— not a battleground.

If.

Slipping onto a chair at the dining table, she lifted her feet to the seat and hugged her knees. She and Majed had to decide what to do about this baby and she had no idea where to start.

A pen and notepad rested in the middle of the table. She pulled them towards her with the thought of writing a list of pros and cons. She'd start with the cons, because there were so many: the pregnancy was unplanned, she was un-employed, so how would she support not just herself but a baby as well? Her mother would have a fit and there'd be no end to the recriminations. Her father would take the opposite stance and think an unplanned pregnancy was an inspired idea. She was only twenty-six—there was plenty of time yet before she needed to start thinking about having children. She was a total screw-up and surely a child deserved better than that for a parent?

There'd be more cons—lots more—but the length of the list had started to dishearten her. She needed something in the pros column to balance it out…just a little bit.

She stared at the page and bit her lip. There had to be one reason to keep this baby. A solid logical reason that made perfect sense. Her throat ached. The page in front of her blurred. She reached out and wrote a single sentence:

I love this baby already.

She stared at the words she'd just written and blinked hard. She did love this baby, but was it enough? A child deserved a better home than Sarah could give it. But, no matter how much she might wish to, she couldn't draw a line through that single entry on her 'pros' list.

Perhaps she should try a different tack and list all of the options available to her instead. Biting back a sigh, she turned the page…only to find that Majed had made a list of his own. Her heart started to pound. Would it be an invasion of privacy to read his list?

Invasion or not, she had no hope of stopping herself.

At the top of the page in bald, ugly print he'd written a single word: *abortion.*

She couldn't stop herself from flinching, even though it had been the first option that had occurred to her too. Even though it was an option she was still considering.

Beneath that he'd written: *adoption.* She swallowed. Did she have the strength for that? If she loved this baby then wouldn't she want the very best for it? Wouldn't she fight to give it the very best, regardless of the cost to her personally?

She froze when she realised that was *exactly* what she'd do. She loved this baby. All she had to work out now was what would be in the baby's best interests.

She pulled Majed's list back towards her. Two hard, dark lines separated those first two items from the rest of his list. Pulling in a breath, she read on…

Majed watched Sarah's eyes widen as she read down the list he'd made. He knew when she'd reached the end of the list because it wasn't possible for her eyes to go any wider.

She glanced across at him and saw him watching her. Something arced in the air between them before she gave him a brave little smile that cracked open something in his chest and started up an ache that he feared would never go away.

He couldn't afford to fall in love with this woman. He couldn't afford to fall in love with anyone. Love clouded one's judgement. And when one's judgement was clouded it put the people one cared about at risk.

He couldn't fall in love with Sarah, but he could look after her.

'Good morning,' she whispered.

Her voice emerged on a rasp, as if her throat was dry, and he threw off his blanket, rose and strode to the kitchen. 'Let me get you something hot to drink. You should've helped yourself.'

'I didn't want to disturb you.'

He came back with glasses of apple juice and steaming mugs of herbal tea. His body cried out for strong black coffee but, if Sarah was avoiding caffeine the way most pregnant women he knew did, then it would be cruel to drink it in front of her.

He nodded at his list. 'I tried to cover every possible option I could think of. Are there any you've thought of that I've missed?'

She shook her head and sipped her tea. He watched carefully for any signs of nausea but she merely closed her eyes and inhaled the steam as if welcoming the warmth into her body. Her clothes looked rumpled from having been slept in, and she had bed hair, but beneath all of that a vitality and vibrancy that had been lacking yesterday had started to emerge.

'You've thought of things that hadn't occurred to me.' She pointed to the very last item on the list. 'That's a bit over the top, don't you think?'

He shrugged but his gut tightened. 'My purpose was to list every option I could think of, without making value judgements.'

He'd spent a lot of time in the West. Four years in the UK at Oxford University with trips to the USA in the summer breaks. For the last four years, he'd worked in Australia. But he'd grown up in Keddah Jaleel—a world of ancient tradition, arranged marriages and duty. He knew exactly what his family would expect of him in this situation.

He had no intention of forcing those expectations onto Sarah but...

'I want you to know that whichever one of those options you settle on, whichever you deem is in your and the baby's best interests, I'll support you one-hundred percent.' He didn't want her to doubt that for a moment.

She set her mug down, a deep furrow marring her brow. 'What?'

'Your happiness is just as important as mine.'

He didn't deserve happiness. He didn't say that out loud, though. It was a sentiment that would horrify her. He nodded at the list. 'None of those options make me unhappy.'

Her raised eyebrow told him she didn't believe him. She pointed towards the top of the list. 'This line here is rather dark. It looks angry. Does that mean you hate the idea of abortion and adoption?'

He tried to keep his face unreadable. 'I've no ethical objection to either. It's just…' He reached out and wrapped her hand in his. 'It's just, I don't dare care for the life growing inside you if those are the routes you're considering.'

She stared at him with such intensity his mouth went dry. The pulse at the base of her throat pounded and he could feel an answering throb start up at the centre of him.

'You care about this baby?'

The question was raw, Sarah's voice full of heartbreak and hope, and he didn't know which one would win out.

He nodded. There wasn't a single doubt in his mind that if Sarah had this child—*if*—he would love it with everything that was inside him.

Then tell her that. You need to give her more.

But he didn't want to pressure her one way or the other. She winced. 'Majed?'

He realised he was all but crushing her hand. He loosened his grip immediately and massaged her hand gently before releasing it. 'Last night I found myself getting excited about the prospect of a baby.' *A grandchild for his parents—what a gift!* 'I know this is completely unexpected. Not in a million years would I have thought… I mean, we were careful.'

'We were. This is so…*unplanned*.'

'But it doesn't follow that it's not a blessing.'

She went still and he chose his next words with care. 'I had to rein in my excitement last night because you deciding not to go ahead with the pregnancy is a valid choice, and an understandable one.'

She sat back and massaged her temples. The conflict he saw mirrored in her face tore at him. Without a word, she reached out and turned over the first page of the notepad. She'd written a list of pros and cons. Only one item was listed under the 'pros' heading. He read it and something fierce gripped his gut. He didn't bother reading her long list of cons. He seized her hand again. 'If you love this baby, Sarah, then you must keep it.'

Her gaze dropped from his. Her hand trembled. She pulled it free and reached for her tea. 'This baby deserves more than I can give it.'

'We're in this together. I'll help you financially. Between us—' He broke off, his heart thundering in his chest. 'You won't deny me access to the child...will you?'

Her mug clattered back to the table. 'Of course not. I wouldn't dream of it—not if you want to be a part of the baby's life.'

'I want that *very* much.' He wanted them to be very clear on that point.

'But, Majed, I'm not talking about the financial arrangements here. I have—' she rolled her eyes '—marketable skills. I don't doubt my ability to get another job.'

It would be so much harder with a baby, though. And they both knew it.

It took a beat longer for what she wasn't saying to hit him. He wanted to take her hand again, to offer her silent support, but she had both hands wrapped tightly around her mug. His heart continued to pound. 'Then tell me what you're really afraid of.'

She lifted her gaze and the shadows in her eyes made his stomach clench. 'I think we need to be completely honest with each other from this point forward, if we're going to have a baby together. Don't you?'

There was so much she didn't know about him. And she'd need to know. He resisted the urge to lower his forehead to the table. 'I agree.'

'I need to be honest with you, even if it means you come to despise me.'

For good or ill, his opinion mattered to her. It was why she'd let him think she'd broken up with Superior Sebastian rather than the other way round. He couldn't let her down now. Gently, he reached out to brush the backs of his fingers across her cheek. 'I could never despise you. The idea is unthinkable.'

She took his hand and squeezed it before releasing it with a smile. 'That was the right thing to say.'

Everything inside him sharpened. He sat back with folded arms, his hand still warm from where he'd touched her. 'Now, if I can only get you to believe it. Come, tell me what you're afraid of.'

She swallowed and her throat bobbed. 'Majed, there's a hole inside me—as if there's something essential that I'm missing. And I try to fill it up with things—like my relationship with Sebastian, a relationship I knew wasn't good for me—in an effort to distract myself from that sense of lacking something. It's why I bounce from job to job. Once I start to feel settled in a job, the emptiness starts gnawing away at me. And…and I have to create upheaval to keep it at bay.'

He stared at her. 'Is that why you invited me back to your apartment that night?'

'No, *that* was something I *wanted* to do. I was feeling jubilant and happy and it felt right.' She met his gaze. 'The night I spent with you, I wasn't thinking about filling up any kind of shortfall or lack inside me. I wasn't trying to distract myself. I'm not sure I was thinking at all. I acted on impulse, yes, but on instinct too.' Her frown deepened. 'I felt as if I was living—as if I were properly alive. It was… exhilarating.'

It merely meant she hadn't had time to become bored with him yet. 'And you're afraid that a baby won't be a big enough distraction? You think you'll find yourself becoming bored with the baby, the way you do with your jobs?'

Shocked eyes met his. 'That's *not* what I mean at all. No. I'm afraid that I'll make the baby the very centre of my life—that I'll use it to fill all those empty places inside me. That'd be wrong. It wouldn't be fair to put that kind of pressure on a child. I have a feeling it would be *shockingly* unfair.'

Her honesty stunned him.

The care she was already taking for her child humbled him.

He had empty places inside him too, but he knew exactly what had caused them—the guilt and responsibility he bore over his brother's death. How did he mean to protect a child from those?

'You sense it in me too, don't you?'

'No.' He shook his head. 'You don't appear to me as if some essential part of you is missing. You don't strike me as lonely, or even as if you're afraid of loneliness.' She had a wide network of friends. He'd seen her with them in the bar. From the outside, Sarah's life seemed full. 'Before Sebastian, you were nearly a year without a boyfriend, yes? You don't strike me as a person who needs to constantly be in a romantic relationship to feel whole.'

'The emptiness has nothing to do with romance or loneliness. If it did, I'd be able to fill it.'

'What does it have to do with, then?'

She shrugged but her gaze slid away. Instinct told him not to push. 'Sarah, you don't strike me as someone who is lacking. You strike me as someone who is searching.'

She swung back to gaze at him. 'Searching for what?'

'I expect you're the only person who can answer that.' Though he'd do anything he could to help her find the answer.

She scrubbed her hands down her face. 'I don't want my...*lack*...to hurt the baby.'

'If we're both aware of it as a potential problem then we can remain on our guards against it—cut it off at the pass, so to speak.'

She bit her lip but it didn't hide the hope that flared briefly in her eyes. 'You make it sound easy.'

'I don't think it'll be easy. I think raising a child must be the most challenging thing a person can ever do in this life. I think it must also be one of the most rewarding.'

She sagged back in her chair. 'You make me believe that I could do it.'

She could do it! And how much he wanted to do it too—with her—should scare him. Instead, it elated him.

She pointed at his list. 'Which of these options is the most attractive to you?'

His heart thundered so loud it was all he could do to hear his thoughts over it.

She tapped a finger to the notepad. 'Do you have a…for the lack of a better term…*favourite* here?'

'Yes.' She'd just been completely honest with him. She deserved the same in return.

'Okay,' she whispered. 'Hit me with it.'

'You want the truth? Right now?'

She moistened her lips. 'What are *you* afraid of?'

'Terrifying you.'

After a beat, she started to laugh. 'Being pregnant terrifies me. Wondering whether I'll be a good mother or not terrifies me. But, Majed, *you* don't terrify me.'

Without another word, he pointed to the last item on the list. 'This is my preference.'

Her quick intake of breath told him she hadn't expected that.

'You want us to marry?' she whispered. 'You want to marry me and take me and the baby to live in Keddah Jaleel with you?'

'Yes.' The word croaked out of him. 'Have I terrified you?'

'Umm…no.'

He didn't believe her. But nevertheless it was time to

tell her the truth. 'Sarah, there's something you need to know about me. My father is the ruling Sheikh of Keddah Jaleel…and I'm his heir.'

Her face remained blank for a disconcertingly long time before she straightened. 'You…you mean that you're…like a king?'

'My father is the king.'

'But you'll be king one day?'

Acid burned the back of his throat. 'Yes.' *Maybe.*

'And if we marry, and our child is a boy, he'll one day be king too?'

He had to force his answer out. 'Yes.'

She folded her arms tightly in front of her. 'Okay, you can now colour me terrified.'

CHAPTER THREE

SARAH WASN'T SURE at what point she stopped listening. Majed's rich tones continued to wash over her but her mind whirled in a million different directions. He was the son of a king. *He was a prince!* And then one of his statements cut through all her confusion, crystallising into an over-arching and urgent question.

'Whoa, wait!' She held up a hand. 'You were sent away from Keddah Jaleel *for your own safety*? Because of border infractions and rebel activity?'

He dragged a hand down his face and she hated how grey he'd gone. 'Majed?'

'Yes.'

'And yet this is a place you want to take me? You're prepared to put your unborn child in danger?'

'No!' His head shot up and his eyes flashed. 'I would never knowingly place you or our child in danger. The skirmishes were minor and quickly smothered, the perpetrators dealt with. It wasn't necessary that I leave, but it put my parents' minds at rest.'

Her heart thumped so hard she swore it would leave bruises. 'Then why have you stayed away from your homeland for the last four years?'

He shot out of his seat to stalk across the room. 'That is not something which I wish to discuss. You have my word of honour, though, that is has nothing to do with fearing for my safety.'

He wanted her to take his word for it? Maybe, if it were only her life at stake here, she would. But it wasn't. She had a baby to consider. She could no longer afford to be reckless or irresponsible.

Rising, she ran her hands over her blouse in a vain effort to smooth out the wrinkles. 'I think it's time I went home.'

Her apartment—Mike's apartment—was only a couple of blocks away. A walk in the early-morning air might help.

Or not. Probably not. But it wouldn't hurt.

His nostrils flared. 'You'll consider my proposal?'

'No.'

Not a single muscle moved and yet he seemed to sag. 'You think the idea too outrageous?'

It was utterly preposterous, yet it wasn't outrage that gripped her. 'I'm not going anywhere near Keddah Jaleel when I've no idea why you've stayed away so long. I know no one there. You'd be my only friend and support, and if I can't trust you…'

Her stomach churned. 'I am not putting myself in that position, Majed. My mother taught me better than that.'

He swung away to pace the length of the room before swinging back to face her. Agitation—anger, perhaps?—crackled from him like a force field. 'An Internet search will provide you with everything you need to know.'

She located her purse and slung it over her shoulder as she made for the door. 'Goodbye, Majed.'

'That is not enough for you?'

She swung back. 'I'm surprised you even need to ask that question. We're going to have a baby and yet you can't be honest with me.' Her hands clenched. 'If you can't see the problem with that, then I'm not going to try and explain it to you.'

His nostrils flared. His chest rose and fell. And for a

moment he looked so forbidding, her mouth went dry. He'd never hurt her, she knew that, but she could suddenly see the legacy of his heritage—the fierce and fearless warriors who'd fought and won innumerable wars on the ancient sands of Keddah Jaleel. Their blood flowed in his veins and, beneath his veneer of polish, that same fierceness resided in Majed's DNA.

'You're going to do it. You're going to keep the baby.'

His words were more statement than question. He smiled and she felt as if she were falling. She opened her mouth and then closed it again, realising that she'd come to a decision in spite of herself. Her heart beat hard. She and Majed would be tied to each other always through this child. And, regardless of what happened between them, the thought of the baby could still make him smile. And that mattered.

She rubbed a hand across her chest, trying to dislodge the ache attempting to settle beneath her breastbone. 'I…' She pulled herself up to her full height. 'Yes, I am. I'm going to have this baby.' If nothing else, this morning had made that crystal clear to her.

And that was something to be grateful for.

He strode towards her, and for a moment she thought he meant to hug her, but he stopped short and she saw shadows gathering in his eyes, ousting the excitement and tenderness that had momentarily lit them.

He dragged both hands through his hair. 'Four years ago my brother was killed by the rebels.'

The floor bucked beneath her feet. Sarah braced herself against the door, pressing her spine back until the hard wood bit into her.

'He'd organised a secret assignation with a woman who couldn't be trusted. It was a reckless and foolish thing to do and he paid heavily for it. Too heavily.'

The anguish in his eyes tore at her. 'Oh, Majed.' She reached a hand towards him but he flinched.

'I loved my brother, Sarah. I've not returned to Keddah Jaleel because I cannot imagine living in my homeland without him.'

She wanted to hug him but everything in his posture forbade it. 'I'm sorry,' she whispered.

He nodded, but all she could see in his face was pain and anger. Her stomach churned in a sickening slow roll. *Oh, no you don't.* This was *not* the time to throw up. Closing her eyes, she rested her head back and concentrated on her breathing.

'Come, Sarah.'

Her eyes sprang open at the touch of warm fingers against her arm.

'Come take a seat on the sofa.'

She couldn't fight the nausea and talk at the same time so she let him lead her across to the plump comfort of the sofa. Once seated, she shoved her head between her knees, murmuring, 'I'll be right as rain in a moment.'

When she was finally sure she'd mastered the nausea, she lifted her head. 'I'm sorry about that. I—'

'I shouldn't have told you in such a way!'

'I'm glad you did tell me.'

'Has it made you more afraid to journey to Keddah Jaleel?'

'Not more afraid, just sadder.' And to her surprise she realised she spoke the truth. 'Your brother...'

'Ahmed.'

She swallowed. 'Did Ahmed not follow proper security protocols? I assume you have security measures in place?'

He nodded. 'It's necessary for any ruling family. But that night Ahmed gave his bodyguard the slip.'

Nobody deserved to pay such a high price for wanting a single night of freedom.

'Why did they kill him?' she whispered. 'What did they hope to achieve?'

'My father is a progressive monarch. At some future point, he'd dearly love to introduce democracy to Keddah Jaleel. There are still those in my country, however, who cling to the old ways.'

'Progressive? Is he working towards gender equality? Will, for example, the daughters of the ruling sheikh ever be allowed to rule?'

For the first time that morning, he smiled—really smiled. 'Ah, Sarah, we're progressive…and we'll continue to work towards a fair and just world for all of our citizens…but change cannot always be introduced as quickly we would like.'

'Meaning?'

'Progress takes time. And we must be seen to respect the traditions of our people, even as we move beyond them. If they believe us to view our heritage as worthless, then we would lose their trust and loyalty. If our child is a daughter, and if she shows an interest in politics, then she'll have some kind of leadership role.'

'But she won't be ruler?'

'I cannot see that happening for the next generation, no. But, if we have a granddaughter, things may be different for her.'

She stared at him and her heart thumped. What a difficult task it must be to lead a country. This man was a prince—one day a ruler by birthright. She had no right telling him what he should and shouldn't do politically, not when she had no notion of what his people held dear, what they valued and what they hoped for.

She swallowed. 'Your family have paid a heavy price for their service to your country, Majed. I'm more sorry than I can say about the loss of your brother.'

This time when she reached out to touch his hand he didn't flinch. Instead, he turned his palm upwards and laced his fingers though hers. The scent of amber and spices—

cloves and cardamom—teased her senses as a thick, pregnant silence wrapped about them. It was all she could do not to chafe the gooseflesh that rose on her arms.

'There is one other thing you need to know.'

His tone lifted the tiny hairs at her nape.

'Ahmed was my *older* brother.'

'Do you have any other siblings?'

He shook his head and that was when she realised what he was trying to tell her. 'Oh!' Her heart started to thump. 'You… Ahmed was supposed to ascend to the throne, not you?'

'Not me,' he agreed.

Wow! Okay. 'And…and that's another reason you haven't wanted to return?'

'Yes.'

And yet he was prepared to face his demons because he had a baby on the way—because he wanted to be a good father. 'I think you'll make a fine ruler, Majed. I know you must miss Ahmed, but you haven't usurped him.'

'I know that in my head. But it's not the way it feels in my heart.'

'What would Ahmed tell you to do?'

He spoke a phrase in Arabic that she didn't understand. But then he laughed and he suddenly looked younger. 'He'd tell me to stop over-thinking things. He'd tell me I need to curb my impatience for change and to tread with respect in relation to the traditional ways.' A sigh shuddered from him. 'He'd tell me to take my place at my father's side. He'd want me to fight for it.'

Fight for it…?

She wasn't sure what that last bit meant but, as she stared into his face, she couldn't agree more with Ahmed's advice. Majed was destined for great things. It was time for him to embrace his destiny.

'Will you come to Keddah Jaleel with me, Sarah? Will

you at least come and see the life you could have there, the
life I can give you and our child?'

'What will your parents think about a baby?'

'It will…' The lines about his mouth deepened. 'It will
bring them joy.'

She had a feeling that there were family issues at play
here that she had no hope of understanding.

'Our unmarried status will not thrill them. It will…
disappoint them. But if you find you like Keddah Jaleel
then maybe you will stay.'

'And marry you?'

'That is my wish.'

'And what kind of marriage do you think we can have?'

'One based on respect and honesty. One based on friendship.'

She pulled in a breath. 'What about love?'

He dragged his hand from hers. She immediately missed
the warmth and connection. He pushed that hand back
through his hair once…twice. 'We said we would be honest, yes?'

She couldn't speak. She could only nod. He was going to
tell her that he could never love her…and she didn't know
why, but she wasn't sure she could bear to hear him say it.

'I do not believe in love.'

She blinked.

'And if I did, I'd not want it in my life.'

What on earth…? So it wasn't that he *couldn't* love her
in particular. It was that he *wouldn't* love any woman at all.

'Love—romantic love—leads people to do wild and
foolish things. It clouds their judgement. I want no part
of that.'

Her mouth went dry. He was talking about Ahmed and
the woman who had entranced him so completely that he'd
thrown caution to the wind.

Oh, Majed.

'I can sincerely assure you, however, that I believe my happiness in marriage with you has a better chance than with anyone else I know. I *like* you, Sarah, and that has to count for something.'

He said that now. But what would happen when he met a woman who stirred his blood? How much would he resent the ties that bound him then—and the woman and child responsible for those ties? Would he become like her father? Would she become like her mother?

She couldn't let that happen.

She moistened parched lips. 'Do you believe in fidelity?'

His eyes flashed. 'I do.' He took her chin in a firm grip and forced her gaze to his. 'I can assure you that, if you marry me, you will not think of other men.'

And then his lips slammed to hers with a force that was far from polite and more demanding than any kiss she'd ever experienced. One hand slid to her nape to prevent her from drawing away, while the other remained at her jaw, holding her still while he plundered her lips with a ruthless and seductive intent that had her melting even as she wanted to resist. The relentless, primal possession continued, sending the blood stampeding through her veins while the strength leached from her muscles until it finally tore his name from her throat.

He lifted his head, his eyes glittering. 'Are we clear on this point?'

She lifted fingers that trembled to swollen lips. That kiss had been an outrageous attempt at domination, yet she wanted him to kiss her like that again...and not stop.

'I'm clear on the fact that you expect fidelity from me. Do you demand it of yourself?'

'Naturally.' His chin tilted at an arrogant angle. 'But then, I expect my future wife to make sure my mind does not stray to other women.'

She tossed her head, dislodging his grip, thrilled and

appalled in equal measure. But before she could give him the put down she was sure he deserved, his lips were on hers again—warm, gentle…playful. They teased and tantalised until her anger had dissolved and she threaded her fingers through his hair to pull him closer.

He obliged until she lay half-sprawled beneath him, their only barrier the thin material of their clothes, his kisses sending something inside her spiralling free. She wanted all barriers between them gone. She wanted to move to the dance he'd taught her six weeks ago. She craved the spiralling pleasure, the adventure of it all, and the peace that followed. She ached…

A whimper broke from her when he lifted his head. He muttered words she didn't understand but could translate all too easily.

There'd be no more kisses today.

He lifted himself away from her and then helped her back into a sitting position with a gentleness that had the backs of her eyes burning.

'I'm sorry.'

He physically removed himself from the sofa, his words emerging clipped and short. If she hadn't heard the regret threading through them, she might've fled in mortification.

'I'm only sorry you stopped.' She'd aimed for levity but fell far short of the desired mark. It was the truth of her words that rang in the space between them rather than humour. What the heck, she'd made a fool of herself over lesser things. 'Why did you stop?'

He moved to sit in an armchair. She'd love to flatter herself that it was because he couldn't trust his control when he was near her, but she wasn't that kind of woman. She didn't inspire that kind of passion in men.

'I don't want to do anything to make you resent me.'

'And…sex can be complicated?'

'That is my experience, yes.'

Hers too, but she and Majed had already been lovers, they were having a baby—he wanted to marry her, for heaven's sake! Surely…?

'From here on, Sarah, it has to be all or nothing. I won't settle for anything less.'

She gulped.

'As the mother of my future child, you're entitled to my respect and consideration.'

Uh huh.

'I don't want… I should hate to come to resent you. We may marry or not—whatever you decide—but I think it important that we do our very best to maintain our friendship.'

'Absolutely.' Desire continued to shift through her in an insistent ache, an itch and prickle in her blood, but she forced herself to focus on his words. Friendship was important. She remembered what it had been like growing up with warring parents. She'd do anything to protect her child from that. But… 'If you don't believe in love, Majed, why should you come to resent me if we became lovers? I don't understand.'

'I have my pride, *habibi*. Just like any man.'

She was starting to suspect he might have more than his fair share. 'Meaning that, if we became lovers and I then chose not to marry you, that would hurt your pride?'

'Deeply.'

Wow. Okay. He really did mean all or nothing. And she had no intention of rousing his resentment. He could think what he liked of her but she had to make sure he never resented their child.

'I'd resent being the tool with which you recovered from a broken heart.'

Her jaw dropped. 'Broken heart? You mean… Sebastian? Oh, *please*! He didn't break—'

'We promised to be honest with each other.' His lips twisted. 'Do not lie to me now.'

Her hands clenched. 'Sebastian did not break my heart!'

She glared at him but Majed's face had gone opaque. 'Perhaps that is what you want to believe. Perhaps that's what you wish were true.'

She shot to her feet. 'That's the kind of privileged-male superiority that seriously ticks me off! Oh, the poor little woman can't possibly know her own mind—she's just a hysterical female! I'll tell her what she really thinks because she's not clever enough to think for herself.'

The lines bracketing his mouth turned white. He shot to his feet too. 'That's not what I meant.'

'It's what you said.'

He raised his arms. 'You want me to believe Sebastian didn't break your heart?'

'Your belief is your own affair. Just…just don't presume to know my thoughts and feelings better than I do myself.'

They were both breathing heavily. Eventually he nodded. 'You are right. That was wrong of me…and stupid. I resent Sebastian—I resent the way he treated you. The only possible explanation I could come up with for why you accepted that treatment was because you were in love with him.'

'There are other reasons.'

'Such as?'

She fell back into the sofa. 'Do we need to talk about this now? There're a whole lifetime of reasons and it makes me tired and ashamed to think of them.'

He sat again too, his eyes dark and intense as they scanned her face. It suddenly occurred to her that maybe he found her just as baffling as she found him. It comforted her a little, but his continuing seriousness made her fidgety. She shot him a smile. 'Perhaps you'll understand if you ever meet my mother.'

'I want to meet your mother.'

That made her laugh, though not in a particularly humorous way.

'Why do you laugh?'

'My mother will try and eat you for breakfast.'

'Meaning?'

'She subscribes to a particularly militant brand of feminism.'

'And you don't?'

'I'm a feminist—don't doubt that for a moment. I believe in equal rights for women, in equal pay and in equal opportunities. I also believe men can be feminists.'

'But your mother doesn't?'

She shook her head. 'She thinks I'm deluded.'

He rubbed his nape. 'I'm the son of the ruling sheikh in a patriarchal society. She's going to hate me.'

She grimaced. 'Pretty much.'

'I see. It won't be a comfortable meeting, then.' He lifted his chin and met her gaze squarely. 'I still want to meet her.'

Brave man.

'And then I want to meet your father.'

'I suspect that'll be impossible. At least, in the short-term. He's in America at the moment. But we can call him if you like.'

'Yes. It's necessary.' For a moment a silence stretched and then he said, 'After that…will you come to Keddah Jaleel and meet *my* family? Will you come and see the life you could have there?'

Her heart started to thump so hard, it was all she could do to breathe. Did she dare?

How can you not? This will be your child's heritage. Whether you stay or not, you owe it to this child at least to experience Keddah Jaleel for yourself.

'Majed…'

He leaned towards her, his face intense and so intent on her that it made her pulse pound in her ears. 'Yes?'

'Do I have your word that, if I want to leave Keddah Jaleel, you and your family won't prevent me?'

He smiled, but it was the saddest smile in the world, and Sarah hated herself for putting it there. 'You've heard horror stories of kidnappings in the Middle East?'

She'd promised him honesty, so she nodded.

He came back to the sofa but he didn't take a seat. Instead, he knelt before her and took her hand in both his own. 'You have my word of honour that you'll be free to leave Keddah Jaleel at any time you choose.' He hauled in a breath that left him pale. 'If you have the baby in Keddah Jaleel and then want to leave, you have my word of honour that you can leave with the child if you wish.'

She saw how much it cost him and she believed him utterly.

'Thank you,' she whispered. 'I...I have something else I want you to promise me.'

'Yes?'

She swallowed. 'If you and I end up hurting each other— I know that's not what either one of us wishes, but this is a situation that has the potential to...matter a lot. And it's unfamiliar territory for us both.'

Midnight eyes bored into hers. 'It doesn't have the *potential* to matter. It already matters a great deal.' He frowned when she remained silent. 'What are you trying to ask of me?'

'I grew up with warring parents, Majed.' She rested a hand on her stomach. 'I don't want that for this child. It would be my worst nightmare.'

His face grew grim. 'I see.'

Her chest clenched. 'I've offended you.'

He shook his head. 'I'm just sorry you had such a difficult childhood.' His gaze met hers, confident, steady and full of belief. 'You and I will never descend to such pettiness.'

How could he be so sure?

'But, if it will set your mind at rest, then you have my word. I will never use this child as a weapon against you. I will always speak of you to this child with respect, whether we are together or not, whether we are friends or not. I promise you this.'

'And I promise it too.'

'No. You need make no such promise. I already know you wouldn't do such a thing.'

She wished she had an iota of his confidence.

'So, Sarah, will you come to Keddah Jaleel with me?'

It was her turn to pull a steadying breath into her lungs. 'Okay, here's what I think we should do.' He allowed her to pull him up to sit beside her, but he refused to relinquish her hand, and she was glad of it. 'We wait until the twelve-week mark in my pregnancy to make sure…' She didn't want to jinx them by saying the words out loud.

Majed nodded. 'Yes, I understand this. You're healthy and young, and I don't envisage that anything will go wrong, but perhaps it would be best to wait.'

She nodded, grateful he'd phrased it so tactfully. 'Then you and I will announce the news to my parents.'

He nodded again.

'And then…and then we go to Keddah Jaleel. Initially for a month.'

'A month?' His eyes flared. 'You'll give me a month?' He lifted her hand to press a kiss to her palm. 'Thank you.'

CHAPTER FOUR

THE ENVELOPE IN Majed's top pocket felt as if it were burning a hole to brand his chest through the thin cotton of his shirt. He glanced at Sarah. Was she ready to go to Keddah Jaleel with him yet?

Three days ago she'd had her twelve-week scan. When she'd asked him if he'd wanted to go with her, he'd said yes with such force it had laid him bare. He dragged a hand down his face. It should've appalled him to reveal such vulnerability but it hadn't. Sarah understood his feelings for this baby. She shared them. She wouldn't toy with his emotions when it came to their child. He knew that in his heart. He knew it in his bone marrow. He held tightly to the knowledge.

Her relief at his affirmative answer had laid her bare too, though. She didn't want to do this parenting thing alone. She wanted her baby to know its father. She wanted her baby to know *him*, and the realisation had set something inside him alight.

And then there'd been the moment they'd seen their baby...

The breath jammed in his throat and his heart started to hammer. *His baby!*

He'd been completely unprepared for the rush of love that had gripped him as he'd stared at the image on the monitor. If asked, he'd have said he already loved this child, and had from the moment Sarah had told him about it, but actually to see the baby…hear its heartbeat…

His hands clenched and unclenched. He'd been ridiculously nervous beforehand. He had no idea why. He wasn't prone to histrionics. He didn't have a predilection for envisioning gloomy outcomes. Sarah was young and the picture of health. There was absolutely no reason why she and the baby should be anything but hale and hearty.

But those moments before the monitor had been turned towards them had felt like an eternity. His heart had lodged in his throat, making his lungs ache with the effort to keep breathing. They ached again now at the memory.

Sarah had felt it too. She'd reached for his hand and had squeezed it with all of her might. He'd understood her fear and he hadn't let go of her hand again until the scan was complete. She'd needed his strength and he meant to give her whatever she needed.

And then the technician had turned the monitor towards them and Sarah's grip had changed—strong, still, but charged with relief…and with awe and excitement. In that instant he hadn't known what was more beautiful—the child on the screen or the love that unfurled across Sarah's face in a warm, golden glow as elemental and awe-inspiring as a sunrise. It had stolen his breath. It had made him ache.

And then she'd met his gaze and her smile had been so big and so *real* that all the breath had flowed back into his body. Her smile had included him so completely and utterly that he hadn't been able to resist it. It had said, *this is our child. Look what we've made. Isn't it beautiful?*

Suddenly they weren't two people thrown together in difficult circumstances trying to work out the best way forward, but two people looking at the life they'd created. In that moment the shadowy, insubstantial bond they shared had crystallised, cementing them together. No matter what happened in the future, they were parents of this child. And they were determined to do whatever was best for it, regardless of the expense to themselves.

He glanced across at her again. They'd taken to spending Monday nights together—dinner out at one of the many local restaurants followed by coffee and conversation, or sometimes a movie back at Sarah's apartment. They always sat—or sprawled—on adjacent sofas, careful not to touch. Sarah dropped into the bar several times a week—just like she used to—but somehow they'd not managed to recapture their old camaraderie.

Because you slept with her. And you want to sleep with her again.

He didn't just *want* it—he *ached* with it. It plagued his dreams at night. It teased and tormented him. But…

He lifted his chin. He refused to allow passion to cloud his judgement or sway his decisions. He'd been blindsided by desire and lust before and it had cost his brother his life. He would *not* let that happen again.

He stared at his hand. The memory of the way she'd gripped it during the scan rose again in his mind. Sarah wanted what was best for this child. With a deep breath, he pulled the envelope from his pocket and slid it across to her.

'What's this?' With a glance at him, she took it…and then stilled. He watched the bob of her throat as she swallowed and a familiar thirst rose through him. The friendship they'd been trying to establish for the last seven weeks did nothing to cool the stampede of heat in his blood, or dispel the ache that gripped him when he gazed at the plump promise of her bottom lip. He craved to suck that lip into his mouth, bite down gently on it, before laving it with his tongue. He…

'These are tickets to Keddah Jaleel.'

He pulled his mind back from X-rated visions of Sarah naked, to find her staring at him with wide eyes. Perspiration prickled his top lip. 'Are you really surprised?'

'I... Well, I guess I shouldn't be.'

But she was. Maybe he should've led up to this more gently. 'The date is open-ended. You, of course, get to decide when we fly out.'

'Have...have you organised a replacement manager for the bar?'

He nodded. His second-in-command was ready to step up to the job whenever Majed asked it of him. He'd spoken to Mike, and Mike had no objections.

Sarah bit her lip as she stared at their tickets. He understood her anxiety, but her vulnerability caught at him. Although they were constantly careful not to touch—other than that isolated incident during the scan—he was tempted to move across to her sofa and take her in his arms. His pulse quickened. *Don't be an idiot.* 'What are you worried about?'

'That your family will hate me.'

'They won't hate you. That'd be impossible.'

'But they might disapprove of me. They might be disappointed in us both.'

'If they are, they'll be too polite to say so in front of you.'

She managed a short laugh. 'I wish I could promise you the same good manners from my mother.'

This child would go a long way to healing his parents' hearts. He longed to alleviate their pain. Nothing and no one could ever replace Ahmed in their lives, and his father might never be able to look at Majed in the same way again—not since the details surrounding Ahmed's death had emerged—but he'd dote on a grandchild. It seemed the least Majed could do. In time, his father might even find a way to forgive him.

But what if Sarah didn't want to stay?

The thought burned a path of acid through him. His hands clenched. He'd have to return to Australia with her, turn his back on Keddah Jaleel and any hope of becoming his father's heir…and on any hope there might be a way he and his father could repair their relationship. Darkness— thick and black—tried to settle over him. He did what he could to beat it back. He'd do what he needed to do. His child's wellbeing and happiness came before all else.

He lifted his head, recalling the way Sarah had gripped his hand during the scan and the deep love that had trans- formed her as she'd stared at the image of their baby. A deep-seated recognition coursed through him. Like him, Sarah would do what was right for this baby, regardless of the personal cost to herself. She wanted her baby sur- rounded by love. She'd never deny it a father who loved it, a father who wanted to be an integral part of its life.

He pushed his shoulders back and found he had to fight a fierce smile. He could offer this baby and her a life of un- paralleled luxury and opportunity. For their child's sake she wouldn't be able to turn her back on all that Majed could provide—the privileged life he could offer their child— even if she cared nothing for such things for herself.

She'd come to the same conclusion once she'd been to Keddah Jaleel and had fallen in love with his family, his country and his people. Her loyalty to her child would win out. But with Sarah a gently-gently, softly-softly approach would be best. He had no desire to force her hand. She needed to feel that she'd made the decision herself, that she hadn't been led…that she was free from pressure and expectation. She needed to come to the conclusion in her own time, not his. And he'd do everything in his power to facilitate that.

He loved this child. He wanted to be a part of its life. She knew that and it meant something to her. She'd do the right thing.

Sarah scrolled through the calendar on her tablet. 'I only need to give the temp agency a week's notice. So…' She shuffled to the end of her sofa nearest to him and he moved to the end nearest to her. 'What if we have dinner with my mother this coming Saturday night…? And we can talk to my father that evening too. And then…and then we could fly out to Keddah Jaleel on the following Saturday? It should give us ample time to get ourselves organised.'

'Perfect. I'll let my parents know to expect us then.'

'Are you going to tell them about the baby?'

'We'll do that together once we arrive—face to face.'

Her smile trembled and he broke their unspoken no-touching rule to reach out and grip her hand. 'It'll be okay, I promise. Just give it a chance.'

'And I thought that you choosing dress-making as a career choice was your greatest mistake!'

Beside Majed, Sarah flinched.

Irene Collins fixed first her daughter and then Majed with a martinet's stare that managed to make him feel he was ten years old again and on the receiving end of a serious scolding from his paternal great-grandmother, who hadn't held with Majed's father's form of parenting. She hadn't been a 'spare the rod' woman. She'd terrified both him and Ahmed.

Irene Collins terrified him in a similar fashion now.

Don't be a coward.

He'd been tutored in the art of diplomacy. He should find this interview—confrontation—relatively easy. Relative, say, to mediating between warring nations, or introducing a new system of government into his homeland, this *should* be a doddle.

But it wasn't.

'Let me see if I have this right,' Irene repeated—she even insisted that Sarah call her Irene. 'Not only are you pregnant, but you're going to *voluntarily* allow this man to escort you to his country *in the Middle East*?'

'His name is Majed, Mother, and I'd appreciate it if you'd maintain some semblance of civility and use it.'

It hadn't taken him long to figure out that, whenever Sarah wanted to annoy Irene, she called her 'Mother'.

'Majed isn't some stranger I picked up in a bar on the spur of the moment and had a random one-night stand with. We've been friends for quite some time. And, whatever else happens, we mean to maintain that friendship. I...' Sarah lifted her chin. 'I insist you treat him with respect.'

Go, Sarah! Something akin to admiration warmed his chest. In her own way she was just as strong as her mother. He wondered if she realised that.

Irene folded her arms. 'At least you got rid of that ridiculous specimen you were dating previously. What was his name?'

Majed's lip curled. 'Sebastian.'

Irene—her spine ramrod-straight—eyed him from her armchair opposite the sofa where he and Sarah sat. Although she evidently shared Majed's opinion of Superior Sebastian, he couldn't detect an ounce of softening in her gaze. Sarah had told him that Irene was the area manager for a building society. He was simply grateful she wasn't his boss.

He yearned to reach out and take Sarah's hand—offer her support, provide a united front—but she looked as untouchable as her mother. It occurred to him then that she might've kept Sebastian around so long simply to annoy her mother. Childish, undoubtedly, but understandable.

Irene flicked a piece of lint from her trousers. 'Have you spoken to that patriarchal, profiting pillock of a father of yours?'

Majed choked.

'Not yet.'

That seemed to unbend Irene a fraction.

Sarah didn't elaborate further and Majed didn't blame

her. They were planning to speak to Sarah's father tonight. He started to see why she'd made him promise never to let their child become caught in a tug-of-war battle between them. His heart ached for the young Sarah who'd had to suffer through all of that.

'I take it you're well?'

'Very. I've had a little morning sickness, but that seems to have passed. The baby is due in October.'

Irene stuck out her chin. 'You know my feelings on men.'

Sarah glanced at Majed. 'Irene doesn't believe a man is necessary to a woman's happiness.'

He met Irene's gaze. 'You don't believe in love?'

'Romantic love? No.' Her raised eyebrow challenged him. 'Do you?'

He believed in it. He just didn't want it. 'My parents have a very successful marriage, but their union was arranged by their families. It has made me see that love is not a necessary component for a successful marriage. I believe mutual respect, shared values and friendship are far more important—and will bring more long-term happiness to one's life. My parents value and respect each other deeply.'

Love could be such a fleeting emotion—an emotion that in his experience was worth neither the heartache nor the upheaval. 'They have been wonderful role models. My childhood was very happy.'

'And are *they* happy?'

His gut clenched. He could feel his face turn wooden. 'Several years ago my brother died. They have had a difficult time since then.' How did one learn to accept the unacceptable, adjust to the un-adjustable?

Irene sat back a fraction, an almost imperceptible sigh infinitesimally loosening her shoulders. Sarah leaned forward, as if sensing that Majed needed a moment's respite—a moment to re-gather his resources. For the last four years he'd managed to avoid any mention of Ahmed, but in the last few weeks he'd been forced to acknowledge his brother's death. And each time it felt as if a sword were slashing his vitals.

'There's more you should know.'

'Dear God, don't tell me you're considering marrying this man, Sarah? Don't be such a little fool! It's completely unnecessary. I'll make sure you're looked after, that you have everything you need—you and the baby.'

Irene's unswerving show of support comforted a part of him that he hadn't known needed comforting. Irene might be tough and uncompromising but she loved her daughter.

'You cannot be serious!' Irene shot to the edge of her chair when Sarah remained silent. 'I raised you with more street smarts than that!'

'That's my own concern.' Sarah stuck out her chin. 'I haven't made a decision yet. The *more* you need to know is that Majed's father is the ruling Sheikh of Keddah Jaleel and that...'

She gripped her hands together, her white knuckles betraying her nervousness.

'Majed is his heir.'

Majed *should* be his heir, Majed corrected silently. If his father disowned him completely then that would change. It was too difficult to try and explain. They'd travel to Keddah Jaleel and he'd discover if he still had a place there.

'I see.' Irene took several agitated turns about the room before resuming her seat. 'What do you know about Keddah Jaleel?'

'I know where it is on the map. I know its climate, its primary industries and the name of its major river.'

She did?

'But I won't pretend that's what you want to know. You mean, what do I know about the politics of the place.' She pressed her hands together. 'Majed's father and uncles are transitioning the country to a democracy with a view to their family becoming a constitutional monarchy—much like Great Britain. At the moment Sheikh Rasheed—Majed's father—is something midway between an absolute ruler and a prime minister.'

'And from where have you had this? From Majed himself?'

Sarah actually laughed. 'For heaven's sake, Mum, you taught me better than that.'

Her 'Mum' sounded far more natural—and affectionate—than her previous 'Irene's or 'Mother's.

Irene's gaze speared to him. 'I assume there's an under-representation of women in both civic and industry leadership roles in your country?'

'Yes, but—'

'No buts! It's appalling.'

'No more appalling than it is in this country.' It took an effort to keep his voice level. 'It's an issue my father is working hard to address, but this kind of change doesn't happen overnight. Currently we're making more university places available to women.' He straightened. 'We intend to have the best educated female population in the world.'

'Which will do them no good if they're not allowed to use their education to better their own situations.'

'That will come.' He found himself on his feet, his fierce love for his country and his people rising through him. 'Tell me what it is that you really fear. Why are you worried about Sarah's visit to Keddah Jaleel?'

Irene stood too. She stabbed a finger at his chest. 'I'm *worried* that once you get her there she'll be a virtual prisoner. I'm *worried* that you and your family will compromise her reproductive autonomy. I'm worried that you'll take the child and that if Sarah proves troublesome—and, believe me, my daughter knows how to be troublesome—you'll imprison her…or worse.'

He swore softly in his native tongue. 'Madam, I am not a barbarian. Nor are my family or my fellow countrymen.

Sarah—and her child—will be free to come and go as and when they choose. It's true that I hope Sarah will marry me but I would never force her.'

'A marriage that will be more to your benefit than hers.'

'A marriage that will be *mutually* beneficial.'

'Mum!' Sarah hissed. Grabbing Majed's arm, she tugged him back down to the sofa beside her. 'I'm going to visit Keddah Jaleel for a month but I've made no decision beyond that.'

Irene smoothed a hand down her trousers and sat. 'It occurs to me that the wife of the ruling sheikh could do a lot of good in Keddah Jaleel.'

No doubt she meant in relation to women's rights. It occurred to him that he hadn't really considered the political implications of marrying Sarah. All he'd thought about was how a grandchild would help to heal his parents' hearts. Marrying Sarah could be the final nail in the coffin of Majed's hope to work alongside his father for his country's betterment.

Would his countrymen accept Sarah?

He pushed his shoulders back. If Sarah accepted his proposal of marriage then they'd have to. Somehow he'd make it work.

They hung up from the call they'd just had with Sarah's father, and for a moment Majed didn't know what to say.

'I did warn you,' Sarah said.

Dear God, she'd had to grow up with these people? His heart ached at the thought of the young girl she must've been, and all she must've suffered being at the centre of the tug-of-war between two such embittered people—people who'd once claimed to love each other.

'He liked you,' she offered.

'Only after discovering your mother didn't approve of me.' He'd actually called Irene a 'ball-busting old witch'.

'He didn't even congratulate you on the baby.' He'd just gone off into ugly torrents of laughter when he'd imagined the look on Irene's face as she'd heard their news.

'He offered me money instead.'

He knew people showed their love in different ways, but…

He shoved his shoulders back. Nobody in Keddah Jaleel would treat Sarah with unkindness or disrespect; he wouldn't let anyone turn her into a pawn in a game. He'd make sure of it.

He made his smile gentle, calm…encouraging. 'Are you ready to come to Keddah Jaleel now?'

She gave a half-laugh that tightened his chest. 'Yes, it's time for me to face the dragons on your side of the fence.'

'No dragons,' he promised. At least, not for her. He'd draw all their fire on himself if need be. It was the least that he could do.

CHAPTER FIVE

'No! You're joking!'

Sarah stopped dead on the tarmac to stare at him, and he had to swallow back a laugh. 'No joke,' he assured her.

Her eyes widened even further. 'You have your own private jet?'

'It belongs to my country, not to me or my father personally.' But his father *had* very thoughtfully provided it for them. That had to be a good sign.

'So, what you're telling me is that we're travelling in that?'

She pointed at the sleek jet gleaming in the mid-morning sun and he nodded. 'Lovely, isn't it?' With a laugh, he took her arm. 'Wait until you see inside. It's amazing. Mind your step. The stairs are steep.'

He waved the flight attendant away and buckled Sarah into an armchair-sized seat himself, taking delight in her simple astonishment and growing awe. *It's for the plane, remember, not for you.*

He buckled himself into the seat beside her. 'What do you think?'

She ran her hand over the cream leather of the seats and pulled her feet from her sandals to dig her toes into the plush carpet. 'I understand textiles are a big industry in Keddah Jaleel.'

'We're proud of our textile industry—justifiably so.

We have some of the finest artisans in the Middle East. We make exquisite carpets, beautiful silks and the finest cottons. Only the best materials and most skilled workers were employed for the kitting out of the jet.' He glanced at the stewardess standing nearby. 'Even the flight attendants' uniforms have been made locally. Would you like a pre-flight drink?'

Sarah ordered a lemonade and then pointed with a shy smile at the stewardess's scarf. 'That is truly lovely.'

The stewardess returned with glasses of lemonade and sparkling mineral water, as well as a complimentary scarf for Sarah, who went into immediate raptures over it. Her cheeks grew pink when she became aware of Majed's scrutiny. 'I'm sorry.'

'Don't apologise. I'm pleased it finds favour with you.'

'I dreamed of being a designer…once upon a time.'

He recalled Irene's scathing, *And I thought you choosing dress-making as a career was your greatest mistake!* He remembered the way Sarah had flinched.

'I soon wised up on that front, but I still have a passion for fabric and cloth.'

He fought back a frown. 'What do you mean, wised up? Why did you not pursue this passion?'

She rolled her eyes. 'Because passion doesn't always translate to talent. One needs more than enthusiasm.' She shuffled upright in her seat and touched her glass to his. 'To a good flight.' She sipped and then let out an exaggerated sigh. 'Real crystal?'

He nodded. 'Real crystal.'

'This is how you live in Keddah Jaleel?'

He tried to see the luxury through her eyes. He hadn't missed it, but maybe he'd taken it for granted. 'The economy of Keddah Jaleel is flourishing. It allows the Sheikh a great deal of…'

'Opulence? Luxury? Splendour?'

'Comfort,' he countered. 'You have to understand that a display of this kind of statesmanship is designed to impress, to give a sense of largesse, to showcase the country's prosperity.'

'Is that another way of saying "to show off"?'

He chuckled. There was something about Sarah that made him feel young. That made it easy to laugh. 'I see I'm going to have to teach you the art of diplomacy.'

Despite her teasing, though, he could see that the jet, the luxury and the respect afforded him from the flight crew impressed her. And he meant to push every advantage he had at his disposal. 'We're very fortunate to be able to enjoy such a lifestyle. If you choose to, Sarah, you can enjoy all of this too.'

Rather than wriggling with excitement, or staring at him with wide eyes, her gaze slid away and she sipped her drink, rubbing her free hand across her chest as if to ease an ache. He'd read that pregnant women often suffered from heartburn. 'Do you feel unwell?'

'I'm fine.' She turned back with a smile that didn't quite reach her eyes. 'What did my mother say to you before we left last night?'

He allowed the abrupt change of subject. He didn't doubt that it had been preying on her mind. 'She told me that she had a lot of resources at her disposal—that she knows important people—and if I thought I could hold you against your will then I had another thing coming.'

She winced. 'I'm sorry.'

'Don't apologise. I don't blame her for her fears, or for doing what she can to ensure your safety.' He sipped his drink before sending her a sidelong look. 'She said that the two of you have a code word...and so I'd better watch myself.'

That got a laugh from her. 'We do.'

He turned to her more fully. 'Really? What is it?'

'My mother taught me better than that, Majed,' she chided, piquing his curiosity further. 'It's a secret—just between her and me. That's the point of it.'

She surveyed him for a moment, head cocked to one side. 'You know, it wouldn't hurt us to have a code word too. Just in case.'

'Just in case of what?' He laughed. 'So I can rescue you if one of my relatives starts to bore you half to death or…?'

'Oh, no! A code word isn't to be used for trivial things, but only in the direst of circumstances. If one of us utters it, or writes it down, or somehow or other telegraphs it to the other, then it means they're in terrible trouble and to get help. We're talking big help here, Majed—like the police.'

He stiffened. 'I'll let no harm come to you in Keddah Jaleel, Sarah. I swear. Are you frightened?'

'I'm nervous about meeting your parents. I'm not frightened for my life or my freedom. But it's a fact of life that people—women—are murdered every day. Random events happen. It never hurts to have a code word.'

He supposed not. But the thought of Sarah needing one disturbed him. He didn't want his perturbation to worry her, so he forced himself to smile. 'You're right. It won't hurt.' *And if it'll put her mind at rest…*

He turned back to find her staring at his mouth, as if totally mesmerised. On cue, a roaring hunger surged through him. She could take him from laughing, to perplexed, to arousal in less than three beats of his heart. She shook herself, her cheeks turning pink. 'You and your father are important men. Don't you have code words with each other… with your bodyguards?'

He couldn't answer for his father but as for him… 'No.'

'Then you should.'

If the future panned out the way he wanted it to, he'd consider it. Until then… 'Let's create one now. It can't be something we'd use in normal conversation?'

'No.'

He stared at her face, at the colour of her lips. 'Coral... Will that suffice, do you think?'

'Coral?' She nodded. 'Perfect.'

If Sarah had been impressed by the deference Majed had been treated to from the moment they'd arrived at the airport in Melbourne, it was nothing to how impressed she was at the pomp and ceremony he received once they'd landed in Keddah Jaleel.

She'd had a brief impression of blazing sands, a glittering ocean and an unexpectedly green belt of land before the plane had descended. She'd turned to Majed and had said stupidly, 'You have beaches!'

The closer they'd got to Keddah Jaleel, the more morose Majed had become. She knew his thoughts must be with Ahmed but she didn't know how to comfort him. She sensed he wouldn't welcome any attempts on her part to intrude into his solitude. He'd been so solicitous towards her, so supportive, that she'd remained quiet and left him to the privacy of his thoughts.

But her words now made him laugh. 'You're surprised, *habibi*?'

Heat curled in her abdomen. She liked it when he called her that. She liked it a little too much. She fought back a frown. 'I shouldn't be, I suppose. I mean, I looked Keddah Jaleel up on the map. I knew it wasn't land-locked.' But beaches hadn't occurred to her.

'My family has a villa on the coast which we sometimes use for vacations. We could spend a few days there, if you would like.'

'That sounds...wonderful.' Australia was renowned for its beaches. It was one of the things she thought she'd miss if she moved to Keddah Jaleel.

If.

Nerves immediately made her stomach churn. Then the plane was on the ground and her entire body turned to jelly. *Please let his family like me.*

Upon landing, Majed's conviviality fled. He became almost grim. She knew he must be going through a hundred different kinds of hell, and she refused to trouble him with her own anxieties—they seemed so paltry in comparison—but…

She slid her hand into his. 'Majed, I know you're thinking about Ahmed and missing him, but this is your home. You have happy memories and associations here too. You're *allowed* to be happy that you're back.' He shouldn't feel guilty about that.

Dark eyes turned to meet her gaze. 'This country is in my blood, and it's leaping to be back here, fired with something more elemental than joy—a recognition that this is where I belong.' His brows drew together, his eyes dark with confusion. 'I didn't expect that.'

Wow. Sarah had never felt that about any place.

'I've stayed away too long.'

He glanced at their linked hands, and a sigh shuddered out of him, and before her eyes he transformed into another man—the same, yet different. He became taller, broader, more serious…and, if it were possible, more tempting. His spine straightened, his jaw lifted and hardened, and determination filled his eyes. She suddenly saw a man who was destined to be king.

It should make her want to flee.

Her heart started to pound as all her mother's dire warnings bombarded her, even as something traitorous softened in her stomach. If she married Majed, she'd have him in her bed every night. She moistened parched lips.

You can't make such an important, life-altering decision based on hormones.

There was no denying, however, that the thought was an alluring one.

Seductive.

Tempting.

'Sarah!'

Majed's sharp tones snapped her back, and she realised she hadn't been attending to a single word he'd said. She swallowed, and prayed he hadn't deciphered the directions of her thoughts. 'I'm sorry.'

His eyes flashed. 'Never mind—the journey has been a long one.'

She couldn't help thinking that it took all his patience to keep his tone level and gentle. She swallowed again. All her life she'd tried people's patience. Now, it appeared, she'd try Majed's. 'What were you saying?'

His eyes scanned her face before he spoke. 'My parents will receive us at the palace, but there'll be a small reception on the ground here at the airport to welcome me home.'

He undid her seatbelt and helped her to her feet. She had to lock her knees to keep them from shaking.

'There are protocols it'd be best for you to follow.'

'Such as?'

'Remain a few paces behind me. Don't address me unless I speak to you first.'

She took a step away from him, her stomach rebelling. What had she let herself in for?

His chin shot up. 'Don't look at me like that. I hate this as much as you do, but this is only until we get to the palace. If I take you out there on my arm, like I wish to, we'll have an entire country thinking we're engaged.'

The flight attendant stood waiting patiently in the doorway. Majed turned and snapped a few rapid-fire words at her, and she immediately withdrew, quietly closing the door behind her.

She'd done his bidding, just like that. Without asking questions or demurring or…anything!

It hit her then that Majed would one day be a king. He might not hold the title at the moment, but he'd been bred to rule.

And she…? She was a nobody!

And here he was, advancing on her with a determined light in his eye, and she found herself giving way before him.

'Have you come to a decision yet, *habibi*? Would you perhaps like to be married to the ruling sheikh and live a life of privilege and luxury?'

'Don't be ridiculous.' But her words emerged breathily… huskily….as if she were inviting him to…

The backs of her legs hit the long bench-seat, and she'd have sprawled along its length if Majed hadn't reached out and pulled her against the hard, masculine length of his body.

'You look at me with such hungry eyes that…that I'm tempted to undress you right now—to make love to you until you beg me not to stop.' His hands drifted down to her hips with seductive slowness. 'Until you cry out my name at the pleasure I can give you.'

His fingers curled into the flesh of her hips, sending coursing flames of desire licking through her veins, and she swayed into him. He held her so close, she could feel the hard length of him pressing against her belly. Both their chests rose and fell too quickly.

She tossed her hair and met his gaze. 'If we make love now, Majed, I can promise you that I won't be the only one crying out my pleasure.'

His nostrils flared, his gaze narrowing in on her lips. 'And afterwards I'd take you out there on my arm.'

She pulled air into lungs that felt as if they were going to burst. 'Then you'd risk looking a fool in the eyes of your countrymen if I decide to not stay in Keddah Jaleel. I'm sorry, Majed, but you can't seduce me into submission.'

'Are you sure about that?' One side of his mouth hooked up in a deliciously wicked grin. 'You bring out the barbarian in me. I find myself tempted to take up your challenge.'

One of his hands travelled from her hip to her armpit, brushing the side of her breast with delicious intent that had her biting her lip as her nipples pebbled into hard nubs that pressed against the thin cotton of her blouse. He stared at them in hunger…and triumph.

Suddenly, she *wasn't* sure, and it frightened her like nothing else had. She wrenched herself out of his arms. 'Positive!'

He stared at her for a moment and then gave a curt nod. 'That's better. You have colour in your face again.'

Her jaw dropped. *He'd…he'd done that on purpose?*

Before she could tell him what she thought of his tactics, he'd turned on his heel and strode out of the plane, leaving her to scrabble her composure into place and scramble after him.

'That was a dirty, rotten trick.' She started the moment the limousine pulled away, the tinted glass shielding them from the crowd's curious gaze, the soundproof barrier between them and the driver securely in place.

'It was, but we were running out of time.' He sent her a sidelong glance. 'But none of it was lies. I'd very much like to…'

'Don't!' She pointed a finger at him. 'Enough of that.'

He took her hand and laced his fingers through hers. 'The fact is, there's a lot at stake here, and appearances are important. I want to shield you as much as I can from unwanted attention and curiosity. For that to happen, you need to be almost invisible—in the same way a brisk, efficient aide would be invisible.'

What he'd done hit her then, and she couldn't help but be grateful for it. If she'd appeared on that welcome committee's red carpet looking nervous…as if she wanted to run…she'd have drawn attention to herself and questions would've been asked. The sense of outrage he'd evoked in her, along with his assured, autocratic arrogance, had protected her from that. Still…

'Couldn't you have just explained all of that to me?' She wasn't stupid. She'd have understood.

'I tried to, but you weren't listening.'

Heat burned her cheeks. She'd been too busy fantasising about Majed to pay attention to anything he'd been trying to tell her. And if she hadn't been such a complete and utter twit she'd have realised there would be protocols it would be best for her to follow.

She was such a flake—a screw-up. What on earth made her think she could successfully move in the same circles as Majed? If he married, he needed an assured diplomat at his side…not someone like her.

'Are you going to be sick?'

His concern tugged at her. 'I'm fine. Just appalled at my own naivety. You better tell me how to address your father and mother, and any other protocols I should be aware of.' Majed had shown her nothing but wholehearted support. The least she could do in return was not embarrass him.

She listened intently as he gave her a quick rundown on palace protocol.

She moistened her lips. 'And what kind of…welcome can I expect from your parents?'

'In public, they'll be very formal, and I expect they'll rarely address you.'

'In private?'

Majed's cheekbones, high and angular, suddenly seemed to stand out in stark relief to the rest of his face. His eyes went pitch-black. Generous lips pressed into a hard line.

'My father is a reserved man. He keeps his true feelings under lock and key.'

Right. She shouldn't expect a warm welcome from him, then. She glanced at Majed out of the corner of her eye. His relationship with his father sounded complicated.

'My mother is the opposite—effervescent and warm. She'll take you under her wing and treat you like a baby chick.'

Her lips twisted. 'Nothing like the welcome you received from my mother, then.'

He laughed, and the hard lines of his face momentarily softened, but he stared out of the window and not at her. 'Look.'

He pointed and she followed the line of his finger. Her jaw dropped.

'The royal palace of Keddah Jaleel.'

On a hill to their right, overlooking the city of Demal—the capital of Keddah Jaleel—stood an enormous palace of white stone and gleaming blue enamel. It had a huge central dome made of silver that gleamed in the sun. There was a cascade of descending half-domes, vaults and ascending buttresses. Numerous slender minarets rose into the sky with a grandeur and grace that left Sarah breathless.

She'd researched Keddah Jaleel's history and geography, its climate and economy. She'd read about Demal's religious diversity and knew that it boasted several mosques, a Catholic cathedral and several Buddhist temples, but she hadn't thought to research its royal palace.

'It's…amazing.'

'We're rather proud of it.'

'It looks like a cross between a fortress and something from the *Arabian Nights*.'

His eyes glowed. 'It has seen a lot of history.'

And then they were gliding through the towering gates and being ushered into the inner sanctum of the palace grounds. An enormous fountain stood in the middle of a generous square that was lined with date palms and drenched with the scent of jasmine and cloves. The water sent a rainbow arcing through the air, fragile and yet beautiful against the fierce blue of the sky. She wasn't sure she'd ever seen anything more beautiful in her life.

She stood to one side and did her best to look deferential, trying to keep her eyes on the ground, rather than darting from side to side to take in all the splendour. Majed held an arm out towards her. 'Come.'

He led her through one of the nearby arches and along a corridor that afforded her glimpses of exotic courtyards and grand rooms.

'We've been lucky to be spared a formal reception.'

She couldn't tell from his tone or his expression whether he considered that a good thing or not.

'Instead we've been summoned to my parents' private apartments.'

Sarah's heart immediately hammered up into her throat. She'd thought she'd have a chance to freshen up before meeting Majed's parents.

He smiled down at her. 'You don't need to be afraid. They're rulers, but they're also people like you and me. Just be yourself.'

Oh, right. She could just imagine them being impressed by a complete and utter flake.

They were halfway across a courtyard—shadier and more beautiful than any other she'd so far seen—when a woman came flying across from the building opposite. 'Majed! Majed, my son!'

The woman flung her arms around Majed and held him tight. Sarah watched them embrace and a lump unexpectedly lodged in her throat. This woman hadn't seen her son in the flesh for four years. Sarah felt like an intruder.

'You must be Sarah?'

She glanced around to find a pair of dark eyes, identical to Majed's, surveying her. 'Your Highness, I…'

She went to curtsey, but he held up his hand. 'You must call me Rasheed.' And to her utter amazement he embraced her, kissing her on both cheeks before holding her close. 'Thank you for bringing my son back home to us, my dear,' he whispered in her ear.

Sarah found herself hugging him back.

CHAPTER SIX

WHEN HIS MOTHER finally loosened her arms from about his neck, Majed turned to greet his father, his insides coiling up tight.

To his surprise, one of his father's hands rested on Sarah's shoulder, and it was evident from the relief in her eyes and the pink in her cheeks that he'd greeted her warmly.

Majed let out a pent-up breath before bowing formally, as was the custom, and when he straightened he found his father's warmth had retreated behind an impenetrable wall of reserve. Even though it was what he expected, it made Majed's gut clench. 'Hello, Father—it's good to see you.'

'Hello, Majed.' He nodded towards Majed's mother. 'It is good to see your mother so happy.'

He felt the sting of the reprimand like a whip against bare flesh. *How could you be so heartless as to make your mother suffer?* He understood immediately what his father hadn't said—that Majed's presence did not make *him* happy. He'd tolerate his son's presence for his wife's sake and that was all.

Sarah glanced at Majed and his father and back again, her brow crinkling. He didn't blame her for her confusion. Should he have given her a clearer picture of how things stood between him and his father?

In all honesty, he hadn't known if things had changed dur-

ing his absence, whether his father's attitude had softened…
or whether he'd still feel the same way.

His hands clenched. Evidently it was the latter.

Evidently he still held Majed responsible for his brother's
death.

And why shouldn't he? Majed still blamed himself. He
didn't deserve forgiveness, but there was still the possibility that he could bring some measure of light into his
parents' lives.

He gestured Sarah forward. 'Mâmâ, this is my friend,
Sarah Collins.'

'Your Highness.'

Sarah curtsied in the fashion of his people and he stared
at her in surprise—when had she learned to do that?

'It's a great honour to meet you.' And then she held her
tongue. One did not speak to the Sheikh or Sheikha unless addressed first.

To his further surprise, his mother didn't embrace
Sarah. She didn't even offer her hand. She merely said,
'I hope you'll be comfortable during your stay.' And then
she turned back to him. 'Majed, you owe your mother a
little of your time, surely? Come now to my sitting room.
We have so much to catch up on. You must give me time
to feast my eyes upon you.'

What on earth…? He glanced back at Sarah.

'The servants will see to your friend.'

Sarah smiled at him and nodded, encouraging him to go,
but he sensed the nerves behind that brave little smile—
saw the way she pressed her hand to her stomach, as if to
protect her child from an unseen force. *His child*. Sarah deserved his consideration. He wouldn't abandon her at the
first available opportunity.

'I'm sorry, Omme.' He used the formal term for mother.
'I'd prefer to attend to Sarah myself. Please give us half an

hour to freshen up after the flight and we'll meet with you and Abii in his private sitting room.'

'As you wish.'

It was all he could do not to wince at the coldness that threaded his mother's voice or the way she swept from the courtyard. Very few people denied the Sheikha her wishes...except on occasion her sons. She did deserve better from him, but she'd understand once she learned that Sarah was pregnant.

His father's eyes flashed a reprimand in Majed's direction but he touched Sarah's arm in a courtly gesture of leave taking and told her he looked forward to speaking with her more, before he too set off in the same direction as his wife.

When they disappeared from view, Sarah spun to him. 'You should've gone with her, Majed. She's not seen you in four years.'

He glanced meaningfully towards a shady corner where a servant waited patiently. Sarah swallowed and bit her lip, but nodded her understanding—they weren't alone and anything she'd prefer not to be overheard needed to wait. She didn't speak again until the servant had led them to the guest quarters. As Majed had requested, Sarah had been given the best suite of rooms.

The servant melted away at a signal from Majed and Sarah glanced at him with a raised eyebrow. 'Is it okay to speak now?'

'I know you wish to berate me for not going with my mother but, Sarah, my first duty is to you.'

Her face turned wooden. 'Duty?'

He bit back a sigh. 'I didn't mean it that way. I don't see you as a duty. But I promised you every care and consideration while you were here, and I meant it. I've no intention of failing you—abandoning you—the moment we arrive.'

'I'd have understood.'

'I know, but...' He raked a hand through his hair, want-

ing desperately to change the subject. 'What do you think
of your quarters?' She had a sitting room, a bedroom and a
lavish bathroom, all decorated in mother-of-pearl and lapis
lazuli. 'Do you approve of them?'

She glanced around, her hands twisting together.
'They're very beautiful—rooms fit for a princess.'

If she married him, she would be a princess.

As if realising that, some of the colour leached from her
face. Was it the thought of marrying him that caused it, or
the thought of becoming a princess?

And, if it were the latter, why would that frighten her?
He'd had women tell him that becoming a princess was a
dream, a fantasy akin to winning the lottery.

'There are things here I don't understand…undercurrents
with your parents.'

'I… Yes. I thought that in four years things might've
changed, but…' But it was as if no time at all had passed.
And he felt damned to hell because even now, at any moment, he expected Ahmed to sweep into the room and pull
him into a bear hug.

Sarah strode across to an arched window. Her room had
a view onto a beautiful courtyard, but when she turned
back to face Majed he realised she'd not even seen it. He
could see her wishing herself a million miles from him
and Keddah Jaleel.

In three strides he was in front of her and gripping her
shoulders. 'Trust me, Sarah, please. I don't have time to
explain it all to you now. We're expected soon in my father's private sitting room. What I can say is that I didn't
go with my mother because I wished to present a united
front with you first. I don't want them to doubt where my
loyalty lies. I want to tell them our news and then I'll humour my mother with as many private interviews as she
wants. I promise.'

She pulled in a breath and finally smiled, but he saw

what it cost her. 'Please tell me I have time to shower and change?'

'Only just. I'll be back to collect you in twenty minutes.'

She nodded. 'You're right. We should get this over with as soon as possible.'

He reached out to trace a finger down her cheek. The memory of their almost-kiss on the plane flared back to life between them. He dragged his hand back from temptation. 'You're not facing a judge, jury and executioner, *habibi*.'

She rolled her eyes, but he suspected it was more an effort to ignore—and deny—the heat flaring between them than anything else. 'No, it's just your parents. And they're *way* scarier.'

And yet, somehow, she could still make him laugh.

'So you are pregnant, then? It's as we feared, Rasheed.'

Majed's heart pounded when his mother strode to the window, her back ramrod-straight. He'd expected his father to be the one to pace, the one whose voice would be strained with disapproval.

Before Majed could speak, Sarah said, 'Your Highness—'

'We do not stand on ceremony in here, Sarah,' Rasheed said. 'In private you must call me Rasheed and my wife Aisha.'

Sarah blinked. 'That's very kind of you. I—'

'And you must allow me to offer you my felicitations.'

To Majed's surprise his father rose, took Sarah's hand to bring her to her feet and embraced her. If he hadn't seen it with his own eyes, he wouldn't have believed it.

'Congratulations, Majed.'

Majed shook the hand his father offered him, feeling as if he'd stepped into a dream.

'Do the two of you plan to marry?'

Sarah glanced at him and it was only the steadiness reflected in her eyes that unglued his tongue from the roof of his mouth. He read her intent to step into the breach if needed, but he had no intention of appearing weak or feeble in front of either her or his father. 'We've not decided yet.'

His father sat with a heavy sigh. 'It will be a great scandal if you do not.' His glance towards Sarah, however, was not unkind.

'Nonsense.' Aisha spun around. 'These things can be hushed up.'

Rasheed continued as if Aisha hadn't spoken. 'I know things are done differently in your country, Sarah, but it will be a scandal whichever path you choose.'

His mother's eyes flashed and Majed readied himself to intervene as she came storming back towards them, her eyes fixed on Sarah. 'You will steal my son from me!'

'Mother!'

'No, Majed, don't.' Sarah swallowed and nodded, but not in agreement with his mother. 'That's what my mother accused Majed of too, though she phrased it differently. And it's not my intention to steal your son from you, Aisha. I've come to your country to see…to see if there's a place for me here. To see if I could live here.'

His mother stilled for a moment. With a smooth, graceful motion she sat and folded her hands in her lap, although her chest rose and fell furiously. 'You would consider moving to Keddah Jaleel rather than forcing my son to turn his back on his birthright?'

Rasheed shot to his feet and started to pace. And, though he cast a dark glare at her, Aisha stoically ignored him.

Sarah nodded. 'It's why I'm here.' She turned to Rasheed, who still paced, a frown darkening his face. 'I want you to know that your son has acted honourably. He's asked me to marry him. It's I who have yet to come to a decision.'

Majed moved to stand beside Sarah. 'I'll not have Sarah

pressured. She'll have the freedom to make up her own mind without interference.'

Sarah stared at him with those big blue eyes as if he were a super-hero. It made him stand taller.

His mother waved an imperious hand. 'Oh, do please sit down, Majed. You're looming and it makes my neck ache.'

He saw Sarah seated first and then sat beside her. All the while he was aware of his father's dark gaze.

Aisha cleared her throat. 'Sarah will be free to make up her mind. As free as the rest of us are.'

He stiffened. 'She's not bound by our laws.'

'No, but you are, my son. And Sarah needs to be aware of the repercussions to you of her decision. It's only fair that she knows all the facts before she makes a decision.'

Sarah stared at Majed and then Aisha. 'What repercussions?'

Majed took her hand—a show of solidarity—but his heart pounded and his nerves stretched tight. 'I'm interested to hear those myself.'

She squeezed his hand and it helped to steady the nerves jangling through him.

His mother shot him a sharp look. 'You know them as well as I do. If you do not marry the woman who bears your child, our people will see it as a sign of weakness and moral degradation. Your father has fought for reform in this country and he needs an heir who is strong—who is seen by the people to be strong. There are those still wedded to the old ways who would use any perceived sign of weakness as a reason to incite civil unrest.'

His heart pounded. At least his mother saw a role for him in the governance of his country. *If he married Sarah.*

Sarah's white-knuckled grip on his hand tore at him and, while he appreciated the truth of his mother's words, he wished she'd held her tongue. 'You need to decide what will be best for you, Sarah—for you and the baby—not for me. And there is time yet before that decision needs to be made. Don't forget that.'

Her grip eased and she nodded. Her low, 'Thank you,' pierced him. He admired her courage in the face of his parents' stateliness, and her veneer of steadiness in the face of her own panic.

'But it *will* need to be made. And *soon*.'

'Mâmâ!'

'And…and if I do decide to marry Majed…?'

His heart clenched with a fierceness that took him off guard—part possessive triumph and part primal, masculine desire that she would be in his bed, that he would have the right to make love with her every single night.

He rubbed his nape and tried to get his rampaging hormones back under control. He was no better than his marauding forebears!

'If I marry Majed will your people see him as a strong ruler—will they see him as someone who can take their country into the future? Will they follow him?'

'It's impossible, my dear.' Rasheed moved back to his seat. 'Our people will never accept a Western woman as their Sheikha.'

Each of his words pounded into Majed like blows. The fact they weren't true made no difference.

'They would come round if *you* showed your support!' his mother all but shouted in Arabic. 'She could show our women a new way, a way forward.'

In Arabic, his father told her to hold her tongue. Majed had never heard him speak to her in such a hard tone before.

Majed squared his shoulders. 'So you still do not see a place for me here? You refuse to countenance me as your heir?'

'I—'

'Stop!' Sarah surged forward to stare into the older man's face. 'What are you doing?' she whispered, and this time it was Majed who felt he didn't understand the undercurrents in the room.'

'You are welcome here, Sarah, but you are an outsider.'

'She's not an outsider.' Majed shot to his feet. 'She's bearing your grandchild.'

His father's chin lifted and his eyes flashed. 'And as such she is entitled to my care, my consideration and my assistance. She also has my gratitude. But it is the same now as it was four years ago, Majed. I plan to make your cousin, Samir, my heir. You are free to return to the West.'

Sarah stared at Rasheed in growing horror. What was he doing?

And why was he doing it?

From the stricken expressions on Aisha and Majed's faces, not only had he hurt them—'gutted' would be a more precise description for them—but he was going against some kind of traditional royal protocol.

'You cannot!' Aisha had gone deathly pale. 'The ruling sheikh hasn't done that in over two hundred years, Rasheed!'

'Hush, Aisha, it's for the best.'

How could this possibly be for the best?

Thank you for bringing my son home.

No!

Sarah clapped her hands, turning all eyes to her. She made herself smile—not over-brightly, because she couldn't manage that, but enough to cover her confusion. 'Majed, your mother has long desired a private interview with you. She hasn't had the opportunity for four long years. Surely it's time to grant her wish now that we've announced our news?'

Majed opened his mouth but she cut him off. 'I'll be perfectly fine. I'm not a child that needs looking after. Besides, I'm very much looking forward to getting to know your father better.'

Rasheed's head came up. 'As much as I echo that sentiment, I'm afraid it will not be possible this afternoon. I have state business that demands my attention.'

A likely excuse if she'd ever heard one! 'You don't have ten minutes to spare for the mother of your future grandchild, sir?'

She hoped he'd correctly interpret the almost-glare she sent him. If he didn't give her ten minutes of his time now, she'd speak her mind in front of everyone…and she had a feeling he'd hate that.

But she refused to hold her tongue. She and Majed might not love each other—and they might not marry—but he was her friend and she was on his side.

'How delightful,' Rasheed murmured. 'I'm sure I could spare you ten minutes, my dear.'

They were said pleasantly enough, but Sarah had a feeling his words were forced out through gritted teeth.

Majed and Aisha left, and Rasheed led her into an even more splendid room than the one they'd just left. But if he thought the pomp and splendour would intimidate her then he was sadly mistaken. 'What on earth are you doing?' She rounded on him. 'You've lost one son. Why on earth would you want to banish another?'

He paled at her words but drew himself up to his full height and stature. 'You know nothing of the politics of my country or my family.'

'Oh, no you don't, Rasheed.' She was too het up to stand still. She paced up and down in front of him and stopped to point a finger at him. 'You might be supreme ruler of Keddah Jaleel, but at the moment you're simply Majed's father. I care about Majed and I care what happens to our baby.'

His gaze lowered to where her hand curved about her abdomen and before her eyes he seemed to age. Her heart thumped. Biting back something rude, she took his arm and led him to a sofa embroidered in such rich cloth it almost distracted her from her aim of talking sense into Rasheed.

'I know you love your son, so why would you banish him from the homeland he loves?'

The older man stiffened. 'I do not banish him.'

'That's exactly what you're doing if you deny his right to ascend to the throne when the time comes.'

Rasheed stare back at her stonily.

Had nothing she'd said made any impact on him? She gripped her hands together. 'Would it really be so problematic if the heir took a Western bride?'

His gaze slid away.

'If the answer to that question is yes…' She swallowed. 'Then the solution is simple. I'll leave Keddah Jaleel and never return. I'll deny Majed all access to his child.'

Rasheed surged to his feet. 'You cannot do that. It would kill my son.'

The way he'd said 'my son' gave her hope.

'And, as Aisha said, it can all be hushed up. No one need ever know that Majed has a child. If we take that course of action, it should surely remove what you see as a major stumbling block to Majed succeeding you.'

The Sheikh's chest rose and fell. 'You cannot deny him his child!'

She didn't know what she was searching for… 'Though, I suppose, Majed and I could continue to live here in Keddah Jaleel. I'm certain Majed could find a role here, even if it wasn't as the supreme ruler.'

Rasheed's face tightened and he slashed a hand through the air. 'That is out of the question!'

Behind the anger she sensed something else but she wasn't sure what. Fear? Resentment? Regret? Her mouth dried. 'Do you really think Majed would make such a poor ruler?' Did he not know his son at all?

Rasheed's chin shot up and for a moment she swore she

saw affront in his face, before it became opaque and calm once again—his statesman's face, she suspected. He lifted his arms. 'What do you want of me, Sarah Collins?'

What did she want? She pushed her shoulders back and refused to dwell on the fact that she was berating a supreme ruler and interfering in the politics of a country she didn't understand. 'I want you to give Majed a chance.'

'A chance to do what?'

She moistened parched lips. 'A chance to prove that he should be your heir.'

'And if I do not do this?'

'Then I'll leave. And I'll make sure I never see Majed again.'

Her heart thumped. What on earth was she doing? What if the Sheikh told her to go now and pack her bags?

She pressed a hand to her stomach and glanced about the stately room. 'I refuse to be responsible for denying Majed his birthright.'

'Instead you will deprive him of his child!'

'It is you, sir, who tells us this situation is impossible.'

He rose to stalk about the room. Something in the slant and set of his shoulders reminded her of Majed so much that an ache pressed against the backs of her eyes.

Rasheed swung around but his stately reserve crumbled when he stared at her. 'My dear, do not cry.'

She lifted her hands to her cheeks, surprised to find them wet. A lump stretched her throat as she tried to mop them up. 'I'm sorry.' To her mortification the words emerged on a sob. 'Pregnancy hormones—they're making me all…all emotional.'

He sat down beside her and patted her hand. 'Do not distress yourself. It cannot be good for you or the baby.'

'Oh, Rasheed, don't you want to know your grandchild?'

'Of course I—'

He broke off and folded his arms, his brow lowering. 'You are either very clever or very ingenuous.'

She dried her eyes. 'I suspect I can be both at different times, but I'm not trying to trick you into admitting anything you don't want to. I'm just wanting to do what is best for my baby. And the best for Majed. And myself too.'

'In that order?'

She smiled. 'Now I think it's you who's trying to be clever. The baby comes first. As for the rest...' She lifted her shoulders and let them fall.

For a moment, silence stretched between them. Sarah's heart thumped and her temples ached. On impulse she reached out and touched Rasheed's arm. 'I'm sorry Ahmed is no longer with you. I wish he were. I know how much Majed wishes it too.'

Rasheed went grey but he didn't pull his arm away. She must be breaking a hundred royal protocols but she didn't care. 'I can't imagine the pain of losing a child.'

'I pray you never will.'

She met his gaze. 'Please don't punish Majed because he isn't Ahmed.'

A wall came down in those eyes and Sarah couldn't help feeling she was missing something significant, some piece of the puzzle that would give her the clue she needed to understand. Before she could try and work it out, Rasheed had risen and was offering her his arm. She took it and followed him as he led them back the way they'd come.

Aisha and Majed broke off when she and Rasheed entered what Sarah guessed must be Aisha's private sitting room. One glance at Rasheed's face and they rose. If possible, their faces grew even more serious.

'Zawj?'

Husband. It was one of the few Arabic words Sarah knew.

Beside her she could feel the tension radiating from Rasheed. 'Majed, Sarah has convinced me to reconsider my position.'

Aisha clapped her hands beneath her chin, her eyes glowing.

'She has convinced me to give you a chance.'

'A chance, sir?'

'You have the next month to prove that you're willing and able to step into my shoes, to prove you should be the heir to the throne of Keddah Jaleel—to prove that you can rule with courage and love.'

Relief ripped through Sarah. Majed's expression, though, turned opaque.

He gave his father a short bow. 'I will not let you down, Bábá.'

Had Majed and Aisha heard the Sheikh's sigh? Something in it tugged at Sarah's heart.

'Sarah.' The Sheikh turned to her. 'If my son does prove himself worthy, you need to know this...'

'Yes, sir?'

Her heart started to thump. Would he banish her and the baby?

'To ascend the throne, Majed must marry you.'

Her heart leapt into her throat to pound there, making it impossible to speak.

'This is not blackmail. It is the tradition of our people. It is the only way Majed will be able to maintain the respect and loyalty of his subjects. Do you understand?'

She couldn't speak but she managed to nod.

'If you'll excuse me now...'

The Sheikh left and Majed immediately moved to her side, his eyes scanning her face. 'You're pale. And you're shaking. Come, sit down.'

He pressed a glass of cold water into her hand and she sipped it gratefully.

'Are you feeling better?'

Dark eyes peered into hers but she could read nothing in them. It was as if Majed had closed himself off from her. Why didn't he look happy or relieved, or something positive?

'Would you like to see a doctor?'

'Don't fuss, Majed. I'm fine. It's just… I've never… Well, your father…'

'The situation has been nerve-racking, yes?' Aisha supplied.

The warmth in her smile settled Sarah's nerves more than anything else could have done. 'Exactly. But I think perhaps the worst is over now.'

Aisha reached out and patted Sarah's hand. 'I think so too. Majed, you should take Sarah back to her room to rest for a bit. I'm looking forward to getting to know you better, Sarah.'

Majed didn't speak on the long walk back to Sarah's quarters. Not once. He didn't speak until he'd seen her seated in her sitting room. 'What did you say to my father?'

She lifted a shoulder and let it drop, trying to smile. 'Probably things that in the olden days would've had me beheaded.'

His lips lifted, as if by rote, but the smile didn't reach his eyes. Her stomach started to shrink.

'We've not had capital punishment in Keddah Jaleel for more than a century.'

'That's a…um…comfort.'

He didn't even attempt to smile this time. His eyes blazed into hers. 'Sarah?'

His tone was even but relentless. It told her he meant to get an answer to his earlier question, and he meant to get it soon.

She bit back a sigh. 'I told him that if he didn't give you a chance to prove yourself that I'd…um…'

He folded his arms. 'That you'd…?'

She swallowed, her throat suddenly dry. 'That I'd leave Keddah Jaleel and…and deny you all access to the baby.'

The lines about his mouth turned an ominous shade of white. 'I see.'

She suppressed a shiver as his eyes froze over.

'Did you mean that?'

'I don't know.'

'So you *lied* to him?' The light in his eyes was utterly relentless. 'Either that or you've lied to me.'

'I was just trying to make things…better.'

'Better?' He stared at her as if she spoke a language he didn't understand.

She lifted her chin. *In for a penny...* 'And I told him it wasn't fair to punish you for not being Ahmed.'

His mouth dropped open. 'You. Did. *What?*'

He flung his arms outwards, each word shooting from him with bullet-like precision, piercing her with his incredulity and censure. He paced the room, letting forth a torrent of Arabic that she didn't understand but which sounded far from complimentary, and her shoulders started edging up.

He swung back. 'You've no idea what you've done, do you?'

Evidently not.

'You've all but promised to marry me if he makes me his heir. You've all but promised him and my mother that you'll raise our child here in Keddah Jaleel. And if you don't keep your word now you'll break their hearts all over again. Not only have they lost a son, but now they must lose a grandchild?'

'No, I—'

'You told him I want to be his heir and you've promised him I'll fulfil the role!'

He paced the room, muttering imprecations under his breath. She tried to claw her panic back under control. All she'd done was defend him, stick up for him. What was so bad about that?

He turned, his eyes black. 'You've made all of these promises on our behalf and neither one of us yet knows if we can keep them, let alone live up to them!'

Her mouth dried. 'You don't want to be the ruling sheikh?'

His hands slammed to his hips. 'Do you know yet if you want to marry me?'

No.

'Precisely,' he shot back at her, as if he'd read that thought on her face.

She'd thought she was making things better. Instead she'd made them worse. *Flake. Disappointment. Failure.* The words pounded at her, making her feel small and stupid.

He slashed a hand through the air. 'You've no idea in what you're meddling. You shouldn't have interfered!'

That put steel back into her spine. 'Then why don't you tell me? Why don't you fill in the blanks I'm so obviously missing? In Australia you told me you were your father's heir, and then I get here and find out there's a whole big question mark over the issue. If you don't give me all the information, Majed, how on earth do you expect me to negotiate the situation here?'

He didn't want her negotiating the situation! He'd negotiate it for both of them.

Even as he thought it, though, he knew he wasn't being fair.

Sarah hadn't meant to put him in a difficult position. All she'd done was fight for the chance she thought he wanted. She'd stuck up for him, had shown loyalty…and he was railing at her like a martinet.

'It's all well and good for you to reprimand and slam me, but I at least told you what to expect from my mother.'

Her eyes flashed. 'I didn't throw you in at the deep end without any warning!'

Yes...but she'd told Rasheed to stop punishing him for not being Ahmed. He wanted to drop his head to his hands and howl.

Her chin shot up. 'You don't trust me, do you? Despite all your promises of friendship and whatnot, you don't trust me enough to tell me what's going on here.'

She moved in closer, her eyes continuing to flash. Her scent bombarded him and he had to grit his teeth against it.

'How on earth do you think we're going to successfully co-parent if you keep important information from me?'

His heart pounded so hard his chest started to hurt.

She folded her arms, her glare increasing. 'Why does your father have such an issue with you becoming the next sheikh? And don't even think of putting me off, Majed. Whether you like it or not, this is going to affect our baby. You *will* tell me the truth.'

Or what? She'd leave?

He bent at the waist, hands braced against his knees to draw deep, ragged breaths into his lungs.

When he glanced up, he found she'd pressed a hand to her brow as if to keep a headache at bay. She was pregnant. She needed to rest—for her own sake and for the baby's too.

She won't rest until you tell her every loathsome, repugnant detail.

He straightened. 'I hate talking about this.' The words left him on a growl but that didn't seem to perturb her in the least.

'That much is evident.'

He motioned for her to take her seat again. 'To understand my father's attitude, you need to become better acquainted with the circumstances surrounding Ahmed's death.'

CHAPTER SEVEN

SARAH'S KNUCKLES TURNED WHITE. 'I know this can't be easy to talk about.'

Yet she still meant to make him utter the words out loud. Majed swung away. 'I told you it was a woman who was responsible for leading Ahmed to the rebels.'

'Yes.'

He stared at a spot on the wall and forced himself to continue. 'I was the one who introduced Fatima to the palace... and to Ahmed.'

Her gasp—loud in the silence of the room—speared into him.

'My father blames me for that. As he should.'

'No, Majed, you're wrong. Even a stranger can see—'

'Let me finish!' The words left him on a bellow, but he couldn't help it. 'There's more to this sordid story yet.' *So much more.* 'I was the one dating Fatima.' His lips twisted and he finally turned to face her, steeling himself for the condemnation and pity he expected to see. 'I was the one who fancied himself in love with her.'

Her jaw slackened. 'She betrayed you with Ahmed?'

Yes. Which meant Ahmed had betrayed him too.

His skin felt as if it were on fire. He tried to bury the pain coursing through his chest, pounding at his temples, threatening the strength of his knees. 'Obviously the rebels' sights were initially set on me, but when Fatima found she had access to a greater prize—the Sheikh's actual heir—she took her chance.'

She stared at him and it was almost impossible not to shift under that gaze. It made him tense...and the tension made him cruel. 'Have I satisfied your curiosity?'

Her head reared back. 'Curiosity? Is that what you think this is?' She shot to her feet. 'I can't believe you let me go in front of your parents without telling me this. I'd never have said the things I said to your father if I'd known.' She dragged her hands through her hair. 'How insensitive and... and *cruel* he must think me.'

She broke off to pace. His heart thumped. She was right—it hadn't been fair. But talking about Ahmed and Fatima tore the very heart out of his chest and...he couldn't bear it.

His heart pounded. Sarah had stood up for him. She'd had the courage to defend him. A strange warmth filtered into his veins, warming him from the inside out. Majed loved his father but he knew how intimidating Rasheed could be. Sarah had promised him friendship and she'd delivered. While he...he dragged a hand through his hair... he'd put her in an impossible situation.

He pinched the bridge of his nose. 'I'm sorry.'

She swung back. 'Because you're afraid I'm going to leave?'

His hands fell back to his sides. 'Because I promised you friendship and I fell at the first hurdle.'

She stilled.

He moved across and took her hands. 'You deserved better from me. You deserved my full disclosure. I've been weak. Talking about Ahmed is...it's very painful for me. I've avoided talking about this for the last four years. I can see now how wrong that was. I'm sorry my weakness put you in such a difficult position.'

Her hands trembled. 'Wow, you can do a really good line in guilt when you want to.'

She said it to make him smile and he did his best to oblige her. 'I'm an expert.'

He said that to make her smile, and something in his chest started to ache when she managed a weak one.

'I want you to know I'm grateful for the opportunity to work with my father.' He squeezed her hands lightly and then released her, stepping away before he pulled her into his arms and tried to erase the events of the day in the mind-boggling pleasure of making love with her. It might work in the short term, but in the long term it would probably prove a disaster. He had no intention of doing anything that might make her leave. He did his best to banish the images from his mind. 'You'll stay?'

She stared at him for a long moment, before nodding. 'For the moment.'

His knees almost gave out in relief and gratitude. 'Thank you.' *Do not kiss her!* 'I should leave you now. You should get some rest.'

'Sarah?'

Majed tapped on the open door to Sarah's sitting room. She glanced up from her seat on the sofa where she was flicking through a magazine. She closed the magazine and sent him a guarded smile that had his chest cramping. She gestured him into the room. 'Good morning.'

'Did you sleep well?'

She started to nod and then slumped back. 'About as well as you did, I expect.'

'Things will get easier. I promise.'

She nodded.

'Which makes what I'm about to say all the harder.'

She tossed the magazine to the coffee table. 'You better give it to me straight. I've been banished or—'

'Nothing of the sort. My mother can't wait to show you about the palace and introduce you to the women of the family.'

'But your father?'

'I haven't spoken to him since our interview yesterday.' He grimaced. 'However, ten minutes ago one of his aides informed me that I'm to take up the mantle of my royal duties today.'

She straightened. 'Oh, wow. But…that's good, isn't it?'

He didn't know. He hoped so.

'But you're feeling bad because you believe you're abandoning me?'

Bingo.

'Don't worry about me, Majed. I'll be fine.' She suddenly smiled. 'I expect your mother will make sure of that.'

So did he. It was just… *He'd* wanted to be the one to introduce her to his country.

'I can tell them it's impossible for me to take up my duties until next week.'

'You'll do nothing of the sort!' She shot to her feet. 'It's obvious this is a test.'

'Of my—?'

'Of *our* determination and…and steadfastness.'

She made it sound as if his father was trying to scare them away. She could have a point.

'Do you have time to talk?'

He'd make time. 'Yes.' He sat.

She sat too. 'I've been going over things.'

He didn't want her going over things. He didn't want her worrying and stressing. He wanted her… He bit back a sigh. He wanted her to fall in love with Aisha and his country, and to leave all the hard stuff to him.

But Sarah wasn't built like that. So he'd simply have to find a way to ease her mind about whatever was worrying her.

'I want to have a *difficult* talk.'

He lifted his chin. He had no intention of shying away from a difficult discussion again. He set his shoulders. 'Shoot.'

She pulled in a deep breath. 'You think your father holds you responsible for Ahmed's death.' She moistened her lips. 'You think…you think he can't forgive you.'

She was spot on, but his throat had closed over and he couldn't speak. He nodded.

'I think you're wrong.'

The certainty in her voice had him glancing up. He fought the urge to yell and fling wild words at her. She didn't deserve his anger. She deserved his gratitude. If it weren't for her, they'd be back on a plane bound for Australia, and who knew when he might've stepped foot on home soil again?

She moved to stand in front of him and he realised he'd shot to his feet. He stood there with hands clenched at his sides, breathing heavily. His feeling of vulnerability appalled him but he could not do anything about it. Talking about the events of four years ago had ripped the scab off a wound that would never heal and it made him want to tear at rock with his bare hands.

She reached up and touched his cheek, laid her hand flat against it, and her warmth seeped into him, helping to ease the storm raging in his soul.

'You've suffered so much. You all have. My family is fractured but that's because my parents have allowed their bitterness to consume them. It means I can recognise that kind of vitriol. There's something different happening with your family, Majed. I'm not sure what it is, but between us maybe we can work it out.'

And then she removed her hand and retreated back to the sofa, staring at him expectantly. Swallowing, he nodded and took the seat beside her. 'I'm listening.'

Her gaze never wavered. 'This is going to take courage from you.'

He stiffened. 'I am no coward.'

'*Emotional* courage.'

His jaw clenched. Was that her opinion of him? 'As I said, I'm not a coward.'

'But your feelings have been hurt. You believe your father blames you for Ahmed's death because you blame yourself. That's colouring your judgement.' She lifted a hand skyward. 'You think I've just called you a coward when I don't believe that for a moment.'

His head rocked back. His mouth dried. 'I wasn't aware I took offence so easily. My apologies.'

'I don't want your apologies, Majed. I want you self-aware and concentrating. Something is happening here and we need to get to the bottom of it.' She dragged in a breath. 'My child's happiness depends on it.'

'*Our* child,' he corrected.

She stilled and then nodded. 'Our child.'

'Go on.'

Those steady eyes of hers speared him again. 'You need to put your sense of guilt and blame to one side for the moment—discount them if at all possible. Can you do that?'

He couldn't explain why, but her calm logic helped to ease the storm raging within him even further until it was nothing more than a distant rumble on the horizon. 'I can try.'

Her smile anchored him.

She turned to him more fully. 'The first words your father spoke to me were, "thank you for bringing my son home".'

His jaw dropped. His heart started to thud.

'And then, to you, he acted all cool and regal and distant.'

He recalled her bafflement at the meeting and it started to make sense.

'Why would he hide his joy, his happiness, at seeing you *from* you? It makes no sense.'

If what she said was true...

'Of course, you were just as cool and regal and distant in return.'

His mouth dried. Should he have given his father more? He suddenly saw what she meant by emotional courage. Did he have the courage to allow himself to be completely vulnerable to his father...and risk rejection? Again.

'I told your father that if it were truly impossible for you to rule with a Western wife I'd return to Australia without you, deny you access to the baby, and we could all keep the baby's paternity secret.'

His hands clenched so hard his entire frame shook. 'Did you mean that?' *She'd deny him his child?*

'Keep your mind focussed on your father for a moment.' Her voice had gone sharp. 'He was utterly horrified that I would even consider doing such a thing.'

His breath got caught midway between his chest and throat.

'He told me I couldn't do it. He said denying you your child would kill you.'

He had?

'If you had to choose between your kingdom or your child, Majed, which would you choose?'

'My child.' He said it without hesitation.

'And your father knows that.'

Hence the reason for his reprieve.

'Because I'm pregnant, my mind is filled with thoughts of our child. My love for it...all I'd endure and suffer for it if I had to. So when I look at your father and find his words and actions in relation to you in such conflict, I ask myself, what's causing it? I ask myself, what does he fear?'

Majed's first thought was that his father feared his second son wasn't up to the task of leading his country. But that was the old guilt—the doubts Sarah had asked him to put to one side.

'What kind of father was he when you were growing up?'

'Loving.' He half-smiled at the memory. 'He was strict too, but he was also loving. He made time for his family, despite the many demands of his position. He said his family was his strength.' Ahmed's death had struck him and revealed his most vulnerable site—it had devastated him.

Majed tried to breathe through the pain raking his chest. 'It's possible he's still grieving. Perhaps he's not yet ready to move on. Nobody can replace Ahmed. The idea is ludicrous but...'

'But someone will need to step up and be ruler when your father's reign comes to an end,' she finished for him.

Was it possible that Rasheed didn't blame Majed for Ahmed's death? Could it simply be that his younger son's presence reminded him so forcefully of his older son's absence? It was a possibility Majed hadn't considered. His heart pounded so hard he found it difficult to breathe. 'I have to make this right. I'm not sure how, but my father deserves peace.'

She nodded and it hit him then that if it weren't for her he'd have never had this insight into his father. He'd have continued to wallow in a sea of self-pity. Sarah had forced him to look beyond his own hurt and instead of despair he'd discovered hope. He gripped her shoulders. 'I cannot thank you enough. I hadn't thought of looking at it in a different way.'

'You don't need to thank me. I'm simply trying to make things as good as they can be for our baby.'

His mind was no longer on the baby but on her. It occurred to him now that he wanted to marry her for *her*, not just because of the baby. He wanted her in his bed every night. She might not be a native of Keddah Jaleel but she'd make him a fine wife.

As if aware of the direction of his thoughts, she scrambled out of his grip and across to the sideboard to pour herself a glass of water. He followed. He didn't mean to, but something stronger than rational thought made him move across to her. Without giving himself time to think, he swept the swathe of hair from her neck to press a kiss there.

Her gasp arrowed straight to his groin.

The glass clattered to the counter and both her hands clutched the sideboard, as if for support.

He grazed his teeth lightly across her earlobe, breathing her in deeply.

'What...what are you doing?'

Her chest rose and fell. She wanted him just as much as he wanted her. He couldn't explain the craving in his blood where she was concerned but it helped that she felt it too. 'I am kissing you, *habibi.*'

'But...why?'

She stiffened, so he ran his hands from her shoulders down to her hips, pulling her back against him so she could feel the hard length of him against her back, glorying when she arched into the kisses he pressed to her neck. 'I want you, Sarah. I want you like I've never wanted any woman before.'

A moan broke from her lips. 'You said you wanted all or nothing.'

And she couldn't promise him that yet...

They both stilled. For a moment the next move hung in the balance. He could make love to her now, as his aching flesh longed to, with no promises made. Or...

With a groan, he stepped away from her and the action felt like a physical pain. 'I'm sorry. Forgive me. I forgot myself.' Regardless of what his barbarian forebears might've done, he couldn't seduce Sarah into marriage. She needed to make that decision with her head, not her hormones.

She was going to be the mother of his child.

She'd won him a major concession from his father.

She didn't deserve pressure or coercion. She deserved his support.

He glanced at his watch. 'It's time for me to go. An aide will be along in half an hour to take you to my mother. I wish you an enjoyable day.'

With that, he turned on his heel and strode from the room.

One week later Majed strode along the corridor leading to the women's quarters. He had aunts and cousins who lived here and others who often came to visit. He hoped they'd taken Sarah to their bosoms, praising their life in Keddah Jaleel and making her want to live here too.

He'd not spent anywhere near enough time with her this week. He'd wanted to introduce her to the delights of his country but instead he'd found himself swamped with royal duties—meeting overseas delegates, taking part in trade negotiations, overseeing the introduction of a science, technology, engineering and maths syllabus at a new women's university in the capital.

He'd relished every moment of it. But it didn't change the fact he hadn't spent enough time with Sarah.

Maybe she was relieved with the current state of affairs. Maybe she was as afraid as he was that they'd give into the overpowering temptation of their desire for each other... afraid of the consequences that might bring.

His mother had kept him abreast of Sarah's activities—most of which she'd taken upon herself to arrange. Earlier in the week they'd visited a master artisan at his textile shop. Majed's lips lifted. Sarah had waxed lyrical about all she'd seen. The artisan had sent her back to the palace with bolt upon bolt of material. She'd been overwhelmed at the generosity. Little did she realise the prestige that came with the title Royal Supplier.

His mother and several of her aides had taken Sarah on a tour of the undercover markets. She'd returned smelling of incense and he couldn't help wishing he'd been able to share the experience with her—to witness her delight and curiosity. Rather than talk about her own experiences, though, she wanted to hear about his.

Did she recognise his new sense of purpose? Did she sense that he'd found the place where he belonged? For the last four years he'd felt cut adrift from all that mattered. Now he felt as if he were finally fulfilling his destiny. And that was all down to her.

Without a single doubt in his mind, he knew now he wanted to be his father's heir. He wanted to lead his country into the future and see his father's—and Ahmed's—vision for Keddah Jaleel become a reality.

He'd stayed away for so long in an attempt to bury the pain of his father's perceived rejection and in the process he'd buried his true desire—that he wanted to take over the throne from his father when the time came. This was his destiny.

Did she sense all that? Did it frighten her?

If so, she gave nothing away. What she wanted to know was if he and his father had *talked* yet.

So far, Majed had to answer in the negative. He'd spent a great deal of his time in his father's company, but never alone. Twice he'd requested a private interview but both times he'd been stonewalled. He'd ask again soon. Eventually Rasheed would grow used to his presence. And then, maybe, they could work on rebuilding their personal relationship.

Music drifted from the large common room at the end of the corridor. It wasn't traditional Keddah Jaleely music. It wasn't even Arabic music. It was... He frowned. And then he laughed. It was kitsch Western pop music.

He moved to the doorway and his grin widened at what he saw. Half a dozen women—his mother included—were following Sarah's lead in a series of dance moves that had them all laughing and breathless.

The pop music was completely out of place in this room with its richly coloured decorative tiles, arched windows and carved columns, yet the women had such large smiles and the music was so much fun that he had no words for the sense of wellbeing that flooded him. Sarah was...

Dear God! He gulped. She was wearing a traditional Bedouin dancing girl's costume in pale blue with a silver-and-lapis-lazuli medallion belt riding low on her hips. The costume left her belly bare and drew the eye to her generous curves.

Desire fireballed in his abdomen. He backed up a step. He shouldn't intrude...

'Majed!'

His mother's greeting prevented his retreat.

The other women in the room all spun to him with smiles of welcome. Sarah sent him a half-grin—as if to share the joke of a disco in an Arabic palace with him—but a moment later her cheeks flamed pink and she attempted to cover her bust, and all that delicious cleavage, with her folded arms... Then she seemed to realise that her stomach was bare and her hands flew down to cover it.

She stood there staring at him with eyes too big for her face, one foot rubbing the top of her other in delicious awkwardness, and a wave of tenderness washed over him. Her pregnancy hadn't started to show yet, but he'd done research on the Internet and he knew that she'd develop a baby bump within the next couple of weeks.

He couldn't wait to feel the baby kick. He hoped she'd let him share that with her.

'Majed,' his mother murmured in an undertone. 'It's impolite to stare.'

He started to find that Sarah's cheeks had gone even redder. The other women didn't know why Sarah was here, but there'd be speculation. They knew Sarah was his friend.

And now he'd added fuel to the fire.

Sarah cleared her throat. 'We've been having a cultural exchange. Your cousins have been teaching me how to belly dance.'

He noticed then that Sarah wasn't the only one wearing a traditional dancing girl's costume.

'While I've...' Her grin peeped out again.

'While you've been polluting their ears and minds with *pop music.*'

She shook her hair back, feigning superiority. 'I'll have you know that this isn't just any pop group, thank you very much. They're *the* pop group.'

As she spoke, she strode over to a nearby chair and pulled on a shirt that buttoned down the front, hiding all her delicious curves from sight. Majed wanted to go down on his knees and beg her not to.

Sarah's pulse fluttered in her throat like a crazy, wild thing. The hungry twist to Majed's lips, the way he surveyed her as she buttoned her shirt—the gleam in his eyes—made her want to incite him to action—make him haul her into his arms and kiss her. And not stop.

Dangerous.

The word whispered through her.

But delicious.

Very.

But she had her baby's welfare to consider and muddying the few rational thought processes she could muster with hormones... Well, it would be irresponsible. And she was trying so very hard to leave that part of herself behind.

She pulled in a breath. She needed to create a better family for her baby than she'd had. She would not give her child a legacy of warring parents and bitterness—a sense of always being pulled in two different directions. They all deserved better than that.

Friendship first.

She pasted on a smile. 'We've been having a lot of fun today. Your family's hospitality is boundless. An offhand comment about needing to buy a pair of wireless speakers, or a wistful remark that my sewing machine is in Australia, and—*voilà!*—these items seem to magically appear!'

He blinked and a sigh welled through her. He had such beautiful eyes.

'Sewing machine? You've taken up your old hobby again?'

'Oh!' She shook herself. 'Just a…whim.' She waved what she desperately hoped was a nonchalant hand through the air. His eyes narrowed and she rushed on. 'After coming home with all that gorgeous cloth the other day, I…'

'Come and see what this remarkable girl can seemingly whip up out of thin air.'

Aisha took Majed's arm and led him towards the other end of the room where two sewing machines and an over-locker had been set up for Sarah's benefit. Her pulse went into hyper-drive. 'Oh, I'm sure Majed isn't the least interested in my silly little bits and bobs.'

He glanced at her, one devastating eyebrow cocked. 'Then you'd be wrong.'

'Bits and bobs!' Aisha scoffed. 'Majed, the girl is an absolute marvel. She could be an artisan herself.'

Ha! Sarah's heart crunched up tight. She gave what she hoped was a light laugh. 'A flattering exaggeration.' But it was still an exaggeration.

Aisha's brow furrowed. She said something low to

Majed that Sarah didn't catch but it had his gaze turning thoughtful.

'Look at this.' Aisha held up the piece Sarah had spent the morning working on. 'Is it not stunning?'

Majed took the creation, his hand travelling thoughtfully over the material, and Sarah had to force her attention away from his hands…and the thought of how they'd feel if they moved over her naked flesh with the same appreciation. A shiver shook through her.

'Granted, it's pretty.' She shifted her weight from one foot to the other. 'But that's really down to the material. It's flawless. And a delight to work with.'

He turned to her. 'This is…it's remarkable! Why must you put it down?'

She snapped her mouth shut, her heart pounding.

'I'd no idea you could do such fine work. What inspired this piece?'

It was a riff on a kaftan. Many of the women in the palace wore gaily coloured kaftans. But this one had a Western influence. 'I was just playing with the idea of East meets West.'

She had to swallow. She did all she could to tamp down the old enthusiasm that rose through her. Nothing could come of it. It would only lead to disappointment. She had a baby on the way, for heaven's sake! She'd given up such folly long ago.

'And?'

She shrugged. 'I love the style of dress here—the long kaftan shirts and the loose, flowing trousers, the long, sheer scarves. They look so comfortable, but I love Western styles as well. I wanted to create something I could wear that was…' She searched for the word.

'A compromise?'

'A complement—the best of both worlds.'

'We want her to make us all one.'

She gestured to the piles of fabric nearby. 'I'd be delighted to. All you need to do is choose the material you'd like.'

Sarah reached out and took the tunic from Majed. 'It's not really finished yet. I've not finished off the seams properly and…and other things.' She showed him a seam to prove her point. 'But we've just been playing and experimenting and having some fun in the process.'

He opened his mouth but she hurried on. 'How has your morning been? I'll warrant ours has been more enjoyable.'

'The kaftan is not the only thing Sarah has made this morning.'

To Sarah's discomfit, Aisha handed Majed a tiny baby's nightie made from the softest cotton threaded with a yellow silk ribbon at the bodice. 'The detail is breath-taking,' Aisha continued. 'Just look at these pintucks.'

She doubted Majed knew what a pintuck was. In fact she doubted Majed even heard his mother. She couldn't speak as she stared up into his stunned and suddenly vulnerable face. She knew he was imagining their child in that nightie. He was imagining holding their baby, seeing it for the first time…and the hunger in his eyes hollowed out her heart.

He loved this child as much as she did.

How could she deny him the chance to co-parent, to be a part of his child's everyday life?

Could a marriage based on friendship be enough?

And desire. Friendship *and* desire.

But desire didn't last…

She snapped back when Aisha said her name, to find everyone surveying her. 'I'm…I'm sorry. I was a million miles away.'

Aisha smiled but Sarah wasn't sure why. 'Would a cruise down the River Bay'al be to your liking this evening? The worst of the day's heat will be gone and it's cool on the river. And very pretty. We're rather proud of it.'

How could she say no to that? 'I'd love to. It sounds wonderful.'

A gleam briefly lit Majed's eyes. 'I'll collect you at six,' he said, before turning on his heel and disappearing.

'It sounds delightful.' She turned back to Aisha with a determined smile. 'What shall we wear?'

'Not we, my dear—*you*.'

It would be just her and Majed? A traitorous pulse leapt at the thought. Wouldn't it be dangerous, the two of them alone together…?

She folded her arms. Majed, her *and* all his staff. They wouldn't be alone. She did her best to quash her disappointment.

'I think you should wear this.' Aisha took the tunic from Sarah's limp fingers. 'And I think you should make those trousers you were describing to us.'

Another riff on the ones the women here wore—except a little more fitted and cropped just above the ankle.

'We're eager to see them. We're eager to see what they'll look like on. Please, my dear, put us out of our suspense.'

'By all means.' Everyone had been so kind that it was the least she could do. And she had a feeling that keeping busy for the rest of the day would be a very good idea. When she sewed the rest of the world fell away, and she found she needed the comfort of that today.

She turned to the piles of fabric. 'We have so much to choose from and—'

'But only this will do.'

Aisha pulled forth a black silk, so finely made it was almost sheer. Sarah could imagine how decadent it would feel against her skin—like a lover's caress. She could imagine Majed's eyes darkening in appreciation when he saw her in them. It would set off the myriad blues in the tunic perfectly. Without a word, she took the fabric, spread it out and set to work.

* * *

'I need to pinch myself.' Sarah kept her voice low, not wanting to disturb the twilight hush of the river. To the west the sky was a burst of orange, slowly shading to breath-taking pinks and paler mauves. All the colours were reflected in a river that was millpond-smooth. Something about it eased the burning in Sarah's soul.

'You like it?'

Majed's caramel voice bathed her skin in a warmth that lifted all the fine hairs on her arms. 'Like it?' She started to laugh. What wasn't there to like? They were drifting down the river on a slow-moving barge reclining on a bed of silken cushions beneath a canopy of blue-and-silver satin. The luxury was unimaginable and the scenery stunning. '*Like* is far too weak a word. I…' She swallowed. 'I can't believe how beautiful it is.'

Date palms, tall, majestic and seemingly ancient, lined the riverbanks. Beyond them stretched a fertile flood plain green with crops. Majed had told her the river was a hub of activity during the day, with trading boats that travelled from the south, but at the moment it was quiet with only an occasional pleasure craft or tradesman's boat to share its great breadth with them. The palace security patrol ensured that nobody could approach the barge.

'It is beautiful.' Majed turned to her, surveyed her from beneath lazy brows. 'You're beautiful too, *habibi*. I'm honoured to share this with you.'

Majed wore traditional robes and a headdress, and her heart had nearly stopped when she'd first clapped eyes on him. He looked like a stranger—a beautiful, exotic stranger. His robes highlighted the masculine breadth of his shoulders and the lean, hawk-like angles of his face.

A great thirst welled up inside her. 'Um…thank you.'

He rested back against the cushions on one elbow and turned more fully to her. A pulse started up in her abdomen. With a deliberate finger, he reached out and traced a path from her knee to her mid-thigh. She sucked in a breath. 'What are you doing?'

The smile he sent her could only be described as wolf-ish. 'I like to touch you…and the clothes you wear invite me to touch them. Was that not your intention?'

'Of course not.' Her pulse hammered. *Liar.* 'Don't be ridiculous.'

'That's a shame.'

He held out a dish of delicacies to her—locally made Turkish delight that melted on the tongue, dates that were fatter and more luscious than any she'd ever had and a pastry, whose name she couldn't pronounce, which was filled with nuts and honey and tasted of the gods. Normally she'd have eaten her fill, but not this evening. Majed unsettled her too much. 'No, thank you.'

He selected a pastry and bit into it slowly, his tongue snaking out to collect a stray flake from his lips, his gaze on hers the entire time. He made a murmur of appreciation that was so lover-like, heat flooded her cheeks. She swallowed convulsively. 'What are you doing?' she whispered. She wanted to look away, but she couldn't.

He finished the pastry slowly, deliberately…and with obvious relish. 'I promised myself that I wouldn't pressure you one way or the other into marriage with me, Sarah, but I think that was a mistake.'

'Oh, I don't! I think—'

His finger against her lips halted her words. 'I think you ought to know how invested I am in you marrying me. I think you ought to know how much I want you in my bed.'

She jerked away from him, her heart thumping hard. 'Stop it.'

'Why? Because when I talk to you like this you find it hard to hold onto your own restraint? Find it impossible to ignore your body's demands?' He smiled, as if he'd read the affirmative answer in her face. 'Good. I burn for you, *habibi*, and I want you burning for me too.'

He leaned towards her, dredging her with the scent of amber and spice. 'If I were an old-time sheikh I'd order the sides of this canopy lowered until we were cocooned in our own private world and I'd have my wicked way with you until you were replete with pleasure.'

The picture he created was so vivid in her mind, her lips parted to draw in more air.

He leaned back. 'You're lucky I'm a more civilised man than my forebears.'

Was she?

Of course she was!

Her heart thumped. It took a moment for her to master her voice. 'You forget we have a baby to consider.'

His nostrils flared. 'I do not forget that for a moment. Our child is always on my mind.'

Of course it was. He wanted the baby, not her. She couldn't forget that.

Oh, no, he wants you too.

In his bed but not in his heart. Could she settle for that? She cleared her throat. 'Be that as it may, we need to decide what will be best for this baby.'

'And why do you doubt that marrying me won't be in our baby's best interests? If you marry me our baby will have a privileged life. He or she will want for nothing. Every opportunity will be open to him or her. What could be better than that?'

His eyes flashed and an answering frustration pierced her. 'Parents who love each other,' she shot back.

He rolled into a sitting position. 'That is impossible. Besides, your parents must've loved each other once and looked what happened to them. We can give our child a more solid foundation. We can give it parents who respect each other.'

Respect? She bit back a sigh. Respect was *important* in a relationship. So why did it sound so…dreary?

'We can give this child a family, Sarah. Brothers and sisters.'

She'd wanted a tribe of siblings when she was growing up. She could have all the things she'd wanted from a family *now*…if she put aside girlish daydreams and fantasies.

It didn't seem too much to ask, did it?

CHAPTER EIGHT

'I will do everything in my power to make you happy, Sarah. I mean that.'

The expression in his eyes told her he meant his words. He was no longer trying to convince her through the force of their desire for each another. He was no longer trying to cloud her judgement by leaning in too close and making her blood leap and her pulse pound.

It should've made her happy! Majed was vowing to do everything in his power to ensure that she and their child would have not just a good life but a wonderful life.

Except give you his love.

She swallowed. Why did that have to matter so much? Love would come. It would evolve naturally from mutual respect and friendship.

Oh, but it would be a pale imitation of what she'd expected whenever she'd thought about love and marriage in the past.

But…

Maybe Majed was right. Their relationship would never descend into the bitter acrimony that her parents' marriage had. Hadn't she vowed to do anything to spare her child that?

'Tell me more about this old design ambition of yours.'

She glanced across at him. He half-reclined against the cushions and stared out at the river as the barge slid across the water. He looked lazy, at ease…almost slumberous. It occurred to her that she'd not seen him the slightest bit relaxed since they'd arrived in Keddah Jaleel. It soothed something inside her.

She crossed her legs and reached for a piece of Turkish delight. 'Oh, it was just a phase—like wanting to be a fire-fighter when I was ten or a mermaid when I was seven.'

'You wanted to be a mermaid?'

His slow grin warmed her blood…and her heart. Pressing both hands to her chest in exaggerated longing, she said, 'Desperately,' making him laugh. And then she popped the Turkish delight into her mouth before it melted in her fingers.

He leaned forward to pour her a glass of exquisite home-made lemonade. 'How old were you when you decided you wanted to be a designer?'

'Fourteen, I think.' It was hard to feign nonchalance but she did her best. 'I always loved making things—as a kid I loved anything crafty.' The desire to make pretty things had always lived inside her, but it wasn't until she'd discovered sewing that it had really flared into life, filling her with a sense of purpose. 'I intended to study design at university.'

'You didn't?'

'I started.' She sipped her lemonade, hoping its sweet-ness would help counter the bitterness of the disappoint-ment that could still rise up inside her all these years later, reminding her what a flake she was…what a failure.

Her heart thumped and she risked a quick glance at Majed's profile. He deserved a better wife than she'd ever make—a more polished and accomplished wife.

'You started?'

His gaze speared hers, belying the laziness of his pos-ture, and for a moment it felt as if he were plumbing the depths of her soul and laying bare all her secrets. She dragged her gaze from his, feigning interest in a passing cargo boat.

She forced herself to continue. 'I completed a year of study.' And, according to her marks and her teachers, she'd been doing well… 'But in the summer break my mother organised for me to be an intern with Inguri Ishinato.'

He refilled her glass. 'The famous designer?'

She nodded and made herself smile. 'She's wonderful, isn't she?'

'I don't know. Some of her creations seem outrageous for outrageousness' sake. But I understand that she has an enviable reputation.'

'Oh, she was a name all right. Working at her studio opened my eyes.'

'You didn't enjoy your experience there?'

Quite the contrary. She'd loved it but…

'You decided it wasn't the right career for you?'

She rolled her eyes in an attempt to mock herself, doing her very best to smile with wry self-awareness. 'If we hadn't sworn to be honest with each other, I'd be tempted to lie now and save my battered ego, but the truth is I don't have the talent to be a designer. At the end of the internship Inguri took me aside and told me I was a very competent seamstress, but that my design talent was mediocre at best.'

Majed shot into a sitting position. 'She what?'

'She suggested I'd find it more rewarding to make dress-making a hobby rather than a career, and more profitable to find work in a different field.'

He stared at her. 'So you quit design school?'

His disbelief made her fidget. 'It seemed the wisest course of action.'

'Wise?'

He stared at her with such unmitigated astonishment her shoulders started to hunch.

'One setback! You let one person's opinion dissuade you from pursuing your dream?'

She'd bet once Majed set his sights on something he wouldn't let anything or anyone dissuade him. But she wasn't like him. 'It wasn't just any person, Majed. It was a world-class designer whose opinion I valued.' Inguri Ishinato had been her hero.

He folded his arms, his nostrils flaring in the twilight. Her heart lurched. The man was magnificent, truly magnificent. But she wished he wouldn't stare at her like that.

'My mother had been warning me for years that the industry was cutthroat and fickle...and how difficult it would be to earn a decent living. So I decided to be sensible.'

'And learn office administration instead?'

His lip curled and he spat out the words as if they tasted bad on his tongue. She shoved her shoulders back. 'It's a skill that's always in demand. The qualification I got ensures I'll always be able to find work. You can scoff at that all you like, Majed, but it's something I refuse to take for granted.'

'But does it fill your soul? Does it chase the emptiness away?'

She flinched and threw up an arm as if to ward off his words. How could he use her confession against her like this? It was...cruel!

He reached out, his fingers shackling her wrist. 'Is it really that easy to deter you from striving towards what you want? Do you really lack the confidence—the courage—to try?'

He stared at her...almost in fury...and her mouth dried.

'If I started a campaign to undermine your confidence in your ability to be a good mother, would you give way so easily?'

'Don't be ridiculous!' She shook off his hand. 'That's completely different.' She *loved* this baby.

You loved designing too.

His face turned cold and pitiless. 'Your mother didn't appear to approve of your career choice. Did you never question her hand in helping you to acquire this internship with Inguri Ishinato?'

His meaning was clear and her stomach clenched. 'My mother would never sabotage me like that.'

'She didn't need to sabotage you. She simply put a single roadblock in your path. And you crumbled with barely a whimper.'

He was wrong about that. It was just that she'd kept her whimpers to herself.

'I haven't seen a sewing machine in your apartment. I've never even heard you speak about designing or sewing until recently.'

'My equipment was packed away in my move. I haven't got round to unpacking it.'

The fact of the matter was that she hadn't had the heart to look at her sewing machine after Inguri's pronouncement. She'd put her things away and had let the emptiness grow. She'd resisted the temptation to dabble—how could she just dabble when it meant so much more to her than that? She'd not been able to face it until here, now, in Keddah Jaleel, where her old world had dropped away. With all of that delicious fabric tempting her…calling to her. Today when she'd sewn, she'd felt at peace—and whole—for the first time in years.

There had been one other time.

The pulse fluttered in her throat. When she'd made love with Majed, the empty places inside her had filled then too.

But that had to have been an illusion.

'You have a fear of failure.'

The disgust in his voice snapped her spine straight. 'Everyone is afraid of failure, Majed, even you.'

'It won't stop me from trying, from striving, from doing my very best and giving my all.'

Her heart started to thump. Did he think her incapable of those things?

Well...aren't you?

She didn't give her all in her work—it was so darn boring and unchallenging that she found it hard to remain engaged—but her employers deserved better than that. The realisation made her reach out a hand to steady herself against the cushions.

She didn't give her all in her relationships either. She was always waiting for someone to find fault with her. If they didn't, she saved them the time by pointing out her myriad flaws first—all under an umbrella of humour and self-deprecation, of course. But it created a distance inside her that was impossible to breach.

She swallowed. Was that what she wanted to teach her child?

At nineteen she'd let someone deter her from following her dream and she hadn't felt whole since. And yet, not once had she dared to resurrect her dream.

Because she lacked courage.

When had she settled for being a flake and nothing more than a flake?

'I want to be the best father I can be to our child. I want to be the very best role model I can be.'

The iron in his voice pounded at her.

'I also want to be happy. I want to show my children that they can be happy too. You, Sarah—I think you're afraid of being happy.'

Pain radiated out from her chest to all her extremities—even the tips of her fingers and the soles of her feet ached. 'I'd like to return to the palace now.'

Her words emerged clipped and short...distant. Without even looking at her, Majed gave the order to return to the palace. They didn't speak a single word to each other again until they reached the palace and Majed gave her a clipped, 'Goodnight.'

Her throat had closed over so she couldn't return the pleasantry. Not that it mattered. He strode off so fast, he'd not have heard it anyway.

Sarah returned to her rooms to find one of Rasheed's aides waiting for her. 'Sheikh Rasheed understands from the Sheikha that you have a desire to become acquainted with the palace protocols and duties surrounding the role of the Sheikha?'

'Um…' She stared at the file the man held out to her. It was so thick!

'He had this compiled for your benefit.'

She took it, her heart sinking. 'Please thank His Highness for me. It was very considerate of him.'

The aide bowed and left.

Sarah carried the file to the desk and stared at it. Majed's reproof rang in her ears before she'd even lifted the cover.

As she read, her heart sank further and further.

Sarah didn't clap eyes on Majed for the next two days. Her lips twisted as she sewed the seam for a sleeve. No doubt he was trying to find a way tactfully to retract his offer of marriage. The thought made her heart burn though she didn't know why. It would make things simpler all round if he did.

The plan had been for her to shadow Aisha these past two days but, for reasons she wasn't privy to, those plans had been cancelled. At Majed's command, perhaps? But nor had Aisha gone about her duties, leaving Sarah to the mercy either of her solitude or the other women's ministrations. Instead, she declared herself on holiday and spent her time in the women's quarters with Sarah and whoever else felt like joining them. They all urged Sarah to work at her sewing machine, to show them the things that she could make, to teach them some of the techniques they admired.

She complied gladly, though Majed's reproof about being afraid to be happy constantly rang in her ears. Sewing—making clothes, handbags, cushion covers and other soft furnishings—*did* make her happy. Why had she denied herself this pleasure so completely? Why had she turned her back on it?

'May I have a word, Sarah?'

Majed's voice sounded next to her and she jumped, nearly sewing her finger to the tunic she was making for Aisha.

'Forgive me, I didn't mean to startle you.'

He didn't look angry, for which she gave thanks. Instead he looked… Actually, she couldn't decipher his expression. But she could guess the contents of the conversation they were about to have and she couldn't prevent her heart from sinking.

This is for the best.

Of course it was, but…

She stood. 'Of course.'

She expected him to lead her to a quiet corner of the room but he led her out to a private courtyard instead. A fountain tinkled in the quiet air and the cool shade beckoned a welcome invitation. She gave a low laugh. 'You've chosen a pleasant spot for your unpalatable news, Majed.' She appreciated that, appreciated his thoughtfulness in providing her with this shield of privacy.

'I don't know what you mean. What *news* do you think I have come to give you?'

He'd accused her of a lot of things—being afraid of failure, of not fighting hard enough for what she wanted—all true. But she refused to be a coward now. She turned to face him. 'After our discussion on the river the other evening, I expect you've come to retract your marriage proposal.'

He paused in the act of motioning her to a bench padded with brightly coloured cushions. 'You are most wrong, *habibi*.'

The whispered promise of the endearment softened her stomach. She wanted to sit, to move away from his overpowering masculinity and the need it sent rocketing through her, but he took her hand and she found she couldn't move a muscle.

'Would that news have been unpalatable to you?'

Oh, um... Before she could concoct a reply, he lifted her hand and pressed a kiss to her wrist at the point where her pulse jumped and jerked. He grazed it with his teeth and she could barely contain a gasp.

'I'm fully committed to marrying you, Sarah Collins. The final decision rests with you. If you choose to not marry me, it will hurt me very much.'

She reclaimed her hand. It would hurt his pride, not his heart.

Though, that wasn't completely true. It would hurt him if she denied him his child. Not that she'd ever do that, but... It would hurt him as much as it would hurt her, and that knowledge plagued her.

'No, *habibi*, I came to apologise.'

Apologise!

'For the things I said two evenings ago. It was wrong of me. It shames me to remember them. I've no right to judge you. I've had privileges you could only have ever dreamed about. I've had parents who encouraged me to strive for whatever it was I wanted. The disparity in our backgrounds...' He shook his head. 'I had no right to call you a coward.'

He sat and, resting his elbows on his knees, he dropped his head to his hands and muttered what she suspected was some kind of curse in his native tongue.

She sat too and touched his arm. Warmth immediately

sparked through her fingers and she reefed her hand back. 'There was truth in your accusations, Majed. I didn't want to admit it then, but—'

'No!'

He spun to look at her and slowly he straightened. Something in his eyes made her mouth dry.

'You're no coward. You lack confidence, that's all. And it's *that* which made me so angry. Not at you,' he rushed to reassure her, 'but at the circumstances in your life that have robbed you of believing you've the right to chase your dreams, that have prevented you from recognising and taking pride in your own talents.'

The regret in his face touched her.

'I'm sorry I railed at you like I did. I—'

'Stop, Majed. Stop feeling so bad about this. I accept your apology. I also accept that there was truth in some of your words—even if I didn't like hearing them.'

He took her hand. 'But the failings aren't your fault. You've not had anyone to believe in you and encourage you…until now.'

Something in his tone… She straightened. 'What do you mean *until now*?'

'I've invited the master artisan you visited the other day to view the things you've been making for my mother and the other women. He's with them now.'

Sarah shot to her feet, her heart pounding. 'You've done what?'

She'd only just rediscovered her love for all of this. She wasn't sure she could bear anyone putting a dampener on her joy just yet and telling her she had only a mediocre talent. Which made no sense at all, because she hadn't had any delusions of grandeur while she'd been playing with all of that gorgeous fabric. And that was what it had felt like— playing. There'd been joy, freedom and fun, nothing more.

'You're angry with me?'

You promised honesty.

She swallowed. 'Hiding behind anger would be easier than facing the truth.'

She went to stride away—to pace up and down the court-yard—but he caught hold of her hand and, before she knew what he meant to do, she found herself tumbled onto his lap. Warm arms encircled her. Warm lips hovered just cen-timetres from hers…so tantalising and tempting. The scent of amber and spice surrounded her.

'I enjoy having you in my arms, *habibi*, and I could very easily lose myself in you this very minute.' The words growled out of him. 'But that would be unforgivable.'

She'd forgive him!

He stroked the length of her jaw with one lazy finger. Beneath it her blood heated. 'You're afraid the artisan will damn your work with faint praise.'

She nodded, not trusting herself to speak.

He stared down at her solemnly. 'I don't know what he'll say. He's promised to provide an honest assessment, that's all.'

Her heart jerked in her chest.

'But I want you to know that, whatever he says, my opin-ion of you won't change.'

She stilled.

'I'll still admire you, regardless of his assessment of your skill. I'll still enjoy your company and the way you make me laugh. I'll still think you intelligent, warm and generous.'

Very carefully—as she was sitting in his lap and they needed to be careful when they were this close to each other—she shuffled into a more upright position. It brought their mouths closer together. His gaze rested on her lips for a moment. He swallowed and she saw the effort it cost him to control himself. A ripple of triumph quivered through her.

His lips curved. He said something she didn't understand then. 'If you agree to marry me, I'll look forward with much pleasure to our wedding night.'

'You'd make me wait that long?'

'It is the custom of our people. I must honour you with every token of reverence and esteem. But there can be pleasure to be found in delayed gratification.'

He leaned forward and grazed his teeth across her ear. Heat shot straight to her core and need pounded through her with a prickling awareness that made her want to press against him to assuage the ache, to inflame him, to incite him to lose control. If she did that... The fat file Rasheed had sent to her rose in her mind. Biting back a sigh, she pressed a hand to Majed's chest and pushed him back. Beneath her palm his heart raced just as hard as hers.

He glanced into her face and murmured something under his breath. 'This is a dangerous game we are playing. Come.' He gently lifted her to her feet. 'Let us go and see what our artisan has to say.'

Us. Our. The sense that they were somehow in this together lent strength to her knees. She pushed her shoulders back and ignored the craven urge to flee. She'd face this with the same courage that Majed faced the future.

The moment they entered the common room, an elderly man raced over to them, his face alight. 'Your Highness Sheikh Majed, who is this talent you have found? What is his name? I would take him for my apprentice in a heartbeat if he is free to engage in such study.'

'Arras, that is a great honour.' Aisha moved to stand beside him, sending Sarah a speaking glance. 'You have to understand that Arras has not taken on an apprentice in more than five years.'

The older man shook his head. 'I am getting old and I'm not as patient as I once was. I give my time now only to the extraordinary. And, while some of this work is raw and undeveloped, it has a great energy and sophistication that mark it as an exciting talent.'

Sarah couldn't believe her ears. She'd forgotten to pull her hand from Majed's upon entering the room, and she gripped it now as if her life depended on it. She didn't care what rumours it would excite among the women.

Arras glanced at their linked hands and he broke out into a radiant smile. 'It is this lovely young lady who possesses this talent, yes?'

'It is.'

The pride in Majed's voice as he introduced them made everything inside her feel bright, as if she had her own internal sun. 'You…you really like my pieces, Arras? You think they have promise?'

'I do, yes! Come, come.' He hustled her over to the table that held the pieces Aisha had evidently assembled for him. 'I'm impressed with the East-West fusion of this tunic…'

They spoke for nearly two hours, the rest of the world receding as they discussed design principles and techniques. Before he left, Arras pressed his card into her hand. She promised they'd talk again soon.

When he was gone, it was only she and Majed left in the common room. He sat on a deeply cushioned sofa but he rose when her gaze founds his.

She pressed a hand to her chest. 'You did this for me?'

She didn't know what to say. She was absurdly close to tears. How could she thank him for all he'd done? He'd helped her to overcome her worst fear. And in facing it she'd discovered that her most cherished wish could come true. That it was true—she had a unique and remarkable gift—and she no longer intended to deny it. In that moment the emptiness that had been a constant part of her since she'd given up on her dream vanished. She'd found what she was destined to do.

Could she do that *and* be Majed's Sheikha?

'I told you I'd do whatever I could to make you happy. I meant that.'

'Wouldn't your people have a problem with the Sheikh's wife doing...that?' She waved a hand towards her sewing machine. 'With her having a career beyond her royal duties?'

'I see no reason why they should.'

She stared at him and her heart started to pound, thumping relentlessly against the walls of her chest. Wind roared in her ears, blocking out everything but the truth. She loved Majed. She loved him heart and soul. She loved *his* heart and soul. She loved his kindness, his sense of honour and his unselfishness. She loved his confidence and his ability to solve problems, his ability to meet obstacles with his head held high. She loved his...big-heartedness.

A vice tightened about her chest. But he didn't love her. *Does it matter?*

She swallowed. Of course it mattered. But it didn't mean she couldn't marry him.

Rasheed's fat file rose in her mind, and a sigh pressed against her throat, but she refused to let it escape.

'Sarah?'

She shook herself. What on earth was she doing just standing here like a dummy? She made herself smile and then she strode across to him. Placing her hands on his shoulders, she reached up to press a kiss to his cheek. His eyes glittered, his lips parted and for a moment she thought he'd sweep her into his arms and kiss her senseless. She stepped back quickly, the blood thundering in her ears. 'I...' She had to swallow. 'Nobody has ever done such a thing for me before. I can't tell you how much it means to me.' She shrugged, unable to find the words. 'You're an amazing man. I feel lucky and blessed to know you.'

'I feel exactly the same way about you.'

Not *exactly*. And that stung in ways she hadn't known

possible. But she did have his friendship and his respect. And there was little doubt that he desired her.

He reached out, as if to touch her cheek, but his hand fell short and dropped back to his side. She knew why. The spark between them was too strong. A single touch could unleash a raging inferno. But there was too much at stake. She couldn't get this wrong. This wasn't something she could screw up.

Her hand curved about her abdomen, unconsciously protective. For once in her life she had to be as unlike a flake as possible. Majed's eyes lowered to where her hand rested. When he lifted them they glowed with a possessive pride.

'You make me believe impossible things are possible,' she blurted out.

He nodded. 'Good.'

'I...I need to go somewhere quiet and process all of this.' She turned and made for the door.

'Sarah.'

She pulled in a breath before turning to face him again.

'There is time. You have time. I don't want you feeling pressured. I don't want you feeling stressed.'

Even now, when he must sense how close her capitulation was, he thought first of her welfare.

He didn't love her, but maybe she had enough love for both of them.

She had to work out what she wanted. And then, somehow, she had to find the courage to fight for it. With a nod, she left.

Majed stood in front of his father. For the last three weeks he'd worked tirelessly at his father's side. The older man hadn't given him a single word of praise, but he had sought Majed's opinion on several tricky issues. Majed didn't flatter himself that it was because his father valued his opinion. It was all part of a larger test. He just didn't know yet if he'd passed or not.

He squared his shoulders. He'd given it his all. He'd made no secret of the fact he wanted a role in taking Keddah Jaleel into the future. He'd held nothing back.

'Greetings, Samir.'

Majed's gut clenched as his cousin—older than Majed by two years—entered the stateroom. Everyone else had been ordered to leave, even the Sheikh's most trusted aides.

The cousins clapped each other on the shoulder in greeting. Majed loved and trusted his cousin.

'As you both know,' Rasheed started, 'I intend to choose one of you to be my heir.'

'Sir—' Samir started, but Rasheed held his hand up for silence.

'As you must be aware, I have long favoured you, Samir. You're smart and steady, and loyal to the people of this country. You'd lead our people well.'

'Thank you, but—'

Again that hand rose, demanding silence.

Majed glanced at his cousin's profile. Samir didn't want the title—not at what he considered to be Majed's expense. Last week the two of them had engaged in a long and serious discussion on the topic.

'Majed, in these past weeks you've proven yourself adept and surprisingly canny in foreign affairs.' Rasheed's lips momentarily pressed into a thin line. 'Additionally, Samir has informed me that if he does become ruler of Keddah Jaleel he envisages a role for you among his trusted advisors.'

It was the role he'd have played if Ahmed had lived. It was what he'd been trained and groomed for. There was no hiding the displeasure in his father's eyes, however, at that prospect.

Majed wanted to throw his head back and howl. Did his

father still hold him so comprehensively responsible for Ahmed's death? Would he never forgive him? Did the sight of his younger son still cause him so much pain?

To spare his father, maybe he should leave Keddah Jaleel for good. *Which would kill your mother.*

It was all he could do to stop his shoulders from sagging.

In the next moment he pushed them back. What of his child's destiny? Did his child not have the right to know and love this land as much as Majed did? He'd fight any battle for his child's welfare and honour.

Rasheed blew out a breath, his dark eyes troubled. 'Majed, if Sarah agrees to marry you, then the throne will one day be yours.'

A fierce gladness gripped him. His father had seen his worth! Majed would work tirelessly to prove to his father that his faith had not been misplaced. 'Thank you, Bábá.'

'I believe you're as committed to bringing democracy to this country as both I and Ahmed.'

Pain raked his heart at the mention of his brother but he forced his chin up. 'I am. I'd infinitely prefer that Ahmed were here, but he's not.' He broke off, fighting the burning in his throat. 'Thank you for giving me the opportunity to prove myself.'

At Majed's mention of Ahmed, Rasheed lowered himself to the seat behind his desk, his hand covering his eyes. When he lifted it away, Majed was shocked to see how old his father looked. He wasn't old! He was only sixty-three!

'Majed, if Sarah decides not to marry you, I'd ask that you leave Keddah Jaleel.'

Ice tripped down Majed's spine, vertebra by vertebra.

'I'll not make it an order, but there will be a scandal that our enemies will do their best to use against us. I cannot let that happen. I'll not allow your brother's death to be in vain.'

CHAPTER NINE

'THIS IS AMAZING!'

Majed glanced across at Sarah as she peered out of the helicopter's windows, straining against her seatbelt in her efforts to take in the view, and was glad he'd taken the time away from his duties to show her more of the land he loved.

They'd been in Keddah Jaleel for three weeks and two days now. He needed to know if Sarah had come to a decision. He needed to know if she was going to marry him.

Don't pressure her. You've no right to pressure her.

His grip tightened about the helicopter's control stick. It was one of the most difficult things he'd ever done—maintaining this façade of patience and calm, of not doing all he could to sway her decision...or to not sway it more than he already had.

But if she left Keddah Jaleel with his child...

His stomach lurched. He couldn't bear the thought.

He knew she wouldn't keep their child from him. There'd be visits and holidays, but he wanted to be a part of their child's everyday life—an integral part, not a figure on the edges.

He swallowed. He'd shown her the beauty and luxury of life at the palace—the lifestyle she could enjoy as his wife. He'd tried to show her the kind of consideration and respect she would receive from him as her husband. He'd demonstrated that she could pursue her dreams and carve out a career for herself here too.

He hadn't pointed out how much more difficult it would be for her if she decided not to marry him, if she returned to Australia instead. His heart clenched at the thought. She already knew those difficulties—had lived through them with her own mother. Even if they shared custody, life would still be far more difficult.

For them both.

He'd avoided mentioning how much her decision would affect his own destiny.

That'd be emotional blackmail.

He hadn't mentioned the scandal that'd break once it was known that the Sheikh's only son had a child out of wedlock. He hadn't told her of the press storm that would explode, the fact it would follow her to Australia…or that an intense media interest—and presence—would follow their child throughout his or her life.

He refused to terrorise her with such horror stories. At the moment her health had to be his primary concern. She should be entitled to make her decision in peace.

'This is such a contrast to Demal.' She breathed.

Her awe reached him through the headsets they wore. He manoeuvred the helicopter lower so she could observe the landscape at closer quarters.

'This is what I imagined Keddah Jaleel would look like.'

They'd left behind the capital with its fertile coastal plain, green fields and glinting river to pass over the high hills to the west. Here the topography changed dramatically to an arid rocky landscape that eventually merged with seemingly endless dunes of shifting, golden sand. A heat haze shimmered in the distance.

He glanced at her again. 'What do you think of it?'

'It's utterly terrifying. Like Australia's Great Sandy Desert. I can't imagine how awful it would be to find yourself stranded alone in it.'

He opened his mouth to tell her she need never fear such a thing when she swung to him.

'It's utterly magnificent. It's so...*beautiful.*'

She saw the same beauty in this landscape as he did and something inside him shifted. He feigned preoccupation with the myriad dials on the helicopter's control panel, but his heart started to pound. This woman had an uncanny ability to get beneath his skin.

He'd dismissed it as desire. Well...he hadn't exactly *dismissed* it.

He wanted her. His desire for her burned through him, hot and fierce. It kept him awake at night. He hadn't *dismissed* that desire but he'd used it to explain away his other reactions to her—other more disturbing reactions.

He clenched his jaw. She was carrying his child. It was only natural he should feel possessive and protective but he couldn't allow that to compromise his common sense, his caution or his ability to reason—the way those things had been compromised with Fatima. The way Ahmed's ability to make good decisions had been overset by his brother's girlfriend.

That Ahmed had betrayed Majed demonstrated the evil that accompanied such a passion. It showed the selfishness and the potential for self-destruction that resided at the heart of such passion. He ground his back molars together. He wanted no part of that kind of love again. He'd dig out every grain he found forming within and he'd destroy it.

If Sarah married him, he'd become Keddah Jaleel's ruling Sheikh. Sarah's welfare, their children's welfare and his people's welfare would rest with him. It would be his duty to protect them and keep them safe. They deserved the very best he could give them. They deserved his very best efforts. He would not fail them.

'Majed?'

Sarah stared at him with pursed lips, a question in her eyes. She'd been speaking but he hadn't been attending to her words. He swallowed. He wouldn't allow himself to fall in love with her, but nor would he neglect her.

Visions of exactly how he wouldn't neglect her rose in his mind. Heat and perspiration prickled his nape. He needed a long, cold drink. 'I'm sorry, *habibi*. It's been a long time since I flew a helicopter. It's requiring more concentration than I remembered.'

The purse of her lips became more pronounced—*those luscious lips!*—and an ache stretched through him, pulling his nerves taut. A teasing light deepened the blue of her eyes. The fact she was oblivious to his preoccupation should've comforted him but it only strained his muscles further.

'Exactly how long has it been since you flew a light aircraft? Should I be worried?'

He laughed—how could she make him do that? 'I think we can risk it. There's the oasis now. See how it emerges from the desert like a jewel?'

An hour later they were sitting beneath a fringed canopy that protected them from the fierce heat of the sun. A small breeze made the fringe dance and cooled their hot flesh as it made its way across the deep pool of water in front of them. They sat on silken cushions scattered across a brightly coloured carpet that Sarah had spent an inordinate amount of time studying. That was, until she'd suddenly spun to him and started pelting him with questions. How many people lived at this oasis? How many people did it service? How did the people here make a living? How many oases like this one were scattered across the Keddah Jaleely desert?

He'd answered each of her questions as best as he could

until he found the opportunity to ask one of his own. 'From where does all of this interest spring?'

She glanced out at the water before taking her time to select a date, but something in her face had become shuttered. He leaned towards her. 'Sarah?'

Her shoulders suddenly drooped. 'I feel so utterly ignorant about everything, Majed—Keddah Jaleel's people, your country's history, its geography…and everything! There's so much to learn.'

He started to laugh. 'You don't need to learn it all at once. You don't need to learn it at all if you don't want to.'

She rose and he found himself staring at a very rigid back. Glancing around, he dismissed the attendants. They melted away without a sound. Rising, he moved behind her. Placing his hands on her shoulders, he pulled her back against him.

For a moment he thought she might resist, but then she softened and nestled back, and he had to grit his teeth at the desire that fired through him. 'Would you like to tell me what's troubling you?'

He felt rather than heard her sigh. 'Not really.'

Instead of pressing her, he simply pulled her more firmly against him, one of his arms encircling her just below her collarbone, and he just held her, running his other hand from her shoulder to her elbow and back again in an attempt to give her comfort…and a safe haven in which to relax. They stood like that for a long time, staring out at the sparkling sheet of water. Very slowly, the tension drained from her. A fierce gladness gripped him. He always wanted her to find comfort in his arms.

Eventually he said, 'In another five days we'll have been in Keddah Jaleel a month.'

She nodded and her hair tickled his face. 'The time has whizzed by so quickly. More quickly than I thought it would.'

Did she mean she wasn't yet ready to make a decision?

'But I know in five days' time you'll ask me again if I'll marry you.'

There was something in her voice. He turned her to face him. 'Do you doubt my desire to marry you?'

She searched his eyes and then shook her head. 'No.'

He couldn't help it. He traced his right hand from her shoulder and up the clean length of her throat to cup her jaw. Her pulse quickened beneath his fingers and his own leapt in response. 'Do you doubt our ability to deal well with each other?'

She shook her head again and the warm slide of her skin against his fingers pulled something tight inside him.

'No, I don't doubt that. The fact is...'

The sudden vulnerability in her eyes caught at him, though he sensed she tried to shield it from his sight. 'The fact is?'

Her lips lifted as if they couldn't help it. 'The fact is I...I like you.'

Both of his hands cupped her face as he wrestled with the sudden fierce joy that gripped him. 'You like me?'

'I know it doesn't sound like much, but—'

'It is everything!' And then he couldn't help himself. He kissed her. He'd meant it to be nothing more than a swift press of his lips to hers, but her surprised gasp sent warmth washing across his lips and he found he couldn't pull away. He dipped his head again, his tongue plundering her softness and warmth, and then she was pressed against him, her fingers entwined in his hair, and Majed found himself lost to sensation.

From somewhere he eventually found the strength to pull back.

Her chest rose and fell as deeply and quickly as his. She touched trembling fingers to her lips and then shot him a shaky smile. 'And I know how much you also like me.'

A laugh burbled in his chest. It would be fun being married to this woman. 'I desire you greatly, *habibi*. I've made no secret of it. But I want you to know that I *like* you too. You've honesty and integrity, and those things are diamonds to me. I think you'll be a wonderful mother—I see the care you already take of our child and it humbles me. A man could ask no more than that. And yet you know how to laugh too, how to make me laugh. I do not think you know how much I value you.'

'Oh!' She pressed a hand to her heart and swallowed. He could see how furiously the pulse in her throat worked. He reached out and brushed his thumb across it. 'Your heart is racing.'

'Isn't yours?'

In answer, he took her hand and pressed it to his chest. 'It races like a wild thing.'

'No man has ever treated me the way you do, Majed. Even when you're angry with me, you still show me kindness and...respect.'

'It's my intention to always do so.' She'd not been shown enough kindness in her life. If she let him, he'd do his best to make that up to her.

'I've a very big question to ask you, Majed. I beg that you'll answer me truthfully.'

His mouth dried but he nodded. They'd promised each other honesty. He wouldn't fail her now.

'Could the people of Keddah Jaleel eventually accept a Western woman as their Sheikha? Would your rule survive that?'

Her earlier unspoken worries made sudden and perfect sense. He nodded, not in assent but in recognition of her concern. 'This is a question I've had to consider carefully. I know it is not *romantic* to admit as much.'

'We're something other than a romance, Majed.'

Her tone was crisp, yet...did she mind? Did she miss

romance so very badly? It was true that women loved romance and he'd tried to give her the façade of it—the sunset cruise on the river, this picnic at the oasis…he'd shower her with such treats for the rest of her life. She deserved them. But the two of them weren't a love match. And he couldn't pretend otherwise.

But she *liked* him, and even now that knowledge thrilled him.

'We're something better than a romance,' he told her.

Her gaze dropped from his but when she spoke her voice was steady. 'Yes, we're going to be parents.'

He pulled in a breath. She understood. 'I've thought hard on this issue, Sarah. I'll not do anything that will hurt you or our child, or that'll hurt my country.'

Her gaze met his again. 'It's a big ask.'

'But not an impossible one. I won't lie—there'll be some among the more conservative sections of Keddah Jaleely society who'll try and make an outcry if I marry you— who'll attempt to create outrage in the general population, accuse my father and me of not holding to or valuing the old ways—but we can weather that.'

'How?'

He admired her need to understand. He respected it. If she married him, his people would become her people. And they'd be lucky to have her as their Sheikha. 'My father is popular with our people and his rule is strong. He's only sixty-three. Our line has, thus far, been blessed with good health and long life.'

Realisation dawned in her eyes. 'His rule could last for another twenty years.'

'Or more. Our people will have a chance to get to know you.'

'To grow used to me.'

'While I work side by side with my father, taking on more and more of his duties as he gets older.' In the same way Sarah would take over more and more of his mother's duties. None of them would throw Sarah in at the deep end. Everyone would have ample time to grow used to the idea.

She nodded. 'I see.'

'So what do you say, Sarah? Will you marry me?'

Will you marry me?

The words pounded at her. He needed an answer. Maybe not right at this moment but in a few days' time. And she'd have to give him one.

Her mouth dried. She'd spent several days shadowing Aisha as the other woman had gone about her duties. Sarah's hands clenched and unclenched, that fat file of Rasheed's rising in her mind to plague her. How could she hope to live up to Aisha's grace and confidence? How could she live up to Aisha's inspiring speeches, wise words and innate dignity as she'd visited countless schools, libraries business centres and hospitals?

Majed has told you there'll be time. She didn't need to step into the Sheikha's role immediately…or even in the near future. There'd be time and opportunity to learn all she needed to know.

She'd moved away from Majed to stride around the perimeter of the awning. She turned back to him now. Leaning against one of the tent poles, she curled her fingers around it for support. If she married him, their baby would grow up living with two parents who loved it. *You'll both still love it, even if you don't marry.* But Majed's family were in a privileged position and if she didn't marry Majed she'd be denying her child that position. Could she do that?

And, if she didn't marry him, Majed would be passed over for the throne.

It's not a woman's role constantly to martyr herself in the service of others.

That was her mother's voice, and she agreed with the

sentiment, but one could hardly call living in the lap of luxury and getting a chance to study design under a master artisan an act of martyrdom.

What do you *want?*

She loved Majed.

Would marrying a man who didn't return her love become an exercise in self-destruction?

Only if you let it.

What *did* she want?

She stared at Majed. He hadn't moved. He watched her closely but he didn't say a word. He didn't try to pressure her, just gave her the time she needed. He...waited. In that moment she knew exactly what she wanted. And for perhaps the first time in her life she meant to fight for it.

She lifted her chin. 'Yes, Majed, I will marry you.'

He moved towards her so swiftly she barely had time to draw a breath. He reached out, as if to grip her shoulders or take her hands, but stopped short. She didn't know whether to be disappointed or relieved.

His eyes throbbed into hers. 'Do you mean that?'

Behind the hope she sensed his vulnerability. 'Yes.'

He stared at her, as if he could barely believe it. 'Do you want to consider it for a few more days before we make the announcement?'

'I see no reason for that. You've given me plenty of time to think about it and I'm grateful for that.' She swallowed. 'But now that I've made up my mind I've no intention of changing it.'

'I want to kiss you.' His chest rose and fell. 'But I'm afraid that if I do I won't be able to stop. And we will be seen.' He swallowed, his hands opening and closing convulsively. 'I want the people of Keddah Jaleel to hold you in the highest regard—the way I do. So...'

She blew out a breath, doing what she could to hide her

disappointment. 'Well, you better not kiss me, then. But how long do we have to wait for the wedding night?'

She wasn't ashamed of her desire for him, and when his eyes flashed an ache burst to life inside her.

'We'll make it a short engagement.' He took her hand and pressed a kiss to her palm. 'You'll not regret this, *habibi*, I promise you that. Is there any other promise you'd like to extract from me?'

Her palm tingled from the heat of his lips. He didn't release it either and she found it hard to concentrate. 'I...' She swallowed. 'I'd like us to mean our wedding vows.'

'I wish that too.'

A frown suddenly built through her.

'Sarah, why are you strangling my hand?'

Oh! She loosened her grip but he refused to allow her to pull away. 'Are your wedding vows here in Keddah Jaleel the same as the ones we have in Australia? I'll promise to love, honour and cherish you but I refuse to have "obey" in there. This is the twenty-first century and my mother taught me better than that.'

She broke off when he started to laugh. 'We can have whatever you want. I promise.'

She pulled in a breath. 'I just want us to promise to do our best to look after each other.'

He stilled. And then he lifted her hand to his lips again. 'That is not a promise for which you need to wait until our wedding day. I can promise that to you now.'

If she hadn't already fallen in love with him, she would have in that moment. And, when his lips touched her smouldering flesh, she swore that this time they left a mark.

'We must have a betrothal ball!'

Aisha clapped her hands, her delight at Sarah and Majed's announcement a balm to Sarah's nerves, even as the thought of being the focus of a formal event stretched them tight again.

She turned to her prospective father-in-law. Rasheed had paled, the lines bracketing his mouth deepening. His evident lack of pleasure at their news cut at her. She glanced at Majed. How much more deeply must it cut at him?

Rasheed rallied, though. Lifting his chin, he said in formal tones, 'I felicitate you both.'

Her heart gave a sickening thud in her chest. 'Thank you,' she managed to murmur.

Majed stared at his father for a long moment and then bent at the waist to rest his hands on his knees, as if someone had punched him in the stomach. 'Bábá, if it causes you so much pain to see me in Ahmed's place then I will step aside.'

The older man's nostrils flared. 'You'd leave Keddah Jaleel?'

'He'll do no such thing!' Aisha cried.

Majed straightened, meeting his father's stare. 'I'll take up the role I'd have had if Ahmed were still alive. I'll become Samir's advisor instead.'

Nobody said a word.

'Maybe,' Majed started, 'when you see me in my rightful role, you won't be reminded so strongly of the son you lost. Maybe then you'll find peace.'

Sarah shot forward. 'Your rightful place is as your father's heir!' She hadn't known she believed those words until she'd uttered them.

Rasheed lowered himself to an armchair as if his legs would no longer hold him. Sarah dropped to her knees in front of him and gripped his hand. 'I know you love Majed.'

He met her gaze but she didn't understand the heartbreak reflected in his face.

'Your son has taught me a lot this past month about finding my courage.'

He sent her a half-smile. 'You think I lack courage, my dear?'

'I think your heart has been broken and it hasn't mended yet.' Her eyes filled. 'Majed would mend it for you if he could,' she whispered.

Rasheed nodded as if he knew that.

Sarah had no idea how to help mend it either. Her knees hurt. Her back hurt. Her heart hurt. 'What would Ahmed say to you at this moment?'

She rose and took a step back. 'What words of comfort or wisdom would he offer you? What advice would he give?' She gripped her hands together. 'Who would *he* choose to take his place?'

The silence became so deep, Sarah thought she might drown in it. 'I'm sorry,' she finally managed, their white faces spearing into her. 'I had no right to say anything. Please forgive me.'

Majed drew her to his side. 'You're a part of this family now. You have every right to speak up. The decisions we make now will affect you and our child's life and destiny.'

Rasheed's head came up at the word 'destiny'. 'Ahmed would have chosen you to take his place, Majed.'

She could feel the tension crackle from Majed. 'Are you sure about that, sir? Because I'm not.'

Her jaw dropped.

And then Majed turned on his heel and strode from the room.

After three panicked beats of her heart, Sarah swung back to Aisha and Rasheed. 'Will you please excuse me?' she said, before scurrying after Majed.

She caught up with him in the long corridor that led towards the private apartments.

'Not now, Sarah.'

Yes, now, but she didn't say the words out loud. Instead,

she faked a cough and pressed a hand to her stomach. 'Will you be a gentleman and see me back to my room?'

He pulled to a halt and glared at her, so she faked another cough for good measure.

'That is not convincing. You're aware of that, no?'

She didn't say anything and eventually he shook his head, but the lines that tightened his mouth eased a fraction. 'You won't be able to make me laugh today, Sarah. So, pray, don't even try.'

She slipped an arm through his and turned him right at the end of the corridor towards her rooms, instead of letting him go in the other direction. 'We're in this together, remember, Majed.'

'That doesn't mean either one of us will not desire solitude from time to time.'

'You can have your solitude in due course, just not right at this moment.'

They'd entered her sitting room but she didn't release him. He glanced at their linked arms and then raised an eyebrow.

'Are you going to run away the moment I let you go?'

His nostrils flared. 'Of course not.'

She let him go and he strode across the room to pour her a glass of water. 'For the tickle in your throat,' he said with a wry twist of his lips.

She sipped it and tried to think of a way to ask him non-confrontationally what he'd meant back there with Rasheed.

'You want to know why I said I'm far from convinced that Ahmed would choose me to take his place.'

She coughed for real this time. She hastily set her glass down and nodded.

'And I'll get no rest until I tell you want I meant, is this right?'

She shrugged. 'Pretty much.'

His chest rose and fell. 'You'll make me say the words out loud?'

Dear God! The expression in his eyes—the pain in them—raked through her. She went to him and pressed her hand to his heart. 'Majed?'

'He betrayed me, Sarah. He knew how I felt about Fatima and yet he still…'

She ached for him.

'I've tried to forgive him. The price he paid far exceeded the crime but…but it doesn't change the fact that he betrayed me—*his own brother*!'

His hand covered hers, his eyes dark and full of confusion. 'He didn't choose me then, and I cannot see that he'd choose me now.'

He peeled her hand away. 'And why should it matter so much still anyway?'

With those words he strode towards the door. His figure blurred as she stared after him. 'Because you still love him.'

He halted and she could almost physically see him count to three before he spun back round. He strode back to her and gripped her shoulders. 'I sent him to his doom! I'm responsible for the misfortune that has befallen my family. How can I possibly take his place with that knowledge weighing on my heart?'

He'd have whirled away again except she captured his face in her hands. 'That's not true. Ahmed made his own choices the day he died. They were poor choices on more than one level. You're entitled to your anger and disappointment, but the fact you still love him—that his opinion still matters to you—tells me he must've been a good man.'

Tears fell down Majed's cheeks unchecked. Her throat thickened and her eyes filled.

'Majed, that makes me think he'd have been truly sorry to have hurt you. It makes me think he'd have sought your forgiveness if he'd lived.'

Anger, pain and despair all warred in his face.

'The two of you were deceived by a clever but wicked woman. Isn't it time you forgave him for that? Isn't it time you forgave yourself?' She pulled in a breath. 'If your positions were reversed, wouldn't Ahmed forgive you?'

CHAPTER TEN

IF THEIR POSITIONS were reversed…?

Majed stared at Sarah. His chest rose and fell, a band tightening about it. He'd have never betrayed Ahmed with a woman. *Never!*

What if Ahmed had met Sarah first?

His hands clenched and unclenched and a shout of pure, possessive outrage boiled up inside him.

'What if Ahmed had brought home a girl who tempted you beyond all reason? What if she let slip that, while she respected your brother, she wasn't really happy…that she didn't love him? What if all her words and actions made you think she had an overwhelming desire for you? Would you have done nothing?'

He stared at Sarah and a chasm opened up before his feet. He couldn't recall the power of his passion for Fatima. Not any more. It had been swallowed by pain—the pain of Ahmed's betrayal, and the utter devastation of Ahmed's death. But the desire he had for Sarah burned like an all-consuming flame through him now. An irrational part of his brain told him he'd kill anyone who touched her.

It's because she carries your child.

Was it?

He took a step away from her, finding it hard to breathe.

'Majed?'

'What you say is true.' He had to force himself to speak,

but as he did the resentment that had festered in his chest for the last four years started to drain away. And he let it. He gave thanks for it. He didn't want to hold onto it. He wanted to remember the Ahmed he'd laughed and schemed with…the brother he'd loved with all his heart.

'I can see now how Fatima manipulated us both. Such passion is dangerous.' He took another step away from her. 'It's why I'll never again allow such a passion in my life.'

She took a step towards him but he held up a hand to tell her to keep her distance. Her frown deepened. 'Love doesn't have to be destructive.'

He wasn't taking that risk.

'It's high time I forgave Ahmed. You're right about that. It's been weak and foolish of me to hold onto my sense of injury for so long.'

'You've been neither weak nor foolish!'

Her voice was sharp but he was too busy building a wall about himself—a wall to contain the uncomfortable feelings she roused in him—to heed it.

'What about yourself?'

'What do you mean?'

Her eyes flashed. 'You've forgiven Ahmed. Will you now forgive yourself?'

For introducing a viper into his family's nest? Never!

She folded her arms and glared. She could glare all she liked but she couldn't change the past or undo the mistakes he'd made.

'So…' Her hands slammed to her hips. 'If your father felt responsible for this incident with Fatima, you'd want him wracked with guilt, to lash himself with blame for the rest of his life?'

He'd started to turn away, wanting to escape from her and her too-difficult questions and demands, to escape the far too simple demands of his body, but he swung back now. 'You talk nonsense! My father is in no way responsible.'

She thrust out her chin, her eyes flashing. 'He's the senior member of your family, isn't he? He sees it as his duty to protect you all.'

His mouth dried. *No!*

'It was *his* palace security that failed.'

Majed's heart thumped.

'How old were you, Majed—twenty-five? Your father was a vigorous fifty-nine-year-old who had more experience of politics, rebels and women than either you or your brother. What if he feels he should've protected you better?'

'That is not true! He has always been the best of men and the best of fathers!' The words bellowed from him. 'He has nothing to reproach himself for. Do you hear me? *Nothing!*'

'I know.'

Her soft voice filtered through the tempest roaring through him. He stilled and met those clear blue eyes. 'You do?'

'He has nothing to blame himself for, Majed, and neither do you.'

His heart thumped and pain radiated from his chest. 'I don't wish to speak about this any more today.'

She stared at him for a long moment. That damned lock of hair did that beguiling almost-falling-into-her-eyes thing and he had to bite back a groan. 'Okay,' she finally whispered.

He pulled in another breath. He couldn't leave her with such fraught words simmering between them. 'I'm glad beyond words that you've agreed to marry me.'

The smallest of smiles touched her lips. 'You're such a big, fat liar. At the moment you're wishing me to the blazes. I expect *glad beyond words* is far too strong for this particular moment. But, I know you were glad. And I know you'll be glad about it again.' She lifted a shoulder and let it drop. 'I can live with that.'

Miraculously, some of the knots inside him loosened.

How did she do that? Without giving himself time to think, he seized her shoulders and pressed a kiss to her forehead. 'Thank you.'

Her quick intake of breath speared straight to his groin. And he released her—fast.

She moistened her lips. 'We're going to fight sometimes. You know that, right?'

He took a careful step away from her and considered her words. 'When we feel we're in the right, neither one of us wants to give way.'

She blew out a breath. 'Just as long as you haven't deluded yourself into thinking you're gaining yourself a restful wife.'

He found himself laughing. 'No, *habibi*, I haven't. A restful wife wouldn't suit me. Besides, it'll be fun to make up after our spats.'

'I'm counting on it.'

She waggled deliberately provocative eyebrows at him and that made him laugh anew. He took another step away from her. 'I must go now.'

She nodded but he felt her eyes follow him as he left the room. He left with a lighter heart than he could've thought possible. And with much to ponder.

Still, it was all he could do not to sweep back into her room and kiss her soundly.

A week later they held the betrothal ball. Majed wore traditional robes that bore the royal insignia in blue and silver. A scimitar in a gilded scabbard set with precious gems hung at his side.

His breath snagged when he caught his first sight of Sarah for the evening.

His. His. His. The word drummed through him in a possessive tattoo.

The traditional tunic that Arras, the master artisan, had

made especially for the occasion flowed over Sarah's body in a fall of silken temptation that had him curling his hands into fists. A headdress of precious gems and gold rested against her hair and a ruby the size of a walnut dangled low on her forehead, making her look exotic, unfamiliar... and utterly desirable.

Her eyes went satisfyingly round when she saw him, making his breath jam in his chest. It was her smile, though, that speared him. It was more beautiful than the ruby on her brow.

He lifted her hands to his lips, kissing both of them, letting his lips linger against her soft flesh. She smelled of honey and lavender. 'All the men of my country will envy me when they see you.'

'You...' Her breath hitched as she surveyed him. 'You look amazing, Majed. The single women of Keddah Jaleel will be in mourning that you're no longer eligible.'

She stood in the reception line beside him and welcomed the invited dignitaries and guests who came to congratulate them, charming them all with her warmth and her attempts to speak in Arabic. He hadn't even known she'd been having language lessons! She kept up a *sotto voce* commentary that had him biting back inappropriate laughter, but her grip on his arm betrayed her nervousness.

'You're doing brilliantly,' he assured her. 'Everyone is enchanted.'

'You great big fibber. It's obvious that the jury is still out in some quarters.'

He followed her gaze to the three older gentlemen standing on the other side of the room, all heads of important Keddah Jaleely families. 'We'll win over Omar and Youssef eventually but nothing we do will win Hamza's acceptance.'

She turned that clear blue gaze to him, one eyebrow raised, and he shrugged. 'Back before I was born, Hamza had great hopes that his sister would marry my father. Their family is an old one and the match would have been politically savvy.'

'But your father married Aisha instead. And they've been very happy.'

He squeezed her hand. 'We will be happy too.'

'Of course.'

But her voice wobbled and he gazed at her sharply. 'Come, you should rest for a bit.'

'Oh, but surely that'd be rude and—'

'Nonsense.'

After a quick word with his mother, he bore Sarah off to an empty antechamber and made her sit and drink a glass of the pomegranate juice she'd grown so fond of. 'Not having second thoughts, are you, *habibi*?' He'd do whatever was necessary to reassure her, to quieten her fears and doubts.

'Of course not!'

Her shock calmed the burning in his chest.

'I find being in the spotlight nerve-racking, that's all. Public engagements intimidate me.'

'They'll get easier,' he promised, taking the seat beside her.

She sent him a shaky smile. 'I hope very much you're right about that. Aisha has said the same.'

She'd spoken to his mother about this? He leaned towards her. 'You're truly worried about appearing in public?'

'Doh!' She rolled her eyes but she smiled as she did so. 'You've been born to all of this. I know I'm going to make mistakes and…'

'And?'

'And I don't want them to reflect badly on you. I'm… I'm not used to this level of attention.'

And she didn't like it. The revelation disturbed him. He'd been focussing on all the good things he could give her, the life of luxury she could live if she married him, without considering the sacrifices she'd also have to make.

She shrugged. 'There's a price to be paid for having such a privileged life, and I'll do my best not to let you down.' She drained her glass and started to rise. 'Come, we should get back out there and—'

He pulled her back down beside him. 'You'll have lots of help, Sarah, and you won't have to take on the Sheikha role for many years yet. You'll have the opportunity to grow comfortable in the role.'

She sat back, evidently recognising the worry in his face. 'I know that too. It's why I'm still here. The thought of being Sheikha filled me with fear at first—especially when I realised all that the role entailed.' She glanced down at her hands. 'I don't have a great track record when it comes to holding down a job, so even considering taking on the role seems a cheek.'

'But?'

She glanced up. 'But if I get the chance to follow my design dream...'

'Which you will.'

'Well, that gives me strength.' She frowned. 'And a measure of confidence. If I can be good at that, then maybe I can be good at...at other things. The fact is I'd sacrifice a lot to follow my dream.'

His heart thumped. She was sacrificing a lot.

'You've made that possible for me. It only seems fair that I do what I can to help make your dream come true too. You've the right to follow in your father's footsteps.'

'And you've made that possible for me.'

Taking his hand, she held it against the gentle swell of her stomach. 'This baby has made it possible—for the both of us.'

His hand curved protectively about her. And then he froze, his gaze spearing to hers. She laughed. 'Did you feel that? It was the baby kicking. I believe he or she agrees with me.'

He couldn't speak and she rested her hand over his. 'Majed, instead of running away, I've decided to face my fears and fight for the life I want. It won't always be easy, but I'm aware of that…and you should be too. Please stop worrying that I'm going to change my mind. I'm not having second thoughts. I promise.'

He wondered if he'd ever wanted any woman more than he wanted her in that moment.

She started to laugh then pressed a hand to the centre of his chest and pushed him gently back. 'Oh, no, you don't! You're *not* going to ruin my lipstick. Not tonight.'

So he told her in a rush of Arabic exactly what he wished to do with her. And what he'd do once they were married.

Her eyes widened and her breath quickened. 'You'… I only understood about a fifth of what you just said but… you're a wicked man, Majed.'

He laughed and took her hand to lead her back out into the grand reception room, pleased with the renewed colour in her cheeks and the sparkle in her eyes.

Majed glanced up from his desk when a knock sounded on the door. He always kept the door to his office partially ajar when not in a private conference. His father's aide stood there, his face grim. Majed motioned him in.

'Your father would like to see you.'

'When?'

'Immediately.'

Majed did his best to hide his surprise. His father rarely requested to see him—their meetings, summits and conferences were all arranged well in advance and entered into Majed's diary by efficient secretaries.

He logged out of his computer and rose, his senses sharpening when the grim expression on the aide's face didn't abate. What on earth…? Was something wrong? He knew better than to question the man—his loyalty to Rasheed was absolute and his adherence to palace protocols unshakeable.

He entered his father's library, the aide close at his heels. A sense of dread settled in his chest when he saw his father was alone. 'What's the matter?' Fear clenched his gut tight. 'Sarah...?'

'Sarah is well. This has nothing to do with her. Please sit.'

The sense of relief didn't last. The expression on his father's face chilled Majed's heart. 'Abii?' *Father?*

'There's no easy way to convey this news to you, Majed. There has been a sighting.'

Rasheed broke off to drag a hand down his face. Majed leaned towards him. 'Of...?'

'Fatima.'

He couldn't move. He couldn't speak. His heart pounded so hard he thought it might burst.

'We thought she was dead, yes,' Rasheed continued, as if he could read the questions burning in Majed's mind. 'But her body was never discovered.'

They'd thought she'd died, caught in the crossfire between the rebels and the Keddah Jaleel special force that had put down the insurrection. The military had searched the rubble and caves for her body but it had never been found.

'What does she want?' His voice didn't sound as though it belonged to him.

Rasheed's mouth whitened. On his desk his hands clenched to fists. 'Intelligence believes she wants revenge on you.'

On him? He shot to his feet. 'She's the one who led my brother to his death! If anyone wants revenge it should be me.'

Rasheed stared at him stonily, as if frozen. 'When our

forces crushed the uprising, her husband and brother both lost their lives.'

Majed fell back into his chair. Against his father's wishes, he'd led those forces. He swallowed. 'She was married?'

His father gave a heavy nod.

Dear God. He and her, they'd… He swallowed. 'This woman is unstable.'

Rasheed met Majed's eyes. 'And very, *very* dangerous.'

The blood pounded in his ears. If she wanted revenge on him, then there was every chance that she'd target Sarah. Fear almost immobilised him, cramping his chest and gut. 'Sarah must leave.' The words croaked from him. 'We have to get her out of Keddah Jaleel.'

'You must try and think clearly! Sarah will be safest here in the palace. So will you.'

No! He had no intention of hiding in the palace. He meant to find the woman and wring her neck with his bare hands! 'The palace is *not* safe. Fatima infiltrated it once before. I don't doubt that she could do so again.'

'Majed, I—'

He slammed to his feet, his heart burning and his throat constricting. 'She won't go after Sarah if she believes our engagement to be broken.' She'd go after him instead.

Rasheed's gasp sounded loud in the deathly quiet of the room. 'You cannot do that! You'll shame both her and yourself in the eyes of our people.'

He didn't care. He'd suffer any indignity to keep Sarah safe. He'd suffer any fate. The thought of losing her, of Sarah no longer being in the world… He couldn't stand it!

His father surged to his feet. 'This is madness! She will not go. She is committed to you. She is committed to Keddah Jaleel.'

'She won't go if she knows the truth.' He knew that in the very marrow of his bones. Sarah had her flaws but she was brave—she'd stare danger in the eye and would do what she could to defeat it. He cared for her and their child passionately, and he feared he'd allow his compulsive need for her to cloud his judgement.

He muttered a curse and started to pace. Such need was too dangerous for a man in his position. It put people at risk—people such as Sarah and the baby.

He swung back to glare at the other two men in the room. 'But we will not tell her the truth. Do you understand me?' He met the men's gazes individually. 'Not a single whisper of this is to reach her ears. Do you hear me?'

He trembled with the force of his emotions but could do nothing to contain them. Rasheed finally gave a heavy nod and his advisor followed suit.

Majed let out a breath, some of the tension easing out of him. He'd ensure that Sarah and the baby were safe. 'Leave it to me. I know exactly how to make Sarah leave.'

It wouldn't be pretty, but it would be better than Sarah dying at a crazed woman's hand.

And the sooner he did it, the better. Without another word he strode from his father's library, his heart growing heavier with every step.

'Sarah!'

Sarah swung round from where she and the women of the female quarters were enjoying a gossipy morning tea. They were bringing her up to date on the political leanings of many of the people she'd met on the night of the betrothal ball. Along with their bad habits, the skeletons in their closets and their secret ambitions.

From what she could tell, no one in Keddah Jaleel had a secret they could call their own.

The smile of welcome that sprang to her lips wavered when she saw the expression on Majed's face. Good Lord!

What on earth could be wrong? One of the women beside her murmured what sounded like a prayer.

Sarah stood.

'May I have a word?'

The words snapped from him, short and clipped. Without a word, she followed him from the room, automatically searching her mind for some palace protocol she might've breached in the last few days. She'd been so careful!

She glanced at him and something cold touched her heart. In Arabic, she said, 'Majed, you look so grim.'

Startled eyes met hers. 'Your Arabic is improving.' He spoke in his native tongue too.

'Shukraan.' Thank you. 'My pronunciation is getting better. I need others to speak slowly to catch what they're saying, but I'm finally starting to believe it'll come and that one day I might be fluent.'

His lips pressed together into a thin line. She didn't understand. Normally he'd be pleased, would congratulate her on her progress. Something weighed heavily on his mind. She'd love to make him laugh—just for a moment—to help lighten his load.

She glanced at him again from the corner of her eye. 'Mind you, we won't mention my written Arabic. Still, I love looking at the script. It's very beautiful, but my tutor keeps telling me it's not aesthetic appreciation he wants from me.' She gave an exaggerated shrug of self-deprecation. 'What on earth could he mean, I wonder?'

Nothing. *Nada. Diddly-squat.*

'If I could find a way to communicate the written word via my sewing machine, I expect it'd make everyone's lives easier.'

He led her to her suite of rooms and then swung to her with a frown. 'I'm sorry?'

He hadn't heard a word she'd been saying! She swallowed. 'It was nothing important.' She sat because she had a feeling she'd need to sit for this conversation.

Majed poured her a glass of iced water and set it on the coffee table…and then paced.

Sarah ignored the water. 'Will you tell me what's on your mind?'

'I'm trying to find the words.' He swung back briefly, his eyes hooded. 'I don't wish to hurt your feelings. I want to give you as little pain as possible.'

'Oh, this sounds promising.' She folded her arms but it did nothing to allay the dread that settled in her stomach.

He sat and went to take her hand but she tugged it free and moved further down the sofa away from him, until she was wedged tight against its corner. 'I don't want you to touch me, not when you look at me like that.' *As if he pitied her.*

'As you wish.'

She could barely believe it when he moved away from her to the sofa opposite. This had the classic hallmarks of a break-up scene. But…that couldn't be possible, surely? They were going to be married in two weeks!

'There's been more political backlash than we expected at my choice of bride. Certain parties are bringing more pressure to bear on my father than we expected.'

'But you both foresaw this would happen.'

'Not to this extent.'

She tried to beat back the panic that wanted to seize hold of her. 'You said Rasheed's rule was strong, that it could withstand a certain amount of disapproval.'

He swung out of his seat to pace again, his face twisting in…fury. Her heart cramped so suddenly it was all she could do to keep breathing. Was he furious with her because…she was questioning him?

'My father is unwell. I don't want him taxed with having to fight this particular fight. It now appears I'll have to take on the role of ruling sheikh sooner than expected.'

She shot to her feet. 'Oh, Majed, I'm so sorry! Is there anything I can do?'

Agonised eyes met hers. 'Go quietly.'

It took a moment for the import of his words to sink in. She sank back to the sofa, her legs shaking too hard to support her. 'Are you…? You're breaking off our engagement?' It took all her courage to ask the question.

He couldn't meet her eyes and maybe that hurt worst of all.

'Yes.'

Acid burned her throat. 'So in the end you choose your kingdom over your child?'

He loved this child. She knew he did.

'My father needs me.' His hands clenched. 'And a man in my position must be prepared to make sacrifices.'

'And what about when this child needs you?' She pressed a hand to her stomach. His eyes followed the movement. 'You promised me friendship and…and respect.' She'd believed him… 'That was all lies?'

He slashed a hand through the air. 'You'll want for nothing. The child will want for nothing. You have my word.'

The child. No longer *our* child.

'Your word means nothing!' She surged to her feet. 'That's neither respect nor friendship. It's simply you doing your paternal duty and nothing more. It's what any man should do.'

She strode around the coffee table until she stood toe to toe with him. 'You love this child, I know you do, but now you mean to deny it?' If he wanted to be ruler he couldn't admit to having an illegitimate child. It would outrage his people.

Rasheed's words came back to her. *You cannot deny him his child. It will kill him.*

She swallowed and tried to rein in her pain and fear. 'If your father needs to step down then couldn't you...couldn't Samir step into the role? I know it means you wouldn't be ruler, but you'd be a trusted advisor. You'd still have a privileged role leading Keddah Jaleel into the future...and you'd get to keep your child!'

He didn't have to marry her but he could still have a relationship with their child. Surely that was better than the alternative?

'Samir doesn't want to be ruler.' He stared at her with pitiless eyes. 'And why should his life be ruined as well?'

He meant marrying her would ruin his life. Colour leached from the edges of her vision. She retreated to the window and concentrated on pulling in one deep breath after another.

'Your instinct about your unsuitability as Sheikha was, as ever, unerring. I should've heeded it. I'm sorry.'

Flake. Disappointment. Failure. The accusations speared into her. It was obvious she'd been living in Cloud Cuckoo Land. Had she seriously thought she could measure up to the demands that would come with being the wife of such an important man?

'I know I've disappointed you.'

How she hated that voice—so smooth, calm and rational.

'All I can do is tell you I'm sincerely sorry. But, Sarah, this was never a love match. Your pride has been hurt, perhaps, but your heart remains intact.'

She turned at that and lifted her chin. 'Is that what you think, Majed?' She made her voice as pitying as she could. 'Then you'd be wrong. You might have your heart under lock and key, but I'm much freer and more generous with mine.'

He paled. His hands clenched and unclenched.

'The only reason I agreed to marry you—the *only* reason—is because I love you.' She gave a short laugh

that nearly choked her. 'You once accused me of cow-
ardice but what an act of courage that was—you'll have
to agree—to consent to marry a man who I knew didn't
love me back. I never realised I could be so...*optimistic*.'

If possible the lines about his mouth went even whiter,
stark in his tanned face.

'I won't let you off the hook that easily. My baby and I
will be perfectly fine without you in our lives, but I refuse
to allow you to operate under the misapprehension that you
haven't hurt us, because you have—deeply.'

He stood there frozen, his nostrils flaring and his hands
clenched at his sides. 'There are no words to convey the
depths of my sorrow at having caused you such pain.'

At least none that he was prepared to utter out loud. She
simply raised an eyebrow—a show of bravado. 'Evidently.'

'I'll make your travel arrangements.'

She turned away to stare down into the serene courtyard below. If he thought she'd thank him for saving her
the trouble of making the arrangements, he was very much
mistaken. When she finally turned back, he was gone.

She pressed one hand to her heart, the other curved
about her stomach. She couldn't think. All she could do
was feel. And she didn't want to! Pain scored through her
as if a thousand whips flayed her heart. The taste of blood
filled her mouth, as her teeth clamped down on her lips to
bite back the cries that rose through her. How was it possible to feel so much? How could she bear it?

'Sarah!'

Sarah came back to herself to find Aisha gently shaking
her arm. She still stood at the window. The shadows of the
courtyard had shifted and lengthened. How long had she
been standing here—an hour...maybe more?

'Come.' Aisha led her to a seat and pressed a glass of

water into her hand. 'Drink, please. You must think of the baby.'

Oh, yes! She couldn't fall ill. She wouldn't allow her heartbreak to harm her baby's health. She drank the entire glass of water in three gulps. 'I'm sorry, I…'

What could she say—*your son has broken my heart and I'm in shock*? Aisha was his *mother*.

Aisha's eyes narrowed. 'What did Majed say to you? What has he done? I've not been able to get near either Rasheed or Majed all afternoon. They've locked themselves away in meetings.'

She pulled in a breath and told herself to not cry—it would only upset Aisha. 'Majed has broken off our engagement. I'm to return home to Australia.' Except Australia didn't feel like home any more. Nowhere felt like home.

Aisha rattled off an angry spate of exhortation in her native tongue. 'My son…he is a fool! He loves you and yet he tries to send you away. Why does he do this?'

'He doesn't love me, Aisha. He never did. But I know he loves this baby.'

'Pah, this is nonsense of which you speak. Tell me everything my son said to you.'

She stared into her now empty glass, tapping her index fingers against it. *Fight for the life you want.*

She lifted her gaze to Aisha's. 'You really think Majed loves me?'

'Of course he loves you. It's in his eyes when he looks at you. It's in his every action—though I do not know if he is aware of it himself. He has been frightened of love since that wicked Fatima.'

Sarah's fingers curved into claws. If she were ever to come face to face with the other woman, she'd quite cheerfully scratch her eyes out.

'But you are unsure of his love for you and this is why you let him send you away.'

She'd started to think that, given time, Majed might start to feel something deeper for her. But, that aside, she knew how much he wanted to be a part of his child's life and…

That could *not* have changed so comprehensively.

Aisha shook her head. 'And this is why you do not put up a fight.'

Sarah shifted on the sofa to face Aisha squarely. 'You just said he *tries* to send me away.' She moistened her lips. 'Are you saying that, if I don't want to go, he can't make me?'

Aisha's shoulders went back and her chin came up. 'He is not supreme ruler yet. And I can assure you, my dear Sarah, that the current supreme ruler will *not* dare countermand me on this.'

Her confidence and outrage almost made Sarah laugh.

'Now come, tell me all that Majed said.'

So she told her, finishing with, 'I'm sorry that Rasheed is not well.'

'Pah! It is nonsense. Rasheed has been living too much of the high life, but he is as fit as a fiddle. His gall bladder was removed earlier in the year, but he has recovered beautifully. He is a very vigorous man still, I assure you.'

Sarah's cheeks warmed when she realised exactly what Aisha meant. Aisha patted Sarah's hand with a laugh. 'Just as his son is vigorous…and virile.'

Dear Lord! Where to look?

'But there is something else at work here.'

Like what? If Majed and Rasheed weren't frightened for their country or their rule, what had them so spooked?

'And these men—' Aisha waved her hand through the air '—they think that they can organise the world according to their whim, expect it to run according to their demands and design. Well, they cannot rule us.' She fixed Sarah with her dark eyes. 'Do you have the courage to fight, Sarah?'

Her mouth went dry. Majed didn't want her. And she

had no intention of begging him for his love. That would be… It would be too humiliating!

But he did love the life growing inside her. Only a very strong fear would have him sending his child away.

She pressed her fingertips to her temples. Was she just trying to find excuses to make his rejection hurt less? 'Your son doesn't think I can make a suitable Sheikha.'

'What do *you* think?'

Her fears pounded at her. *Failure. Hopeless. Flake.*

But she lifted her head. Majed had deliberately played on her deepest fears. He'd said things deliberately to distance her. Why would he do that?

There was a mystery here and she needed to solve it.

Did she dare…?

Her heart pounded and her mouth went dry. She loved Majed. If he truly wanted to turn his back on her and their child, then she'd leave. But first she had to make sure.

She lifted her chin. 'I think I could make a fine Sheikha.'

'Bravo.'

Sarah reached out and clasped the other woman's hand. 'Aisha, I have a plan—but I'm going to need your help.'

CHAPTER ELEVEN

'What the hell do you think you're doing?'

Majed stormed into Sarah's bedroom. It was all he could do not to step forward, throw her over his shoulder and toss her onto a plane himself. Slamming his hands to his hips, he glared at her. She glanced round from the suitcase open on her bed, not looking the least perturbed at his martial tone. That damned lock of hair fell forward, brushing her cheek, making him want to reach out and touch it…touch her.

She gestured to the suitcase as if what she was doing was self-evident. 'Packing.'

His entire body started to shake. 'To go home to Australia?' The words growled out of him in a voice he didn't recognise. They'd been supposed to emerge as a command. Instead they sounded more like a question.

She sent him a look of such pity it made him want to shake and hug her at the same time. 'Don't play the fool, Majed. It doesn't suit you.'

The fool? He started to shake even harder.

'Your mother rang not two minutes ago.'

No doubt to warn her he was on the warpath.

'So I know you're aware of our plan.'

'She's a treacherous—'

He broke off at the glare she sent him. Anger would evidently get him nowhere. He drew himself up to his full imposing height. Thrusting out his jaw, he forced a coldness into his eyes and voice that he was far from feeling. 'I forbid it.'

She stared at him…and then she started to laugh. *To laugh!*

'You've met my mother. Do you honestly think she raised me to put up with nonsense like that? Oh, if only she were here now. She'd have a field day with you.'

She straightened and stuck out one hip. It drew his attention to the shape of her…to her lush curves and the delights her body held. The need to sweep her up in his arms, to kiss her and make love to her, nearly overcame him. But if he did that she'd know—she'd know how he felt about her—and then she'd never leave. *It would put her in danger.*

That was why this kind of passion was so dangerous. It flouted all reason and common sense. Sarah *had* to leave. There was no other way to keep her safe. He would not allow his passion for her to endanger her further than it already had.

'I'm sorry, Majed, but the moment you broke off our engagement you lost any right to make demands of me— reasonable or otherwise.'

She flipped the lid of her suitcase closed and zipped it up before glancing at her watch. 'You don't have to marry me—that's your right. But you've no right to tell me where I can live or what I can do. You've shown me that I can have a wonderful life in Keddah Jaleel.'

She shrugged. And smiled. *Smiled!*

'I don't have to be married to you to study design and textiles under Arras. I can live here in Keddah Jaleel and give my child a thorough grounding in his or her Keddah Jaleely heritage. We can holiday in Australia. It appears, Majed, that I can have it all.'

But what if Fatima got to her? They couldn't risk it!

He straightened, stiffening every muscle. She'd said she loved him. It would be a dastardly card to play… But her

172   SARAH AND THE SECRET SHEIKH

safety was paramount—it was his only priority—and he'd stoop as low as he had to. 'And what about me? You said you cared for me.'

She went to lift her suitcase to the ground but he stepped forward, brushed her aside and did it for her. 'You shouldn't be lifting anything heavy. It's not good for the baby.'

She sent him an odd look—an assessing look—and then nodded, as if satisfied about something. 'Then I'd be grateful if you placed it by the door.' And then she swept past him, out of her bedroom and into the sitting room. 'As for what about you, Majed, I expect you can have it all too. You can marry some Arabian princess that your people will endorse.'

He didn't want to marry an Arabian princess. He wanted to marry Sarah!

Sweep her into your arms. Tell her you love her. You can find another way to keep her safe.

What other way? Marrying him would place her in danger and he wouldn't allow that.

'And you can be supreme ruler of Keddah Jaleel, be king of all you survey and live a blessed life.'

He didn't want a blessed life. He wanted…

If he turned his back on Keddah Jaleel, would Fatima still want her revenge? He squared his shoulders. It wasn't a chance he was prepared to take. Sarah's life was too precious to risk as a stake in such a dangerous game.

'That won't happen once word gets around that my mistress has borne a child out of wedlock.'

'Aisha is confident we can hush that up.'

'You're a fool if you believe that. You want to revenge yourself on me! You want to dash my hopes. I don't know why it should surprise me. After all, it was the way you were raised.'

Her head reared back and he knew he'd scored a point, but it gave him no pleasure.

'I don't see it'll make any difference where I live. You still mean to deny your child. I'll lie for you publicly. So you don't need to fear—your reputation will remain intact.'

'I don't care about my reputation!' He roared the words, fear making his extremities throb.

She came to stand in front of him, her blue gaze unwavering. 'Then what is this about? Would you care to tell me the truth?'

If he told her the truth, she'd stay.

He made his voice ice-cold. 'It's about not being constantly reminded of a mistake that I'd prefer to forget.'

Her quick intake of breath speared into his heart. *I'm sorry,* habibi. *I'm sorry, my love.*

'Cruelty isn't your style, Majed. It doesn't suit you any better than stupidity.' She turned away and wound a scarf—a scrap of sheer chiffon—about her neck. 'Demal is a large city. I doubt our paths need ever cross.' She glanced again at her watch. 'If you'll excuse me, my driver is here.'

What on earth…? She couldn't go to his mother's villa! It was on the other side of the city. He shoved his shoulders back. 'I may not be able to force you to leave Keddah Jaleel, but my father can.'

Her answering laugh infuriated him.

'Good luck with that. He'll have to get through Aisha first, and I don't like his chances. Goodbye, Majed.'

She didn't even offer him her hand.

And then she was gone.

It took two hours before Majed could see his father. His father's aides had to physically restrain him from breaking in on the delicate negotiations Rasheed had been involved in with the delegates from a neighbouring nation. But, when Rasheed was finally back in his office, Majed stormed in and, ignoring everyone else in the room, slammed a fist to the desk. 'You must banish Sarah from Keddah Jaleel! You must have her deported to Australia! She must leave!'

Rasheed stared into Majed's face and then with a few quiet words dismissed everyone else from the room. He motioned to a chair. 'Sit!'

Majed didn't want to sit, but the expression on his father's face had him biting back his anger and planting himself on the chair. 'Has there been news of Fatima?'

'Not yet. I've ordered a dozen men from the special forces unit to be placed around the perimeter of your mother's villa.'

'Have you told her about Fatima?'

The older man hesitated. 'I didn't want to stir up bad memories. She's suffered enough on account of that woman.'

Majed dragged in a breath. 'You could stop this all now if you sent Sarah home.'

Rasheed rested his head in his hands. When he lifted it again, the fine lines fanning from his eyes had deepened. Majed's heart started to pound. His father looked so...tired.

Rasheed lifted his chin but his sigh sounded about the room. 'Do either of us have the right to make that decision for her?'

'It'll keep her safe!'

'But it will make her unhappy.'

He couldn't deny it...

'How would you feel, Majed, if someone made that decision for you? Would you not be outraged? Would you be able to forgive it?'

Something in his father's voice had a cold hand tightening about his heart. 'What are you talking about?'

'Did you not wonder why I sent you away when Ahmed was killed?'

Acid burned the back of his throat. 'You said it was for my own safety. You said I had to leave to save my mother from more fear and worry. When you didn't ask me to return, when you didn't *speak* to me, I believed it was because you held me responsible for Ahmed's death.'

The older man shook his head heavily. 'I never held you responsible, Majed. It was my fault that palace security was breached.'

'That's not true!'

'Before Ahmed's death, I'd never really understood how dangerous it was to be the son of the ruling sheikh. Oh, I understood it academically, but it had never felt real until that moment. And I knew then that the danger and fear would be present forever. I understood that you were also in danger.'

Majed's heart gave a sickening kick in his chest. 'You... you sent me away and encouraged me to stay away because...'

No. His father would not be cruel enough to let him think he blamed him for Ahmed's murder.

'Because I was afraid of what would happen to you otherwise? Yes. I couldn't face the thought of losing you the same way I had lost Ahmed.'

Majed surged out of his chair. The world no longer felt solid beneath his feet. He lurched from one side of the room to the other. 'But Keddah Jaleel is my home. It's where I belong.'

Rasheed's shoulders drooped, as if a heavy weight pressed down on them.

'I...I thought you blamed me for everything!'

Those shoulders sunk further. 'I know.'

He fell back into his seat, not believing what he was hearing. 'How could you let me go on believing that?'

'I considered it a small price to pay in return for your safety.'

'*Small?* I—' Blood thundered in his ears.

'Your Sarah, although she's not aware of it, made me see

how wrong I was. She made me realise I was placing *my* need to keep you safe above *your* happiness. I told myself that you would suffer in the short term but would become reconciled to it all eventually and live a full and long life. And, son...' he met Majed's gaze '...I want that life for you more than anything. But... I placed the demands of my own heart above yours. I'm only starting to see now how wrong that was. I am truly sorry, Majed. I do not know if you will ever be able to forgive me.'

There could be no denying his father's sincerity. He leapt up again, the agitation coursing through him demanding an outlet. 'I... A year ago I'd have stormed out of here and... and I don't know when I'd have spoken to you again.' *If ever.* 'But now that I have a child of my own on the way—' now that he had Sarah '—I'm starting to understand the power of fears I'd not considered before.'

He went to his father and embraced him. 'I forgive you, Bábá. But if you ever do anything like that again...'

Rasheed hugged him back. 'I am glad to have you at my side once again, Majed. You may rest assured that I will never again interfere in your destiny in such a way.'

A weight lifted from Majed—a weight he'd been carrying for four years—making him feel both freer and stronger.

'But...' Rasheed pulled back and met Majed's eyes. 'Can you find the courage to do the same for Sarah?'

He froze. He wanted her safe!

Like your father wanted you safe.

He had no right to take away her autonomy, no right to make decisions on her behalf without her knowledge. His hands clenched. But how would he bear it if he lost her?

He shook his head and spun away. He had to keep her safe, whatever the cost.

But...

He raked both hands through his hair. If his father had

held to that course of action, Majed would be back in Australia by now with a wound that would never heal burning in his soul.

He spun back. 'I want to keep her safe!'

'Then work with her to do that,' Rasheed said. 'Not against her. I've had to learn to do that with your mother. And I have to learn to do it with you.'

Majed let his father's words sink in. His heart pounded when he recognised the expression in Rasheed's eyes. Adrenalin flooded every atom. 'You love Mâmâ?'

'Yes.'

'I don't mean simply feel affection for—?'

'I love your mother with every atom of my being!'

It took an effort of will to prevent his jaw from sagging. 'But…your marriage was arranged.'

Rasheed's eyes flashed. 'I fell in love with her the moment I saw her. My father knew that.' His lips lifted in a sudden and sweet smile. 'I made sure he knew it. It's why he selected her from among the other possible choices.'

'You married her because you *loved* her?' Not out of duty, as he'd always thought. The world moved on its axis a fraction. It was love that had made his parents' marriage so strong, not duty, respect or friendship.

'Yes, my son.'

Majed's heart hammered. It suddenly hit him. The real reason he'd wanted to marry Sarah—the reason he'd hidden from himself—was because he loved her, heart and soul. Like his father loved his mother. It was the same reason he'd tried to send her away.

Dear God, had he ruined everything? He spun on his heels. 'I have to go to her. I have to tell her the truth.'

He prayed to God she'd forgive him for what he'd almost done.

He prayed to God that he could keep her safe.

* * *

Sarah swam a lazy lap in the sumptuous pool before turning on her back to float. The pool house was attached to Aisha's villa and, the moment she'd seen it, she hadn't been able to resist a dip. She stared up at the tiled ceiling and allowed the cool water to soothe her. The combination of colours—sage-green, cream and dusky pink—helped to ease the burning that gripped her soul.

Majed had been so angry!

She blew out a breath and tried a relaxation breathing exercise, but she couldn't concentrate. She frowned up at those lovely tiles. Something had lain beneath Majed's anger. Had it been fear? She'd thought so...until he'd turned icier than the Arctic. She shuddered now, remembering it. If she let them, her insecurities would get the better of her, but she couldn't heed them. They'd misdirect her.

What do you know for certain?

One: Majed wasn't a cruel man—it wasn't in his nature—yet he'd been deliberately cruel to her.

Two: he might not love her, but his friendship had been sincere. She'd stake everything on that.

Three: he loved this child. She touched a hand to her stomach. *He loves you, little one.*

So...what could he be afraid of if, indeed, it was fear prompting this out-of-character behaviour?

She made a face. It was possible he did fear for his reputation, but she didn't think so. It didn't ring true somehow. In the same way his cruelty hadn't rung true.

So, if he didn't fear for himself, it had to be that he feared for his father's safety...or his mother's.

She frowned. Or hers and their child's. But, if that were the case, why hadn't he told her?

Her heart started to hammer. She straightened and brought her hand down hard, the slap sending water high into the air. *Of all the...!* Because he knew it wouldn't work!

He knew it wouldn't make her leave. Her nicely cooled skin heated up again in temper and she slapped her other hand down on the water. Did he think her a child?

A movement in the far corner of the pool house snagged her attention. She turned to find herself staring at a slim and stunningly beautiful woman. All of the hairs on her nape lifted. It suddenly occurred to her exactly the kind of danger Majed might have been trying to protect her from.

Oh, Majed, why didn't you tell me?

Her pulse raced and her heart thundered. She wanted to sink beneath the surface of the water and pretend that nothing bad could happen but...

She had a baby to protect.

She bit back all physical signs of panic that might alert this intruder to her fear. A thread of steel shot through her. She wouldn't let anyone harm her baby. 'Hello,' she said in Arabic. 'May I help you?'

'You are Sarah?'

The woman's English was good, though thickly accented. Sarah considered lying but since the betrothal ball her picture had featured in all of Keddah Jaleel's newspapers. 'Yes.'

'My name is Fatima.'

Then she held up a gun and pointed it directly at Sarah.

Sarah's heart hammered in her throat but she merely resumed floating. *Show no fear. Don't freeze up. Keep thinking.* '*The* Fatima, I presume? I've been curious to meet you.' She cocked her head to one side and considered the other woman. 'You're as beautiful as I thought you must be.'

The woman smirked her satisfaction. 'You have heard of me, then?'

'Oh, yes. You have them all in a flap at the palace at the moment.'

She stiffened and glanced behind her. 'They know I'm in Demal?'

Sarah assumed so. It would explain Majed's ridiculous behaviour. 'They have nothing concrete—at least, not that they've told me. Just rumours.'

Fatima tossed her mane of glorious black hair. 'The security of Aisha's villa is appalling. I could not believe how easy it was to break in.'

Keep her talking.

'Ah, there's a perfectly good explanation for that.'

'Which is?'

Very slowly, Sarah shook her head. 'You first, Fatima. I'll satisfy your curiosity if you satisfy mine. Why are you pointing that gun at me? What threat do you think I pose?'

'Threat?' She gave a scornful laugh. 'None! You are just a pampered Western girl.'

She was neither pampered nor a girl. But she let it pass. She wasn't the one holding a gun. 'So why do you want to shoot me?'

'Revenge,' she purred. 'Majed killed my husband and my brother. He will know the agonies I suffered when I kill his bride.'

Her stomach gave a slow, sickening turn. 'Well, as he broke off our betrothal yesterday, it appears I will no longer be his bride.'

The gun waved wildly in the air. 'You lie!'

'I wish.' She gestured around the pool house—*slowly*. 'It's why the security around here is so lax. You see, Majed was very much hoping I'd be on a plane to Australia by now. He's livid that I'm not. He thinks I'm going to cause him trouble. It's all been rather unpleasant. I couldn't remain at the palace any longer. That's why I'm here.'

Fatima stared at her as if she didn't know whether to believe her or not. She hitched up her chin. 'What kind of trouble could you cause?'

An avid look, almost of madness, had come into Fatima's

eyes. Sarah had to repress a shudder. 'Look, do you mind if I get out? It's getting a little chilly in here.'

She might have very little chance of getting the gun away from Fatima on dry ground, but she had no chance at all in the pool.

Fatima motioned with the gun towards the steps at the far end of the pool. 'Any sudden movements…'

'I get the picture.'

Sarah moved up the steps—slowly—until she was no longer in the water and was clearly visible. She turned side-on and stood there dripping, touching a hand to her stomach. 'I think you can see the kind of trouble I could cause.'

Fatima's eyes went wide.

Sarah pointed to her towel—slowly—and then reached for it and started drying her hair—slowly. 'I'm afraid that if you kill me you'll be doing Majed a service rather than an injury. With one bullet you could make this nightmare go away for him.'

Please let her swallow this nonsense.

The gun wavered. 'Why should I believe you?'

'Why risk it when you can verify the truth in the next day or two? I expect the broken engagement will make the headlines. And I'm probably being a little hard on Majed. If you kill me, he will feel guilt and regret, but he won't be heartbroken…and he will be relieved.'

Maria, Sarah's bodyguard who was posing as a maid, entered the pool house. Sarah had thought her own private bodyguard an over-the-top measure, but Aisha had insisted, and she gave thanks for it now. Maria pulled up short when she saw that Sarah wasn't alone. Fatima had pulled the gun down by her side where it was hidden by the material of her tunic. Sarah wanted it to remain there.

Show no fear. 'Ah, Maria, this is…Sinna, an acquaintance of mine. Would you be kind enough to bring us some tea? Or would you prefer coffee?' She turned to Fatima. 'Strong Turkish coffee?'

Fatima gave a short sharp nod.

'Right, Turkish coffee for Sinna, and I'll have some of that lovely chicory coffee.'

Chicory was the code word she and Maria had set up and, to her credit, Maria didn't so much as bat an eyelid. 'Very good, miss. Also, His Highness Majed is on the phone.'

Sarah blew out an exaggerated breath. She had to maintain this charade. 'Can you tell him I'm not available? You can repeat that, as long as he meets my demands, I won't go to the press. Oh, and can you tell him he'll find his mother's coral necklace in the top drawer of the dresser in the guest-room I was using?' She glanced at Fatima. 'The last thing I need is for the palace to accuse me of being a thief.'

'Yes, miss.'

Maria disappeared and Sarah pulled on a blouse. 'She's German. I think they're afraid I'll corrupt a nice Keddah Jaleely girl.'

'She's probably spying on you.'

Sarah shrugged. 'Suits me. If she tells Majed I'm not alone, he'll leap to the conclusion that I'm talking to the press. That suits me nicely.'

'Why didn't you give me away?'

She nodded at the gun. 'Call me sentimental, but I'd prefer not to be shot. I'd prefer that Maria wasn't shot either, even if she is spying on me. She's just a servant girl.'

To her relief, some of Fatima's agitation—the fanatical light in her eyes—receded. 'What are these demands you're making of Majed?'

She gestured across to the patio furniture. 'Shall we sit?' She led the way and hoped that Fatima would follow, her heart pounding. 'Just money.'

Fatima sat. 'A lot?'

Sarah sat too. 'I think it's a lot. I've asked for a million dollars. I don't care that Majed wants to deny his paternity, but he can jolly well ensure that the child is financially secure.'

'You should've asked for more.'

She still held that damn gun in too secure a grip for Sarah to risk trying to take it from her. 'You think? How much would you have asked for?'

'Two million. In American dollars.'

She feigned dismay. 'I said Australian dollars.'

Fatima snorted her disgust. 'You have no idea what you're doing!'

Sarah slumped back. 'I'm a rank amateur.' *Wasn't that the truth!* 'I've never tried to blackmail anyone before. I—'

She broke off when Maria entered with a clattering tea tray but, before she reached the table, footsteps sounded on the far side of the pool house. Majed strode in, all tall and powerful-looking with those broad shoulders and strong thighs, and Sarah's heart leapt into her mouth. He was such a big target!

'Oh, look, my two favourite women.'

Her gaze snagged with his. Had he heard the nonsense she'd been feeding Fatima? How long had he stood out there listening? She hoped he had the entire villa surrounded with police and bodyguards.

'Plotting my demise, no doubt.'

Don't lose it now! 'Checking up on me, Majed?' She made her words a taunt.

He raised an eyebrow, but she could practically feel his eyes scanning her for signs of hurt or injury. 'Do you blame me, *habibi*? I like to keep my enemies close.'

Fatima rose and pointed her gun at him. 'I'm going to enjoy killing you, Majed.'

He moved towards them slowly with panther-like grace

and Sarah's heart pounded. She wanted to shout, *'Turn and run!'*

'Will you kill me quick or will you make it slow, I wonder?'

A scream pressed at the back of her throat. She could see he was playing for time as Maria manoeuvred herself into position behind Fatima, but he was putting himself in such danger!

With a superhuman effort Sarah pulled herself together. She would not let this crazed woman kill the man she loved!

'Do you want to know how Tabor died? Shall I tell you the gory details? Do you want to know whose name he shouted in his death throes?'

Dear God, he was deliberately taunting Fatima to keep her attention on him.

Fatima paled and her face tightened. She cocked the revolver.

No! Nobody was going to kill Majed. She wouldn't allow it.

At that precise moment, Maria flung steaming hot coffee and it hit Fatima in the centre of her back. Fatima screamed, rearing back automatically in reaction, giving Sarah the split-second chance to bring her hand down hard on Fatima's arm in a karate-chop move her self-defence teacher had taught her when she was eleven…and thirteen…and fourteen… and again at seventeen.

The gun slid across the floor and she kicked it away, before catching Fatima in an arm lock that left the furious woman immobilised and screaming in frustration.

'You lied to me!'

She didn't bother responding. She couldn't.

In the next moment, Maria had taken over and a dozen men surged into the pool house. Fatima was handcuffed, hauled to her feet and dragged from the room.

Sarah found herself swept up into strong arms and Majed's lips were pressed to her ear, murmuring words that sounded like a prayer. Arms and lips that made her feel safe, cherished...and loved.

Tears pricked the backs of her eyes. He didn't love her, but he had risked his life for her, and she clung to him now. *He was safe. He was safe.*

'Shh, *habibi*, the danger is now past.'

It was only then that Sarah realised she was crying. 'I—I thought she was going to kill you,' she hiccupped.

He lifted her into his arms, carried her into the house and took her into the sitting room, where he settled on the sofa with her ensconced securely on his lap. He held her close, his hands making soothing circles on her back. She finally pushed herself up a little to stare into his face. 'You were so brave. My heart nearly stopped when you walked in. I wanted to yell at you to run.'

'You were the one who was brave.' He smoothed her hair back from her face, cupping the back of her head and staring at her with such admiration she almost believed he cared for her.

Of course he cares for you. Just don't mistake it for more.

'The way you played for time...played on her prejudices and need for revenge... It was so clever! And you appeared so calm. I was in awe of you.'

'I was shaking inside.'

'I knew you were brave but I've never been more afraid than in that split second when you brought your hand down on Fatima's arm.' His hands gripped her shoulders, his fingers digging into her flesh as his face twisted. 'All I could think was that Fatima would injure you badly—she's expert in martial arts. But you disabled her so quickly and then had her in an arm lock before I was even halfway to you. I—' his hands gentled '—I was never more proud of anyone in my life. Where did you learn to do that?'

Sarah suddenly found that she could laugh. 'My mother, of course. Every year from the age of eleven through to eighteen she bought me a course of self-defence lessons for my birthday. I guess some of it stuck.'

'She is a wise woman. I will tell her so next time I see her.'

Sarah moistened suddenly dry lips. 'Fatima is the reason you tried to send me away?'

His eyes darkened and the lines about his mouth momentarily deepened. 'Yes.'

She tried to shift away but he wouldn't let her. She turned her face towards the door. 'Don't you want to go after them—the guards—to make sure that the woman who killed your brother is—?'

'I don't care about her! I don't care about my revenge! I care about you. I…I care about you, *habibi*.'

She stilled. Her heart thudded. She finally found the courage to turn back and face him. He looked so ragged and vulnerable that she wanted to pull his head down to her shoulder and comfort him the way he'd just comforted her.

'I'm sorry I lied to you, Sarah. It was my father who made me realise how wrong I was.'

She blinked. 'Rasheed? What did he say? I…I thought he wanted me gone too.'

'No, *habibi*, he wanted *me* gone. For the same reasons I tried to make you leave Keddah Jaleel.'

Her heart gave a sudden kick of recognition. 'He'd lost one son. So…he wanted to keep the other one safe. And that's why he sent you away?'

He nodded. 'But you made him see how wrong he was.'

'Me?' she squeaked.

'You forced him to recognise that my home and destiny— my happiness—would always be linked to Keddah Jaleel. He saw that I'd never be happy anywhere else, although I might be safer elsewhere. He realised that he had no right to interfere in my destiny in such a way.'

She leaned back into him. 'Wow.'

'He made me realise I couldn't rob you of your choices and your freedoms either.'

She pulled in a breath. 'You realised that if I knew the truth—that Fatima was on the warpath—that I wouldn't agree to leave.'

'My fear put you in danger. I'll never forgive myself. I should've confided in you and we should've come up with a plan to keep you safe.'

She nodded.

His eyes bored into hers. 'I learned also another valuable lesson.'

Her heart started to race with a different kind of tempo. 'Oh?'

'I can see now how love can make you strong, if you let it.'

Two beats passed before his words sank in. He continued talking but she didn't hear his words. 'Whoa, wait!' She sat bolt-upright in his lap. 'Did you just say...*love*?'

Midnight eyes stared into hers. His lips curved in a way that made her pulse pound. 'But of course, Sarah. Surely you must know now that I love you?'

She could only stare. And then she could only shake her head.

Very gently he took her face in his hands. 'Little one, you are the light of my life. I love you with all my heart and soul—and very soon I will love you with my body... if you'll let me. If you'll still marry me.'

Of course she was going to marry him...

'I've been fighting it for a long time.' His face darkened. 'I was stupid. I thought love made men weak and easy to manipulate. Not being true to love is what makes a man weak. I allowed my fear of love, and my fear of being betrayed, to rule me. It is those things that made me weak. And it could've ended in disaster. If you had come to harm...'

His regret and self-recriminations tugged at her. She touched his cheek. 'I'm safe, Majed. We're both safe and the threat has been dealt with.'

His hands caressed her from shoulder to wrist, making her shiver. 'Because of your code words.'

'Because we worked as a team.'

He stilled, his gaze burning into hers. 'I want us to always work as a team. I will not make the same mistakes again. I swear that to you. Can you forgive me, *habibi*?'

Her breath jammed in her lungs. 'Say it again.'

He pulled in a breath, his expression intense, his eyes not leaving hers. 'I am sorry. I will never—'

'No, not that.'

He stared into her eyes and then he smiled. 'I love you, Sarah Collins. I love you with all that I am. I will love you forever.'

Warmth radiated through her chest, his words leaving her feeling weightless and grounded at the same time.

'If I promise to honour our vow of love, will you marry me?'

'Yes,' she breathed. 'A million times yes. I love you, Majed.'

She lifted her face to meet his kiss, her arms winding about his neck. She was no longer afraid of having to hide her love from him, no longer overwhelmed at all she felt for this amazing man.

Firm lips captured hers and he kissed her so thoroughly, with such tenderness and intensity, that it made the blood pound in her ears. It left her in little doubt of the depth of his feelings for her.

The baby suddenly kicked, as if to share in her joy, and with a laugh she took his hand and laid it on her abdomen.

'Who'd have thought we would all end up here like this? Who'd have thought an…accident would end so happily?'

'No, *habibi*, not an accident. This baby might not have been planned but it was no accident. It was destiny. It brought you to me, and you brought me home.'

She touched her hand to his cheek, placing her other hand over his on her stomach. 'This baby has helped me find a home—a place where I belong. It has helped me find my courage. While you showed me that I should never give up on my dreams.'

'This baby is a blessing.'

She couldn't argue with that. Reaching up, she pressed a kiss to his cheek. 'Please tell me we can marry soon.'

His eyes gleamed. 'We will be married very soon, *habibi*. I can promise you that.'

And then his lips claimed hers in a kiss that left her breathless, and looking forward to the future with more anticipation than she'd ever dreamed possible.

* * * * *

CLAIMING
HIS SECRET
ROYAL HEIR

NINA MILNE

To the memory of my very lovely 'Nanni'—
I still miss you.

CHAPTER ONE

August 15th—Online Celebrity News with April Fotherington

Who will be the new Lycander Princess?

All bets are off!

It's official! Lady Kaitlin Derwent is no longer a contender for the position of Lycander Bride—the people's favourite aristo announced that her new squeeze for the foreseeable future is Daniel Harrington, CEO of Harrington's Legal Services.

Who'd have thought it?

Exit Lady Kaitlin!

So Prince Frederick, ruler of Lycander, is on the lookout for a new bride.

Who will it be?

Will it be the type of woman who graced his arm and his bed back in his playboy days, before the tragic death of his older brother and the scandalous death of Prince Alphonse, his flamboyant father, in a house of ill repute propelled him to the throne?

FREDERICK II OF the House of Petrelli, Prince and Ruler of Lycander, stopped reading and pushed his screen across the ornate carved desk, resplendent with gilt—a royal gift from an English monarch of yore.

The phrase pounded his brain—*tragic death of his older brother*—but he forced his features to remain calm, and made himself focus on the man standing in front of him: Marcus Alrikson, his chief advisor. After all, he needed all the advice he could get.

'I don't understand what the problem is—this article is nothing more than a gossip fest. And it's old news.'

Marcus shook his head. '*That* is the problem. The article serves to remind the people of your past.'

'Don't you mean my sordid, scandalous and immoral past?' Might as well tell it like it is, he thought.

'If you like,' Marcus returned evenly. 'The bigger problem is that we both know you are holding on to the crown by your fingertips. The people did not want you on the throne because of your past—so any reminder causes damage.'

'I understand that.'

The all too familiar guilt twisted his insides—the people had wanted his brother on the throne. Axel had been born to this. He would have been the ideal ruler to bring prosperity and calm to the land after their father's turbulent rule.

But Axel was dead and buried—victim of a car crash that should have been Frederick's destiny. Frederick should have been in that car on his way to a State dinner; instead he'd asked Axel to step in and take his place and his big brother had—no questions asked. So Frederick had attended a party on board a glitzy yacht to celebrate a business deal…and Axel had died.

The dark secret tarnished Frederick's soul, weighted his conscience.

And now Lycander was stuck with the black sheep of the royal line and the people were threatening to revolt. Bleak determination hardened inside him. He would keep the crown safe, whatever the cost—he owed that at least to Axel's memory.

'So what do you suggest?'

'I suggest you find a new bride—someone like Lady Kaitlin. Your proposed alliance with Kaitlin was a popular one. It showed the people that you had decided to settle down with a suitable bride, that you'd changed—proof there would be no repeat of your father's disastrous marriages.'

'I *have* decided to settle down.' To bind himself to a lifestyle he'd once sworn to avoid and the formulation of a cold-blooded alliance undertaken for the sake of the throne. 'But Kaitlin is no longer an option—she has fallen in love with another man.'

Irritation sparked inside him. He wished Kaitlin well, but it was hard to believe that the cool, poised Lady Kaitlin had succumbed to so foolish an emotion.

'Which is not good news for Lycander.'

Marcus resumed pacing, each stride swallowing up a metre of the marble floor, taking him past yet another portrait of one of Frederick's ancestors.

'Kaitlin was the perfect bride—her background is impeccable and she reminded the people of Lycander brides of the past.'

Unlike the succession of actresses, models and gold diggers Frederick's father had married.

'The people loved her.'

Unlike you.

The unspoken words hovered in the air between them.

'I understand all this. But Kaitlin is history.'

'Yes. And right now the press is *focused* on your history. That article zones in on your former flames—the actresses, the socialites, the models. Giselle, Mariana, Sunita... Hell, this reporter, April, even tried to track them down.'

Frederick froze.

Sunita.

Images flashed across his mind; memory reached across the chasm of tragedy.

Sunita.

Shared laughter, sheer beauty, almond-shaped eyes of a brown that veered from tawny to light, dependent on her mood. The raven sheen of her silken hair, the glow of her skin, the lissom length of her legs.

Sunita.

The woman who had left him—the woman he'd allowed to go…

Without preamble, he pulled his netbook back towards him, eyes scanning the article.

But where is Sunita now?

This is where it becomes a little mysterious.

Mere weeks after the end of her relationship with the Prince of Lycander—which, according to several sources, she ended abruptly—Sunita decided to 'take a break' from her highly lucrative modelling career to 'rediscover her roots'.

This involved a move to Mumbai, where her mother reportedly hailed from. But the trail ends there, and to all intents and purposes Sunita seems to have vanished.

'Frederick?' Marcus's voice pulled him from the article and he looked up to see his chief advisor's forehead crease into a frown. 'What is it?'

'Nothing.' Under the sceptical gaze Frederick shrugged. 'It just sounds unlike Sunita to give up her career.'

Sunita had been one of the most ambitious people he knew—had been defined by that ambition, had had her career aspirations and goals mapped out with well-lit beacons. The idea of her jacking it all in seemed far-fetched at best.

Marcus drummed his fingers on his thigh. 'Could her disappearance have anything to do with you?'

'No.'

'What happened?'

'We spent a few weeks together—she moved on.'

'*She* moved on?'

Damn. 'We moved on.'

'Why?'

Keep it together. This is history. 'She decided to call it a day as she'd garnered sufficient publicity from our connection.'

Marcus raised his eyebrows. 'So she used you for publicity?'

'Yes. To be fair, she was upfront about that from the start.'

More fool him for thinking she'd changed her mind as time had gone on. He'd believed their time together, the long conversations, the laughter, had meant something. Well, he'd been wrong. Sunita had been after publicity and then she'd cut and run. Yet there had been something in her expression that morning…a transitory shadow in her tawny eyes, an errant twist of her hands that had belied the glib words dropping from her lips. But he hadn't called her on it.

Enough! The past was over and did not bear dwelling on because—as he knew with soul-wrenching certainty—it could not be changed.

Marcus's dark blue eyes met his as he resumed pacing. 'So weeks after this publicity stunt she disappeared off the modelling scene? That doesn't make sense.'

It didn't. But it had nothing to do with him. Two years

ago Sunita had affected him in ways he didn't want to remember. He'd missed her once she'd gone—an unheard-of weakness he'd knocked on the head and buried. Easy come, easy go. That was the Playboy Prince's motto. Sunita had gone—he'd accepted it. And then, mere months after her departure, Axel had died and his life had changed for ever.

'I'll look into it,' Marcus said. 'But right now you need to focus on this list. Potential brides. A princess, a lady and a *marquesa*. Take your pick.'

Frederick accepted the piece of paper but didn't so much as glance down. 'What do you mean, "look into it"?'

'If there is any chance of potential scandal we need to shut it down now. So I plan to find Sunita before April Fotherington or any other reporter does.'

'Then what?'

'Then I'll send someone to talk to her. Or go myself.'

'No!' The refusal came with a vehemence that surprised him. However it had ended, his time with Sunita had marked something—his last moments of joy before catastrophe occurred, perhaps. He didn't want her life tainted…didn't want Marcus or his minions to find her if she didn't want to be found.

'It needs to be done.' Marcus leant forward, his hands on the edge of the desk. 'I understand you don't like it, but you can't take even the smallest risk that there is a scandal floating around out there. The crown is at stake. The throne is rocking, Frederick, and if it topples it will be a Humpty Dumpty scenario.'

Great! A Humpty Dumpty scenario—exactly what he needed. Of course he could choose to ignore the warning, but that would be foolish. Marcus knew his stuff. The sensible option would be to allow Marcus to go ahead, investigate and deal with any problem. But for some reason every fibre of his being cavilled—dammit, stupid though it sounded, it wasn't the *honourable* thing to do.

A small mocking smile tilted his lips as he faced his chief advisor. Frederick of Lycander—man of honour. Axel would be proud of him. 'Fine. *I'll* check out Sunita.'

Marcus's blue eyes narrowed. 'With all due respect, that's nuts and you know it. The press will jump on it.'

'Then let them jump. I'm the boss and this is what's going to happen.'

'Why?'

'Because it's the right thing to do.' And for once he'd like to stand on a tiny wedge of the moral high ground. 'What would Axel have done? Sent you in to spy on a woman he'd dated?'

'Axel would never have got himself into a position where it was necessary.'

'Touché. But I have and I will deal with it.' His brain whirred as he thought it through. 'I can schedule a trip to Mumbai—I'd like to follow up on how the Schools for All project is rolling out anyway.'

It was a project set up by Axel, but Frederick had taken it over and had every intention of making it into a success.

'I'll locate Sunita, confirm there is no scandal, and then I'll come back and find a wife from your shortlist. No argument.' A mirthless smile touched his lips. 'Don't worry. I'll be discreet.'

August 17th, Mumbai

Sunita stared down at the screen and reread the article for approximately the millionth time in three days as a mini-tornado of panic whirled and soared around her tummy.

She told herself that she was climbing the heights of irrationality. April Fotherington *hadn't* found her—she was safe here in this spacious, anonymous Mumbai apartment, surrounded by cool white walls and the hustle and bustle of a city she'd come to love. Soon enough the flicker of interest the article might ignite would die out. No one had discovered her secret thus far—there was no reason to believe they would now. She was safe. *They* were safe.

But she couldn't help the sudden lurch of fear as she gazed round the living room and the evidence of the life she'd created. Signs of her baby son were everywhere— a wooden toy box in the corner, the cheerful play mat by the sofa, board books, beakers… She knew all too well how quickly life could change, be upended and destroyed.

Stop. No one would take Amil away. Alphonse of Lycander was dead, and he had been the greatest threat—a man who had fought virulent custody battles for four of his children and used his position and wealth to win them all. She had no doubt he would have done the same for his grandchild—would have used the might and power of his sovereignty to win Amil.

Just as Frederick still might.

The peal of the doorbell jolted her from her thoughts and a scud of panic skittered through her. It couldn't be her grandmother and Amil—they had only left a little while before. *Chill.* They could have forgotten something, it could be a neighbour, or a delivery or—

Only one way to find out.

Holding her breath, she peered through the peephole.

Shock dizzied her—she blinked and prayed the man at her door was a figment of her overheated imagination, brought on by reading the article so many times. The alternative was too ghastly to contemplate. But, however many times she blinked, Prince Frederick of Lycander was still right there.

What to do? What to do? Ignore him?

But what if he waited outside? What if he was still there when Amil came back? Or what if he went away and returned when Amil was here? What if he was here to take Amil?

Enough. She had not got this far to give up now. She was no longer that ten-year-old girl, reeling from her mother's death, powerless to stop the father she had never known from taking her. No longer that eleven, twelve, thirteen-year-old girl at the mercy of her stepmother and sisters who had graduated with honours from *Cinderella* school.

She'd escaped them without the help of a handsome prince and left that feeling of powerlessness far behind. No way was she going back there—especially now, when her son was at stake.

Adrenalin surged through her body as she did what life had taught her—moved forward to face up to whatever was about to be thrown at her. She might dodge it, catch it, or punch it, but she would confront it on her own terms.

True to her motto, she pulled the door open and raised her eyebrows in aloof surprise. 'Your Highness,' she said. 'What are you doing here?'

Stepping out into the communal hall, she closed the door behind her, searching his gaze for a sign that he knew about Amil.

'I came to see *you*. April Fotherington wrote an article saying you'd vanished.'

Sunita forced herself not to lean back against the wall in relief. Instead, she maintained her façade of reserve as they stood and studied each other. Against her will, her stomach nosedived and her hormones cartwheeled. Memories of the totally wrong sort streamed through her mind and fizzed through her veins as she drank him in. The same corn-blond hair, the same hazel eyes...

No, not the same. His eyes were now haunted by shadows and his lips no longer turned upward in insouciance. Prince Frederick looked like a man who hadn't smiled in a while. Little wonder after the loss of his brother and his father, followed by a troubled ascent to the throne.

Instinctively she stepped closer, wanting to offer comfort. 'I saw the article. But before we discuss that, I'm sorry for your losses. I wanted to send condolences but…'

It had been too risky, and it had seemed wrong somehow—to send condolences whilst pregnant with his baby, whom she intended to keep secret from him.

'Why didn't you?'

The seemingly casual question held an edge and she tensed.

'If all your girlfriends had done that you'd still be reading them now. I didn't feel our brief relationship gave me the right.'

Disingenuous, but there was some truth there. For a second she could almost taste the bitter disappointment with herself for succumbing to the Playboy Prince's charms and falling into bed with him. Hell—she might as well have carved the notch on his four-poster bed herself.

She'd woken the morning after and known what she had to do—the only way forward to salvage some pride and dignity. End it on *her* terms, before he did. It had been the only option, but even as she had done it there had been a tiny part of her that had hoped he'd stop her, ask her to stay. But of course he hadn't. The Playboy Prince wouldn't change. People didn't change—Sunita knew that.

Anyway this was history. *Over and done with.*

'I am offering condolences now.'

'Thank you. But, as I said, that's not why I am here.'

'The article?'

'Yes. I'd like to talk—perhaps we could go inside.'

'No!' *Tone it down, Sunita.* 'This is my home, Frederick, my private sanctuary. I want to keep it that way.'

He eyed her for a moment and she forced herself to hold his gaze.

'Then where would you suggest? Preferably somewhere discreet.'

'In case the press spot us and tips me as the next candidate for Lycander Bride?'

The words were out before she could stop them; obscure hurt touched her with the knowledge he didn't want to be seen with her.

'Something like that. You're my unofficial business.'

For a moment there was a hint of the Frederick she'd known in the warmth of his voice, and more memories threatened to surface. Of warmth and laughter, touch and taste.

'My official reason for this trip is charity business— I'm patron of an educational charity that is rolling out some new schools.'

The tang of warmth had disappeared; instead impatience vibrated from him as he shifted from foot to foot.

'Are you sure we can't talk inside? It shouldn't take long. All I want is the solution to April's mystery.'

Sunita checked the hollow laughter before it could fall from her lips. Was that *all* he wanted? Easy-peasy, lemon-squeezy.

'I'm sure we can't talk here.'

Think. But coherent thought was nigh on impossible. Raw panic combined with her body's reaction to his proximity had unsettled her, sheer awareness wrong-footed her. *Think.* Yet her mind drew a blank as to any possible location, any café where she and Amil weren't regulars.

Fear displaced all other emotion—Frederick must not find out about Amil. Not now, not like this. One day, yes, but at a time of her choice—when it was right and safe for Amil.

'I'll just grab a coat and we can go.'

'A coat?'

'It's monsoon season.'

Sunita turned, opened the door, and slipped inside, her mind racing to formulate a plan. She'd always been able to think on her feet, after all. If Frederick wanted a solution to the mystery of her disappearance from the modelling scene, then that was what she would provide.

Grabbing her phone, she pressed speed dial and waited.

'Sunita?'

'Hey, Sam. I need a favour. A *big* favour.'

CHAPTER TWO

FREDERICK WATCHED AS she opened the door and sidled out. Coatless, he couldn't help but notice. What was going on? Anyone would think she had the Lycander Crown Jewels tucked away in there. Hell, maybe she did. Or maybe something was wrong.

Disquiet flickered and he closed it down. He'd vowed emotion would not come into play here. He and Sunita were history—the sole reason for his presence was to ensure no scandal would touch Lycander and topple him, Humpty Dumpty-style.

They exited the building and emerged onto the heat-soaked pavement, thronged with an almost impossible mass of people, alive with the shouts of the hawkers who peddled their wares and the thrum of the seemingly end-less cars that streamed along the road. Horns blared, and the smell of cumin, coriander and myriad spices mingled with the delicate scents of the garlands of flowers on offer and the harsher fumes of pollution.

Sunita walked slightly ahead, and he took the oppor-tunity to study her. The past two years had done nothing to detract from her beauty—her hair shone with a lustre that should have the manufacturer of whatever brand of shampoo she used banging at her door, and her impossibly long legs and slender waist were unchanged.

Yet there was a difference. The Sunita he'd known had dressed to be noticed, but today her outfit was simple and anonymous—cut-off jeans, a loose dark blue T-shirt and blue sandals. It was an ensemble that made her blend in with the crowd. Even the way she walked seemed altered—somehow different from the way she had once sashayed down the catwalk.

Once.

And therein lay the crux of the matter. The more he thought about it, the more he recalled the vibrant, publicity-loving, career-orientated Sunita he'd known, the less possible it seemed that she had traded the life path she'd planned for an anonymous existence. His research of the past two days had confirmed that mere weeks after Sunita had ended their association she'd thrown it all away and melted into obscurity.

'How did you find me?'

'It wasn't easy.'

Or so Marcus had informed him. Sunita's agent had refused point-blank to respond to his discreet enquiries, but Marcus had ways and means, and had eventually procured the address through 'contacts'—whatever that meant.

'Was it my agent? Was it Harvey?'

'No. But whoever it was I promise you they did you a favour.'

'Some favour.'

'You mean you aren't happy to see me?' he deadpanned.

A shadow of a smile threatened to touch her lips and he fought the urge to focus on those lips in more detail.

'Pass.'

Raising an arm, she hailed a taxi and they waited until the yellow and black vehicle had screeched through the traffic to stop by the kerb.

Once inside she leant forward to speak to the driver.

'Sunshine Café, please,' she said, and then sat back. 'I'm taking you to meet the solution to your mystery. The reason I stayed in India.'

Her eyes slid away from him for a fraction of a second and then back again as she inhaled an audible breath.

'His name is Sam Matthews. He used to be a photographer, but he's moved here and set up a beach café.'

'A boyfriend?'

Such a simple answer—Sunita had given it all up for love. A small stab of jealousy pierced his ribcage, caught him unawares. *Get real, Frederick.* So what if she walked straight into someone else's arms, into the real thing? That had never been his destiny. *Know your limitations. Easy come, easy go.* Two stellar life mottos.

'Yes.'

'Must be some boyfriend to have persuaded you to throw away your career. You told me once that nothing was more important to you than success.'

'I meant it at the time.'

'So you gave up stardom and lucre for love.'

A small smile touched her lips. 'Yes, I did.'

'And you're happy? Sam makes you happy?'

Her hands twisted on her lap in a small convulsive movement. She looked down as if in surprise, then back up as she nodded. 'Yes.'

A spectrum of emotion showed in her brown eyes—regret, guilt, defiance,—he couldn't settle on what it was, and then it was gone.

'I'm happy.'

Job done. Sunita had a boyfriend and she'd moved on with her life. There was no dangerous scandal to uncover. A simple case of over-vigilance from his chief advisor. He could stop the taxi now and return to his hotel.

Yet…something felt off. He could swear Sunita was

watching him, assessing his reactions. Just like two years ago when she'd called it a day. Or maybe it was his own ego seeing spectres—perhaps he didn't *want* to believe another woman had ricocheted from him to perfect love. Sunita to Sam, Kaitlin to Daniel—there was a definite pattern emerging.

He glanced out of the window at the busy beach, scattered with parasols and bodies, as the taxi slowed to a halt.

'We're here,' she announced.

What the hell? He might as well meet this paragon who had upended Sunita's plans, her career, her life, in a way he had not.

Damn it. There was that hint of chagrin again. Not classy, Frederick. Not royal behaviour.

Minutes later they approached a glass-fronted restaurant nestled at the corner of a less populated section of sand, under the shade of two fronded palms. Once inside, Frederick absorbed the warm yet uncluttered feel achieved by the wooden floor, high exposed beam ceiling and polished wooden tables and slatted chairs. A long sweeping bar added to the ambience, as did the hum of conversation.

Sunita moved forward. 'Hey, Sam.'

Frederick studied the man who stood before them. There was more than a hint of wariness in his eyes and stance. Chestnut wavy hair, average height, average build, light brown eyes that returned his gaze with an answering assessment.

Sunita completed the introduction. 'Sam, Frederick—Frederick, Sam. Right, now that's done...'

'Perhaps you and I could have a drink and a catch-up? For old times' sake.'

The suggestion brought on by an instinctive unease, augmented by the look of reluctance on her face. Something wasn't right. She hadn't wanted him to so much as peek into her apartment, and she could have simply *told* him about Sam. Instead she'd brought him here to see him, as if to provide tangible proof of his existence.

'Sure.' Sunita glanced at her watch. 'But I can't be too long.'

Sam indicated a staircase. 'There's a private room you can use upstairs, if you want to chat without attracting attention.'

'Great. Thank you,' Frederick said, and stepped back to allow the couple to walk together.

Their body language indicated that they were...*comfortable* with each other. They walked side by side, but there was no accidental brush of a hand, no quick glance of appreciation or anticipation, no chemistry or any sign of the awareness that had shimmered in the air since he himself had set eyes on Sunita.

They entered a small room with a wooden table and chairs by a large glass window that overlooked the beach. Sam moved over to the window, closed the shutters and turned to face them. 'If you tell me what you'd like to drink, I'll have it sent up.'

'You're welcome to join us,' Frederick said smoothly, and saw the look of caution in Sam's brown eyes intensify as he shook his head.

'I'd love to, but we're extremely busy and one of my staff members didn't turn up today, so I'm afraid I can't.'

'That's fine, Sam. Don't worry,' Sunita interpolated—and surely the words had tumbled out just a little too fast. Like they did when she was nervous. 'Could I have a guava and pineapple juice, please?'

'Sounds good—I'll have the same.'

'No problem.'

With that, Sam left the room.

'He clearly doesn't see me as a threat,' Frederick observed.

'There is no reason why he should.'

For an instant he allowed his gaze to linger on her lips and he saw heat touch her cheekbones. 'Of course not,' he agreed smoothly.

Her eyes narrowed, and one sandaled foot tapped the floor with an impatience he remembered all too well. 'Anyway, you came here to solve the mystery. Mystery solved. So your "unofficial" business is over.'

Were her words almost too airy or had he caught a case of severe paranoia from Marcus? 'It would appear so.' He watched her from beneath lowered lids.

'So, tell me more about your official business—the schools project.'

'My brother set up the charity—he believed every child deserves access to an education, however basic.'

It had been a philanthropic side Frederick hadn't even known Axel had had—one his brother had kept private. Because he had been a good man…a good man who had died—

Grief and guilt thrust forward but he pushed them back. The only reparation he could make was to continue Axel's work.

'So, I'm funding and working with a committee to set up schools here. Tomorrow I'm going to visit one of the new ones and meet the children.'

'That sounds incredible—there's so much poverty here, and yet also such a vibrant sense of happiness as well.'

'Why don't you get involved? That would be great publicity for the organisation—I could put you in touch.'

For a second her face lit up, and then she shook her head. 'No. I'm not modelling at the moment and…'

'I'm not suggesting you model. I'm suggesting you get involved with some charity work.'

'I… I don't want any publicity at the moment—'

'Why not?'

'I… Sam and I prefer our life to be out of the spotlight.'

This still didn't make sense. Sunita had thrived in the spotlight, been pulled to it like a moth to a flame. But before he could point that out, the door opened and a waitress appeared with a tray.

'Thank you.' Sunita smiled as the girl placed the drinks on the table, alongside a plate of snacks that looked to range from across the globe. Tiny pizzas topped with morsels of smoked salmon nestled next to crisp, succulent *pakora*, which sat alongside miniature burgers in minuscule buns. 'These look delicious.'

Once the waitress had exited, Frederick sampled a *pakora*, savoured the bite of the spice and the crunch of the batter around the soft potato underneath. 'These are delicious! Sam runs an excellent kitchen.'

'Yes—he and…he has made a real success of this place.'

'You must be proud of him.'

'Yes. Of course.'

'Are you involved with the restaurant?'

'No.'

He sipped his drink, with its refreshing contrast of sharp and sweet. 'So what do you do now? Do you have a job?'

'I…'

Fluster showed in the heat that crept along her cheekbones, the abrupt swirling of her drink, the over-careful selection of a snack.

'I'm a lady of leisure.' Her eyes dared him to challenge her, but he couldn't help it—a snort of disbelief emerged. Sunita had been a human dynamo, always on the go, abuzz with energy, ideas and vibrancy.

'For real?'

'Yes.' Now her fingers tapped on the table in irritation. 'Why not? I'm lucky enough that I can afford not to work—I pay my own way.'

An undercurrent of steel lined her words—one he remembered all too well. 'Just like you did two years ago.'

It had become a standing joke—she'd refused point-blank to let him pay for anything, had insisted they split every bill down the middle. The one time he'd been foolish enough to buy her a gift, she'd handed it back.

I don't like to feel beholden. It's my issue, not yours. Keep it for your next woman. I pay my own way.'

Apparently she still did.

He raised his hands in a gesture of peace. 'Where you get your money from is none of my business. I just can't imagine you doing nothing all day.'

'That's not how it is. I have a very fulfilling life.'

'Doing what?'

'None of your business. You came here to find out why I disappeared. I've told you—I fell in love, I've settled down, and I want to live my life quietly.'

Instinct told him there was something askew with the portrait she painted. Tension showed in the tautness of her body; but perhaps that tension had nothing to do with him.

'My chief advisor will be relieved—he is worried there is some mystery around your disappearance that could damage me.'

For a fraction of a second her knuckles whitened around her glass and then her eyebrows rose in a quizzical curve. 'Isn't that a tad far-fetched? To say nothing of egotistically paranoid?'

'Possibly,' he agreed, matching her eyebrow for eyebrow. 'But it also seems extremely far-fetched to me that you walked away from your career.'

'Well, I did.'

Frederick waited, but it appeared Sunita felt that sufficed.

'So you confirm that your retreat and subsequent dramatic change of lifestyle have nothing to do with me?'

Her glance flickered away and then she laughed. 'We spent one night together two years ago. Do you *really* think that your charms, manifest though they were, were sufficient to make me change my life?'

Put like that, he had to admit it sounded arrogantly self-involved. And yet... 'We spent more than one night together, Sunita.'

A wave of her hand dismissed his comment. 'A publicity stunt—nothing more.'

'OK. Let's play it your way. I can just about buy it that those weeks were all about publicity for you, but what about that night? Was *that* all for publicity?'

These were the questions he should have asked two years ago.

Her gaze swept away from him. 'No. It wasn't. I didn't intend that night to happen.'

'Is that why you left?'

It was as though the years had rolled back—he could almost imagine that they were in that five-star hotel in Paris, where they'd played truant from the glitzy party they'd been supposed to be at. Attraction had finally taken over and—

Whoa! Reel it in, Frederick!

'Yes, that's why I left. I broke my own rules. By sleeping with you I became just another notch on your bedpost—another woman on the Playboy Prince's conveyor belt. That was never meant to happen.'

'That's not how it was.'

'That's *exactly* how it was.' Tawny eyes challenged him.

'And if I'd asked you to stay?'

'You didn't.'

Her voice was flat and who could blame her? The point was that he hadn't. Because it had been easier to believe that she'd never cared, to stick by his *easy come, easy go* motto.

'But this is all beside the point—there was never a future for us. People don't change.' Her voice held utter conviction. 'You were The Playboy Prince...'

'And *you* were very clear that you had no desire for a relationship because you wanted to focus on your career. Then, just weeks later, you met Sam and realised he was the one and your career was no longer important?' It was impossible for Frederick to keep the scepticism out of his voice.

'Yes, I did.'

'So you changed.'

'Love changes everything.'

Damn it—he'd stake his fortune on the sincerity in her voice, and there was that irrational nip of jealousy again.

'So, yes,' she continued, 'I met Sam and I decided to take a break, and the break has extended to a couple of years. Simple. No mystery. That's what you came here to discover.'

Now her tone had lost the fervour of truth—he was nearly sure of it.

'You promise?' The words were foolish, but he couldn't hold them back.

She nodded. 'I promise...'

He studied her expression, saw the hint of trouble in her eyes and in the twist of her fingers under the table.

'No scandal will break over Lycander.'

'Then my work here is done.'

Yet an odd reluctance pulled at him as he rose from the

chair and looked down at her, sure now that there was *more* than a hint of trouble in her eyes. *Not his business.* She'd made a promise and he believed her. He had a country to run, a destiny to fulfil…

'I wish you well, Sunita. I'm glad you've found happiness.'

'I wish you well too.'

In one lithe movement she stood and stretched out a hand, caught his sleeve, stood on tiptoe and brushed his cheek with her lips. Memory slammed into him—her scent, the silken touch of her hair against his skin—and it took all his powers of self-control not to tug her into his arms. Instead, he forced his body to remain still, to accept the kiss in the spirit it was being given—whatever that might be—though he was pretty damn sure from the heat that touched her cheeks that she wasn't sure either.

'I…goodbye.' Once again her hands twisted together as she watched him.

'Goodbye, Sunita.'

He headed for the door, stopped at her audible intake of breath, half turned as she said his name.

'Yes?'

'It…it doesn't matter. It was good to see you again.'

That only confirmed that she had intended to say something else, but before he could respond Sam entered and glanced at them both. 'All OK?'

'Everything is fine.' Sunita's voice was over-bright now. 'Frederick is just leaving.'

Minutes later he was in a taxi, headed back to the hotel. But as the journey progressed doubts hustled and bustled and crowded his brain. Something was wrong. He had no idea what, and it most likely had nothing to do with him. Quite possibly he had the wrong end of the stick. Undoubtedly wisdom dictated that he should not get involved. Sunita was more than capable of looking out for herself, and she had Sam to turn to. But what if Sam was the problem?

Hell.

Leaning forward, he gave the driver Sunita's address.

Damn it all to hell and back! Sunita strode the length of her lounge and resisted the urge to kick a bright red bean bag across the room. Venting wouldn't stem the onrush, the sheer *onslaught* of guilt, the veritable tsunami of distaste with herself.

Why, why, *why* had he turned up? Not telling Frederick for two years had been hard enough—lying directly to Frederick's face was another ballgame altogether. Especially as it was a face that mirrored Amil's—the angle of his cheekbone, the colour of his eyes, the subtle nuances that couldn't be ignored.

The guilt kept rolling on in and her stride increased. *Focus*. Concentrate on all the sensible, logical justifications for her actions.

The decision to keep Amil a secret had been one of the toughest she had ever faced, but it was a decision she still believed to be right. She'd done her research: the Lycanders had a track record of winning custody of their children and hanging the mothers out to dry.

Frederick's father, Prince Alphonse, had fathered five children by four wives; his first wife had died, but he'd fought and won vicious custody battles against all the other three.

Ah, pointed out her conscience, *but Alphonse is dead, and in any case Frederick is Amil's father.*

But Frederick was also his father's son, and who knew what he might do? The scandal of an illegitimate baby was the last thing Lycander's Prince needed at this juncture, and she had no idea how he would react.

She didn't like any of the possible scenarios—from a custody battle to show his people that he looked after his own, to an outright and public rejection of Amil. Well, damn it, the first would happen over her dead body and the second made her shudder—because she knew exactly how awful that rejection felt and she wouldn't put Amil through it.

But the Frederick she'd seen today—would he be so callous?

She didn't know. Her thoughts were muddled by the vortex of emotion his arrival had evoked. Because something had warmed inside her, triggering a whole rush of feelings. Memories had swooped and soared, smothering her skin in desire. Flashes of his touch, of their shared joy and passion...all of that had upended any hope of rational thought or perspective. Just like two years before.

When she'd first met Frederick she'd expected to thoroughly dislike him; his reputation as a cutthroat businessman-cum-playboy had seen to that. But when he'd asked her to dinner she'd agreed to it for the publicity. And at that dinner he'd surprised her. At the next he'd surprised her even more, and somehow, as time had gone on, they had forged a connection—one she had tried oh, so hard to tell herself was nothing more than temporary friendship.

Hah!

And then there had been that *stupid* tug of attraction, which had eventually prevailed and overridden every rule she'd set herself.

Well, not this time.

To her relief the doorbell rang. Amil's arrival would put an end to all this.

She dashed to the door and pulled it open, a smile of

welcome on her face. A smile that froze into a rictus of shock.

'Frederick?'

She didn't know why she'd posed it as a question, since it clearly *was* Frederick. Her brain scrambled for purchase and eventually found it as she moved to swing the door shut, to hustle him out.

Too late.

He stepped forward, glanced around the room, and she could almost see the penny begin to drop—slowly at first, as cursory curiosity morphed into deeper question.

'You have a baby?'

His hazel eyes widened in puzzlement, and a small frown creased his brow as he took another step into her sanctum. His gaze rested on each and every item of Amil's.

'Yes.' The word was a whisper—all she could manage as her tummy hollowed and she grasped the doorjamb with lifeless fingers.

'How old?'

Each syllable was ice-cold, edged with glass, and she nearly flinched. No, she would not be intimidated. Not here. Not now. What was done was done, and—rightly or wrongly—she knew that even if she could turn back time she would make the same decision.

'Fourteen months.'

'Girl or boy?'

'Boy.'

Each question, each answer, brought them closer and closer to the inevitable and her brain wouldn't function. Instead, all she could focus on was his face, on the dawn of emotion—wonder, anger, fear and surely hope too?

That last was so unexpected that it jolted her into further words. 'His name is Amil.'

'Amil,' he repeated.

He took another step forward and instinctively she moved as well, as if to protect the life she had built, putting herself between him and her home.

'Is he mine?'

For an instant it was if the world went out of focus. She could almost see a line being drawn in the sands of time—this was the instant that separated 'before' and 'after'. For one brief instant she nearly took the coward's route, wondered if he would swallow the lie that Amil was Sam's. Then she realised she could not, *would* not do that.

'Yes. He is yours. Amil is your son.'

Now she understood the origins of a deafening silence. This one rolled across the room, echoed in her ears until she wanted to shout. Instead she waited, saw his body freeze, saw the gamut of emotion cross his face, watched as it settled into an expression of anger so ice-cold a shiver rippled her skin.

Panic twisted her insides—the die had been cast and she knew that now, whatever happened, life would never be the same.

CHAPTER THREE

STAY STILL. FOCUS ON remaining still.

The room seemed to spin around him, the white walls a rotating blur, the floor tilting under his feet. Good thing he didn't suffer from seasickness. Emotions crashed into him, rebounded off the walls of his brain and the sides of his guts. His heart thudded his ribcage at the speed of insanity.

A child. A son. *His* child. *His* son.

Fourteen months old.

Fourteen months during which his son had had no father. Anger and pain twisted together. Frederick knew exactly what it was like to have no parent—his mother had abandoned him without compunction in return for a lump sum, a mansion and a yearly stipend that allowed her a life of luxury.

Easy come, easy go.

Yes, Frederick knew what it was like to know a parent was not there for him. The anger unfurled in him and solidified.

'My son,' he said slowly, and he couldn't keep the taut rage from his voice.

He saw Sunita's awareness of it, but she stepped forward right into the force field of his anger, tawny eyes fierce and fearless.

'*My* son,' she said.

Stop.

However angry he was, however furious he was, he had to think about the baby. About Amil. Memories of the horrendous custody battles his father had instigated crowded his mind—Stefan, Emerson, Barrett—his father had treated all his sons as possessions.

'*Our* son,' he said.

The knowledge was surreal, almost impossible to comprehend. But it was imperative that he kept in control—there was too much at stake here to let emotion override him. Time to shut emotion down, just as he had for two long years. Move it aside and deal with what had to be done.

'We need to talk.'

She hesitated and then nodded, moving forward to close the front door. She watched him warily, her hands twisted together, her tawny eyes wide.

'How do you know he's mine and not Sam's?'

The look she gave him was intended to wither. 'I'm not an idiot.'

'That is a questionable statement. But what you *have* shown yourself to be is a liar. So you can hardly blame me for the question, or for wanting a better answer than that. How do you know?'

Her eyes narrowed in anger as she caught her lower lip in her teeth and then released it alongside a sigh. 'Sam isn't my boyfriend. He has a perfectly lovely girlfriend called Miranda and they live together. I asked him to fake it to try and explain to you why I left the modelling world.'

'Is there a boyfriend at all?'

She shook her head. 'No.'

So there had been no one since him. The thought provoked a caveman sort of satisfaction that had no place in this discussion. Sunita had deceived him to his face in

order to hide his son from him—now was not the moment
to give a damn about her relationship status. Apart from
the fact that it meant Amil was his.

*Hold it together, Frederick. Shelve the emotion...deal
with the situation at hand.*

'Why didn't you tell me?'

Sunita started to pace. Her stride reminded him of a
caged animal.

'Because I was scared.'

Halting in front of him, she looked so beautiful it momentarily pierced his anger.

'I know how hard this must be for you, but please try
to understand I was terrified.'

For an instant he believed her, but then he recalled her
profession, her ability to play to the camera, and he swat-
ted down the foolish fledgling impulse to show sympathy
and emitted a snort of disbelief.

'Terrified of what? What did I ever do to make you
fear me?'

The idea was abhorrent—he'd witnessed his father in
action, his delight in the exertion of power, and he'd vowed
never to engage in a similar manner. Thus he'd embarked
on a life of pleasure instead.

'It wasn't that straightforward. When we split obviously
I had no idea I was pregnant. I found out a few weeks later
and I was in shock. I did intend to tell you, but I decided to
wait until I got to twelve weeks. And then your brother died.
I *couldn't* tell you then, so I decided to wait some more.'

Now her expression held no apology, and her eyes met
his full-on.

'And?'

'And obviously there was a lot of press at the time about
Lycander. I did some research, and it's all there—your father fought custody battles over every one of his children

except Axel, and that was only because Axel's mother died before he could do so. Your mother never saw you again, his third wife fought for years before she won the right even to *see* her son, and wife number four lost her case because he managed to make out she was unfit and she had to publicly humiliate herself in order to be granted minimal visiting rights.'

'That was my father—not me.'

'Yes, but *you* had become the Lycander heir. Are you saying your father wouldn't have fought for custody of his grandson? Even if you'd wanted to, how could you have stopped him? More to the point, would you have cared enough to try?'

The words hit him like bullets. She hadn't believed he would fight for the well-being of their child. She'd thought he would stand back and watch Alphonse wrest his son away.

He shook his head. *Do you blame her?* asked a small voice. He'd been the Playboy Prince—he'd worked hard, played harder, and made it clear he had no wish for any emotional responsibilities.

'I would *never* have let my father take our child from you.' He knew first-hand what it felt like to grow up without a mother. All the Lycander children did.

'I couldn't take that risk. Plus, you didn't want to be a father—you'd made it more than clear that you had no wish for a relationship or a child.'

'Neither did you.'

His voice was even, non-accusatory, but she bristled anyway, tawny eyes flashing lasers.

'I changed.'

'But you didn't give me the chance to. Not at any point in the past two years. Even if you could justify your deceit to yourself when my father was alive, you could have told me after his death.'

His father's death had unleashed a fresh tumult of emotion to close down. He'd had to accept that he would now never forge a relationship with the man who had constantly put him down—the man who had never forgiven him for his mother's actions. And on a practical level it had pitchforked him into the nightmare scenario of ascension to the throne.

But none of that explained her continued deceit.

'I read the papers, Frederick. You have had enough to contend with in the past year to keep your throne—the revelation of a love-child with me would have finished you off. You were practically engaged to Lady Kaitlin.'

'So you want my *gratitude* for keeping my child a secret? You've persuaded yourself that you did it for me? Is that how you sleep at night?'

'I sleep fine at night. I did what I thought was right. I didn't want Amil to grow up knowing that he had been the reason his father lost his throne, or lost the woman he loved. That is too big a burden for any child.'

The words were rounded with utter certainty.

'That was not your decision to make. At any point. Regardless of the circumstances, you should have come to me as soon as you knew you were pregnant. Nothing should have stopped you. Not Axel, not my father, not Kaitlin— *nothing*. You have deprived him of his father.'

'I chose depriving him of his father over depriving him of his mother.' Her arms dropped to her sides and a sudden weariness slumped her shoulders. 'We can argue about this for ever—I did what I thought was best. For Amil.'

'*And* you.'

'If you like. But in this case the two were synonymous. He needs me.'

'I get that.'

He'd have settled for any mother—had lived in hope that one of the series of stepmothers would give a damn. Until he'd worked out there was little point getting attached, as his father quite simply got rid of each and every one.

'But Amil also needs his father. That would be me.'

'I accept that you are his father.'

Although she didn't look happy about it, her eyes were full of wariness.

'But whether he needs you or not depends on what you are offering him. If that isn't good for him then he doesn't need you. It makes no odds whether you are his father or not. The whole "blood is thicker than water" idea sucks.'

No argument there. 'I *will* be part of Amil's life.'

'It's not that easy.'

'It doesn't matter if it's easy.'

'Those are words. Words are meaningless. Exactly *how* would it work? You'll disguise yourself every so often and sneak over here to see him on "unofficial business" masked by your charity work? Or will you announce to your people that you have a love-child?'

Before he could answer there was a knock at the door and they both stilled.

'It's my grandmother…with Amil.' Panic touched her expression and she closed her eyes and inhaled deeply. 'I don't want my grandmother to know until we've worked out what to do.'

Frederick searched for words, tried to think, but the enormity of the moment had eclipsed his ability to rationalise. Instead fear came to the podium—he had a child, a son, and he was about to meet him.

What would he feel when he saw Amil?

The fear tasted ashen—what if he felt nothing?

What if he was like his mother and there was no instinctive love, merely an indifference that bordered on dislike? Or like his father, who had treated his sons as possessions, chess pieces in his petty power games?

If so, then he'd fake it—no matter what he did or didn't feel, he'd fake love until it became real.

He hauled in a deep breath and focused on Sunita's face. 'I'll leave as soon as you let them in. Ask your grandmother to look after Amil tonight. Then I'll come back and we can finish this discussion.'

Sunita nodded agreement and stepped forward.

His heart threatened to leave his ribcage and moisture sheened his neck as she pulled the door open.

A fleeting impression registered, of a tall, slender woman with silver hair pulled back in a bun, clad in a shimmering green and red sari, and then his gaze snagged on the little boy in her arms. Raven curls, chubby legs, a goofy smile for his mother.

Mine. My son.

Emotion slammed into him—so hard he almost recoiled and had to concentrate to stay steady. Fight or flight kicked in—half of him wanted to turn and run in sheer terror, the other half wanted to step forward and take his son, shield him from all and any harm.

'Nanni, this is an old friend of mine who's dropped in.'

'Good to meet you.' Somehow Frederick kept his voice even, forced himself to meet the older woman's alert gaze. He saw the small frown start to form on her brow and turned back to Sunita. 'It was great to see you again, Sunita. 'Til later.'

A last glance at his son—*his son*—and he walked away.

Sunita scooped Amil up and buried herself in his warmth and his scent. She held him so close that he wriggled in protest, so she lowered him to the ground and he crawled towards his play mat.

'Thank you for looking after him.'

'I enjoyed it immensely. And thank *you*, Sunita, for allowing me to be part of Amil's life. And yours.'

'Stop! I have told you—you don't need to thank me.'

Yet every time she did.

'Yes, I do. I was neither a good mother nor a good grandmother. You have given me a chance of redemption, and I appreciate that with all my heart.'

'We've been through this, Nanni; the past is the past and we're only looking forward.'

Her grandmother's marriage had been deeply unhappy—her husband had been an autocrat who had controlled every aspect of his family's life with an iron hand. When Sunita's mother had fallen pregnant by a British man who'd had no intent of standing by her, her father had insisted she be disowned.

Sunita could almost hear her mother's voice now: *'Suni, sweetheart, never, ever marry a man who can control you.'*

It was advice Sunita intended to take one step further— she had no plans to marry anyone, *ever*. Her father's marriage had been a misery of incompatibility, bitterness and blame—an imbroglio she'd been pitchforked into to live a Cinderella-like existence full of thoughtless, uncaring relations.

'Please, Nanni. You are a wonderful grandmother and great-grandmother and Amil adores you. Now, I have a favour to ask. Would you mind looking after Amil for the rest of the evening?'

'So you can see your friend again?'

'Yes.'

'The friend you didn't introduce?'

Sunita opened her mouth and closed it again.

Her grandmother shook her head. 'You don't have to tell me.'

'I *will* tell you, Nanni—but after dinner, if that's OK.'

'You will tell me whenever you are ready. Whatever it is, this time I will be there for you.'

An hour later, with Amil fed and his bag packed, Sunita gave her grandmother a hug. She watched as the driver she'd insisted on providing manoeuvred the car into the stream of traffic, waved, and then made her way back up-stairs... To find the now familiar breadth of Frederick on the doorstep, a jacket hooked over his shoulder.

'Come in. Let's talk.'

He followed her inside and closed the door, draping his dark grey jacket over the back of a chair. 'Actually, I thought we could talk somewhere else. I've booked a table at Zeus.'

Located in one of Mumbai's most luxurious hotels, Zeus was the city's hottest restaurant, graced by celebrities and anyone who wanted to see and be seen.

Foreboding crept along her skin, every instinct on full alert. 'Why on earth would you do that?'

'Because I am taking the mother of my child out for dinner so we can discuss the future.'

Sunita stared at him as the surreal situation deepened into impossibility. 'If you and I go out for dinner it will galvanise a whole load of press interest.'

'That is the point. We are going public. I will not keep Amil a secret, or make him unofficial business.'

She blinked as her brain crashed and tried to change gear. 'But we haven't discussed this at all.'

This was going way too fast, and events were threaten-ing to spiral out of control. *Her* control.

'I don't think we should go public until we've worked out the practical implications—until we have a plan.'

'Not possible. People are already wondering where I am. Especially my chief advisor. People may have spotted us at the café, and April Fotherington will be wondering if my presence in Mumbai is connected to you. I want the truth to come out on *my* terms, not hers, or those of whichever reporter makes it their business to "expose" the story. I want this to break in a positive way.'

Sunita eyed him, part of her impressed by the sheer strength and absolute assurance he projected, another part wary of the fact he seemed to have taken control of the situation without so much as a by-your-leave.

'I'm not sure that's possible. Think about the scandal— your people won't like this.' And they wouldn't like *her*, a supermodel with a dubious past. 'Are you sure this is the best way to introduce Amil's existence to your people?'

'I don't know. But I believe it's the right way to show my people that this is *good* news, that Amil is not a secret. That I am being honest.'

An unpleasant twinge of guilt pinched her nerves— *she* had kept Amil secret, *she* had been dishonest. She had made a decision that no longer felt anywhere near as right as it had this morning.

'So what do you say?' he asked. 'Will you have dinner with me?'

The idea gave her a sudden little thrill, brought back a sea of memories of the dinners they had shared two years before—dinners when banter and serious talk had flown back and forth, when each word, each gesture, had been a movement in the ancient dance of courtship. A courtship she had never meant to consummate...

But this meal would be on a whole new level and courtship would not be on the table. Wherever they held this discussion tonight, the only topic of conversation would be Amil and the future.

And if Frederick believed this strategy was the best way forward then she owed him her co-operation.

'Let's get this show on the road.' An unexpected fizz of excitement buzzed through her. She could *do* this; she'd always relished a fight and once upon a time she'd revelled in a show. 'But I need to change.'

'You look fine to me.'

His voice was deep and molten, and just like that the atmosphere changed. Awareness hummed and vibrated, shimmering around them, and she had to force herself to remain still, to keep her feet rooted to the cool tiles of the floor. The hazel of his eyes had darkened in a way she remembered all too well, and now it was exhilaration of a different sort that heated her veins.

Stop.

All that mattered here was Amil and his future. Two years ago she had tried and failed to resist the magnetic pull that Frederick exerted on her—a pull she had distrusted, and this time would not permit. Whatever her treacherous hormones seemed to think.

Perhaps he realised the same, because he stepped backwards and nodded. 'But I appreciate you want to change.'

'I do. You need a show, and a show is exactly what I can provide. Luckily I kept some of the clothes from my modelling days.'

Even if she'd never once worn them, she loved them still. Silk, chiffon and lace, denim and velvet, long skirts and short, flared and skinny—she had enjoyed showcasing each and every outfit. Had refused to wear any item that didn't make her soul sing. And now there was no denying the buzz. This was what she had once lived for and craved. Publicity, notice, fame—all things she could spin and control.

Almost against her will, her mind fizzed with possibility. Amil was no longer a secret, no longer in danger—they could live their lives as they wished. She could resume her career, be Sunita again, walk the catwalks and revel in fashion and all its glorious aspects. Amil would, of course, come with her—just as she had accompanied her mother to fashion shoots—and Nanni could come too.

Life would take on a new hue without the terrible burden of discovery clouding every horizon. Though of course Frederick would be part of that life, if only a minor part. His real life lay in Lycander, and she assumed he would want only a few visits a year perhaps.

Whoa! Slow right down, Suni!

She had no idea what Frederick's plans were, and she'd do well to remember that before she waltzed off into la-la land. She didn't know this man—this Frederick.

Her gaze rested on him, absorbed the breadth of his body, his masculine presence, the determined angle of his stubbled jaw, the shadowed eyes crinkled now in a network of lines she thought probably hadn't come from laughter. Her breath caught on a sudden wave of desire. Not only physical desire, but a stupid yearning to walk over and smooth the shadows away.

A yearning she filed away under both dangerous and delusional as she turned and left the room.

CHAPTER FOUR

FREDERICK CHANGED INTO the suit he'd had delivered to him whilst he was waiting and prowled the flat on the lookout for evidence of Amil's life.

Amil. The syllables were still so unfamiliar—his only knowledge of his son that brief glimpse a few hours earlier. But there would be time—plenty of time—to catch up on the past fourteen months. Provided Sunita agreed to his proposition—and she *would* agree.

Whatever it took, he would make her see his option was the only way forward.

He paused in front of a framed photograph of Sunita and a newborn Amil. He looked at the tiny baby, with his downy dark hair, the impossible perfection of his minuscule fingernails, and the utter vulnerability of him twisted Frederick's gut.

Shifting his gaze to Sunita, he saw the love in her brown eyes clear in every nuance, every part of her body. Her beauty was unquestionable, but this was a beauty that had nothing to do with physical features and everything to do with love.

Perhaps he should feel anger that he had missed out on that moment, but his overwhelming emotion was relief—gratitude, even—that his son had been given something so vital. Something he himself had never received. *His* mother had handed him straight over to a nanny and a few scant years later had disappeared from his life.

For a long moment Frederick gazed at the photo, trying to figure out what he should feel, what he *would* feel when he finally met Amil properly, held him... Panic hammered his chest and he stepped backwards. What if he was like his mother—what if he quite simply lacked the parenting gene?

The click of heels against marble snapped him to attention and he stepped back from the photo, turning to see Sunita advance into the room. For a moment his lungs truly ceased to work as his pulse ratcheted up a notch or three.

Sunita looked... It was impossible to describe her without recourse to a thesaurus. *This* was the woman he remembered—the one who dressed to catch the eye. But it wasn't only the dress with its bright red bodice and gently plumed skirt that showcased her trademark legs. The bright colour was toned down by contrasting black satin panels and silver stiletto heels. It was the way she wore it—she seemed to bring the dress alive. And vice versa. A buzz vibrated from her—an energy and sparkle that epitomised Sunita.

'Wow!' was the best he could do as he fought down visceral desire and the need to tug her into his arms and rekindle the spark that he knew with gut-wrenching certainty would burst into flame. To kiss her senseless...

What the hell was he thinking? More to the point, what part of himself was he thinking *with*?

Maybe he was more like his father than he knew. Alphonse had always put physical desire above all else. If he'd been attracted to a woman he'd acted on that attraction, regardless of marriage vows, fidelity or the tenets of plain, common decency. The last ruler of Lycander had believed that *his* desires were paramount, and it didn't matter who got hurt in the process.

Frederick wouldn't walk that road. He never had—that, at least, was one immoral path he'd avoided.

His business with Sunita was exactly that—*business*. He had an idea to propound, an idea he would not mix with the physical.

'You look fantastic.'

'Thank you. I know it sounds shallow, but it is awesome to dress up again.'

She smoothed her hand down the skirt and her smile caught at his chest.

'You look pretty good yourself. Where did the suit come from?'

'I had it delivered whilst I was waiting.'

'Good thinking, Batman.'

Her voice was a little breathless, and he knew that she was as affected as he was by their proximity. Her scent teased him, her eyes met his, and what he saw in their deep brown depths made him almost groan aloud.

Enough.

Right now he had to focus on the most important factor, and that was Amil. Irritation scoured him that he could be letting physical attraction come into play.

He nodded to the door. 'We'd better go.'

Sunita wanted, *needed* this journey to come to an end. Despite the spacious interior of the limo, Frederick was too...*close*.

Memories lingered in the air, and her body was on high alert, tuned in to his every move, and she loathed her own weakness as much now as she had two years before. She needed to distract herself, to focus on what was important—and that was Amil.

The day's events had moved at warp speed and she was desperately trying to keep up. The truth was out, and it was imperative she kept control of a future that she could no longer reliably predict.

Frederick wanted to be a real part of Amil's life—he had made that more than clear. But at this point she had no idea what that meant, and she knew she had to tread carefully.

The limo slowed down and she took a deep breath as it glided to a stop.

'Ready?' he asked.

'Ready.'

With any luck she wouldn't have lost her touch with the press. In truth, she'd always liked the paparazzi. Her mother had always told her that publicity was a means to measure success, part of the climb to fame and fortune and independence.

They stepped out into a crowd of reporters, the click of cameras and a fire of questions.

'Are you back together?'

'Friends or lovers?'

'Does Kaitlin know?'

'Where have you been, Sunita?'

Frederick showed no sign of tension. His posture and smile were relaxed, his whole attitude laid back.

'At present we have no comment. But if you hold on I promise we will have an announcement to make after dinner.'

Next to him, Sunita smiled the smile that had shot her to catwalk fame. She directed a small finger-wave at a reporter who'd always given her positive press, a smile at a woman she'd always enjoyed a good relationship with, and a wink at a photographer renowned for his audacity.

Then they left the reporters behind and entered the restaurant, and despite the knowledge of how important the forthcoming conversation was a part of Sunita revelled in the attention she was gathering. The simple ability to walk with her own natural grace, to know it was OK to be recognised, her appreciation of the dress and the inner confidence it gave her—all of it was such a contrast to the past two years, during which she had lived in constant denial of her own identity, burdened by the fear of discovery.

The manager beamed at them as he led them past the busy tables, where patrons looked up from their food and a buzz immediately spread. Sunita kept her eyes ahead, noting the dark-stained English Oak screens and latticing that graced the room, the hustle and bustle from the open-plan kitchen where chefs raced round, the waiters weaving in and out, and the tantalising smells that drifted into the eating area.

'As requested, we've seated you in a private dining area where you will be undisturbed. My head chef has arranged a buffet for you there, with samples of all our signature dishes, and there is, of course, champagne on ice—we are very happy to welcome you both here.'

He turned to Sunita.

'I do not expect you to remember me, but when you were a child your mother brought you many, many times to the restaurant I worked in then. Your mother was a lovely lady.'

Memory tugged as she studied the manager's face. 'I *do* remember you. You're Nikhil! You used to give me extra sweets and fortune cookies, and you would help me read the fortunes.'

His smile broadened. 'That is correct—I am very happy to see you here, and I am very sorry about your mother. She was a good woman.'

'Thank you. That means a lot to me. And it would have to her as well.'

It really would. So many people had looked down on

Leela Baswani because she had been a single, unmarried mother, and a model and actress to boot. But her mother had refused to cower before them; she had lived her life and she'd loved every minute of it—even those terrible last few months. Months she didn't want to remember, of watching her mother decline, knowing that soon she would be left alone in the world.

But those were not the memories Leela would have wanted her daughter to carry forth into life. Instead she would remember her as Nikhil did—as a good, brave, vibrant woman.

Nikhil showed them into the private dining room, where a beautifully decorated table laid with snowy white linen held fluted glassware, gleaming cutlery and a simple table decoration composed of an arrangement of glorious white roses.

Sunita looked at them, and then at Nikhil, and a lump formed in her throat. White roses had been her mother's favourite flower—her trademark accessory—and as the scent reached her nostrils she closed her eyes for a second. 'Thank you, Nikhil.'

The manager gave a small bow. 'You are very welcome. Now, both of you enjoy the food. I believe our chef has excelled himself. And I guarantee you complete privacy.'

With one more beaming smile, he left, closing the door behind him.

'I'm sorry about your mother,' Frederick said.

'Thank you.'

'She isn't mentioned in any articles about you except April's most recent one. None of your family is.'

'No. They aren't.'

And that was the way it would stay—she would love to remember her mother more publicly, but to do that would risk questions about her father, and she'd severed her ties

with him years before—the man who'd abandoned her before birth and then reappeared in her life only to make it
thoroughly miserable.

'Anyway, we aren't here to speak of my family.' He
raised an eyebrow and she bit her lip. 'I mean, we are here
to discuss Amil's future.'

'We are. But first shall we help ourselves to food?'

She nodded. No way could she hurt Nikhil's feelings,
but she sensed there was more to Frederick's suggestion
than that. It was almost as if he were stalling, giving himself time to prepare, and a sense of foreboding prickled
her skin—one she did her best to shake off as she made a
selection from the incredible dishes displayed on the table.

There was a tantalising array of dumplings with descriptions written in beautiful calligraphy next to each platter—
prawn and chive, shanghai chicken, *pak choi*... Next to them
lay main courses that made her mouth water—Szechuan
clay pot chicken, salmon in Assam sauce, ginger fried rice...

The smell itself was enough to allay her fears, and she
reminded herself that Frederick had a country to run—
other fish to fry, so to speak. Surely the most he would
want would be to contribute to Amil's upkeep and see
him a few times a year. That would work—that would be
more than enough.

Once they were seated, she took a deep breath. 'Before
we start this discussion you need to know that I will not
agree to anything that feels wrong for Amil. He is my priority here and if you try to take him away from me I will fight
you with my last dying breath. I just want that out there.'

There was something almost speculative in his gaze,
alongside a steely determination that matched her own.
'Amil is my priority too—and that means I *will* be a real
part of his life. That is non-negotiable. *I* just want *that* out
there.'

'Fine. But what does that mean?'

'I'm glad you asked that, because I've given this some thought and I know what I believe is best for Amil's future.'

The smoothness of his voice alerted Sunita's anxiety. The presentiment of doom returned and this time her very bones knew it was justified. Spearing a dumpling with an effort at nonchalance, she waved her fork in the air.

'Why don't you tell me what you have in mind?'

His hazel eyes met hers, his face neutral. 'I want you to marry me.'

CHAPTER FIVE

'MARRY YOU?' SUITA STARED at him, flabberghasted. 'That's a joke, right?'

It must be his opening bid in negotiations designed to throw her into a state of incoherence. If so, he'd slammed the nail on the head.

'No joke. Trust me, marriage isn't a topic I'd kid about. It's a genuine proposal—I've thought it through.'

'When? In the past few hours? Are you certifiably *nuts*?'

'This makes sense.'

'How? There is no universe where this makes even a particle of a molecule of sense.'

'This is what is best for Amil—best for our son.'

'No, it isn't. Not in this day and age. You *cannot* play the let's-get-together-for-our-child's-sake card.'

That was the stuff of fairy tales, and she was damned sure that her mother had been right about those being a crock of manure.

'Yes, I can. In the circumstances.'

'What circumstances?' Her fogged brain attempted to illuminate a pathway to understanding and failed.

'If you marry me Amil will become Crown Prince of Lycander after me. If you don't, he won't.'

The words took the wind out of the sails of incredulity. Of *course*. *Duh!* But the idea that Frederick would marry her to legitimise Amil hadn't even tiptoed across her mind. The whole concept of her baby one day ruling a principality seemed surreal, and right now she needed to cling onto reality.

'We can't get married to give Amil a crown.'

'But we can get married so that we don't deprive him of one.'

'Semantics.' *Think*. 'He won't feel deprived of something he never expected to have.' *Would he?* 'Amil will grow up knowing…'

Her voice trailed off. Knowing what? That if his mother had agreed to marry his father he would have been a prince, a ruler, rather than a prince's illegitimate love-child.

'Knowing that he can be whatever he wants to be,' she concluded.

'As long as what he wants to be isn't Ruler of Lycander.'

Panic stole over her, wrapped her in tentacles of anxiety. 'You are putting me in an impossible position. You are asking me to decide Amil's entire future. To make decisions on his behalf.'

'No. I am suggesting *we* make this decision together. I believe this is the best course of action for Amil. If you think otherwise then convince me.'

'He may not want to be pushed into a pre-ordained future—may not want to be a ruler. Why would we burden him with the weight of duty, with all the rules and obligations that come with it?'

'Because it is his *right* to rule. Just as it was my brother's.'

His voice was even, but she saw the shadows chase across his eyes, sensed the pain the words brought.

'Axel wanted to rule—he believed in his destiny.'

'So you believe this is Amil's destiny?' Sunita shook her

head. 'It's too abstract. We make our own destiny and Amil will make his, whatever we decide to do. I want to make the decision that is best for his wellbeing and happiness—you don't need a crown for either.'

'This isn't about need—this is about his birthright. As my first born son he has the right to inherit the Lycander crown.'

'Even though he was born out of wedlock?'

It was the phrase her grandmother had used to describe Sunita's birth, to try and explain why her husband had thrown their pregnant daughter out.

'I know it is hard to understand in this day and age, Sunita, but in our family a mixed race child, born out of wedlock, was a stigma. It wasn't right, but it was how my husband felt.'

A feeling shared by others. Sunita could still feel the sting of the taunts her half-siblings had flung at her—nasty, insidious words that had clawed at her self-esteem.

Focus. Frederick watched her, his hazel eyes neutral and cool; he was in control and she quite clearly wasn't. Her thoughts raced round a playground of panic, visited the seesaw, spent time on the slide. Being born out of wedlock would have no impact on Amil's life; it was not a reason to get married.

She forced herself to concentrate on Frederick's answer to her question.

'It makes no odds as long as we legitimise him through marriage,' he said. 'Lycander's rules are complex, but clear on that front.'

Oh, Lord. What was she supposed to do? How could she make a decision like this without the use of a crystal ball? Her mother had believed the right course of action had been to hand Sunita over to her father.

'People can change, Suni,' her mother had said. She'd

stroked Sunita's hair with a hand that had looked almost translucent, the effort of even that movement an evident strain. *'I have to believe that.'*

Sunita understood the uncharacteristic thread of sentimentality in her mother over those final weeks. Leela Baswani had wanted to die believing her daughter would be safe and happy, and so she had allowed herself to be conned again by the man who had already broken her heart. She'd allowed herself to believe that people could change.

Well, she'd been wrong. And so was this.

'This is impossible, Frederick. We can't spend the rest of our lives together.'

The very idea of spending a *week* with anyone made her skin prickle in affront—she could almost feel the manacles closing round her wrists. 'Maybe we should get married, legitimise Amil, and then get a divorce.'

Even as the words left her lips she knew how stupid they were.

'No. I want to give Amil a life with both his parents, and most importantly, if he is to rule Lycander, he needs to live in the palace, be brought up to understand his inheritance. And I need a wife—a true consort.'

This was becoming laughable. 'Really, I am *not* wife material—trust me on this.'

His broad shoulders lifted. 'But you *are* the mother of my child.'

Fabulous. 'So you'll make do with me because I come with a ready-made heir? And this whole marriage idea is because we are convenient?' The idea caused welcome anger—an emotion she could manage way better than panic.

'You don't care about Amil as a person—you only care about him as a commodity.'

'No!' Her words had clearly touched a nerve. 'I care about Amil because he is my son and I believe this is his right. I want him to grow up with two parents. And, believe me, this is hardly *convenient*. I intended to present my people with a wife and heir in a more conventional way.'

'Well, gee, thank you. That makes us feel *really* special.'

But she was the woman who had omitted to mention his son's existence—making her feel special would hardly be anywhere on his agenda.

His raised eyebrows indicated complete accord with her unspoken thought. 'There's no point in hypocrisy. If you expect me to go down on one knee, think again.'

'I don't expect anything—especially not a proposal. I don't want to marry you; I don't want to marry anyone.'

'I appreciate that. Until recently marriage has never exactly been high on my to-do list either. Back in the day I had a business to run and a party lifestyle to maintain. But circumstances have changed. For us both. *We* have Amil. *I* now have a country to run. I need a wife and I need an heir…to show the people of Lycander that I have changed. That I am responsible, that I offer stability, that I can put the principality's needs above my own.'

Sunita tried to equate this Frederick with the man she had known. '*Have* you changed?'

'Yes.' The syllable was bleak in its certainty, but despite its brevity it conveyed absolute conviction. 'You can choose to believe that or not, as you wish. But believe this: I need to get married.'

'Well, I don't. I prefer to be on my own.' She didn't want to be tied to anyone—she wanted to be independent and free to make decisions for herself and for Amil. 'Free.' *In control.*

'I understand that.' His jaw set in a hard line. 'But marriage is the only way to secure Amil his birthright and give him two parents one hundred per cent of the time.'

There was a strange undercurrent to his voice, and she realised just how important this must be to him. According to her research, his parents had split when he was three and his father had won sole custody. After that he'd had a series of stepmothers, none of whom had lasted more than a few years. So perhaps it was little wonder he wanted to give his son the kind of stable family he'd never had. For a moment, compassion for the little boy he had once been touched her and she forced herself to concentrate on the present.

'But it wouldn't be good for Amil to grow up and see his parents in an unhappy marriage.'

'Why assume it will be unhappy?'

'Because…' To her own annoyance, not a single reason sprang to mind that didn't sound stupid. Eventually she said, 'You can't expect me to sign up to a life sentence with a man I don't even know.'

'Fair enough. Then let's rectify that.'

He smiled—a smile of the toe-curling variety, like sunshine breaking through a grey cloudbank. And she couldn't help smiling back. But then the moment was gone and the stormy skies reappeared.

'Rectify it how?'

'Let's get to know each other. Bring Amil to Lycander and—'

'No! Once we are in Lycander I have no idea if we will be subject to Lycander law. Which, as far as I can gather, is *you*.'

The smile was a distant memory now, his face set in granite. 'You don't trust me?'

'I don't trust anyone.' After all, if you couldn't trust your own father, who *could* you trust? His promise to her mother that he would look after Sunita, care for her as only a parent could, had turned out to be a bunch of empty, meaningless syllables.

'So we stay here.'

He raised his hands. 'Fair enough. But I can't be away for too long. I can stay in Mumbai for a few days or... Wait, I have a better idea.' The smile made a return. 'How about we go away for a few days? You and me. Away from the press and the politics and the spotlight.'

'You and me?' Panic and horror cartwheeled in her stomach.

'Yes. You and me. I'll put my money where my mouth is—you said you couldn't marry someone you didn't know, so here's the opportunity to spend time with me. Twenty-four-seven, with no distractions.'

'Be still my beating heart.'

Now his smile broadened and this time she was sure her hair curled.

'I *knew* you'd like the idea. Would your grandmother be happy to look after Amil?'

'If I agree to this, Amil comes with us.' A frown touched her brow and her eyes narrowed in suspicion. 'Surely you want to get to know your son?'

'Of course I do. But before we spend time together as a family, we need to know where we stand. I know he is only a baby, but I want him to have certainty and stability.'

The kind of certainty she guessed he'd never known. Again for an instant she wanted to reach out and offer comfort. *What to do? What to do?* In truth she didn't know. She should close this down now—but was that the right thing for Amil?

Frederick wanted to be a real part of his life, wanted to make him his heir. She couldn't in all conscience dismiss it out of hand. More than that, insane though it might be, there was a tiny part of her that didn't want to. That same tiny part that two years ago had wanted Frederick to ask her to stay, to sweep her into his arms and—

Cue mental eye-roll and a reality check. Fairy tales didn't exist. This was for Amil's sake.

'OK. Two days. I won't leave Amil longer than that.'

'Deal. Where do you want to go?'

Sunita thought for a moment. 'Goa.' That would keep it all in perspective—her parents had spent some time in Goa; they'd been happy there, but that hadn't led to a happily-ever-after in any sense.

'OK. Here's how it'll work. I'll have my people pick up Amil and your grandmother now, and bring them to the hotel. Once we make the announcement about Amil the press will converge. I want my son safe here, under royal security protection.'

She could feel the colour leech from her skin and saw that he had noticed it.

'I don't believe he is danger, but his position has changed. No matter what we decide, there will be more interest in him and his life from now on.'

She inhaled an audible breath. 'You're right. I'll call my grandmother and prepare her.'

Pulling her phone out of her bag, she rose and walked to the opposite end of the room.

Frederick watched as Sunita paced the width of the room as she talked, her voice low but animated, one hand gesturing as the conversation progressed.

It was impossible not to admire her fluidity of movement, her vibrancy. At least she hadn't blown the marriage idea out of the water. But he'd known she wouldn't do that—for Amil she had to consider it. What woman would deprive her son of a crown? Yet unease still tingled in his veins. Sunita might well be the one woman who would do exactly that.

Ironic, really—his chief advisor had a list of women who wanted to marry him, and he'd proposed to the one woman who didn't even want to audition for the part of bride.

No matter—he would convince her that this was the way forward. Whatever it took.

His conscience jabbed him. Really? *Whatever* it took? Maybe that was how his father had justified the custody battles.

Abruptly he turned away and, pulling his own phone out, set to work making arrangements.

He dropped his phone back in his pocket as she returned to the table. 'How did your grandmother take it?'

'With her trademark unflappable serenity. I think she suspected—she may even have recognised you earlier and put two and two together. She'll have Amil ready.' Her chin jutted out at a defiant angle. 'I've asked Sam and Miranda as well.'

She really didn't trust him. 'Do you really think I will take Amil from you by force?'

Silence greeted this and he exhaled heavily.

'If you can't trust my morality then at least trust my intelligence. I want you to marry me—kidnapping Amil would hardly help my cause. Or garner me positive publicity in Lycander. You hid Amil from me for two years. I have more reason to distrust *you* than vice versa.'

'Maybe it's best if neither of us trusts each other.'

She had a point.

'Works for me. Whilst we are away Amil will be in your grandmother's charge, with Sam and Miranda as your back-up. But they remain based in the hotel, and if they go anywhere one of my staff goes with them. Does that work for you?'

'Yes.'

'Good. Once they are safely here I'll announce it to the press. We'll leave for Goa tomorrow, after my visit to the school.'

'Whoa! Hold on.' One elegant hand rose in the air to stop him. 'This is a *joint* operation. So, first off, *I* want to make the announcement. And we are *not* mentioning marriage.'

She drummed her fingers on the table and he could see her mind whir. This had always been her forte—she'd used to play the press like a finely tuned instrument, and had always orchestrated publicity for maximum impact with impeccable timing.

'Prince Frederick and I are delighted to announce that fourteen months ago our son Amil was born. Obviously we have a great deal to discuss about the future, which we will be doing over the next few days. My press office will be in touch with details of a photo opportunity with the three of us tomorrow.'

'Photo opportunity?' Three of us…? The words filled him with equal parts terror and anticipation.

'Yes. Better to arrange it than have them stalk us to try and get one. And I assume you want to spend time with Amil before we go?' She clocked his hesitation before he could mask it. 'Is there a problem?'

'No.' *Liar.*

Her eyes filled with doubt. He racked his brain and realised that in this case only the truth would suffice.

'I don't want to upset Amil or confuse him just before you leave him.'

He didn't want his son to believe on any level that it

was his father's fault that he was losing his mother. Even for a few days.

For the first time since his proposal she smiled—a real, genuine smile—and he blinked at the warmth it conveyed. If he were fanciful, he'd swear it had heated his skin and his soul.

'You won't upset him. Truly. How about we take him to the Hanging Gardens? He loves it there—the press can take their photos and then we can take him for a walk.'

'Sounds great.'

But the warmth dissipated and left a cold sheen of panic in its wake. What if the meeting didn't go well? What if they couldn't connect?

Then he'd fake it. If he could close his emotions down—and he was a past master in the art—then surely the reverse would be true too. 'My school visit is planned for seven a.m., so if we schedule the press for midday that should work.'

'I'd like to come with you to the school. It's a cause I'd love to be involved in, and now…now I can.'

Her smile broadened and it occurred to him that, whilst he couldn't condone what she had done, hiding Amil impacted on Sunita's life heavily. She'd lost her career, had to subdue her identity and become anonymous.

Sheesh. Get a grip. Any minute now he'd start to feel sorry for her.

The point now was that Sunita would be an asset to the charity.

His phone beeped and he read the message.

'Amil and your grandmother are in the hotel. So are Sam and Miranda. So let's go and face the press.'

And then he'd face the music. He had no doubt his chief advisor had set up a veritable orchestra.

CHAPTER SIX

'YOU'VE DONE *WHAT*?' Marcus Alrikson, hot off a private jet, scooted across the floor of the hotel suite. 'The whole existence of a secret baby is bad enough—but now you're telling me you have proposed marriage!' Marcus paused, pinched the bridge of his nose and inhaled deeply. 'Why?'

Frederick surveyed him from the depths of the leather sofa. 'Because I have a son, and I want my son to live with me *and* his mother. I realise that flies in the face of Lycander tradition, but there you have it. I want Amil to inherit his birthright. The only way to achieve both those goals is marriage.'

'If this marriage loses you the crown he won't have a birthright to inherit.'

'It won't.' Frederick imbued his voice with a certainty he was far from feeling—but he was damned if he would admit that to Marcus. 'This is the right thing to do and the people of Lycander will see that.'

'Perhaps...but that doesn't mean they will accept Sunita or Amil.'

'They will have no reason not to. Sunita has proved herself to be an exemplary mother. And she will be an exemplary princess.'

Marcus shook his head. 'She is a supermodel with a reputation as a party girl. You have no idea what she may or may not do—she would never have made my list in a million years. She is as far from Kaitlin Derwent as the moon is from Jupiter.'

'And look what happened with Lady Kaitlin. Plus, don't you think you're being a little hypocritical? What about *my* reputation?'

'You have spent two years showing that you have changed. The reforms you are undertaking for Lycander are what the people want. You may have been a playboy with a party lifestyle, but you also founded a global business—Freddy Petrelli's Olive Oil is on supermarket shelves worldwide. At least you partied on your own dime.'

'So did Sunita. And her party days were over by the time we met.'

'Sunita has spent two years hiding your son from you,' Marcus retorted. 'There is nothing to suggest she will be good for Lycander and plenty to suggest she will plunge the monarchy straight back into scandal. She could run off with Amil, file for divorce before the honeymoon is over...'

'She won't.'

He couldn't know that, though—not really. He'd known Sunita for a couple of weeks two years ago. Doubt stepped in but he kicked it out even as he acknowledged the sceptical rise of his chief advisor's eyebrow. 'Or at least it's a risk I am willing to take.'

'It is too big a risk. The women on my list are open to the idea of an arranged marriage—they have been brought up to understand the rules. Dammit, Frederick, we *had* this discussion. We agreed that it was important for the Lycander bride to be totally unlike your father's later choices and more in line with his first wife.'

Axel's mother, Princess Michaela, a princess in her own right, had been a good woman.

'We did. But circumstances have changed.'

'Doesn't matter. You plan to present your people with a bride who may well cause a scandal broth of divorce and custody battles.'

'I have no choice—none of this is Amil's fault.'

'I am not suggesting you turn your back on Amil. Provide for him. See him regularly. But do not marry his mother.'

'No.' It was as simple as that. 'I will be a real father to Amil and this is the way forward. I'm doing this, Marcus—with or without your help.'

Silence reigned and then Marcus exhaled a long sigh and sank into the seat opposite. 'As you wish.'

Sunita surveyed her reflection in the mirror, relieved that there was no evidence of the tumult that raged in her brain. Frederick...discovery... Amil... Crown Prince... marriage... Goa....disaster.

There was potential disaster on all fronts—the thought of marriage was surreal, the enormity of the decision she needed to make made her head whirl and the idea of two days in Goa with Frederick made her tummy loop the loop.

A tentative knock on the door heralded the arrival of Eric, the Lycander staff member who had been dispatched to her apartment the previous night.

'Good morning, Eric, and thank you again for getting my things. I really appreciate it.'

'You're very welcome, ma'am. The Prince is ready.'

She followed Eric through the opulence of the hotel, with its gold and white theme, along plush carpet and past gilded walls, through the marble lobby, past luscious plants and spectacular flower arrangements and outside to the limo. There Frederick awaited her, leant against the hood of the car, dressed casually in jeans and a T-shirt, his blond hair still a touch spiked with damp, as if he'd grabbed a shower on the run.

'A limo? Isn't that a touch ostentatious?'

The flippant comment made to mask her catch of breath, the thump of her heart. 'I promised the children a limo after my last visit—they were most disappointed when I turned up in a taxi.'

He held the door for her and she slid inside, the air-conditioned interior a welcome relief against the humidity, with its suggestion of imminent monsoon rain.

'They are amazing kids—they make you feel…humble.'

Sunita nodded. 'I read up on the charity last night. The whole set-up sounds awesome and its achievements are phenomenal. I love the simplicity of the idea—using open spaces as classrooms—and I admire the dedication of the volunteers. I'll do all I can to raise the profile and raise funds. Today and in the future.'

'Thank you. Axel helped set up the charity and donated huge sums after someone wrote to him with the idea and it caught his imagination. I wish…'

'You wish what?' The wistfulness in his voice touched her.

'I wish he'd told me about it.'

'People don't always like to talk about their charitable activity.' She frowned. 'But in this case surely he must have been pretty public about it, because his profile would have raised awareness.'

'It didn't work like that. My father was unpredictable about certain issues—he may not have approved of Axel's involvement. So Axel kept it low-key. Anonymous, in fact. I only found out after his death because someone from the charity wrote with their condolences and their thanks for all he had done. I decided to take over and make it a more high-profile role.'

'Didn't your father mind?'

Frederick shrugged. 'I don't know. He and I weren't close.' His tone forbade further questions. 'Anyway, in the past two years the number of schools has increased three-fold and I've hired an excellent administrator—she isn't a volunteer, because she can't afford to be, but she is worth every penny. The schools are makeshift, but that has saved money and I think it makes them more accessible.'

His face was lit with enthusiasm and there was no doubting his sincerity. Any reservations she'd harboured that this was simply a publicity stunt designed to show that Frederick had a charitable side began to fall away.

This continued when they arrived at the school and a veritable flock of children hurtled towards the car.

He exhibited patience, good humour and common sense; he allowed them to feel and touch the car, and then promised they could examine the interior after their lessons—as long as their teacher agreed.

A smiling woman dressed in a forest-green and blue *salwar kameez* came forward and within minutes children of differing ages and sizes were seated in the pavilion area and the lesson commenced.

Sunita marvelled at the children's concentration and the delight they exuded—despite the open-air arena, and all the distractions on offer, they were absorbed in their tasks, clearly revelling in the opportunity to learn.

'Would you like to go and look at their work?' the teacher offered, and soon Sunita was seated next to a group of chattering children, all of whom thrust their notebooks towards her, emanating so much pride in their achievements that flipped her heart.

She glanced at Frederick and her heart did another turn. Standing against a backdrop of palm trees and lush monsoon greenery, he was performing a series of magic tricks that held the children spellbound. He produced coins from ears and cards from thin air, bringing gasps of wonder and giggles of joy.

Finally, after the promised exploration of the limo, the children dispersed—many of them off to work—and after a long conversation with the teacher Frederick and Sunita returned to the car for their journey back to the hotel.

'Next time I'll take Amil,' Sunita said. 'I want him to meet those kids, to grow up with an understanding of the real world.'

'Agreed.'

The word reminded Sunita that from now on Frederick would have a say in her parenting decisions, but right now that didn't seem to matter. This was a topic they agreed on.

'There's such a lesson to be learnt there—those children want to learn, and it doesn't matter to them if they have computers or science labs or technology. They find joy in learning, and that's awesome as well as humbling.'

'*All* of this is humbling.'

He turned to look out of the window, gesturing to the crowded Mumbai streets, and Sunita understood what that movement of his hand had encompassed—the poverty that was rife, embodied by the beggars who surged to the limo windows whenever the car slowed, hands outstretched, entreaty on their faces. But it was more than that – you could see the spectrum of humanity, so many individuals each and every one with their own dreams and worries.

'You really care. This isn't all a publicity stunt…part of your new image.'

'This is about a continuation of Axel's work—no more, no less. Don't paint me as a good person, Sunita. If it weren't for Axel I would never have given this so much as a thought.'

The harshness of his voice shocked her, jolted her backwards on the seat with its intensity. 'Perhaps, but you were hardly duty-bound to take over—or to come out here and interact with those children like that.' She couldn't help it. 'Axel didn't do that, did he?'

'Axel *couldn't* do that—he needed to be the heir my father wanted him to be.'

With that he pulled his phone out of his pocket in a clear indication that the subject was well and truly closed.

Sunita frowned, fighting the urge to remove the phone from his grasp and resume their conversation, to make him see that he was wrong—in this instance he *was* a good person.

Back off, Sunita.

Right now she needed to remain focused on whether or not she wanted to marry this man—and what the consequences of her decision would be for Amil. And in that vein she needed to look ahead to the photo call, which meant an assessment of the recent press coverage. So she pulled her own phone out of her pocket.

A few minutes later he returned the mobile to his pocket.

'OK. We'll fly to Goa late afternoon, after the photo call and the trip to Hanging Gardens. As you requested I've sorted out a room near your suite for Sam and Miranda.'

'Thank you. I appreciate that.'

Goa! Sudden panic streamed through her and she pushed it down. She was contemplating *marriage* to Frederick, for goodness' sake—so panic over a mere two days was foolish, to say the least. She needed to focus on Amil.

She glanced across at Frederick, wondering how he must feel about taking Amil out. Perhaps she should ask, but the question would simply serve as a reminder of the fact that he had missed out on the first fourteen months of his son's life.

So instead she faced forward and maintained silence until the limo pulled up outside the hotel.

Frederick stood outside the hotel bedroom door. His heart pounded in his chest with a potent mix of emotions—nervousness, anticipation and an odd sense of rightness. In two minutes he would meet Amil. Properly. Terror added itself to the mix, and before he could turn tail and flee he raised his hand and knocked.

Sunita opened the door, Amil in her arms, and he froze. He didn't care that he was standing in the corridor in full sight of any curious passers-by. All he could do was gaze at his son. *His son.*

Wonder entered his soul as his eyes roved over his features and awe filled him. *His son.* The words overwhelmed and terrified him in equal measure, causing a strange inability to reach out and hold the little boy. His emotions paralysed him, iced his limbs into immobility, stopped his brain, brought the world into slow motion.

Determination that he would not let Amil down fought with the bone-deep knowledge that of course he would. He wasn't equipped for this—didn't have the foundations to know how to be a parent, how not to disappoint.

But he would do all he could. He could give this boy his name, his principality, and perhaps over time he would work out how to show his love.

Amil gazed back at him with solemn hazel eyes and again panic threatened—enough that he wrenched his gaze away.

'You OK?' Sunita's soft voice pulled him into focus and he saw understanding in her eyes, and perhaps even the hint of a tear at the edge of her impossibly long eyelashes.

'I'm fine.'

Get a grip.

He had no wish to feature as an object of compassion. So he kept his gaze on Sunita, absorbed her vibrant beauty, observed her change of outfit from casual jeans and T-shirt to a leaf-print black and white dress cinched at the waist with a wide red belt. Strappy sandals completed the ensemble.

'Babababababa!' Amil vouchsafed, and a well of emotion surged anew.

'Do you want to hold him?'

'No!' *Think*. 'I don't want to spook him—especially just before the photo call.'

It wasn't a bad cover-up, but possibly not good enough to allay the doubts that dawned in her eyes.

'You won't. He's fairly sociable. Though obviously he doesn't really meet that many strange me—' She broke off. 'I'm sorry. Of all the stupid things to say that took the cake, the biscuit and the whole damn patisserie.'

'It's OK. I am a stranger to Amil—that's why I don't want to spook him.'

His gaze returned to the baby, who was watching him, his eyes wide open, one chubby hand clutching a tendril of Sunita's hair.

'We need to go.'

'I know. But first I have a couple of questions about the press conference and the Kaitlin question.'

Frederick frowned. 'What question would that be?'

'A couple of reporters said, and I quote, that you are "broken-hearted" and that perhaps I can mend the chasm. Others have suggested you would welcome a dalliance with an old flame as a gesture, to show Lady Kaitlin you are over her.'

'I still don't understand what your question is.'

'Two questions. *Are* you heartbroken? *Are* you over her?'

'No and yes. I need to get married for Lycander. My

heart is not involved. Kaitlin understood that—our relationship was an alliance. When that alliance became impossible we ended our relationship. Since then she has met someone else and I wish her well.'

Sunita's expression held a kind of shocked curiosity. 'That's *it*? You were with her for *months*. You must have felt *something* for her.'

Momentary doubt touched him and then he shrugged. 'Of course I did. I thought that she would be an excellent asset to Lycander.'

Kaitlin's diplomatic connections had been exemplary, as had her aristocratic background. She'd had a complete understanding of the role of consort and had been as uninterested in love as he was.

'I was disappointed when it didn't work out.'

'Yes. I see that it must have been tough for you to have the deal break down.' Sarcasm rang out from the spurious sympathy.

'It was—but only because it had an adverse impact on my position as ruler.'

And that was all that mattered. His goal was to rule Lycander as his brother would have wished, to achieve what Axel would have achieved. Whatever it took.

'So all you need to know about Kaitlin is that she is in the past. My heart is intact.' He glanced at his watch. 'And now we really need to go.'

A pause and then she nodded. 'OK. This is our chance to change the mixed reaction into a positive one. An opportunity to turn the tide in our favour.'

'You sound confident that you can do that.'

'Yup. I'm not a fan of bad publicity. Watch and learn.'

One photo call later and Frederick was looking at Sunita in reluctant admiration. He had to hand it to her. By the end of the hour she had had even the most hostile reporter

eating out of her hand. Somehow she had mixed a suggestion of regret over her actions with the implicit belief that
it had been the only option at the time. In addition, she had
managed to make it clear that whilst two years ago Frederick had been a shallow party prince, now he had morphed
into a different and better man, a worthy ruler of Lycander.

No doubt Marcus had been applauding as he watched.

Hell, even *he* had almost believed it. *Almost*.

'You did a great job. And I appreciate that you included
me in your spin.'

'It wasn't spin. Everything I said about you was true—
you *have* worked incredibly hard these past two years, you
have instigated all the changes I outlined, and you *do* have
Lycander's future at heart.'

The words washed over him like cold, dirty water—if
the people of Lycander knew where the blame for Axel's
death lay they would repudiate him without compunction,
and they would be right to do so. But he didn't want these
thoughts today—not on his first outing with Amil.

He glanced down at Amil, secure now in his buggy,
dressed in a jaunty striped top and dungarees, a sun hat
perched on his head, a toy cat clasped firmly in one hand.

'Amamamamam…ma.' Chubby legs kicked and he
wriggled in a clear instruction for them to move on.

Sunita smiled down at her son. 'I think he wants to get
going—he wants to see all the animal hedges. They seem
to utterly fascinate him.'

As they wandered through the lush gardens that
abounded with shades of green tranquillity seemed to be
carried on the breeze that came from the Arabian Sea, and
for a moment it was almost possible to pretend they were
an ordinary family out for the day.

Sunita came to a halt near a topiary hedge, one of many

clipped into the shape of animals. 'For some reason this is his favourite—I can't work out why.'

Frederick studied it. 'I'm not sure I can even work out what it is. I spotted the giraffe and the elephant and the ox-drawn cart, but this one flummoxes me.'

Sunita gave a sudden gurgle of laughter. 'I know what Amil thinks it is. Amil, sweetheart, tell Mu— Tell us what the animal does.'

The little boy beamed and made a *'raaaah'* noise.

Frederick felt his heart turn over in his chest. Without thought he hunkered down next to Amil and clapped. 'Clever boy. The tiger goes *"rah".*'

'Raaah!' Amil agreed.

And here it came again—the paralysis, the fear that he would mess this up. He'd never managed any other relationship with even a sliver of success. Why would this be different?

Rising to his feet, he gestured around the garden. 'This is a beautiful place.'

'I used to come here as a child,' Sunita said. 'It's one of my earliest memories. I loved the flower clock.'

She pressed her lips together, as if she regretted the words, and Frederick frowned. Her publicity blurb skated over her childhood, chose to focus instead on her life after she'd embarked on her career. Almost as if she had written her early years out of her life history...

'Come on,' she said hurriedly. 'This morning isn't about my childhood. It's about Amil's—let's go to the Old Woman's Shoe.'

Five minutes later Frederick stared at the shoe—actually an enormous replica of a boot. As landmarks went, it seemed somewhat bizarre—especially when the words of the nursery rhyme filtered back to him.

There was an old woman who lived in a shoe.
She had so many children she didn't know what to do.
She gave them broth without any bread,
Then whipped them all soundly and sent them to bed.

'Isn't this a slightly odd thing to put in a children's playground?'

'Yes. But I loved it—I used to climb it and it made me feel lucky. It was a way to count my blessings. At least I didn't live with a horrible old woman who starved me and beat me!'

At least. There had been a wealth of memory in those syllables, and for a daft moment he had the urge to put his arm around her and pull her into the comfort of a hug.

As if realising she had given away more than she had wanted, she hastened on. 'Anyway, I looked up the rhyme recently and it turns out it probably has political rather than literal connotations. But enough talk. This is about you and Amil. Do you want to take Amil into the shoe? I'll wait here with the buggy.'

The suggestion came out of nowhere, ambushed him, and once again his body froze into immobility even as his brain turned him into a gibbering wreck.

'I think that may be a little bit much for him. He barely knows me.' *Think.* 'We haven't even explained to him who I am.'

The accusation in his own voice surprised him—and he knew it masked a hurt he didn't want her to see. Because it exposed a weakness he didn't want her to know. *'Never show weakness, my son.'* The one piece of paternal advice he agreed with. *'Show weakness and you lose.'* Just as all his stepmothers had lost. Their weakness had been their love for their children—a weakness Alphonse had exploited.

Heat touched the angle of her cheekbones as she acknowledged the truth of his words. 'I know. I'm not sure what you want to do. I don't know what you want him to call you. Dad? Daddy? Papa?'

In truth he didn't know either, and that increased his panic. Sunita stepped towards him, and the compassion in her eyes added fuel to the panic-induced anger.

'But remember, he is only fourteen months old—I don't think he understands the concept of having a dad.'

The words were a stark reminder of her deception.

'Amil doesn't understand or *you* don't?'

The harshness of his voice propelled her backwards, and he was glad of it when he saw the compassion vanish from her expression.

'Both of us. Give me a break, Frederick. Until yesterday it was just Amil and me. Now here you are, and you want to marry me and make Amil the Crown Prince. It's a lot to take in.'

For an instant he empathised, heard the catch in her voice under the anger. But this was no time for empathy or sympathy. Now all that mattered was the knowledge of what was at stake.

'Then take it in fast, Sunita. You chose to hide Amil from me and now you need to deal with the consequences of that decision. Most people wouldn't think they were so bad. *I* am the one who has missed out on the first fourteen months of my son's life. *My son.* I am Amil's father and *you* need to deal with it.'

There was silence, broken only by the sound of Amil grizzling, his eyes wide and anxious as he looked up at Sunita.

Oh, hell. Guilt twisted his chest. What was *wrong* with him? This was his first outing with Amil and he'd allowed it to come to this. Shades of his own father, indeed.

He squatted down beside the baby. 'I'm sorry, Amil. Daddy's sorry.' Standing up, he gestured to the Old Woman's Shoe. 'You take him up. I'll wait here with the buggy. I've upset him enough—I don't want to compound my error.'

Sunita hesitated, but then Amil's grizzling turned to tears and she nodded assent.

'OK.' Leaning down, she unbuckled Amil and took him out. 'Come on, sweetheart. Let's try some walking.'

Frederick watched their progress and determination solidified inside him. He might be messing this up big-time, but he would not concede defeat. At the very least he would give his son the chance to be a prince. Their outing to the Hanging Gardens might be a disaster, but going to Goa wouldn't be.

By the end of their time there Sunita would agree to marry him.

CHAPTER SEVEN

SUNITA LOOKED ACROSS the expanse of the royal jet to where Frederick sat. There was no trace of the man she'd glimpsed mere hours ago in the Hanging Gardens—a man who had exhibited a depth of pain and frustration that had made her think long and hard.

Another glance—he still looked cool, regal and remote, and she couldn't read any emotion or discern what thoughts might be in his mind. Which would make what she had to say all the more difficult.

For a moment she nearly turned craven. *No.* This was the right thing to do and she would do it.

'Frederick?'

'Sunita.'

'Can we talk?'

'Of course.' He pushed his netbook across the table, rose and crossed to sit in the luxurious leather seat next to hers. 'Shoot.'

'I've thought about what you said earlier. About me having to accept that you are Amil's father.'

He raised a hand. 'It doesn't matter. I shouldn't have said what I did.'

'It *does* matter. I don't see how we can even consider a future together until we resolve our past. So I want to say I'm sorry.'

She twisted her hands together on her lap, recalling Frederick's expression when he'd looked at Amil as if his son was the most precious being in the universe.

'I'm sorry you missed out on Amil's first months.'

However justified her decision, Frederick could never have that time back—would never be able to hold his newborn son in his arms, see his first smile, run his finger over his gum to reveal that first tooth.

'I'm sorry.'

'OK.'

'But it's *not* OK, is it?'

'No.' He closed his eyes, then reopened them. 'No. It isn't OK that you hid my son's existence from me.'

'I couldn't take the risk.'

'Yes. You could have. You *chose* not to.'

Rationalisations lined up in her vocal cords but she uttered none of them. Bottom line—he was right. Her choice had meant Frederick had missed out on something infinitely precious.

'Yes, I did. And all the reasons I gave you earlier were true. But it's more than that.'

She inhaled deeply. She had no wish to confide this to him—she wasn't even sure she wanted to acknowledge it herself. But there it was again—the memory of the way Frederick had looked at Amil, the fact that he wanted to be part of his son's life and wanted to create a stable family unit. He deserved a true explanation.

'I thought history was repeating itself. I thought you would be like…' Her voice trailed off, her brain wishing it could reverse track and pull the words back.

'Like who?'

The gentleness of his voice surprised her—gave her the momentum to carry on.

'Like my father. He was a Londoner, on holiday in India

with a group of friends when he met my mother. They fell in love—or so she believed. She fell pregnant and she *did* choose to tell him, and all she could see was a tornado of dust as he disappeared. Straight back, road-runner-style, to his fiancée in London.'

Even now the enormity of her father's selfishness had the power to stun her—he *must* have understood the repercussions. They would have been complex enough in any culture, but in India there had been added layers of complication that transcended even betrayal and heartbreak.

Understanding showed in the expression on Frederick's face. 'That must have been tough for your mother.'

'Yes. It was. It changed the entire trajectory of her life. Her family was horrified and threw her out—she was only nineteen, and she had to fend for herself in a society which by and large had condemned her. And a lot of that is down to my father and his rejection of her—and me. I know we were in different circumstances—you didn't lie to me— but I knew you didn't want children. I didn't want to hear you say the same words my own father had—I didn't want Amil to feel the sense of rejection I did.'

Sunita forced herself to hold his gaze, to keep her tone level. This verged on the excruciating—touchy-feely confidences were not her bag at all.

'It seemed better, easier, less painful, to bring Amil up on my own. I figured what *he* didn't know and *you* didn't know wouldn't hurt anyone.'

There was a silence, and then he reached out, touching her forearm lightly. 'I'm sorry for what happened to your mother and to you. I promise you—I will never reject Amil.'

There could be no doubt as to the sincerity in his voice, and in the here and now she believed he meant every word. But she knew that good intentions did not always turn into actions. Her father must have once believed the empty promises he'd made to make up for his past, to be a good parent.

'It will not happen,' he repeated, as if he sensed her doubts. 'And now let's put the past behind us. I wish you had told me about Amil earlier, but I do understand why you made the choices you did. I believe now that we need to move forward, put the past behind us and focus on our present and our future. Deal?'

He held out his hand and Sunita looked down at it. So perfect—strong, masculine, capable... Capable of the gentlest of caresses, capable of...

Close it down, Sunita.

Too late—images scrambled her mind and for a moment she was unable to help herself. She closed her eyes, let the sensation dance over her skin. But it was more than desire—she knew that this deal signified understanding and forgiveness, and that made her head whirl as well.

Then she opened her eyes and reached out, clasped his hand and worked to still the beat of her heart. 'Deal,' she said. The syllable emerged with way too much violence, and she dropped his hand as if it were burning her. Which in a sense it was.

She looked down, then sneaked a look up at him—had he seen her reaction? Of course he had. It didn't take a forensic degree to know that. Embarrassment flushed her skin even as she couldn't help but wonder if this stupid physical reaction was a mutual one.

Her gaze met his and against all odds her pulse quickened further. His hazel eyes had darkened, the heat in them so intense her skin sizzled as her hormones cartwheeled.

Nothing else mattered except this.

Her lips parted as he rose, and his eyes never once left hers as he held out a hand. Without thought she put her hand in his, and he tugged her up so they stood mere centimetres apart.

Oh, so gently, but with a firmness that neither expected nor brooked denial, his hands encircled her waist and pulled her body flush against his. The feel of him, of the hard, muscular wall of his chest, made her gasp, and she looped her arms round his neck, accidentally brushing the soft skin on his nape.

An oath dropped from his lips and then those self-same lips touched hers and she was lost.

The kiss oh-so-familiar and yet so much more than before; the tang of coffee and the hint of strawberry jam, the sheer rollick of sensation that coursed her blood, made her feel alive and made her want more. He deepened the kiss and she pressed against him, caught in this moment that felt so damn right.

Stop. What the hell was she doing?

She wrenched out of his arms so hard she nearly tumbled over, putting a hand out to steady herself against the back of the chair.

For a moment silence reigned, broken only by the sound of their jagged breathing. Sunita tried to force herself to think through the fog of desire that refused to disperse. She couldn't let herself succumb to him again—she *couldn't*. Two years ago she'd lost her self-respect—now she could lose even more than that. Her attraction was a weakness he could play on—something that might cloud her judgement when she needed it most.

'I'm sorry. That was stupid.'

He ran a hand down his face, almost as if to wipe away all emotion, all desire, and when he met her gaze his expression was neutralised. 'No need to be sorry. That was a *good* thing.'

'How do you figure that out?'

'Because it proves we have physical compatibility. That's important in a marriage.'

His words acted like the equivalent of a bucket of ice-cold water and she slammed her hands on her hips. 'So that kiss was a deliberate ploy? A way to make the marriage more acceptable to me?'

'It wasn't a deliberate ploy, but it wasn't a mistake either. Mutual attraction is a benefit in a marriage. A bonus to our alliance.'

A benefit. A bonus. Any minute now he'd tell her there was some tax advantage to it too.

Sheer outrage threatened at his use of their attraction as a calculated move to persuade her. More fool her for believing he had been as caught up and carried away as she had. This *was* the Playboy Prince, after all.

'Well, I'll bear that in mind, but given that you have found "physical compatibility" with hundreds of women, I'm not sure it counts for much. Now, if you'll excuse me, I'll just go and freshen up.'

Frederick resisted the urge to put his head in his hands and groan. Then he considered the alternative option of kicking himself around the private jet.

Kissing Sunita had not been on the agenda—but somehow her beauty, her vulnerability, her honesty had overwhelmed him, and what he had meant to offer as comfort had turned into the type of kiss that still seared his memory, still had his body in thrall.

Dammit. He would *not* let physical attraction control him as it had his father—that way led to stupid decisions, poor judgement calls and people getting hurt. Yet during that kiss his judgement could have parachuted off the plane and he wouldn't have given a damn.

Then, to compound his original stupidity, he had

morphed into a pompous ass. Words had flowed from his tongue as he'd fought the urge to pull her straight back into his arms and resume proceedings. What an idiot. And then there had been her reference to his past. The truth was, even back then Sunita had been different from his so-called 'hundreds of women'.

He looked up as she returned to the room, her brown eyes cold, her expression implacable as she headed back to her chair and reached down into her bag for a book.

Hell. Now what? This was not going to plan and he didn't know how to retrieve it. Did not have a clue. He was so far out of his comfort zone he'd need a satnav and a compass to find his way back.

'Sunita?'

'Yes.'

'That kiss…'

'I think we've said all that needs to be said about it. As far as I am concerned, I plan to erase it from my memory banks.'

'Fine. But before you do that I want to clarify something. You mentioned my "hundreds of women"—for starters, that is an exaggeration. Yes, I partied hard and, yes, there were women, but not as many as the press made out. But, any which-way, those days are over and they have been for a long time. I was never unfaithful to any woman and I plan on a monogamous marriage.'

Clearly his default setting today was 'pompous ass', so he might as well run with it.

'So you'd be faithful for the duration. For decades, if necessary?'

The scepticism in her tone rankled.

'I am always faithful.'

'But your relationships have only lasted a few weeks

at a time—that's hardly much of a test. Variety was the spice of your life.'

'Very poetic. Let's take it further, then—I believe it's possible to have variety *and* plenty of spice with one woman.'

'Then why didn't you ever try it before?'

Damn. Poetic *and* sharp.

'Because short-term suited me—I didn't want physical attraction to develop into any expectations of marriage or love. I never offered more than I could give and the same goes now. I can offer marriage and fidelity, but not love.'

'I still don't buy it. Most people are faithful *because* of love—if you don't believe in love what would motivate you to be faithful?'

'I will not repeat my father's mistakes. He went through women like a man with a cold does tissues. Any beautiful woman—he thought it was his right to have her, whether he was already in a relationship or not, and it led to a whole lot of strife and angst. So I will not plunge Lycander into scandal and I will not hurt my children or humiliate my wife. That is nothing to do with love—it is to do with respect for my country and my family.'

'OK.'

Sympathy warmed her eyes and the moment suddenly felt too weighted, too heavy, and he cleared his throat. 'I thought you might want to know more about Lycander—after all, it will be your new home and your country.'

'I'd like that. I do remember some of what you told me two years ago. Rolling countryside, where you can walk and smell the scents of honeysuckle and almost taste the olives that you grow. You made the olive groves come to life.' She hesitated, and then asked, 'What happened to your business deal? The one you hoped would go through two years ago?'

Her words caused him to pause. Sunita had been one of the very few people he'd spoken to about his dreams. Ever since he was young he'd been focused on breaking free of his father's money—sick and tired of the constant reminders that he relied on his father's coffers for his food, his clothes, the roof over his head.

Then, at twenty-one, he'd come into the inheritance of a run-down, abandoned olive grove. And as he'd walked around it had been as if the soil itself had imparted something to him, as if the very air was laden with memories of past glories, of trees laden with plump lush olives, the sound and whir of a ghostly olive press.

That was where it had all started, and over the years he'd built an immensely profitable business. Two years before he'd been in the midst of a buy-out—he'd succeeded, and taken his company to the next echelon. That had been the deal he'd been celebrating—the reason he'd handed over the state function to Axel, the reason Axel had died.

Guilt and grief prodded him and he saw Sunita frown. *Focus.* 'The deal went through.'

'So who runs your business now?'

'A board of directors and my second-in-command—I have very little to do with it any more.'

'That must be hard.'

'That's how it is. Lycander needs my attention, and its people need to see that they come first. The principality isn't huge, but we have beaches, we have vineyards, we have olive groves. I know I'm biased, but our olives are the best in the world—they have bite…their taste lingers on your tongue—and the olive oil we produce is in a class of its own. As for our grapes—I believe the wine we produce rivals that of France and Spain. Lycander has the potential to be a prosperous land, but right now it is a vessel of past glories. My father increased taxes, lowered the minimum wage—did all he could to increase the money in the royal coffers without a care for the effect.'

'But couldn't anyone stop him?'

'No. In Lycander, the ruler's word is law—he has the final say on the governing of the land. Of course there are elected advisors, but they have no legislative power and the monarch can disregard their advice. So effectively everything hinges on having a ruler who genuinely cares about Lycander and its people.'

'That sounds like a whole heap of responsibility. For you. *And* to wish upon Amil.'

'It is, but I think it needs to be seen in context. In the past, when everything worked, it was easier—right now it is harder. But I will make sure I set things to rights. I know what needs to be done. I will make the laws fair, I will reduce taxation rates and I'll stop tax evasion. I want the divide between the wealthy and the poor to be bridged. I—'

He broke off at her expression.

'You can pick your jaw up from the ground.'

She raised her hand in admission. 'OK. Busted. I *am* surprised. Two years ago you were passionate about your business, but you didn't mention politics or social beliefs. Now your enthusiasm, your beliefs, are palpable.'

The all too familiar push and pull of guilt tugged within him.

'This isn't about my enthusiasm or my beliefs. It is about Axel—it's about fulfilling a promise. The people and the country suffered under my father's rule. The real reason there was no rebellion was that they knew one day Axel would succeed him, and that kept the unrest at bay. Axel had a vision—one that I *will* make happen.'

That had been the promise he'd made in his very first speech and he would fulfil it.

'What about *your* vison? The way you speak of Lycander—I can hear your pride in it.'

'I never had a vision for Lycander. I had a work hard, play hard lifestyle.'

'But you've changed?'

'Yes, I have.'

But the cost of that had been his brother's life.

Her frown deepened. She leant forward and he could smell her exotic scent with its overtone of papaya, could see the tiny birthmark on the angle of her cheekbone.

'I know you will be a good ruler. Whether you rule because it is your duty or because your heart is in it.'

There was silence. She was close. Way too close. And he had had a sudden desire to tell her the truth about his ascent to the throne—a desire mixed with the longing to tug her back into his arms and damn common sense and practicality.

Neither could happen, so he rose to his feet and looked down at her.

'Thank you. But the point I was trying to make is that I will ensure the principality Amil inherits will be a *good* place, with a strong economic foundation. Of course he will still have much responsibility, but I hope it will not be a burden.'

'What if he doesn't want the job? What if he has other ambitions, other aspirations?'

'I would never force him to take the crown. He could abdicate.' He met her gaze. 'Provided we have more children.'

'More children?' she echoed.

'Yes. I would like more children in order to secure the succession.' After all, there was no hope of his brothers ever having anything to do with Lycander. 'To take the pressure off Amil.'

'Is that the only reason?'

'For now. I haven't really got my head around having Amil yet.'

Right now he was terrified about his ability to parent *one* child—it wasn't the moment for a rose-tinted image of a functional, happy group of siblings.

'Do *you* want more kids?'

Sunita hesitated. 'I don't know...' A small smile tugged her lips upwards. 'I haven't really got *my* head around it all yet either. Until yesterday it was just me and Amil. My happiest memories are of my mother and me—just us. After—'

She broke off, looked away and then back at him, and he wondered what she had been about to say.

'Anyway,' she resumed, 'I'm not sure that the whole "happy family" scenario always works. Are you close to your other brothers?'

'No.'

His half-siblings... Stefan, who loathed all things Lycander, had left the principality as soon as he'd reached eighteen and hadn't returned. The twins, Emerson and Barrett, still only twenty, had left Lycander only days after their father's death and hadn't returned.

There was a definite pattern there, and it wasn't woven with closeness. The way they had grown up had made that an impossibility—their father had revelled in pitting brother against brother in a constant circus of competition and rivalry, and in the end Frederick had retired from the field, isolated himself and concentrated on his own life.

'But that was down to our upbringing. I hope that our children would do better.'

Perhaps it was a fruitless hope—there was every chance he would prove to be as useless a parent as his own parents had been, in which case perhaps a large family was a foolish idea.

But now wasn't the moment to dwell on it.

Relief touched him as the pilot announced their descent to Goa before Sunita could pursue the conversation further.

CHAPTER EIGHT

SUNITA'S EYES STRETCHED so wide she wondered if her eye-balls would actually pop out of her head.

'This is incredible.'

In truth it was beyond incredible—and she hadn't even seen the inside of the villa yet.

The drive itself had been unexpected—their chauffeur-driven car had traversed remarkably peaceful roads until they'd reached an idyllic village seemingly untouched by tourism. Winding lanes had displayed a number of villas draped with greenery, and now they had arrived at Sangwan Villa.

The Portuguese-built, newly renovated building was nestled amidst verdant grounds where teak and jackfruit trees thrived, giving the air an evocative smell of leather with a hint of pineapple.

Her gaze rested on the structure itself. With its pillared verandas and high roof it looked like a vision out of a fairy tale.

The thought jolted her. She needed to remember that fairy tales were exactly that—tales, fiction. And most fairy tales had a dark side, a grim under-story, and the myths they were built on didn't have any happily-ever-afters.

'How on earth did you get it at such short notice?'

'It was closed for maintenance—I made it worth the owners' while to postpone the work.'

A woman walked towards them, a smile on her face, her white and green sari very much in keeping with the verdant backdrop.

'Your Highness. Welcome. I am Deepali and I will be looking after you during your stay. Your staff have been settled in and your suites are ready, if you will follow me. I will show you your rooms and then I thought you may wish to have an evening drink by the pool before dinner. There are menus in your rooms—just call through when you are ready.'

'That sounds wonderful,' Sunita said. 'And thank you so much for making this available at such short notice.'

Minutes later she was looking around a sumptuous suite. 'It's beautiful…'

But it was more than that—it was quirky and cosy, with its warm aura countered by the cool of the tiled floor. The sitting area boasted comfy overstuffed armchairs, where she could imagine curling up with a book and a cup of coffee, or simply gazing at the courtyard outside, resplendent with shrubbery. Two steps led down to the bedroom, where a luxurious wooden bed sprawled against decadent red walls.

Her suitcases had been deposited by a large lacquered wardrobe and she opened one, needing the confidence fresh clothes would give her. A floaty dress with a vivid bird print gave her instant cheer, and as she made her way out to the courtyard she allowed herself to revel in the sound of kingfishers and the sight and scent of the opulent lilies in the ornate pond.

Frederick sat on a recliner chair, a frosted beer bottle on the small table behind him and his blond head slightly tipped back to absorb the rays of the evening sun. Her breath caught as her gaze snagged on the strong line of his throat, the strength of his jaw—Adonis could eat his heart out.

But enough voyeurism...

He turned as she approached and smiled, and for a moment the clock turned back, transported her to two years before, when that smile had quite literally bewitched her, causing her to forget common sense and every promise she'd made herself.

Not this time. This time she had her sensible head on.

So she forced her toes to uncurl and sat down next to him, stretched her legs out and exhaled. 'This is a fabulous place.' She swiped a sideways glance at him. 'And you've surprised me.' *Again.*

'Why?'

'It's not what I expected.'

'What *did* you expect?'

'Something busier—a five-star hotel on the beach, with a nightclub.'

'Is that what you wanted?'

'No.'

'I told you, Sunita, I've changed. Plus, this time needs to be for you and me. No distractions. You wanted to get to know me better. Here I am.'

So he was—and the thought had her reaching for the lime drink she'd ordered.

She needed to focus on the practical—on need-to-know, real-life information.

'I need to know what our marriage would mean on a day-to-day level for Amil. What it will be like for him to grow up in a palace, as a Lycander prince. Right now it feels surreal.'

'The state apartments are a bit more opulent than your

average home, I suppose, but otherwise his childhood will be what we make it.'

'Will he go to a nursery?'

'I don't see why not—there will be a certain level of security arrangements, but I can't see a problem with that.'

'And he'll have friends round to play?'

How she'd craved friendship as a child—but there had been no one. Her mixed race heritage, the fact that she was illegitimate, the fact that her mother was a model, had all combined to make school a miserable place of isolation for her. She knew exactly what a solitary childhood could be like, and she didn't want that for her son.

'Yup. Again, subject to security vetting.'

'Is that how it worked for you?'

She sensed the tension in his body.

'It isn't relevant how it was for me,' he said.

He had to be kidding. 'Of course it is. You are a prince who grew up in a palace. You want Amil to do the same. So, did you make friends, have kids round to play? Were you treated differently?'

Discomfort showed as he shifted on his seat, picked his beer up and put it down again without even taking a sip. 'My life…my younger brothers' lives…weren't as straightforward as I hope Amil's will be. There weren't that many opportunities for us to make normal friends. It was better for Axel, because my father sent him to boarding school, and—'

Whoa! 'That is *not* happening to Amil. I will not send him away.'

'I won't rule that out.'

'Yes, you will. I don't care if every Crown Prince since the Conquest was sent to boarding school. Amil isn't going.'

'That is not why I would do it.' Frustration seeped into

his tone. 'In fact, I didn't say I *would* do it. It is simply a possibility I will consider in the future.'

'*No.*'

His voice tightened. 'Different children thrive in different conditions. Axel was educated at boarding school and it didn't do him any harm. I spent a term there and I loved it.'

'In which case, why did you leave?'

'Because my father changed his mind.'

'He must have had a reason.'

'I'm sure he did.'

Despite the even tone of his voice she could sense evasion.

'Do you know what it was?'

'My father's attitude to my education was a little hit and miss. Axel went to boarding school, but the rest of us... We had tutors some of the time, attended a term of local school here and there, or we ran wild. For my father, education wasn't a priority—in the palace or in the principality as a whole. I will change that, but it will take time—that's why I won't rule out boarding school if it is right for Amil.'

'That is *my* decision.'

'Amil is *our* son. *We* will make decisions about his future. Not you or me. Us—together.'

'And what happens if we don't agree?'

'Then we find a compromise.'

'There is no compromise between boarding school and not boarding school. It's black or white. What happens then?'

'I don't know. But we'll work it out.'

'Those are just words. Neither of us has any idea of how to work things out.'

Which was exactly why this was a terrible idea. Co-parenting sucked.

'Fine. Then let's work it out now,' he said.

'How?'

'You tell me exactly why you are so adamant that boarding school is not an option. The truth. My brother loved his boarding school, and the few months I spent there were some of the happiest times of my life. I will not rule it out without reason.'

'I...' Explanations sucked as well, but she could see that she didn't sound rational. 'I'm scared for him. School was an unmitigated disaster for me—because I didn't fit from day one. I was the only mixed race child in my school, and my mother's status didn't help. Plus, quite often she would pull me out of school to go on shoots with her— she had no one to leave me with, you see. I guess I was an obvious target.'

'Were you bullied?'

Although his voice was gentle she could hear an underlying anger, saw the clench of his jaw.

'No. It was much worse. I was ignored. Some girl decided that the best way to treat someone as low down the pecking order as me would be to pretend I was invisible.'

She could still hear it now. The high-pitched voice, so stuck-up and snobbish, the other girls gathering round to listen. 'It is demeaning to even *acknowledge* a dirty girl like her. So we will ignore her. Are we all agreed?'

'My whole experience of school was miserable. The only saving grace was the fact that it wasn't boarding school—that I could go home to my mother. Amil will be different too. He will be royalty—there will be people who are envious of him. I don't want him to be far away and miserable.'

Though in truth there was even more to it than that. There was her bone-deep knowledge that time was infinitely precious—she had had so few years with her mother, but at least they had had the maximum possible time together.

'I don't want him to be far away. Full stop. He is *my* child—I want to see him grow, and I want to be there for him.'

Frederick's hazel eyes studied her expression with an intensity that made her feel he could read her soul.

Then he nodded. 'OK. You get the casting vote on the boarding school question.'

'Why?' Wariness narrowed her eyes at his capitulation.

'Does it matter?'

'Yes. I need to know that you mean it. That these aren't just words to sweeten the marriage offer.'

'Because you still don't trust me?'

She wanted to—she really did—but how could she when there was so much at stake?

'Let's say it would help if I knew what had changed your mind.'

'You've made me realise why I enjoyed boarding school so much. Why Axel thrived there. It was the opposite to your situation. For us it was an escape from our home life—boarding school was a haven of certainty after the chaos of life at the palace. Somewhere I knew what was what, where I had an opportunity to actually get an education. Our home life was erratic, at best. It won't be like that for Amil.'

Sunita's heart ached at the thought of all those young princes, buffeted by the fallout from their father's chaotic lifestyle. 'No, it won't.'

'And by the time he goes to school I *will* have turned education around in Lycander. Teachers will be better paid, the curriculum will be overhauled in a good way, and there will be more money injected into schools everywhere.'

As if embarrassed by his own enthusiasm, he leant back

with a rueful smile that flipped her heart again. A sure case of topsy-turvy heart syndrome. And it was messing with her head, making the idea of marriage more palatable. *Ridiculous.* Marriage equalled tying herself down, committing herself to a shared life, to a fairy tale ending. The idea hurt her teeth, sent her whole being into revolt.

Only that wasn't true, was it? Horror surfaced at the identification of a tiny glimmer of sparkle inside her that desperately *wanted* a fairy tale ending... Frederick, Sunita and Amil, living happily ever after in a palace. Princess Sunita.

'Penny for your thoughts?' His voice interrupted her reverie.

'They aren't worth it.'

They weren't worth even a fraction of a penny—she had lost the plot and it was time to get it back. This marriage deal wasn't off the table, but there wouldn't be any glimmer of fairy sparkle sprinkled on it.

She looked up as Deepali approached from across the courtyard. 'Your meal is ready. The chef has prepared a selection of traditional Goan food—I trust you will enjoy it.'

Sunita managed a smile even as her brain scrambled around in panic, chasing down that stupid, sparkly bit of her that advocated the ringing out of wedding bells. How had this happened? In a little over twenty-four hours he had somehow persuaded her that marriage was not only a possibility but a sparkly one.

Enough. She had to halt this before this fairy tale place wove some sort of magic spell around her—before that stupid sparkly bit inside her grew.

Frederick studied Sunita's expression as she looked round the dining room. Her eyes skittered over the colourful prints on the white walls, along the simple wooden table, and he could almost hear her brain whirring.

Deepali entered and put their plates in front of them. 'Prawn rissoles,' she said, and Sunita inhaled appreciatively.

'They smell marvellous—and I'm sure they'll taste just as good.'

The middle-aged woman smiled. 'I'll pass on your kind comments to the chef.'

Once she'd gone, Frederick watched as Sunita studied the rissole with more attention than any food warranted, however appetising.

'This looks great.' She popped a forkful into her mouth and closed her eyes. 'Fabulous! The reason why melt-in-the-mouth is a cliché. Cumin, with perhaps a hint of coriander, and...'

But even as she spoke he knew that her thoughts were elsewhere. There was an almost manic quality to her culinary listing, and he interrupted without compunction.

'So,' he said, 'you avoided my earlier question about what you were thinking.'

Her brown eyes watched him with almost a hint of defiance. 'I was thinking how surreal this situation is—the idea that two people who don't know each other at all could contemplate marriage. It's...mad.'

'That's why we're here—to get to know each other.'

'We can't pack that into two days—most people take years.'

'And there is still a fifty per cent divorce rate.'

'In which case we are *definitely* doomed.'

'Not at all. All those people who take years...they try to fall in love, decide they've fallen in love, expect love to last. Every action is dictated by love. They heap pressure on the whole institution of marriage *and* on themselves. Our approach is based on common sense and on us both getting a deal we think is fair. Two days is more than enough time.'

He leant over and poured wine into her glass.

'In days gone by it would have been the norm. Throughout Lycander history, rulers made *alliances*—not love matches.'

'Does posterity say whether they worked?'

'Some were more successful than others, but every marriage lasted.'

Until Alphonse had arrived and turned statistics and traditions on their heads.

'For better or worse?' Sunita sounded sceptical.

'I see no reason why we couldn't be one of the better ones—we'd go in without any ridiculous, unrealistic expectations, with an understanding of what each other is looking for.'

'I don't even know what your favourite colour is.'

'Does it matter?'

'I feel it's the sort of thing one should know before they marry someone.'

'OK. Blue.' He raised his eyebrows. '*Now* will you marry me?'

This pulled a reluctant smile from her, but it came with an attendant shake of her head. 'What sort of blue? Royal blue, because it's on the Lycander flag?'

'Nope. Aquamarine blue.'

'Because...?'

'Does there have to be a reason?'

Sunita tipped her head to one side. 'There usually is.'

'So what's *your* favourite colour?'

'Red.'

'Because...?'

'Because it was my mother's favourite colour—I like to

think it was her way of sticking two fingers up at the world that had branded her a scarlet woman. She always wore something red—her sari would maybe have a red weave, or she'd wear a red flower, or paint her toenails red. And as for her lipstick collection...'

'You must miss her.'

'I do. A lot.' She looked down at her plate and scooped up the last of her rissole. 'Anyway, why aquamarine blue?'

Reluctance laced his vocal cords—along with a sense of injustice that a question that had seemed so simple on the surface had suddenly become more complex. *Get a grip.* If this was a hoop Sunita had constructed as a prelude to marriage then he'd jump through it—he'd do the damn hula if necessary.

'It's the colour of the Lycander Sea. When life in the palace became too much I'd escape to the beach, watch the sea. It put things into perspective. Sometimes it was so still, so calm, so serene it gave me peace. Occasionally it would be turbulent, and then I guess I'd identify with it. As a child I was pretty sure Neptune lived off the coast of Lycander...'

OK, Frederick, that's enough. More than he'd intended in fact. But there was something about the way Sunita listened—*really* listened—that seemed to have affected him.

She watched him now, lips slightly parted, tawny eyes serious, but as if sensing his discomfort she leant back before she spoke.

'OK, next question. Star sign?'

'Leo.'

'Me too.'

'Is that good or bad?'

'I really don't know. We'd need to ask Nanni—she is an avid believer in horoscopes. Though I'm not sure why. I think her parents had her and my grandfather's horoscopes read to see if they'd be a good match, and the astrologer was confident they were compatible.'

'Were they?'

'I don't think they can have been. From what my mother told me my grandfather was a tyrant and a control freak, whereas Nanni is a kind, gentle woman. But Nanni herself never speaks of her marriage—and never criticises my grandfather. And she still believes in horoscopes.'

'What about you? Do *you* believe in horoscopes?'

'I think there may be something in it, but not enough that you can base your life decisions on them—that's the easy way out, isn't it? You can just shrug your shoulders and blame fate if it all goes wrong. It doesn't work like that—life is about choice.'

'Yes…' Bleakness settled on him—his choices had cost Axel his life. 'But life is also about the consequences of those choices. Consequences you have to live with.'

'Yes, you do. But in this case Amil's future is in *our* hands—he will have to live with the destiny *we* choose for him. And that is hard. But it's not only about Amil. It's about us as well. You and me. That's why this marriage can't work.'

Her chin jutted out at an angle of determination.

Frederick frowned—but before he could respond the door opened and Deepali re-entered the room, followed by a young man pushing a trolley.

'Fish *recheado*,' the young man announced. 'Made with pomfret.'

Deepali's face shone with pride. 'This is my son, Ashok—he is the chef here,' she explained.

'I thought you might want to know about the dish,' Ashok said.

'I'd love to.'

Sunita smiled her trademark smile and Frederick saw Ashok's appreciation.

'The pomfret is stuffed with a special paste. I used chillies, cloves, cumin and lemon. It is a Goan dish, but *recheado* means stuffed in Portuguese.' Ashok smiled. 'And there is also Goan bread, freshly baked. Enjoy.'

Frederick waited until the mother and son had left the room and then he looked at Sunita.

'Why not?' he repeated.

CHAPTER NINE

'WHY WON'T THIS marriage work?'

Frederick's voice was even, his question posed as if the topic under discussion was as simple as a grocery list rather than the rest of their lives.

Sunita took a deep breath and marshalled the thoughts she'd herded into a cogent argument throughout the starter. 'Would you have even considered marriage to me if it wasn't for Amil?'

There was no hesitation as he tipped his hand in the air, palm up. 'No.'

To her surprise, irrational hurt touched her that he didn't have to give it even a second's thought. 'Exactly.'

'But you *can't* take Amil out of the equation. If it weren't for Amil you wouldn't consider marriage to me either.'

'I get that. But it's different for you. I don't *need* to marry anyone. You do, and you need it to be the right person—for Lycander's sake. A woman like Lady Kaitlin Derwent. I am the *antithesis* of Kaitlin.'

For an insane moment the knowledge hurt. But she was no longer a child, desperately trying to measure up to her half-sisters and always failing. High academic grades, musical ability, natural intelligence… You name it, Sunita lacked it. But in this case she needed to emphasise her failings with pride.

'I haven't got an aristocratic bone in my body, and I don't have the *gravitas* that you need to offer the Lycander people.'

'You are the mother of my son.'

'Your *illegitimate* son. Plus, I was a model. Your father married or was associated with a succession of models, actresses and showbiz people, and all his relationships ended in scandal. Your people will tar me with the same brush.'

'Then so be it. I agree that you do not have the background I was looking for in my bride, but I believe you will win the people over. In time.'

'I don't think I will.' She inhaled deeply. 'For a start, I want to resume my modelling career—and I can't see that going down a storm with the people.'

Or with him. He masked his reaction, but not fast enough—he hadn't taken that into the equation.

'You don't like the idea either?'

'I neither like nor dislike it. I agree it might be problematic for the people to accept, but it's a problem we can work around.'

'But it doesn't *have* to be a problem. Don't marry me— marry someone like Kaitlin…someone with the qualities to be a true consort.'

Even as she said the words a strange pang of what she reluctantly identified as jealousy shot through her veins. *Jealousy? Really?* She didn't even know who she was jealous of. It meant nothing to her if Frederick married someone else. *Nothing.* As for being jealous of Kaitlin—that was absurd.

Sunita forged on. 'You know I'm right. Tell me about your agreement with Kaitlin. What else did she bring to the table apart from her background?'

'This is not a constructive conversation.'

'I disagree. This isn't only about Amil. This is about us as well. Your life and mine. You want to make me a princess—I deserve to know what that entails, what your expectations are. You said it yourself.'

'What I expected from Kaitlin and what I would expect from you are different.'

Ouch. 'In what way?' Ice dripped from her tone as she forked up a piece of succulent fish with unnecessary violence.

'You are two different individuals—of course I would have different expectations.' Frustration tinged his voice, along with what looked like a growing knowledge that he'd entered stormy waters and was in imminent danger of capsizing.

'Well, I'd like to know what you expected from Kaitlin.' *From your ideal candidate*, her treacherous heart cried out.

'Fine. Kaitlin was brought up for this role—she has dozens of connections, she speaks four European languages, she has diplomacy down pat. I planned to use her as a royal ambassador—she would have played a very public role. I also hoped she would be influential behind the scenes—play a part in turning Lycander round, in shaping policy.'

For Pete's sake! Sunita didn't think she could bear to hear any more. Lady Kaitlin had obviously been on a fast track to royal sainthood, and the role of Lycander princess would have fitted her like a silken glove. Whereas Sunita was more fitted for the lost sock that languished behind the radiator.

The realisation hollowed her tummy and she shook her head in repudiation. 'There you have it. I think you owe it to Lycander to marry someone else.'

Surely she'd made her case? She understood that Frederick wanted to be part of Amil's life, but he *had* to see that Sunita was quite simply not princess material.

'No.' His voice was flat. 'I have already considered everything you've said. And, incidentally, you and my chief advisor are in complete agreement. But you are Amil's mother, and that trumps all other considerations. He is my son. I want him to live with me—I want him to be Lycander's Crown Prince after me. I also want him to live with his mother. So marriage is the only option.'

'No, it isn't. What if I decide not to marry you?' He couldn't actually *force* her to the altar. 'You would still be an important part of Amil's life.'

'Stop!'

'What?' Her stomach plummeted as she saw the expression on his face—weariness, distaste, sadness.

'Don't do this.'

'Why not?'

'Because if you don't marry me I will fight for joint custody.'

Joint custody. The words sucker-punched her. 'You promised that you wouldn't take him from me. You said he needs me.'

'I also told you I will be a real part of his life. What would you suggest? A weekend here and there? He is my son as well.'

'Yes. But you'll marry someone else—have another family.'

'And you think that should make me want Amil less—is that the message you want to give our son?'

'No!'

Damn it—she couldn't think. Panic had her in its grip, squeezing out any coherent thought. All she could think of now was losing Amil for half of his childhood. Of Amil in Lycander with a stepmother—whichever new multilingual paragon of virtue Frederick eventually married—and half-siblings.

History on repeat with a vengeance.

Memories of her own humiliations, inflicted by the

hands of her stepmother and her half-sisters—the put-downs, the differentiation, the horror—were chiselled on her very soul. No way would she risk that for Amil.

'I won't agree to joint custody. I *can't*.'

But she could see his point. She had already deprived him of fourteen months of Amil's life—how could she expect him to settle for the occasional week? Regular phone calls and Skype? Would *she* settle for that? Never in a million years.

She inclined her head. 'All right. You win. I'll marry you.'

It looked as if Princess Sunita was about to enter the land of fairy tales. It was a good thing she knew that happy-ever-afters didn't exist in real life.

CHAPTER TEN

'ALL RIGHT. YOU WIN. I'll marry you.'

The words seemed to haunt his dreams, and by the time the distinctive fluting whistle of a golden oriole penetrated his uneasy repose it was a relief to wake up, hop out of the slatted wooden bed and head for the shower. He could only hope the stream of water would wake him up to common sense.

He had won, and there was nothing wrong with winning—it meant he would have a life with his son, would be able to give Amil his principality. That was *good* news, right?

The problem was Sunita's words had not been the only ones to permeate his sleeping mind. His father's voice had also made a showing.

'Every woman has a price. Find her weakness, exploit it and then you win, Freddy, m'boy.'

He switched off the shower in a savage movement. Time to man up. Yes, he'd won—and that was OK. It was a cause to celebrate—*not* the equivalent of what his father had done. *He* was striving to keep Amil with Sunita full-time. He hadn't destroyed a family—he'd created one. Ergo, he was not his father. It wasn't as if he had *threatened* her with joint custody. It had been the only other option—an option he'd known she would knock back.

Rationally, the facts were undeniable. Sometimes in life you had to choose between the rock and the hard place, and he'd done his best to make the rock a comfortable choice for her. He'd offered her the chance to be a princess—most women would have grabbed the baton and run with it.

End of.

Now it was time to figure out the next step.

He pulled on chinos and a navy T-shirt and headed into the courtyard and the early-morning sunshine.

'Over here.'

He heard Sunita's voice and spotted her sitting under the shade of a tree, simply dressed in a rainbow-striped sundress, sunglasses perched atop her raven hair. Sunlight filtered through the green leaves of the banyan tree, dappling her arms and the wood of the table, lighting up the tentative smile she offered as he approached.

It was a smile that seemed to bathe his skin in the warmth of relief, pushing away any lingering doubts about his actions.

'Hey.'

'Hey…' He sat down opposite and surveyed the array of fruit. 'Wow.'

'I know, right? It's hard to know where to begin!'

'I'm not even sure I can name them all.'

'*Chiku*, papaya, guava, pineapple, *rambutan*. They all taste different and they are all delicious.'

He reached for a *chiku*—a fruit he'd never heard of. 'It looks like a potato.'

'Wait until you taste it.'

He halved the fruit to reveal pinkish flesh seeded with a mere three black seeds. He scooped out a spoonful and blinked at the intense sweetness.

'Better than cotton candy.'

She smiled, and once again relief touched him.

'About last night…' he said. 'I know marriage isn't your ideal option, but I am very glad you said yes.'

'It isn't, but it *is* the best option on the table and I've decided to make the best of it. Perhaps if I'd been more upfront two years ago we wouldn't be in this mess. But we are, and I'll do my best to be positive about the marriage idea.'

'Our marriage doesn't have to be a mess. I think we can make this work. For Amil *and* for us.'

A pause, and then she nodded. 'I'll try. So, what's the next step in Project Marriage?'

There was no room for further doubts or any more discussion with his conscience. Project Marriage was what he wanted and what he believed to be right for them all. Yet for some reason he felt restless, as if the beauty of the surroundings was somehow tainted. This was the sort of place where *real* couples should sit and plan their future—couples foolish enough to believe in the concept of love.

'We need a plan, but I suggest we move this discussion to somewhere else. Is there anything you want to see in Goa? We could hit the beach…visit the old quarter…'

In truth he didn't care—he needed to move, to get on with the business of the day away from this tranquil fairy tale setting that seemed to accuse him of having behaved like his father, however much logic told him he hadn't.

Sunita thought for a moment, her tawny eyes dreamy, as if the question needed deeper consideration than it appeared to warrant.

'I'd like to go to the Dudhsagar Falls.'

There was a nuance in her voice he couldn't identify. 'Any reason?'

For a second she hesitated, then she shrugged. 'My parents came to Goa together and they visited the falls. It's one of the few memories my mother ever shared about them both—she said it was important sometimes to remember the happy memories or they would all crumble to dust.'

She picked up a *rambutan*, rolled the lychee-like fruit almost like a dice.

'I'm not entirely sure what she meant, but I'd like to go somewhere she was happy. Even if that happiness was no more than a mirage.'

He had the feeling that right now Sunita missed her mother—and who could blame her? She was about to step into a whole new world that she didn't want to enter.

'I'm sorry you lost her, Sunita.'

'Me too. But I do feel lucky I had her for the time I did.' She hesitated. 'I don't know the details, but I'm guessing you didn't have much time with *your* mum.'

'No.'

Even before the divorce his mother had spent minimal time with him—at least until the divorce proceedings were underway. Then it had all changed, and even now he could remember the glorious happiness his three-year-old self had felt—not the detail, but the joy that finally his mother wanted his company, would hug him, take him out… And then abruptly it had all ceased. She'd gone before the ink had even dried on the papers. The whole 'loving mother' act had been exactly that—an act undertaken to up her settlement.

'I'm sorry.'

'No need. You can't miss what you've never had.'

The words came out rougher than he'd intended, but he didn't want her compassion. He'd got over his mother's abandonment long ago, buried those emotions along with the rest.

Pulling out his phone, he did a check on the falls, scanned the information. 'The falls it is—I'll speak to Security, see how close they can get us. Looks like the official road is closed off because of monsoon season, but I'm sure we can get something sorted.'

'Actually, I wondered if we could do what my parents did and walk along the railway track to get there. Just us— no security. I know they're discreet, but today I'd like to be just Frederick and Sunita—before we get caught up in the reality of being a royal couple.'

The wistfulness in her voice decided him—alongside the fact that, however much he trusted his staff, it made sense to thrash out the details of this marriage in private. Plus if he was being honest with himself, he too wanted to be 'just Frederick and Sunita' for one day. To put aside the burden of ruling and his complex need for this marriage for one day.

'Sounds like a plan.'

Surprise etched her face. 'You're sure?'

'I'm sure. Tell me the route they took and I'll figure it out.'

She grinned. 'I think they came back on a goods train.'

'We can manage that.'

'The Prince and his future consort hopping on a goods train? I like it.'

Her smile broadened and it caught at his heart, causing a sudden unfamiliar tug of hope that perhaps this might all work out.

Sunita glanced up at the sky, and for the first time in the past forty-eight hours her thoughts slowed down as she absorbed the grandeur of the bright grey monsoon clouds.

Most tourists flocked to India in the summer months, but she loved monsoon—always had, even as a child. Loved the drum of the rain, which brought the country much needed water and succour from heat, and lavished verdant green to the trees and fields.

'It doesn't seem possible that there can be so many different shades of green—it makes me wish I could paint, somehow capture all this.' Her outswept arm encapsulated the winding track, the surrounding green and the skies above. 'Photos never seem to catch the reality of it—they look fake, somehow.'

'Then commit it to memory,' Frederick said, putting out a hand to steady her as she stumbled slightly over an awkward rock.

The touch of his hand against hers almost made her gasp out loud, adding an extra level to her already overcrowded senses. In an almost involuntary movement she clasped her fingers around his.

'Like my mother did. She described this walk to me so many times it almost felt like a story.'

Perhaps a real-life fairy tale, in which a moment of happiness had *not* led to a lifetime of happily-ever-after.

'It's odd to think that they walked here once...maybe took the exact same steps we're taking now.' She turned to him. 'You must feel that a lot as a ruler—the idea of history being always around you. Your ancestors' spirits looking over your shoulders.'

For an instant she'd swear a small shiver shot through him, and understanding smote her. Perhaps for him it was the spirit of his older brother that haunted his every move and decision.

Yet his voice was light as he answered, 'I am more worried about current judgement and the opinion of posterity than the line of my progenitors.'

He slowed as they approached a tunnel, half turning for evidence of any oncoming train.

They stepped inside the dark and now it was her turn to shiver at the dank confines. Water trickled down the damp mossy walls and he tightened his grip on her hand. Without thought she moved closer to the strength of his body.

'It's safe. Even if a train does come through there is ample space as long as we keep to the side.'

Yet suddenly it didn't *feel* safe—though it was no longer the train she was worried about. Frederick was too close, and that proximity was playing havoc with her body.

Did it matter any more? They were to be married—their physical attraction could now be acknowledged. The idea jolted a funny little thrill through her—one she short-circuited instantly. Two years ago physical attraction had lambasted her self-control and her pride. No way would she enter *that* thrall again.

As they emerged into sunlight she dropped his hand, under the pretext of tugging her hair into a ponytail, and then turned to him.

'I think we were talking about current judgement and public opinion—and on that topic we need to decide how to announce our engagement.'

For an instant his gaze locked on her hand and then he nodded. 'I think we keep it low-key. I don't want to announce this as a romantic fairy tale—that would be disingenuous, and way too reminiscent of my father's marriages. Every engagement, every wedding was an extravaganza, with proclamations of eternal love.'

'Did he love *any* of them?'

'According to his own criteria he did—but in reality I believe it was little more than lust and an ability to kid himself.'

'Perhaps he did it for children?'

'My father never did anything unless it was for himself.' His tone was factual, rather than bitter. 'But that isn't the point. I don't want to lie and present our marriage as some sort of perfect love story. I'd rather be honest.'

Sunita stared at him. 'That is hardly the most gripping headline—*Prince Proposes to Legitimise Heir.*' Irrational hurt threatened at his reminder that this was the only reason for their union. Well, so be it. 'I don't believe in fairy tales, but I *do* believe in good publicity.'

'So what would *you* suggest?'

'An old flame is rekindled. Prince Frederick of Lycander and Sunita decide to wed! Both the Prince and his bride profess delight at the prospect of being a real family.' Her pace increased slightly. 'I mean, that is just off the top of my head—I'm sure your spin people can work on it. We don't have to profess undying love, but anything is better than indifference.'

Admiration glinted in his eyes and warmed her.

'I'd forgotten what a natural you are with publicity. You've definitely not lost your touch.'

'Thank you kindly, good sir. Publicity is an incredibly powerful tool. I agree that we shouldn't lie to your people, but what you are doing is a good, principled action for your son—the people should know that. Of course they'll be interested in a bit of fun and glitz and a celebration too.' She glanced sideways at him. 'Fun is important—for all of us. I want Amil's childhood to be full of fun and joy—I want him to have a happy path through life.'

'So do I.'

'Good. Then let's show your people that. Let's make sure the engagement announcement is honest, but happy. We've decided to do this, so we need to make the best of it.'

With impeccable dramatic timing the skies chose that moment to open up, and before Sunita could do more than let out a warning cry the rain sheeted down in a torrential downpour.

Sunita tipped her face up and let it gush over her, revelling in the sheer force of Nature as it provided one of life's essentials.

Mere moments later the rain ceased. Blue skies replaced the grey, and sudden shafts of bright golden sunshine shot down, illuminating the droplets of water that hung everywhere. The smell of wet earth permeated the air and it seemed impossible not to smile.

'It's as if someone switched the tap off and the lights on,' Frederick said, a note of wonder in his voice as he looked round.

'That would be Varuna, the god of water. Nanni says that he listens to what the frogs say, and when they croak enough he gives us rain.'

'I think I'm going to like Nanni.'

'Of course you are.'

'So I take it your mother's family eventually relented and took her and you back in?'

'No...' Sunita sighed, feeling the familiar ache of regret and sadness. 'I wish that was how it had played out, but it didn't. They didn't relent.'

Even when they knew her mother was dying.

Anger was suddenly added to the mix. Her grandfather hadn't even told Nanni that their daughter was ill—hadn't given her the chance to say goodbye.

'I met Nanni for the first time when I was pregnant with Amil.' She glanced across at him. 'I don't expect your sympathy, but when I found I was pregnant I felt very alone.'

His expression hardened slightly, but to her surprise she could see an element of frustrated sympathy in his creased brow. 'So you decided to find your mother's relatives?'

'Yes. My mother had left enough information that it wasn't too hard. It turned out my grandfather had died two years before, and Nanni agreed to see me.'

That first meeting was one she would never forget—her

grandmother had simply stared at her, tears seeping from her brown eyes, her hands clasped as if in prayer. And then she had stepped forward and hugged Sunita, before standing back and touching her face as if in wonder, no doubt seeing not just her granddaughter but her daughter as well.

'She was overjoyed and so was I. She has never forgiven herself for not standing up to my grandfather, for letting my mother go, and I think she sees me and Amil as her second chance.'

'It isn't always easy to stand up to a partner if he or she has all the power. Your Nanni shouldn't be too hard on herself.'

'I've told her that. My mother didn't blame her either. Nanni was totally dependent on her husband—money, clothes, food, everything—and he made sure she knew it. If she had left with my mother he would have cut her off from the rest of her family, her children...everyone.' She paused and then turned to him, willing him to understand. 'I won't *ever* let myself get into that position.'

'You won't. Our marriage will be nothing like that.'

'I understand that, but I did mean what I said yesterday— I intend to resume my career. You saw what happened to your mother, your stepmothers. I've seen what happened to Nanni—I will *not* be dependent on you.'

'You won't be. We can set up a pre-nup.'

'In a principality where your word is law? Any pre-nup I sign wouldn't be worth the paper it was written on.'

'OK. You will be paid a salary that goes directly into your personal account—you can move that into another account anywhere in the world.'

'A salary essentially paid by *you*—one you could stop at any moment?'

His lips thinned. 'You really do not trust me at all, do you?'

There was a hint of hurt in his voice, but it was something she could not afford to listen to.

'I can't trust anyone. Think about it, Frederick. What if I decided to take Amil and leave? Would you still pay my salary? What if you turn out to be like your father? What if you fall in love with another woman?' Life had taught her there could never be too many 'what ifs' in the mix. 'Then I'll need money of my own.'

The easy warmth in his hazel eyes vanished, and now his brow was as clouded as a monsoon sky. 'None of those things will happen.'

'That's what you say *now*, but times change—we both know that.'

A shadow flickered across his face and she knew her point had gone home.

'So I must make sure myself that I have enough money in the bank for whatever life throws at me.'

To ensure there was always an escape route—that she would never be trapped like her grandmother had been, as *she* had been as a child.

'That is non-negotiable.'

'Understood.'

'Also, I want to leave Amil with my grandmother when we go back to Lycander.'

'Why?' The syllable was taut. 'Because you think I will snatch him the minute we land on Lycander soil?'

'No. But I won't risk taking him there until we have worked out how our marriage will be received. Also, I can get things ready for him; it will be a big change for him and I'd like to make his transition as easy as possible.'

The idea of not having Amil with her hurt, but she could not—*would* not—risk taking him to Lycander until she was sure of his reception there.

'I'll come back to Lycander with you, and *then* I'll get Amil.'

'OK. But *we* will get Amil.'

She nodded and then there was a silence, broken by a roar in the not so far distance.

'Dhudsagar Falls,' Sunita said. 'We're close.'

By tacit consent they quickened their pace.

CHAPTER ELEVEN

THE SOUND OF the monsoon-inflated waterfalls pounded his eardrums, but even as Frederick anticipated the sight his brain couldn't banish Sunita's expression, the realisation that she still didn't trust him.

Not that he blamed her—after all, his father had used his wealth and power to grind his wives to dust in the courts. All except his mother, who had played Alphonse at his own game and duped him—an act his father had never forgiven her for. Never forgiven Frederick for, come to that. But he wished that Sunita did not think so badly of him. *Enough.* Her opinion shouldn't matter, and in truth she couldn't judge him more harshly than he deserved. But…

His train of thought was broken by her gasp from next to him. 'Any minute now,' she whispered, as they emerged through a tunnel and onto a railway bridge already populated by a few other visitors.

But they had no interest in Sunita and Frederick— because it was impossible to focus on anything other than the waterfalls, both mighty and terrible. No image could do them justice as the four tiers cascaded and roared in torrents of milky-white water, leaping from the edge of towering cliffs and gusting and gushing down the slippery rock slopes.

The spray drenched him but he didn't move, utterly

mesmerised by the power and glory of Nature's creation, cloaked in a rising mist that mixed with the shafts of sunlight to create a rainbow of light.

'It's beyond description.'

Frederick nodded and moved by awe, on instinct, he reached out and took her hand in his. He wasn't sure how long they stood there, but it was long enough that the other tourists dispersed, long enough that another group came and went.

And then Sunita shook her head, as if coming out of a trance. 'We'd better go.'

He wondered what she'd been thinking all that time—perhaps she'd imagined her parents standing in the same spot, their thoughts and emotions, their hopes and dreams as they'd gazed at the might of the waterfalls.

They continued their trek along the railway tracks in a silence that he instinctively respected until he motioned to the adjacent forest. 'Shall we explore in there—it looks peaceful?'

'Good idea.' She glanced up at him. 'Sorry I've been lost in thought—it was just such an awe-inspiring sight.'

'It was.' He reached into his backpack. 'Time for food—or is that too prosaic?'

'Nope. I'm starving. And this looks idyllic—if a little damp.'

'I've brought a blanket, and if we spread it here, over this branch, we can perch on it.'

'Perfect.'

She accepted the wrapped sandwiches.

'Goan green chutney,' Frederick informed her. 'I promised Ashok to tell you the exact ingredients. Coriander leaves, coconut, chili and a little sugar and salt.'

Sunita took a bite. 'Glorious. That boy is talented.' She

surveyed him. 'So you went to the kitchen yourself? I'm surprised that was allowed.'

'Meaning?'

'Meaning your staff seem to think you shouldn't lift a finger for yourself.'

'I've noticed. I *am* trying to re-educate them—in fact I've given them all the day off today. The problem is my father expected to be waited on hand and foot, and that is what all Lycander staff seem conditioned to do. I even have someone who chooses all my clothes.' He grinned. 'Though, to be fair, Kirsten does a better job of it than I could.'

'Well, for the record, no one is choosing *my* clothes for me. That would drive me nuts. I need to fit my clothes to my mood.'

They ate in companionable silence and then Frederick leant forward, unsure why he felt the need to say his next words, but knowing he had to take heed of the urge to show her that their hopes and dreams didn't have to be built on an altar of falsehood and misunderstanding.

'Sunita?'

'Yes.'

She turned her head and his heart did a funny little jump. Dressed in simple khaki trousers and a red T-shirt, with her hair pulled back in a high ponytail, her features make-up free, she looked absurdly young and touchingly vulnerable.

'I understand why you want to go back to your career, and I understand your need for independence, but let's not go into this marriage expecting the worst. We'll be OK,' he said, even as he realised the ridiculous inadequacy of the words.

'You can't know that.' She lifted her shoulders in a shrug. 'But I appreciate the sentiment.'

'There are some things I *do* know, though. I won't turn into my father.' *Please God!* 'I won't fall in love with someone else and take Amil away from you.'

'You can't know that either.'

'I don't do falling in love, and that will not change. As for Amil, I will not take him from you. You have my word.'

'Words are meaningless.'

Her fierce certainty told him that someone had lied to her with devastating consequence, and increased his need to show her that he would not do the same.

'Sunita, I couldn't do it.' The words rasped from his throat. 'I would have done anything to have a mother. I witnessed first-hand what my father did to his wives, how it affected my brothers. I could not, I *will* not let history repeat itself.'

Her whole body stilled, and then she rose and moved towards him, sat right next to him, so close a tendril of her hair tickled his cheek.

'I'm sorry—I know what it's like to lose a mother through death, but for you it must have been pain of a different type…to know she was out there. And your poor mother… to have lost you like that—I can't imagine how it must have felt. Not just your mother but Stefan's and the twins'.'

For a moment the temptation to let her believe the fiction touched him. To let her believe the false assumption that his mother had been wronged, had spent years in grief and lamenting, that his mother had loved him. After all, he had no wish to be an object of pity or allow the ugly visage of self-pity to show its face.

But as he saw the sympathy, the empathy on her face, he realised he couldn't let her waste that compassion. 'My mother didn't suffer, Sunita.'

'I don't understand.'

'My mother sold me out for generous alimony and a

mansion in Beverly Hills. She played my father like a fine fiddle—conned him into believing she would do anything to keep custody of me, would be devastated to lose me. At the time he was still worrying about his popularity—many people hadn't got over the way he'd married my mother mere weeks after his first wife's death. He wanted to hurt her by taking me away—however, he didn't want to come across as the totally cruel husband again, so he offered her a generous settlement and she skipped all the way to the bank.'

'But...' Disbelief lined her face, along with a dark frown. 'How *could* she?'

'With great ease, apparently. Hey, it's OK. I came to terms with it long ago. I didn't tell you because I want to discuss it, or because I want sympathy. I told you because I want you to know that I could never take Amil from you. I know first-hand that a child needs his mother. From my own experience *and* my siblings'. Stefan, Barrett, Emerson—they have all been devastated by the custody battles and having their mothers torn from them. I would not put you or Amil through it. You have my word, and that word is not meaningless.'

'Thank you.' Shifting on the branch so that she faced him, she cupped his face in her hands, her fingers warm against his cheeks. 'Truly. Thank you for sharing that—you didn't have to. And I do believe that right here, right now, you mean what you promise.'

'But you don't believe I'll make good?'

'I...' Her hands dropped to her sides and, leaning forward, she dabbled her fingers in the soil of the forest floor, trickled it through her fingers and then sat up again. 'I don't know.'

She shrugged.

'Perhaps it's my turn to share now. I told you how my

father left when he found out my mother was pregnant. He promised her that he loved her, that they had a future.' She gestured back the way they'd come. 'Maybe he said those words at the falls. Hell, maybe they even sat here, in this very forest. But that promise meant nothing. And, you see, that wasn't the only promise he made.'

'I don't understand.'

'He came back.' Her eyes were wide now, looking back into a past that he suspected haunted her. 'When my mother found out she was terminally ill she managed to track him down. She had no one else. And he came, and he agreed to take me in. He explained that he was married, with two other daughters, but he promised—he swore that I would be welcomed, that I would have a family, that he would love and cherish me. He said that he was sorry and that he wanted to make it up to her and to me.'

The pain in her voice caused an ache that banded his chest and he reached out to cover her hand in his own, hoped that somehow it would assuage her hurt.

'So, after she died…' Her voice caught and her fingers tightened around his. 'He came to bring me to England— to my new family.'

Perhaps he should say something, Frederick thought. But he couldn't think of anything—couldn't even begin to contemplate how Sunita must have felt. The loss of her mother, the acquisition of a father she must have had mixed feelings about, the total upending of her life. All he could do was shift closer to her, *show* his comfort.

'It didn't work out. Turned out his promises didn't materialise.'

'What happened?'

'My stepmother and my sisters loathed me—I knew that from the instant I walked into the house.'

A house that must have felt so very alien to her, in a country that must have felt grey and cold and miserable.

'In a nutshell, he pitched me into a Cinderella scenario. They treated me like I was an inferior being.' She made a small exasperated noise. 'It sounds stupid, because it is so difficult to explain, but they made me feel worthless. I ate separately from them, my clothes were bought from charity shops, while my half-sisters' were new, I ended up with loads of extra chores so I could "earn my keep", and there were constant put-downs, constant reminders that I was literally worthless.' Another shrug. 'It all sounds petty, but it made me feel like nothing—worse than invisible. I was visible, but what they could see made them shudder.'

'It doesn't sound petty—it sounds intolerable.' Anger vibrated through him, along with disbelief that people could be so cruel. 'Was your father involved in this?'

'He was more of a bystander than a participant. He was away a lot on business. I did try to explain to him that I was unhappy, that I felt my stepmother didn't like me, but he simply said that I must be imagining it or, worse, he would accuse me of base ingratitude. Which made me feel guilty and even more alone.'

No wonder Sunita found it hard to take people at their word. Her own father, who had promised to care for her, had instead treated her like muck and allowed others to do the same.

'I'm sorry. I wish I could turn back time and intervene.'

'You can't change the past. And even if you could perhaps the outcome would be worse. Because in the past I got out, I escaped, and I've come to terms with what happened. I can even understand a little why my stepmother acted as she did. She was landed with a strange girl—the daughter of a woman her husband had been unfaithful with, the woman who probably was the love of his life. The gossip and speculation in the community must have been beyond humiliating for her and my half-sisters. So they turned all that anger and humiliation on to me.'

'That doesn't excuse their behaviour, or explain your father's.'

'I think my father was weak and he felt guilty. Guilty over the way he'd treated my mother…guilty that he had betrayed his wife in the first place. And that guilt translated into doing anything for a quiet life. That worked in my favour later on. I got scouted by a model agency when I was sixteen and my father agreed to let me leave home— my stepmother was happy to see me go, sure I'd join the ranks of failed wannabes, so she agreed. I never looked back and I never went back. I never saw them again. The second I could, I sent my father a cheque to cover any costs he might have incurred over the years. As far as I am concerned we are quits. I don't even know where he is.'

So much made sense to Frederick now—her lack of trust, her fears over Amil, her need to be in control. Admiration burned within him that she had achieved so much, was such an amazing parent herself.

These were all the things he wanted to say, but didn't quite know how. So instead he did what he had promised himself he wouldn't do and he kissed her—right there in the middle of the rainforest, with the smell of the monsoon in the air, and the pounding of the waterfall in the distance. He kissed her as if his life and soul depended on it.

Her resistance was brief—a nanosecond of surprise— and then, as if she too were tired of words, of this walk down a memory lane that was lined with sadness, her resistance melted away and her lips parted beneath his.

He tasted the sweet chili tang left by the sandwiches and heard her soft moan. Their surroundings receded. The call of a hornbill, the rustle of the monkeys in the trees above all melted away and left only them, encased in a net of yearning and need and desire.

He pulled her closer, oblivious of the rustle of the blanket, the unwieldiness of the branch they sat on. Nothing mattered but *this*—losing themselves in this moment of sheer bliss as he deepened the kiss, as her hands slipped under his T-shirt so her fingers covered the accelerated beat of his heart.

Who knew what would have happened if a monkey in the tree above hadn't decided to take advantage and scamper down in an audacious bid for the rucksack. It's insistent chatter and the swipe of an overhanging branch brought Frederick back to reality.

A shout from him, a darting movement from Sunita, and the monkey jumped to safety and jabbered at them in indignation.

They met each other's eyes, hers still clouded with desire, and he managed a smile. 'Well saved.'

Then there were no words. They both simply stood there, and he reached out and took her hands in his.

'What now?' he asked.

'I don't know.' She shook her head. 'Yes, I do. Let's walk. And eat and talk. But let's not talk about unhappy things.'

'That sounds good. Only happy topics—all the way back.' He held her gaze. 'And what happens then?'

She stepped forward, stood on tiptoe, and dropped the lightest of kisses on his lips. 'I don't know,' she whispered. 'I really don't.'

For a moment neither did he. Oh, he knew what he *should* do—he should lock this down now. This physical attraction was too intense, too emotional, and he didn't want intensity or emotion to enter their relationship. This marriage was an alliance and he wanted it to last. Succumbing to physical allure, allowing it too much importance, would jeopardise that.

But today he was just Frederick, not the Playboy Prince or the ruler of a principality who had vowed to fulfil his brother's vision. Today they were Frederick and Sunita.

And so he stepped forward and smiled—a smile that was shamelessly predatory and full of promise. 'Then it's lucky that I know *exactly* what to do.'

'What...?' Her voice was even softer than before, her brown eyes wide.

'We're going to walk to the nearest station and catch a goods train, and then take a taxi back to the villa. Then we're going to resume where we've just left off and this time we are not going to stop.' He paused. 'How does that sound?'

He realised he was holding his breath as she tipped her head to one side, and then she smiled a smile that lit her face and ignited a warmth that spread across his chest.

'That sounds perfect. I just hope the goods train is fast.'

Frederick shook his head. 'Anticipation is half the fun.' He held out his hand. 'Let's go.'

'Anticipation is half the fun.'

Sunita wasn't so sure of that. As they walked alongside the train tracks anticipation streamed through her veins, causing her tummy to cartwheel and her pulse-rate to soar. Was *that* fun?

It was hard to tell—her whole body felt tight with need, a yearning that it would now be impossible to quell, and truth to tell she didn't want to. She glanced down at their clasped hands, at the strength of his profile, the jut of his jaw, the lithe assurance he walked with, the whole time aware of his own scrutiny, the desire that warmed his hazel eyes when they rested on her.

They talked—of course they did. Of films and books and politics…of cabbages and kings…but the words seemed to be filtered through a haze of awareness that glistened in the air alongside the sunlit drops of rain that sparkled from the lush leaves.

Their ascent onto a goods train seemed almost surreal as they travelled amidst the bulky cargo, and she gazed out over the variegated greens of paddy fields, the swoop of the Goan valleys, the shimmering grey of the sky, where clouds swelled and perfumed the air with the promise of rain. All the while, even as her senses stored away Nature's munificent beauty, they also revelled in Frederick's proximity, in the knowledge that soon—soon—they would be together, that for a time at least he would be hers.

Careful!

She must not let this get out of perspective, make it into any more than it was. This was a benefit of their marriage deal—a benefit that could be taken or left at will. This was physical—no more no less—and the only reason she was so on edge was because she hadn't felt like this for two years. Not since that night when all her principles had been abandoned and she'd tumbled into bed with him.

'Hey.'

She turned to see his hazel eyes rest on her face.

'You OK? We don't have to do this, you know? We have a lifetime ahead of us…'

But not like this—not as Frederick and Sunita. Today meant something different—she couldn't explain how she knew it, but she knew with soul-wrenching certainty that this was the case.

'I know, but I want this now, today…' She grinned suddenly. 'There is only so much anticipation a girl can take.'

His answering grin removed all doubts; it was a smile

she remembered from two years ago, boyish, happy, and she hadn't seen it once in the past few days.

'It'll be worth it. I promise.'

And as the train slowed to a stop she had no doubt that this was a promise she could rely on.

Twenty minutes later they arrived back at the villa and alighted from the taxi. She glanced around almost furtively, not wanting to meet Deepali or Ashok or anyone. Hand in hand, they practically tiptoed through the garden… And if Deepali did spot them she remained discreetly hidden and they reached Sunita's bedroom safely.

Once inside, she moved to the window and pulled the blackout shutters closed, then turned and moved towards Frederick with an urgency more than matched by his own as he strode forward and pulled her so she was flush against the hard promise of his body.

'The anticipation was great,' she murmured. 'But now it's got old.'

His laugh held a breathless quality. 'Tell me about it!'

And with that he tumbled her back onto the bed, and after that all coherent thought evaporated as sensation took over. The feel of his lips on hers, his taste, his touch against her sensitised skin—all caused her to moan in unabashed joy. His skin under her fingers, his shudder of pleasure, his voice whispering her name, the shucking of clothes, the urgency and the exquisite gentleness, the awe and the laughter and desire such as she had never known, all created a waving, pulsing sense that carried them higher and higher…

Hours later she opened her eyes, realising that she was being gently shaken awake, a hand on her shoulder. *His* hand. She blinked sleepily, and then sat up as the glorious dream dissipated. Frederick stood back from the bed—fully clothed, she noted with a fuzzy disappointment.

'Hey...' she said.

'Hey. Everyone's back—we need to show our faces before they wonder where we are.'

Sunita blinked, tried to compute why it mattered—they were engaged. Surely he wasn't embarrassed. Properly awake now, she propped herself up on one elbow as a sudden awkwardness descended. 'You should have woken me earlier.'

'I thought I'd let you sleep.' Now a small smile quirked into place. 'We expended a lot of energy.'

'So we did.' For a moment relief touched her—maybe she'd imagined the awkwardness.

'But now the day is over and we aren't "just" Sunita and Frederick any more. We are the Prince and his Princess-to-be and we can't repeat this.'

'This?' she echoed, as a spark of anger ignited by hurt flared. 'Define "this".'

His gaze remained steady. 'We can't sleep together again before the wedding. This engagement needs to be seen as completely different from my father's marriages—I don't want the people to believe it is based on physical attraction alone, that their ruler has been influenced by anything other than the good of Lycander.'

'Of course.'

It made perfect sense, she could see that. Of course she could. She could measure every publicity angle with unerring accuracy. This marriage would not play well with Lycander—she herself had pointed that out. So she understood that they needed to downplay their physical attraction and focus on the real reason for their marriage—Amil.

Yet his words felt like a personal rejection, as though

beneath his common-sense approach lay reserve, a with-
drawal.

The knowledge…the certainty that he regretted the day
and its outcome, that he regretted 'this', bolstered her pride,
gave her voice a cool assurance. 'I understand.'

After all, he'd made it clear enough. Their physical attraction was a side benefit, a bonus to their marriage alliance, and she would not make the mistake of reading any
more into it than that.

'I need to get dressed. Shall I meet you in the gardens?'

For a moment he hesitated, and then nodded and headed
for the door. Once he was gone Sunita closed her eyes, an-
noyed to feel the imminent well of tears. Two years before she'd allowed physical attraction to override common
sense, and now it seemed she might have done it again.
But no more.

She swung herself out of bed in a brisk movement and
headed across the room. Pulling open her wardrobe, she
surveyed the contents and settled on a black cold-shoulder
crop top over floral silk trousers. A quick shower, a bit of
make-up and she was good to go.

Once in the gardens, she spotted Frederick in conversation with Eric, saw the hand-over of a package that Frederick dropped into his pocket before he saw her and walked
over.

'Shall we have a quick walk before dinner?' he asked.
'Sure.'

They walked into the sylvan glade, skirting the lily
pond, where two brilliant turquoise kingfishers dived, their
white 'shirtfront' breasts bright in the dusk.

'I wanted to give you this,' he said, and he reached into
his pocket and took out the package, undoing it with deft
fingers and handing her the jeweller's box inside. 'We can't
announce the engagement without a ring.'

She flipped the lid open and gazed inside. The ring had presence; it glinted up at her, a cold, hard, solid diamond. A discreetly obvious ring that knew its own worth—its multi-faceted edges placed it in the upper echelon of the diamond class. A regal ring—perhaps he hoped it would confer a royal presence on her.

Hell, it was the very Kaitlin of rings.

'Did you choose it?'

For a scant instant discomfort showed, but then it was gone. 'No. Kirsten did.'

The woman who chose his clothes. Of course—who better to choose the correct ring for Lycander's bride?

'I asked her to get it done last night. Is there a problem with it?'

'Of course not.'

In an abrupt movement she pulled the ring out and slid it over her finger, where it sat and looked up at her, each glint one of disdain. The ring wasn't fooled—it knew this was not a worthy hand to rest upon.

Sunita glared down at it as she executed an almost painful mental eye-roll. *Note to self: the ring does not possess a personality. Second note: of course I am worthy.*

She summoned a smile. 'Guess we're all set to go.' Even if she couldn't have felt less ready.

CHAPTER TWELVE

Lycander

THE CAR WOUND up the mountain road. Sunita stifled a gasp and Frederick felt a sudden surge of pride as he saw her reaction to Lycander's castle.

'Holy-moly,' she said. 'It's straight out of a fairy tale. Any minute now Snow White will wave at me from a turret or I'll see Rapunzel climb down a tower.'

Something tugged at his heart as he looked at her—something he couldn't identify and didn't particularly want to. Focus on facts…that was the way to go.

'Believe it or not, this castle has been around for centuries. It started out long ago as a wooden fortress and over the years it has been renovated, added to, and here we have it.'

'It's hard to believe I'm going to live there.'

Equally hard to ascertain her opinion on the fact, he thought.

Sunita subsided into silence as they approached the castle and parked in an impressive paved courtyard, complete with fountains, stone lions and an immense marble sundial.

'I'll give you a proper tour later. For now, if it's all right with you, I'll show you to your rooms—I've asked Giselle Diaz, the housekeeper, to get a set of apartments ready.

After the wedding we will move into the state apartments. I'll show you those later—I think you may want to redecorate them.'

Slow down. No need to turn into a tour guide. Come to that, he couldn't help but wonder at the dearth of staff there to greet them. Foreboding touched him—perhaps the no-show was connected to the emergency council meeting he was scheduled to attend right now. Convened to 'discuss'—for that read 'object to'—his marriage.

They reached the apartment suite that would be Sunita and Amil's until the wedding and he scanned it quickly. Clean and polished...welcoming flowers in place. On the surface it all looked fine, but he knew it lacked the extra touches that had abounded the one time Lady Kaitlin had stayed as a Lycander guest. Back then Giselle had been there to greet them, the flowers had been more lavish, the toiletries a tad more luxurious.

Hmm...

'I'll leave you to settle in and I'll be back as soon as I can.'

'Why don't I come with you? My guess is that your council will want to talk to you about our marriage—let's face them together.'

Frederick shook his head. 'I'd rather do it alone. I brokered this marriage—it is my responsibility to explain it to my people.'

A flash of hurt showed in her eyes and then she shrugged. 'As you wish.'

He pushed down the urge to assuage the hurt; this was *his* business and he would deal with it alone.

Fifteen minutes later he looked around the council chamber, which was informally referred to as the tapestry room, due to the needlepoint that lined nearly every centimetre of the walls. The lifework of a princess centuries before, who had toiled whilst her husband had dallied with a string of mistresses.

Each section illustrated a different theme, dominated by war and religion with plenty of fire and brimstone and gore... Presumably it was meant to be an apt backdrop for the discussion of council matters.

'Order!' called one of the council members.

Frederick looked around the table—at Marcus's assessing expression, at the rest of the council's combative stance. 'You requested we meet as soon as I arrived to discuss your concerns. Please enlighten me.'

A middle-aged man rose to his feet. 'This proposed marriage, Your Highness...we do not believe it is a good move.'

'Marcus has kept me apprised of your concerns.' He kept his voice even. 'But this marriage *is* happening.'

'But the people will not like it,' interpolated another council member.

'Sunita is an excellent publicist—I believe she will win them over.'

'How? She is a woman you barely know—a model, the mother of a baby she kept from you—but now that you are on the throne she seems happy to marry you.'

'Shades of your mother...'

'Who said that?' Frederick demanded.

'*I* said it.' The voice came from one of the elder statesmen.

'My relationship with Sunita bears no resemblance to that of my parents.'

'I beg to differ, Your Highness. I was there. Prince Alphonse fell hook, line and sinker for your mother—chased her whilst his wife, the mother of Crown Prince Axel, was dying. Their wedding was an extravaganza pushed forward because the bride was pregnant. Within months of your birth the marriage was floundering; within a few years it had ended in scandal. Your mother played him for a fool.'

White-hot anger roiled inside him. Yet the words were true—a fact he had to face.

'Are you saying that *I* am a fool? What would have happened if you had spoken to my father thus?'

Frederick made a gesture to a guard, who stepped forward without hesitation to a murmur of surprise.

'You would have been marched out and the council would have been shut down until after the wedding.'

He gestured for the guard to stop and rose to his feet.

'But I do not rule as my father did—I have listened to all your concerns and I understand them. Now I tell you this. My marriage to Sunita is to be made in good faith on both our parts. There will be no scandal. There will be no custody battle. This union will endure. This wedding is happening.'

What was he? The Delphi Oracle? But now was no time to exhibit doubt. 'I promise you all that I value your opinion. But you see, ladies and gentlemen, Amil is my son, and if I have a chance to be a father *without* taking my son from his mother then I have to take it. So the wedding will happen and I very much hope to see you all dance at it.'

Further silence, and then Marcus rose to his feet, an enigmatic look on his face. 'I suggest that is the end of this special council meeting.'

As everyone filed out Frederick ran a hand down his face and turned as his chief advisor approached. Frederick shook his head. 'Not now, Marcus. I can't take any more wedding advice.'

The dark-haired man gave a half-smile. 'I wouldn't dare.'

'Now, *that* I don't believe.'

'You should.' Marcus eyed him. 'That is the first time since your ascension to the throne that I have seen you stand up for something *you* believe in.'

'Rubbish. I have stood in this room and fought to convince councillors to support education and tax reform, to close the casinos...'

'I get that. But those were all Axel's policies. This is *your* marriage.'

'Axel would have agreed that I am doing the right thing.'

'Then maybe you and Axel had more in common than I realised.'

For a second his chief advisor's words warmed him—but only for a fleeting second. If Marcus knew the truth he'd never use such words.

Frederick rose to his feet before the urge to confess overcame common sense and tried to rid himself of the grubby feel of deceit.

'Frederick? I'll support you in this, but you will need to make this work. You need to win the public round.'

'I know.'

Luckily, he knew the perfect person to help with that.

Sunita stared down at the diamond ring that sparkled and glistened and weighted her finger. She looked around the apartment that appeared opulent yet felt oppressive, with its heavy faded gold curtains and the bowls of flowers that, though magnificent, emanated a cloying, gloom-laden scent.

These were showrooms—there should be signs and information leaflets to outline the names of the rich and famous who had stayed within these walls, to document the lives of the painters who had created the looming allegorical creations that adorned them.

The furniture was decorative—but the stripes of the

claw-footed chaise longue almost blinded her, and the idea of sitting on it was impossible. As for the bedroom—she'd need a stepladder to get up into a bed that, conversely, seemed to have been made for someone at least a foot smaller than she was.

Well, there was no way she would let Amil live in a showroom, so she needed to make it into a home.

She started to unpack—hung her clothes in the wardrobe, took comfort from the feel of the fabrics, the splash of the colours, every item imbued with memories.

She halted at a knock on the door.

Spinning round, she saw Frederick framed in the doorway, and to her annoyance her heart gave a little pit-pat, a hop, skip and a jump.

'Hi.'

'Sorry, I did knock on the main door.'

'That's fine. How did the meeting go?'

'As well as could be expected. The council understand this marriage. But we need to get the publicity right to prevent a public backlash.'

Sunita moved away from the wardrobe. 'OK. Let's brainstorm.'

Her mind whirred as they moved into the lounge and perched on two ridiculously uncomfortable upholstered chairs.

'We need to make sure the people understand why we have left Amil in India—that it is simply so we can prepare a home for him. I could talk to the local press about my plans to renovate these apartments and the state apartments. I also suggest that before Amil arrives we go on a tour of some of Lycander, so it's clear that I am interested in the country—not just the crown. I won't accept any modelling contracts straight away.'

Even though her agent's phone was already ringing off the proverbial hook.

He rose to his feet, looked down at her with a sudden smile that set her heart off again.

'Let's start now.'

'How?'

'I'll take you on a tour of an olive grove.'

'One of yours?'

For a moment he hesitated, and then he nodded. 'Yes. I'll arrange transport and press coverage.'

'I'll get changed into appropriate clothes for touring an olive grove.' In fact she knew the very dress—a long, floaty, lavender-striped sun dress.

A shot of anticipation thrilled through her.

Stop. This was a publicity stunt—not a romantic jaunt. She had to get a grip. This marriage was an alliance that Frederick had 'brokered'—a word he had used in this very room a mere hour before.

The problem was, however hard she tried—and she'd tried incredibly hard—that anticipation refused to be suppressed by logic or any other device she could come up with.

Perhaps it was simply to do with the glorious weather, the cerulean blue sky, the hazy heat of the late August sun whose rays kissed and dappled the rolling hills and plains of the Lycander countryside. She could only hope it was nothing to do with the man who sat beside her in the back of the chauffeured car.

'So, where exactly are we going?'

'The place where it all started—the first olive grove I owned. It was left to me by a great-uncle when I was twenty-one. I visited on a whim and—*kaboom!*—the whole process fascinated me. The family who lived there were thrilled as my great-uncle had had no interest in the place—they taught me all about the business and that's how Freddy Petrelli's Olive Oil came into being. I expanded, bought up some smaller businesses, consolidated, and now our oil is stocked worldwide.'

'Are you still part of the company?'

'I'm still on the board, but by necessity I have had to delegate.'

'That's pretty impressive—to take one rundown olive grove and turn it into a multi-million-dollar business in a few years.'

'You turned yourself into one of the world's most sought-after supermodels in much the same time-frame. That's pretty impressive too.'

'Thank you—but it didn't feel impressive at the time.' Back then she'd been driven. 'I *needed* to succeed—I would not let my family see me fail. I wanted them to know that they had been wrong about me. I wanted to show them I was my mother's daughter and proud of it.'

At every photo shoot, she'd imagined their faces, tinged a shade of virulent green as they opened a magazine to see Sunita's face.

'That's understandable—and kudos to you for your success. You have my full admiration and, although it may not be politically correct, I hope they choked on envy every time they saw your picture.'

She couldn't help but laugh as a sudden warmth flooded her—it had been a long time since anyone had sounded so protective of her.

Before she could respond further the car came to a halt—and right after that they were mobbed. Or that was what it felt like. Once she had alighted from the car she realised the 'mob' actually consisted of four people—a middle-aged couple, a youth and a young girl—all of whom broke into simultaneous speech.

'The crop has been excellent this year. The olives—they will be the best yet. And last year's olive oil—the gods have blessed it, Freddy!'

'It has been too long, Frederick, too long—how can you have not been here for so long? And why didn't you tell me of this visit earlier? I would have prepared your favourite dishes. Now. Bah... All we have is what I have had time to prepare.'

'Thanks so much for the links to the bikes. Oil, gears, helmets...'

'Frederick, I've missed you! Why haven't you visited?'

There was no mistaking the family's happiness at seeing him, and as Sunita watched Frederick contend with the barrage of comments his smile flashed with a youthful boyishness.

'Pepita, Juan, Max, Flo—I'd like to introduce you to Sunita...my fiancée.'

For a moment the silence felt heavy, and Sunita could feel her tummy twist, and then Pepita stepped forward.

'Welcome, Sunita. It is lovely that Frederick has brought you here. We have all been reading the papers—every article. The little *bambino* looks adorable.'

As she spoke Pepita swept them forward towards a whitewashed villa. Terracotta tiles gleamed in the sunshine and trees shaded the courtyard outside.

'Come—lunch is all ready, Alberto, sort out the drinks. Flo, set the table, Max, come and help me serve.'

'Can I help?' asked Sunita.

'No, no, no. You and Frederick go and sit.'

Within minutes, amidst much debate and chat, food appeared. A bottle of wine was opened, tantalising smells laced the air and Pepita beamed.

'Come and serve yourselves. Frederick, you have lost

weight—I want you to eat. They are not your favourite dishes, but they are still good.'

'Pepita, everything you cook is good.'

Sunita shook her head. 'Nope. Everything you cook is *amazing*.'

It truly was. The table was laden with a variety of dishes. Bite-sized skewers that held tangy mozzarella, luscious tomatoes that tasted of sunshine and basil. Deep-fried golden rounds of cheese tortellini. Freshly baked bread with a pesto and vinegar dip that made her taste-buds tingle. Baked asparagus wrapped in prosciutto. And of course bowls of olives with a real depth of zing.

But what was truly amazing was the interplay between Frederick and the family—to see him set aside his role of ruler, to see him morph back to the man he had been before tragedy had intervened and changed his life path.

There was conversation and laughter, the clatter of cutlery, the taste of light red wine, the dapple of sunshine through the leaves causing a dance of sunbeams on the wooden slats of the table.

Until finally everyone was replete and this time Sunita insisted. 'I'll help clear.'

Frederick rose as well, but Pepita waved him down. 'Stay. Drink more wine. I want to talk to your fiancée alone.'

A hint of wariness crossed his face, but clearly he didn't feel equal to the task of intervention. So, plates in hand, Sunita followed Pepita to a whitewashed kitchen, scented by the fresh herbs that grew on the windowsill. Garlic hung from the rafters, alongside copper pots and pans.

'It is good to see Frederick here,' Pepita ventured with a sideways glance. 'And now he is a father.'

'Yes.' Sunita placed the plates down and turned to face

the older woman. 'I know you must be angry at what I did, but—'

'It is not my place to be angry—this is a matter for you to sort out with Frederick…a matter between husband and wife. I want to tell you that I am worried about him. Since his brother's death we have barely seen him—all he does now is work. I know that he avoids us. There is a demon that drives him and you need to get rid of it.'

'I… Our marriage isn't going to be like that, Pepita…'

'Bah! You plan to spend your lives together, yes? Then that is your job.'

Her head spun as the enormity of Pepita's words sank in. She *was* planning to spend her life with Frederick—her *life*. She wouldn't have another one; this was it.

Closing her eyes, she forced her thoughts to centre, to concentrate on the here and now. 'I'll do what I can,' she heard herself say, wanting to soothe the other woman's worry.

Frederick looked up as Sunita emerged from the house. Her face was slightly flushed from the sun, her striped dress the perfect outfit for a sunny day. Her expression looked thoughtful, and he couldn't help but wonder what Pepita had said—though he was wise enough to have no intention of asking. He suspected he might not like the answer.

Guilt twanged at the paucity of time he had given to this family—people he felt closer to than his 'real' family.

He turned to Juan. 'Is it all right if I take Sunita on a tour?'

'Why are you asking me? It is *your* grove, Frederick— I just tend it for you. Go—show your beautiful lady the most beautiful place in the world.'

Sunita grinned up at him as they made their way towards the fields. 'They are a lovely family.'

'That they are.'

'And it's good to see your royal authority in action.'

'Sarcasm will get you nowhere—but you're right. Pepita wouldn't recognise royal authority if it rose up and bit her. To her I am still the twenty-one-year-old they taught the olive oil business. Right here.'

Sunita gave a small gasp, her face animated as she gazed ahead to where majestic lines of evergreen trees abounded. Olives clustered at the ends of branches clad with silver leaves that gleamed in the sunlight.

'The colour of those leaves—it's like they're threaded with real silver.'

'That's actually the colour of the underside of the leaf. When it's hot the leaves turn light-side up to reflect the sun. When it's cold they turn grey-green side up to absorb the sun.'

'That's pretty incredible when you think about it.'

'The whole process is incredible. The olives are growing at the moment. They won't be ready to harvest for another few months. You should be here for the harvest. It's incredible. The green table olives get picked in September, October, then the ones we use for oil from mid-November, when they are bursting with oil. It is exhausting work. You basically spread a cloth under the trees to catch the olives and then you hit the trees with sticks. The harvest then gets carted off to the mills—which is equally fascinating. But I won't bore you with it now.'

'You aren't boring me. Keep going. Truly.'

Her face registered genuine interest, and so as they walked he talked and she listened. They inhaled the tang of the olives mingled with the scent of honeysuckle carried on the gentle breeze, revelled in the warmth of the sun and the lazy drone of bees in the distance.

It was impossible not to feel at peace here. Impossible

not to note Sunita's beauty—her dark hair shining with a raven sheen in the sunlight, the classic beauty of her face enhanced by the surroundings—and it took all his willpower not to kiss her. That would be a bad move.

She looked up at him. 'I can see why you fell in love with this place—it has a timeless quality.'

'A few of these trees have been here for centuries.'

'And in that time history has played out…generations of people have walked these fields, beaten the trees with sticks, experienced joy and sadness and the full gamut of emotion in between. It gives you perspective.' She gave him a sideways glance and took a quick inhalation of breath. 'Maybe you should come here more often.'

'Because you think I need perspective?'

'Because Pepita misses you.'

'Did she say that?'

'No, but it's pretty obvious. I'd guess that you miss them too.'

'I don't have time to miss them. In the same way I don't have time to come down here—my days in the olive oil industry are over, and I've accepted that.'

'That doesn't mean you can't visit more often.' She stopped now and turned to face him, forced him to halt as well. 'No one would grudge you some down-time. And this place *means* something to you.'

That was the trouble—this place took him off his game, distracted him from his mission, reminded him of a time untainted by guilt, of the man he had once been and could never be again. When Axel had been alive.

Yet he had brought Sunita here today—*why?* The reason smacked into him. He'd succumbed to temptation— one more day of 'just Frederick and Sunita'. *Foolish.* 'Just Frederick and Sunita' didn't exist.

'Yes, it does. It represents the past. A part of my life that is over. For good.'

Reality was the crown of Lycander and the path he had set himself. Axel had died—had been denied the chance to rule, to live, to marry, to have children. The only thing Frederick could do now was honour his memory—ensure his vision was accomplished. Ensure the monarchy was safe and Lycander prospered.

'It's time to get back to the palace.'

CHAPTER THIRTEEN

Two weeks later

SUNITA GAZED AROUND the transformed apartments with satisfaction. It hadn't been easy, but the spindly chairs of discomfort, the antique non-toddler-friendly glass tables, the dark gloomy pictures were all gone—and she didn't care if they *were* by museum-worthy artists. Mostly it hadn't been easy because of the intense levels of disapproval exhibited by nearly every single member of staff she'd asked for help.

In truth, Sunita quite simply didn't get it—she hadn't expected instant love or loyalty, but this condescension hidden behind a thin veneer of politeness was both horrible and familiar. It made her feel worthless inside—just as she had in her stepmother's home.

Giselle Diaz, the housekeeper, looked down her aristocratic nose at her, Sven Nordstrom, chief steward, somehow managed to convey utter horror, and the more junior members of staff had taken their cue from their superiors. Whilst they listened to Sunita's instructions, they did so with a frigid politeness that made her quake.

But she'd stuck to her guns, had ransacked the palace for *real* items of furniture, and tucked away in nooks and crannies she'd discovered some true treasures.

Old overstuffed armchairs, ridiculously comfortable sofas…and now she and Amil had a home, a haven.

Sunita gazed at her son. They had brought him back from Mumbai ten days before and he had settled in with a happiness she could only envy. With a smile, he crawled across the floor and she scooped him up onto her lap.

'What do you think, sweetheart?' She showed him two different fabric swatches. 'Do you like this one or this one? For your new nursery when we move to the state apartments.'

'Dabadabad!' Amil said chattily.

'Shall we ask Daddy? That's a good idea, isn't it?'

Frederick would arrive at any moment—every day without fail he was there for Amil's breakfast and tea, and for bedtime. Otherwise he worked.

Ever since the olive grove he'd been distant, as if he'd built a wall of transparent glass that she couldn't penetrate. He was polite, kind and unfailingly courteous, and it made her want to scream. It also made her wonder what demon drove him to spend nigh on every waking hour in the council room, closeted with advisors, lawyers, education experts or engrossed in legal and constitutional tomes that dated back centuries.

Her reverie was interrupted by the familiar knock on the door.

'Come in.'

Frederick entered and, as happened each and every day, her heart fluttered and she noted the lines of tiredness around his eyes and wished she could smooth them away.

'Adadadadaa!' Amil said, and if she'd blinked she'd have missed the smile that lit Frederick's face—one of pure, unaffected joy—before his expression morphed back to neutral.

'Good evening, Amil. And what have you got for tea today?'

'He has lasagne with carrot sticks. Prepared by his very loving, very lovely potential new nanny.'

Satisfaction pumped a fist inside her as she saw his eyebrows snap together—that had at least got his attention.

'Nanny? You didn't tell me you'd chosen one from the list I gave you.'

The list that had chilled her very bone marrow—a list of extremely qualified, excessively expensive women.

'That's because she isn't on the list. But maybe we could discuss this once Amil is in bed.'

'Sure.'

'Then let's get tea underway.'

She headed to the kitchenette and soon had Amil seated in his high chair.

As she did every day, she asked, 'Would you like to feed him?'

He replied as he did every day. 'No. I'm good, thanks. It looks tricky, and I don't know how you manage to get more food into him than ends up elsewhere.'

True enough, meal times weren't the tidiest of processes—and equally true she *had* worked out a dextrous method of spooning in maximum food—but still… She wasn't sure that his reluctance stemmed from fastidiousness. As for worrying that Amil wouldn't get enough to eat, that didn't ring true either—as she had pointed out, he could always have a second helping.

Perhaps he didn't like the idea of being watched and judged.

'I can go into the lounge whilst you feed him, if you like?'

'I'd prefer it if *you* fed him, if that's OK?'

'Of course.'

Only it wasn't OK. Not really.

Just like it wasn't really OK that Frederick didn't engage in bathtime, didn't take Amil onto his lap for his bedtime story. If it were any other man she would suspect that he didn't care, that he was going through the motions. But that didn't make sense. Frederick had fought tooth and nail to be a full-time father to Amil—risked his throne, defied all advice, was willing to take a less than ideal bride.

'Say goodnight to Daddy.'

The little boy gurgled happily and she walked over so that Frederick could give him a kiss.

'See you in a minute.'

Fifteen minutes later she tiptoed from Amil's room and entered the lounge—then stopped on the threshold and cursed under her breath.

Damn. She'd left her sketchbook open on the table—worse, she'd left it open, so she could hardly blame Frederick for sitting there and studying the page.

'Did you do this?'

'Yes.'

There was little point in denial—it wasn't as if he'd believe that *Amil* had drawn a ballroom dress or an off-the-shoulder top.

'They're good.'

'Thank you—they're just sketches…doodles, really. You know how much I love clothes.'

'These look like more than doodles—you've written notes on fabric and cut. How many of these sketchbooks have you got?'

'It doesn't matter.' No way would she confess the number. 'I've always enjoyed sketching and I've always loved fashion. Ever since my mum took me on a photo shoot with her—I loved the buzz, the vibrancy, but most of all I loved the clothes. The feel, the look, the way they could totally transform a person. Sounds mad, maybe, but I think clothes have power.'

His gaze returned to the sketchbook. 'Have you ever thought about fashion design?'

'No.'

That might be a little bit of a fib, but she didn't really want to discuss it. Her sketches were private—she'd never shown them to anyone and she wasn't about to start now.

'It's just a hobby. I think my forte is wearing clothes, not designing them.'

Moving forward, she removed the sketchpad and closed it with a finality she hoped he would apply to the whole topic.

'Anyway I wanted to talk to you about my nanny idea.'

In truth, she wasn't that keen on a nanny—but she could see that if she planned to model and fulfil her commitments as a Lycander consort then it would be necessary.

'Go ahead.'

'I want to give Gloria Russo the role.'

Frederick frowned. 'I thought she worked in the palace kitchens.'

'She does. That's where I met her. I went down there to sort out how it all works—whether I am supposed to shop, or food is delivered, how and where and when I can cook Amil's food… Anyway, Gloria was really helpful.'

Which had made a novel change from every other staff member.

'She only joined the staff recently, but obviously she has been security vetted.'

'So she used to be a nanny?'

'No.'

'All the people on my list have been trained as a nanny—they have extensive qualifications and experience.'

'So does Gloria—she has four grown-up children. And, most important, Amil loves her already.'

'Amil needs a *proper* nanny.'

Frustrated anger rolled over her in a tidal wave—a culmination of being patronised all week and a need to make her own presence felt in a world she didn't fit into. *Again.*

'*Will* you get your royal head out of your royal behind? Gloria will *be* a proper nanny. She knows how to keep him safe and she knows how to provide love and security and fun. She makes him laugh, but she will also make sure he listens. At least agree to meet her and see her with Amil.'

'As long as *you* agree to meet two people from the list. Then we will make the decision.'

'Deal. You'll like Gloria—I'm sure you will. She is kind and she's down to earth and she's fun. Fun is important.' Something Frederick seemed to have forgotten. 'You must remember that—you used to be the Prince of Fun.'

'That was a long time ago.' His tone implied a lifetime rather than mere months.

'Do you miss it? That lifestyle?'

When there had been a different woman in his bed whenever he wanted, and all he'd had to worry about was where the next bottle of champagne was coming from.

'That life feels like it belonged to someone else. So, no, I don't miss it.'

'I know what you mean. My life before Amil seems surreal sometimes, but there are parts of it that I want to retain—I still love clothes, I'm still Sunita.'

Whereas the Frederick of before—apart from the occasional glimpse—seemed to have vanished completely, remorselessly filtered out by grief and the weight of a crown.

'I know that you have taken on a huge responsibility, and of course you need to take that seriously. But there are aspects of the old Frederick that you should keep. The ability to have fun, to laugh and make others laugh.'

'I've had my quota of fun.' He rose to his feet. 'I have a meeting with Marcus now, so…'

'You have to go.'

Sunita bit her lip, told herself it didn't matter. Why should it? Their marriage was an alliance made for Amil's sake—any desire for his company was both ridiculous and clearly unreciprocated.

'Don't forget about tomorrow. We have a family day out scheduled.'

'It's in the diary.' He looked down at her. 'You are sure you don't want to tell me where we're going?'

'Nope. It's a surprise.'

It was an idea she knew the press would love—the fiancée taking her Prince to a surprise destination with their son. A way of emphasising to the people that their Prince and his Princess-to-be had changed and their party lifestyle was well and truly over.

She smiled at him. 'It will be fun.'

For a moment she thought he would return the smile, but instead he merely nodded. 'Goodnight, Sunita.'

'Goodnight.'

There it was again—that stupid yearning to ask him to stay.

Not happening.

The door clicked behind him as her phone buzzed. Her agent.

'Hi, Harvey.'

'Hey, sweetheart. We need to talk.'

Frederick checked the weather forecast as he approached Sunita's apartments. A sunny and cloud-free day—a typical late-summer day in Lycander, perfect for a 'family day out'. The words had an alien twist to them—family days out had been few and far between in his childhood. And now both anticipation and an irrational fear tightened his gut.

Fear at the level of anticipation, and the knowledge that too much of it was tied up in Sunita, was mixed with the fear of messing it up with Amil. Somehow he had to get these fledgling emotions under control—work out which were acceptable, which he needed to nourish to be a good father and which he needed to stifle before they got out of hand.

He could *do* this—he was a past master at emotional lockdown and he would work it out. He would achieve the balanced, calm marriage alliance he wanted.

Pushing open the door, he entered. Sunita smiled at him and his breath caught. *Beautiful*—there was no other word to describe her. She was dressed in flared, delicately embroidered jeans and a simple dark blue sleeveless top, sunglasses perched atop her head and her hair tumbling loose in a riot of waves. Her vibrancy lit the room—a room that she'd made home.

Clutter without untidiness gave it a feeling of relaxed warmth, as did the overstuffed armchairs and sofas that she had commandeered from somewhere in the palace to replace the antique showcase furniture.

'You ready?' he asked.

'We're ready—aren't we, Amil? Look, it's Daddy.'

Frederick turned his head to look at Amil, who waved his favourite toy cat at him in greeting. And then he twisted, placed his hands on the sofa cushion and hauled himself up so he was standing. He turned and—almost by mistake—let go, tottered for a moment, found his balance, and then took a step…and another step…and another until he reached Frederick and clutched at his legs for balance.

He looked down at his son—his son who had just taken his first steps. Amil had a look of utter awe on his face, as the life-changing knowledge had dawned on him—he could walk! Frederick's chest contracted with pride and wonderment as Amil turned and tottered back, with each step gaining confidence, until he reached the sofa and looked to Sunita for confirmation of his cleverness.

Sunita let out a laugh of sheer delight and flew across the room, scooped Amil up and spun him round. 'What a clever boy!' she said as she smothered him in kisses, before spinning to a halt right in front of Frederick.

Something twisted in his chest as he looked at them—a strand of emotion almost painful in its intensity. Sunita's face was slightly flushed, her tawny eyes were bright with happiness and pride, and it filled him with yearning. Like a boy locked out of the sweetshop for ever—doomed always to gaze at the sweets he could never, ever taste.

He forced a smile to his lips and hoped it didn't look as corpse-like as it felt. 'He is a very, *very* clever boy.'

Amil beamed at him and that strand tightened.

Frederick cleared his throat, turned slightly away. 'So, what's the plan?' he asked.

'First up we'll do a little press conference.'

'How can I do a press conference if I don't know where I'm going?'

'You'll have to let me do the talking.' She grinned at him. 'Don't look so worried. There are a million royal duties I am *not* equipped for, but I *am* good with the press.'

The words, though casually stated, held a shade of bitterness, but before he could do more than frown she had headed for the door.

Once in the palace grounds, with a knot of reporters, Amil proudly demonstrated his new ability and she seemed totally at ease.

'Hi, all. I've decided the Prince needs a day off—because even a ruler needs some down-time. So we are off on a family day out—I promise I'll take some pics, which I'll pass on to you. As I'm sure you all appreciate we are still a new family, so we'd appreciate some privacy.'

'And what about you, Sunita? Do *you* deserve a day off? Isn't it true you're headed back to the catwalk?'

'That's the plan—but I'll let you know more about that when I know the details.'

'Don't you feel you should focus on your role as Princess, like Lady Kaitlin would have?'

Frederick felt her tense, sensed her palpable effort to relax. 'Lady Kaitlin and I are two different people, so we are bound to approach the role differently.'

He stepped forward. 'Hey, guys, any questions for me? I'm feeling left out.'

The tactic worked and fifteen minutes later he wound the meeting down. 'OK, everyone, fun though this is, we need to head off.'

Sunita delivered the parting shot. 'Amil, wave to the nice reporters. That would be that one...that one...and that one.'

Not the one who had brought up Lady Kaitlin.

Laughter greeted this, and Sunita smiled. 'Have a great day—and, as I said, the pics will be with you soon!'

Once they were alone, Sunita nodded towards one of the palace cars. 'Hop in. We're off to Xanos Island.' She paused. 'I hope that's OK? Marcus suggested it.'

That surprised him. 'I'd like to take Amil there. Eloise used to take us. Me and Stefan and Axel, and Marcus as well, because he and Axel were best friends.'

'Eloise is Stefan's mother, correct?'

'Yes. She came after my mother, and she truly tried to be a good mother to Axel and me.'

'What happened?'

'Same old story. My father decided to divorce her and it all disintegrated into an awful custody battle. It ended up that she was allowed occasional visitation with Stefan, and only if she agreed not to see Axel or me.'

'That must have been tough on you and Axel.'

'Yes.'

The comprehension that he wouldn't see Eloise again, witnessing Stefan's fury and pain—it had all hurt. The emotions had been painful, until he'd locked the futile grief down, figured out that love could never be worth this type of loss. First his mother, then Eloise—never again.

'But let's not spoil the day—I want to make this a happy memory for Amil.'

'Then let's do that.'

Her smile lit the very air and he forced himself to turn away from it before he did something stupid. Something emotional.

The car slowed down at the small Lycandrian port, and minutes later they boarded the motor boat that would ferry them across. Frederick watched Amil's curiosity and joy at this unprecedented adventure, listened to Sunita as she broke into song and encouraged the Captain to join in.

Closing his eyes, he inhaled the salty tang of the sea breeze, absorbed the sound of her song and the cry of the curlews as they soared in the turquoise blue of the unclouded sky.

Once at the island they alighted and headed over the rocks to the beach, where Sunita produced buckets and spades and a large tartan blanket that she spread out over the sun-bleached sand. Amil sat down and waved a spade with energetic abandon and Sunita grinned as she handed another one to Frederick.

'Right. I thought we'd try and do a sand replica of the

Lycander palace—but I think the hard work may be down to you and me.'

The next hours skated by, and Frederick knew he would add this to his list of happy memories. Preventing Amil from eating sand, building turrets and digging moats, the good-natured bickering over the best way to make the walls secure, Amil walking in the sand, eating the picnic prepared by Gloria—it was all picture-perfect.

'We need to consider Gloria for the role of royal picnic-maker as well as royal nanny.'

'So you really *will* consider her? Give her a fair chance?'

'Of course. But in return I'd like *you* to do something.'

Tawny eyes narrowed. 'What's that?'

'Put a portfolio together and send it to a fashion design college. Or talk directly with an actual fashion house. You said to me that Gloria doesn't need formal qualifications to do the job—maybe you don't either.'

The sketches he'd seen the previous day showed talent—he knew it.

'Those sketches had a certain something about them that I suspect is unique to you—I think you should get them checked out.'

'I'll think about it,' she said, in a voice that was clearly humouring him as she pulled the picnic basket towards her. 'Mmm…chocolate cake.'

Frederick raised his eyebrows. 'Are you trying to change the subject?'

'How did you guess?'

'I'm bright like that. Come on, Sunita, why not send them off? What have you got to lose?'

She looked away from him, out over the dark blue crested waves that sculled gently towards the shore, towards the horizon where a ferry chugged purposefully.

Turning back to him, she shrugged. 'I could lose something precious. Those sketches kept me sane—they were my own private dream growing up. They represented hope that I wasn't totally worthless, not utterly stupid. I don't want to expose them to anyone. I've never shown them to a soul.'

And he understood why—she would have been terrified of the comments from her stepmother or sisters…she would have hoarded her talent and hugged it tight.

'Then maybe now is the time. Don't let them win—all those mean-spirited people who put you down. You've already proved your success to them.'

She shook her head. 'Only through modelling—that's dumb genetic luck, plus being in the right place at the right time. Fashion design requires a whole lot more than that.'

'I understand that you're scared—and I know it won't be easy—but if fashion design is your dream then you should go for it. Don't let them hold you back from your potential. Don't let what they did affect your life.'

'Why not? *You* are.'

He hadn't seen that one coming. 'Meaning…?'

'I think you're scared too.'

'Of what?'

'Of bonding with Amil.'

The words hit him, causing his breath to catch. She moved across the rug closer to him, contrition written all over her beautiful face.

'Sorry. I didn't mean that in a tit-for-tat way, or as an accusation. It's just I see how you look at him, with such love, but then I see how you hold back from being alone with him. You won't even hold him and I don't understand why.'

There was silence, and Frederick knew he needed to tell her. He couldn't bear her to believe he didn't *want* to hold his son.

'Because of dumb genetic luck.'

'I don't get it.'

'When I was eighteen I went to see my mum. I hoped that there had been some mistake—that my father had lied to me, that she hadn't really abandoned me and that there was some reason that would explain it all away. It turned out there was—she explained that she quite simply lacked the parenting gene.'

'She *said* that?'

'Yes.'

Her hands clenched into fists and her eyes positively blazed. 'Is *that* what you're scared of? That you lack the parenting gene?'

His gaze went involuntarily to his son, who lay asleep on the blanket, his bottom in the air, his impossibly long lashes sweeping his cheeks.

He couldn't answer—didn't need to. Even he could hear the affirmation in his silence.

'You don't.' Sunita leaned across, brushing his forearm in the lightest of touches. 'I can see how much you love Amil. You are not your mother *or* your father. You are *you*, and you are a great father—please believe that. Trust yourself. I promise I trust you.' She inhaled an audible breath. 'And I'll prove it to you.'

'What do you mean?' Panic began to unfurl as she rose to her feet.

'He's all yours. I'll see you back at the palace much later. Obviously call if there is an emergency—otherwise the boat will return for you in a few hours.'

Before he could react she started walking across the sand. He looked at his sleeping son. Obviously he couldn't leave Amil in order to chase after Sunita, which meant... which meant he was stuck here.

His brain struggled to work as he watched Sunita disappear over the rocks. If he called after her he would wake

Amil, and that was a bad plan. He stilled, barely daring to breathe as he watched the rise and fall of his son's chest. Maybe Amil would sleep for the next few hours…

As if he should be so lucky.

With impeccable timing Amil rolled over and opened his eyes just as the sound of the boat chug-chug-chugging away reached his ears. He looked round for his mother, failed to see her, and sat up and gazed at his father. Panicked hazel eyes met panicked hazel eyes and Amil began to wail.

Instinct took over—his need to offer comfort prompted automatic movement and he picked Amil up. He held the warm, sleepy bundle close to his heart and felt something deep inside him start to thaw. The panic was still present, but as Amil snuggled into him, as one chubby hand grabbed a lock of his hair and as the wails started to subside, so did the panic.

To be replaced by a sensation of peace, of unconditional love and an utter determination to keep this precious human being safe from all harm—to be there for him no matter what it took.

CHAPTER FOURTEEN

SUNITA GLANCED AT her watch and then back at the sketch-books spread out on the table. Thoughts chased each other round her brain—about Frederick and Amil; she hoped with all her heart that right now father and son had started the bonding process that would last a lifetime.

Her gaze landed back on the design sketches and she wondered whether Frederick had been right—that fear of rejection and self-doubt stood in her way. Just as they did in his. Could she pursue a dream? Or was it foolish for a woman with no qualifications to put her head above the parapet and invite censure? Or, worse, ridicule.

Another glance at her watch and she closed the books, piled them up and moved them onto a shelf. Instead she pulled out a folder—design ideas for the state rooms, where they would move after the wedding.

The door opened and she looked up as Frederick came in, Amil in his arms. There was sand in their hair and identical smiles on their faces. *Keep it cool...don't overreact.* But in truth her heart swelled to see them, both looking so proud and happy and downright cute.

'Did you have fun?'

'Yes, we did.'

'Fabulous. Tea is ready.'

'I thought maybe today *I* could feed him. Do his bath. Put him to bed.'

Any second now she would weep—Frederick looked as if a burden had been lifted from his shoulders.

'Great idea. In which case, if you don't mind, I've got a couple of errands to do. I'll be back for his bedtime.'

Frederick didn't need an observer—especially when Amil lobbed spaghetti Bolognese at him, as he no doubt would. And perhaps she could do something a little courageous as well. She needed to speak with Therese, the snooty seamstress, about her wedding dress.

Lycander tradition apparently had it that the royal seamstress had total input on the design of the dress, but surely the bride had a say as well. So maybe she would show Therese one of her designs.

Grabbing the relevant sketchbook, she blew Amil a kiss and allowed a cautious optimism to emerge as she made her way through the cavernous corridors to the Royal Sewing Room.

A knock on the door resulted in the emergence of one of Therese's assistants. 'Hi, Hannah, I wonder if Therese is around to discuss my dress.'

'She's popped out, but I know where the folder is. I'm sure she wouldn't mind you having a look.' Hannah walked over to a filing cabinet. 'I'll leave you to it.'

With that she scurried to an adjoining door and disappeared.

Sunita opened the folder and stared down at the picture—it was…was… Well, on the positive side it was classic—the designer a household name. On the negative side it was dull and unflattering. There didn't seem to be anything else in the folder, which seemed odd.

She headed to the door through which Hannah had disappeared, to see if there was another file, then paused as she heard the sound of conversation. She recognised Hannah's voice, and that of another assistant—Angela—and then the mention of her own name.

Of course she should have backed off there and then, taken heed of the old adage about eavesdroppers never hearing any good of themselves. But she didn't. Instead, breath held, she tiptoed forward.

'Do you think she knows?' asked Hannah.

'Knows what?' said Angela.

'That that's the dress Therese had designed for Lady Kaitlin—she was dead sure Lady K would marry Frederick. Everyone was, and everyone is gutted she didn't. Even that engagement ring—it was the one they had in mind for Kaitlin. Lady Kaitlin would have been a *proper* princess—everyone knows that. And she would have looked amazing in that dress—because it's regal and classic and not showy. As for Sunita—Frederick is only marrying her for the boy, which is dead good of him. He's a true prince. But Sunita can't ever be a true princess—she'll never fit in.'

Sunita closed her eyes as the flow of words washed over her in an onslaught of truth. Because that was what they were—words of truth. Otherwise known as facts. Facts that she seemed to have forgotten in the past weeks, somehow. She didn't know how she'd started to look at her marriage through rose-tinted glasses. How she had started to believe the fairy tale.

Fact: the sole reason for this marriage was Amil. Fact: Frederick's ideal bride would have been Lady Kaitlin or a woman of her ilk. Fact: fairy tales did not exist.

This must be what her mother had done—convinced herself that a handsome, charming English holidaymaker was her Prince, who would take her off into the sunset and a happy-ever-after. Perhaps that was what her father had done too—convinced himself that he could right past wrongs, that his family would welcome in his bastard child and everyone would live happily ever after.

Carefully she moved away from the door, leaving the folder on the desk, then picked up her sketchbook, and made her way out of the office, back along the marble floors, past the tapestry-laden walls, the heirlooms and antiquities collected over centuries, and back to her apartments.

She took a deep breath and composed her expression—this was a special day for Frederick and Amil and she would not spoil it.

Nor would she whinge and whine—there was no blame to be cast anywhere except at herself. Somehow she'd lost sight of the facts, but she wouldn't make that mistake again.

Entering the room, she halted on the threshold. Frederick sat on an armchair, Amil on his lap, looking down at a book of farm animals with intense concentration as Frederick read the simple sentences, and made all the noises with a gusto that caused Amil to chuckle with delight.

The book finished, Amil looked up and beamed at her and her heart constricted. Amil was the most important factor.

'Hey, guys. Looks like I'm back just in time.' Hard as she tried, she got it wrong—her voice was over-bright and a touch shaky, and Frederick's hazel eyes scanned her face in question.

'You OK?'

'I'm fine.' Walking over, she picked Amil up, hid her face under the pretext of a hug. 'How did tea and bath go?'

'Well, I have spaghetti down my shirt and bubbles in my hair, but we had fun, didn't we?'

'Abaadaaaaada!' Amil smiled and then yawned.

'I'll put him to bed.' Frederick rose and took Amil into his arms. Amil grizzled, but Frederick held on. 'Daddy's putting you to bed tonight, little fella. It'll be fine.'

And it was.

Fifteen minutes later Frederick emerged from Amil's bedroom, a smile on his face, headed to the drinks cabinet and pulled out a bottle of red wine.

Once they both had a glass in hand, he raised his. 'Thank you for today. You were right—I was afraid. Afraid I couldn't be a good parent…afraid I'd hurt him the way my parents hurt me. I thought doing nothing would be better than getting it wrong. Now I really hope that I can be a better parent than mine were, and can create a real bond with my son.'

The words made her happy—truly happy—and she wanted to step forward, to get close and tell him that, show him that happiness. But she didn't. Because close was dangerous—close had landed her in this scenario where she had distorted the facts with perilous consequence.

Perhaps it had been that magical physical intimacy in Goa, or maybe it had been a mistake to confide in him, to share her background and her fears and dreams. Whatever. No point in dwelling on the mistakes. Now it was vital not to repeat them.

So instead she stepped backwards and raised her glass. 'I'll drink to that. I'm so very pleased for you and Amil.'

And she was. But to her own horror, mixed into that pleasure was a thread of misery that she recognised as selfish. Because his love for Amil had never been in doubt—it had simply needed a shift in the dynamic of their relationship. A shift that had highlighted exactly what Sunita was—a by-product, a hanger-on, exactly as she been in her father's family. There only by default, by an accident of birth.

Well, she was damned if she would sit around here for the rest of her life being a by-product.

'Earth to Sunita?'

His voice pulled her out of her thoughts and she manufactured a smile, floundered for a topic of conversation. Her gaze fell on a folder—her plans for the state apartments.

'Would you mind having a look at this? I wanted your opinion before I went ahead.'

She picked up the file, opened it and pulled out the pictures, gazed down at them and winced. Every detail that she'd pored over so carefully screamed happy families—she'd done some of the sketches in 3D and, so help her, she'd actually imagined the three of them skipping around the place in some family perfect scene.

For their bedroom she'd chosen a colour scheme that mixed aquamarine blue with splashes of red. The double bed was a luxurious invitation that might as well have *bliss* written all over it.

She had to face it—her vision had included steamy nights with Frederick and lazy Sunday mornings with a brood of kids bouncing up and down. What had happened to her? This was a room designed with *love.*

This was a disaster. *Love.* She'd fallen in love.

Idiot, idiot, idiot.

Frederick frowned. 'Are you sure you're OK?'

Reaching out, he plucked the pictures from her hand and she forced herself not to clutch onto them. *Think.* Before he looked at the pictures and figured it out. *Think.* Because even if he didn't work it out she couldn't share a room with him—that would take intimacy to insane levels, and Frederick was no fool. He'd realise that she had done the unthinkable and fallen for him.

As he scanned the pictures desperation came to her aid. 'I wondered which bedroom you wanted.'

His head snapped up and his eyebrows rose. He placed

the papers on the table. 'I assumed from these pictures that we would be sharing a room.'

Picking up her wine glass, she met his gaze. 'As I understood it, royal tradition dictates separate bedrooms and I assumed you'd prefer that.' Or at least she *should* have assumed that. 'However, obviously there will be some occasions when we *do* share—hence the design. If you want that bedroom I'll design the second one as mine. But if you don't then I'll take that one and we can discuss how you want yours to be.'

Stop, already. He'd got the gist of it and now she sounded defensive. Worse, despite herself, there was a hint of a question in the nuances of her tone, and a strand of hope twisted her heart. Hope that he'd take this opportunity to persuade her to share a room.

'What do you think?'

He sipped his wine, studied her expression, and she fought to keep her face neutral.

'I think this is some sort of trick question.'

'No trick. It's a simple need to know so I can complete the design. Also, as you know, I'll be giving an interview once the renovations are done, so it depends what you think the people of Lycander would prefer to see. We can pretend we share a room, if you think that would go down better, or...'

Shut up, Sunita.

Just because full-scale panic was escalating inside her, it didn't mean verbal overload had to implode. But she couldn't help herself.

'And then there is Amil to think about. I'm not sure that he should grow up thinking this sort of marriage is right.'

'Whoa! What is *that* supposed to mean? "This sort of marriage"? You say it like there's something wrong with it.'

'There *is* something wrong with it.'

It was almost as if her vocal cords had taken on a life of their own.

'Is this the sort of marriage you want Amil to have? An alliance? Presumably brokered by us? A suitable connection? Perhaps he will be lucky enough to get his own Lady Kaitlin. *Hell.*' She snapped her fingers. 'Perhaps we should get dibs on her first-born daughter.'

'Stop.' His frown deepened as he surveyed her expression. 'What is going on here? We agreed how our marriage would work—we agreed what we both wanted.'

'No, we didn't. I didn't want to get married at all. *You* did.'

'And you agreed.'

'Because there was no other choice.' She closed her eyes. 'There still isn't. But when Amil gets married I don't want it to be like this.'

For her son she wanted the fairy tale—she wanted Amil to love someone and be loved in return and live happily ever after. *The End.*

'There is nothing *wrong* with this.' His voice was urgent now, taut with frustration and more than a hint of anger. 'Amil will see two parents who respect each other, who are faithful to each other, who are polite to each other. There will be no uncertainty, no banged doors and no voices raised in constant anger. He'll have two parents who are there for him—I think he'll take that. God knows, *I* would have. And so would you.'

Touché. He was right. The problem was this wasn't about Amil. It was about her. *She* wanted the fairy tale. Her whole being cried out at the idea of a marriage of civility. Her very soul recoiled from the thought of spending the rest of her life tied to a man she loved who would never see her as more than the mother of his children—a woman he'd married through necessity not choice.

But she'd made a deal and she'd honour it. For Amil's sake. She wouldn't wrest Amil from his father, wouldn't take away his birthright. But neither would she stick around and moon in lovelorn stupidity. The only way forward was to kill love before it blossomed—uproot the plant now, before it sank its roots into her heart.

So she dug deep, conjured up a smile and said, 'You're right. I just had a mad moment.' She gave a glance at her watch. 'Anyway, don't you need to go? I thought you had a meeting about the casino bill?'

He hesitated. The frown still hadn't left his face. 'We'll talk in the morning.'

'Sure.'

Pride kept her cool, enigmatic smile in place as he turned and left the room. Then, ignoring the ache that squeezed her heart in a vicelike grip, she picked up her mobile.

'Harvey. It's me. We need to talk.'

The next morning Frederick approached the door to Sunita and Amil's apartments, forcing his steps to remain measured, forcing himself not to dwell on the previous night's conversation with Sunita. But her words still pummelled his conscience.

I didn't want to get married. You did. There was no choice. There still isn't...'

The unpleasant edge of discomfort bit into him.

Shades of his father.

He knocked on the door and entered, glanced around for Amil. Anxiety unfurled as he looked around and saw only Sunita at the table. 'Where's Amil?'

'With Gloria. I need to talk with you.'

Dressed in a simple white three-quarter-sleeved dress, belted with a striped blue and red band, she looked both elegant and remote. The only indication of nerves was the twist of her hands.

Sudden familiarity hit him—she'd had the same stance two years before, when she'd been about to leave. Panic grew inside him and he forced himself to keep still.

'Is anything wrong?'

'No. I've signed a modelling contract. Effective pretty much immediately. We need to discuss the details.'

'Immediately? But you said you wouldn't sign a contract straight away.'

'And I didn't. The first time the offer came in I refused. But now they have upped the ante and agreed to schedule the shoots around my commitments here. I'd be a fool to pass it up.'

A bleakness started to descend...a strange hollow pang of emptiness. 'What about Amil?'

'The first shoot is in India—in Mumbai. I'll take Amil with me. We can stay with Nanni. Thereafter, whenever I can take him I will, or I will leave him in Lycander with you. Gloria will be here, and I will also ask Nanni if she can come and stay.'

She handed him a piece of paper with her schedule printed out.

Frederick frowned. 'This can't possibly have been arranged since last night.'

'No. Harvey was approached a few weeks ago—right after our first press release. The brand had dropped the model they had planned to use due to her lifestyle. They thought of me. I refused—but now I've changed my mind and luckily they still want me.'

'You didn't think to discuss this with me at all?'

'No. Any more than you discuss state business with *me*. Part of our marriage agreement was that I would resume my career as long as I fitted it around Lycander's needs. I understand some people may not approve, but to be honest with you a lot of people won't approve of me no matter what I do. The people wanted Kaitlin. I can't be her, or be like her. I will not try to fit into a box I'll never tick. I spent too many years doing that.'

Frederick knew there were things he should say, things he needed to say, but the words quite simply wouldn't formulate. All he wanted to do was tug her into his arms and beg her to stay—but that was not an option.

Because Sunita didn't want this marriage—she never had. He'd forced it upon her, caught her between a rock and a hard place. Self-disgust soured his tongue, froze his limbs. He was no better than his father. He had ridden roughshod over her wish not to marry him; he'd inveigled and manoeuvred and blazed down the trail he wanted regardless of her wishes. Worse, he'd bolstered himself with pious justifications.

But it was too late to stop the wedding, to release her from their marriage agreement—it would be an impossibility, the impact on Lycander, on Amil, too harsh.

Just Lycander? Just Amil? queried a small voice.

Of course. It made no difference to him. It *couldn't* make a difference to him

Why not?

The small voice was getting on his nerves now. It couldn't because he wouldn't let it. Over the past few weeks Sunita had very nearly slipped under his skin, and that way led to disaster, to pain and loss, to messy emotions that got in the way of a calm, ordered life. That would ruin this marriage before it even got underway.

The silence had stretched so taut now he could bounce off it. One of the terms of their marriage agreement *had* included her right to a career and he would not stand in the way. So he said, 'I understand. You're right to go.'

He looked down at the schedule again, but couldn't meet her gaze, couldn't seem to quell the spread of cold emptiness through his body and soul.

'I'll talk to Marcus—if you need to miss any functions I'll let him know it's OK. I know how important this contract is for you—anything I can do to help, I will.'

'Thank you. I appreciate that.'

He nodded, and yet still that desolation pervaded him, even as that unsquashable small voice exhorted him to *do* something. *Anything.*

But he couldn't. It wasn't in him. So instead he headed for the door.

One week later—Lycander Council Room

Frederick threw the pen across his desk and watched it skitter across the polished wood. Concentration wouldn't come. The words on the document blurred and jumped and somehow unerringly formed into images of Sunita. *Ridiculous.*

Shoving the wedge of paper away, he sighed, and then looked up at the perfunctory knock on the door.

Seconds later he eyed his chief advisor in surprise. 'What's wrong?'

'Nothing. I thought you could do with a break. You've been closeted in here for hours. Days.'

'A break?' Frederick looked at Marcus blankly. 'Since when do you care about me having a rest?'

'Since you gave up on both sleep *and* food. So how about we grab a beer, shoot the breeze…?'

Frederick wondered if Marcus had perhaps already grabbed a few beers—though there was nothing in the other man's demeanour to suggest any such thing.

'Are you suggesting you and I go and have a beer?'

'Yes.'

'Why?'

Marcus shrugged. 'Why not?'

'Because I'm pretty damn sure you'd rather shoot yourself in the foot than have a beer with me.'

Dark eyebrows rose. 'Feeling tetchy?'

Damn right he was. Sunita had been gone for a week and his whole world felt...*wrong*...out of kilter. And he hated it. He loathed it that he didn't seem able to switch these emotions off. However hard he twisted the tap, they trickled on and on. Relentlessly.

'No. Just being honest. So, what gives?'

'I'm your chief advisor, right?'

'Right.'

'So here's some advice. Go after Sunita.'

'Sunita is in Mumbai on a photo shoot—why would I do that?'

'Because I think you love her.'

Frederick blinked, wondered if this conversation was a hallucination. 'Then you think wrong. You *know* all this—we're getting married because of Amil and for Lycander.'

'You can't kid a kidder. But, more importantly, why kid yourself?'

'With all due respect, has it occurred to you that this is a bit out of your remit?'

'Yes, it has.' Marcus started to pace the office, as he had so many times in the past year. 'But I'm talking to you now as Axel's best friend. I know Axel wouldn't want you to throw this away.'

Guilt and self-loathing slammed Frederick so hard he could barely stay upright. 'Hold it right there. You *don't* know what Axel would want.'

'Yes, I do. He'd want you to get on with life. *Your* life.

Right now you're getting on with Axel's life, fulfilling his vision. I think Axel would want you to fulfil your own.'

Frederick searched for words before guilt choked him. He needed Marcus to stop—he couldn't listen to this any more.

'The accident… Axel's death was my fault. *I* should have been in that car. *I* was meant to go that state dinner. I passed it off to Axel.'

'I know.' Marcus's voice was measured. 'Axel was supposed to meet up with me that night. He told me you'd asked him to go because you had a party to go to. To celebrate a buy-out that no one thought you'd pull off.'

A buy-out he now wished he'd never tried for—if he could have pulled out any domino from the cause-and-effect chain he would. Most of all, though, he wished he hadn't chosen a party over duty.

He watched as Marcus continued to stride the floor. 'So why did you take this job with me? Why didn't you tell me you knew the truth?'

'I did what I believed Axel would have wanted. Axel was my best friend—we climbed trees as boys and we double-dated as young men. A few days before the accident he was trying to get up the courage to ask my sister on a date—he'd joke that he wished he had your charm. He cared about you very much, and he wouldn't have wanted you to punish yourself for the rest of your life.'

Marcus halted in front of the desk and leant forward, his hands gripping the edge.

'You didn't know what would happen—you didn't send Axel to his death.'

'But if I had chosen not to party, not to do what I wanted to do, then Axel would be alive now.'

Marcus shrugged. 'Maybe. But it didn't pan out like that. You can't turn the clock back, but you can make the most of your time now. I think you love Sunita, and if you do then you need to go for it—before you lose her. Axel's death should show you how life can change in a heartbeat—don't waste the life you've got. Axel wouldn't want it. And, for what it's worth, neither do I.'

Frederick stared at him. Emotions tumbled around him—poignant regret that Axel had never had the chance to ask Marcus's sister on a date, grief over the loss of his brother, a loss he had never allowed himself time to mourn, and gratitude that Marcus had given him a form of redemption.

'Thank you.'

There wasn't anything else he could say right now. Later there would be time. Time to grab those beers and sit and talk about Axel, remember him and mourn him. But now...

'Can I leave you at the helm? I need to go to Mumbai.'

'Good luck.'

Frederick had the feeling he'd need it.

Mumbai

Sunita smiled at Nanni across the kitchen, listened to the comforting whirr of the overhead fan, the sizzle of *malpua* batter as it hit the heated pan. Ever since Nanni had first made these sweet dessert pancakes Sunita had loved them.

'You don't have to make me breakfast every morning, Nanni, but I do so appreciate it.''

'If I didn't you would eat nothing. And you do not need to stay in with me every night. I am sure there are parties and social events.'

'I'd rather be here.'

Totally true. She didn't want to socialise; she was too tired. Sleep deprivation, combined with the effort it took to work when all she wanted was to be back in Lycander.

Irony of ironies, she wanted to be in a place that had rejected her, with a man who had rejected her. What a fool she was. But she'd be damned if anyone would know it—she'd dug deep, pulled up every professional reserve and hopefully pulled the wool over Nanni's eyes as well.

'You aren't happy.'

So much for the wool pulling endeavour.

Nanni put her plate in front of her; the scent of cardamom and pistachio drifted upward.

'Of course I am. The job is going great, I'm back in Mumbai, Amil is here and I'm with my favourite grandmother.'

'And yet you still aren't happy. You can lie to me, Suni. But don't lie to yourself.'

'Sometimes you *have* to lie to yourself—if you do it for long enough the lie will become the truth.'

Or that was her theory. And, yes, there were holes and flaws in it, but it was a work in progress.

'That still doesn't make it *actual* truth,' Nanni pointed out with irrefutable logic. 'Do you no longer wish to marry Frederick?'

'I have no choice.'

'Yes, you do. There is always a choice—however hard a one it is. If you do not love him, don't marry him.'

'I *do* love him, Nanni. But he doesn't love me.' Tears threatened and she blinked them back.

'How do you know?'

'Because he has made it pretty clear.'

'By action or word?'

'What do you mean?'

'Love is not all about declarations—it is about demonstration. I told your mother how much I loved her repeatedly, but when the time came for me to show that, to fight for her, I failed miserably.'

'But you still loved her, Nanni, and she knew that. She never blamed you—she blamed her father.'

'At least *he* had the courage of his convictions—he did what he did because he believed it to be right. I was a coward—I loved Leela, but not enough to fight for that love. It is one of the biggest regrets of my life, Suni—that I didn't fight for her, for *you*. So all I would say is think about your Frederick, and if there is a chance that he loves you then fight for that chance.'

Sunita stared down at her somehow empty plate and wondered if she were brave enough—brave enough to risk rejection and humiliation. And even if she was…

'I don't fit, Nanni. Even if he loved me I can't live up to Lady Kaitlin.'

'You don't need to live up to anyone—you just have to be yourself. Now, go,' Nanni said. 'Or you will be late for work.'

Frederick approached the site of the photo shoot, where the Gateway of India loomed in the twilight, its basalt stone lit up to create a magical backdrop, the turrets adding a fairy tale element for the photographer to take full advantage of.

The square was cordoned off for the shoot, and he joined the curious pedestrians who had stopped to watch. The people behind the cordon were packing up, so he slipped under the ropes, ignored the protest of a woman who approached

'Sir, I'm sorry, but…' There was a pause as she recognised him.

'I'm here to see Sunita.'

'Is she expecting you?'

'No. I thought I'd surprise her.'

'And you have.'

He spun round at the sound of Sunita's voice; his heart

pounded, his gut somersaulted. She wore a square-necked red dress, in some sort of stretchy material that moulded her figure and fell to her knees in a simple drop.

'Is everything all right?'

'Yes. I want to…to talk.'

She hesitated and then nodded.

'OK. I'm done here. We can go by the wall over there and look out at the sea, if you like.'

'Perfect.'

'Are you sure everything is all right?' Concern was evident in her tone now, as she looked at him.

'Yes. No. I don't know.'

And he didn't—after all, this could be the most important conversation of his life and he could totally screw it up. He could lose her.

'I need to tell you something.'

'Actually, there is something I need to tell you as well.' Her hands twisted together and she looked away from him, out at the boats that bobbed on the murky water.

'Could I go first?' *Before he bottled it.*

She nodded.

'First I need to tell you about Axel. The accident that killed him—*I* should have been in the car. He took my place because I'd decided to go a party—a celebration of a buy-out deal. He not only took my place, he totally covered for me. He told everyone that it had been his idea, that he'd wanted to attend and I'd given up my place.'

Her beautiful brown eyes widened, and then without hesitation she moved closer to him. 'I am so very sorry. I cannot imagine what you went through—what you must still be going through. But please listen to me. It was *not* your fault—you did not know what would happen.'

'I know that, but…'

'But it doesn't help. I understand. I understand how

many times you must think *if only* or *what if?* But you mustn't. I spent years thinking what if my mother hadn't died? What if she hadn't handed me over to my father? What if I could somehow have won his love? My stepmother's love. My sister's love? It made me question how I felt about my mother and it ate away at my soul—like this is eating away at yours. You can't know what would have happened. Axel might have died anyway. Your action wasn't deliberate—you wished Axel no harm.'

'That's what Marcus said.'

'He's a good man.'

'Yes.'

Frederick took a deep breath, looked at her beautiful face, her poise and grace, the compassion and gentleness and empathy in her gorgeous eyes.

'He said something else as well…'

Suddenly words weren't enough—he couldn't encompass how he felt in mere words. So instead he pushed away from the wall, and when she turned he sank to one knee.

'Frederick…?'

He could taste the sea spray, see the expression on her face of confusion, and hope soared in his heart as he took her left hand in his and removed the huge, heavy diamond—a ring chosen by someone else. He delved into his pocket and pulled out a box, purchased earlier from one of Mumbai's many jewellers.

'Will you marry me? For real. Not for Amil, not for Lycander, but because I love you. Heart, body and soul. Because I want to spend the rest of my life with you, wake up with you every morning. I want to live my life side by side with you. I want us to rule together, to laugh together, to live a life full of *all* the emotions. So, will you marry me? For real?'

His heart pounded and his fingers shook as he opened the box and took the ring out.

Her breathless laugh was caught with joy, the smile on her face so bright and beautiful his heart flipped.

'Yes. I *will* marry you. For real. Because I love you. That's what I wanted to tell you. That I love you. I didn't think in a million years that you could possibly love me back, but I wanted to tell you anyway. Heart, body and soul—they are all yours.'

He slipped the ring onto her finger and she lifted her hand in the air, watching the red and aquamarine stones interspersed with diamonds glint in the light of the setting sun.

'It's beautiful. Perfect.'

'I'm sorry about the other ring.'

'It makes this one all the more special. Did I mention I love it? Did I mention I love *you*?'

He rose to his feet. 'You did, but you can say it as many times as you like—those words won't ever get old.'

'No. Though Nanni says we have to back the words up. That love isn't only words—it's actions.' She stepped forward and looped her arms round his waist, snuggled in close. 'You *are* sure, aren't you? Sure this is real?'

'I have never been more sure of anything. I think I loved you from the start—I just couldn't admit it. Not to you, not to myself. You see, I didn't feel I deserved this joy.'

Her arms tightened around him. 'Because of Axel?'

'Partly. But even before that. I had parents who didn't give a damn—a mother who sold me for a crock of gold and a father who saw all his children as pawns or possessions. Love wasn't in the equation. Then I saw how much pain and angst love can cause—saw how losing Stefan tore Eloise apart. It was the same with Nicky, the twins' mother. My parents, who eschewed love, were happy and everyone else who *did* love was made miserable through that love. So I never wanted love to hold me hostage. I could see that emotions led to misery—that life was easier to control without emotion.

'Even two years ago you were different. But then you left, and Axel died, and I froze every emotion in order to cope. When you came back into my life all the emotions I'd bottled up for years kept surging up and I couldn't seem to shut them down any more. I didn't know what to do. I couldn't succumb to them because that was way too scary and it felt *wrong*. Axel died because of me. He'll never have the chance to live and love, have children, so how could it be right for me?'

'I am so very sorry about Axel, but I am sure he wouldn't have wanted you to give up on happiness.'

'I think you're right. Marcus seems sure of that too. And I know that if anything happened to me I wouldn't want *you* to shut your life down. I'd want you to live it to the full.'

'Nothing will to happen to you.' Her voice was fierce. 'And if it did I would never regret loving you.'

Frederick's heart swelled with the sheer wonder that he would share his life with this wonderful woman—and share it for real. The ups and the downs…everything.

He grinned down at her. 'I am so happy it doesn't seem possible. I never believed in my wildest dreams that you would love me too. I was willing to beg, fight—do what-ever it took to persuade you to give me a chance to win your love.'

'You won that long ago but, like you, it took me a long time to admit it. I think deep down I knew the day I left you on the island with Amil. I couldn't have done that if I didn't trust you completely. And trust… I always thought that was for mugs and fools. My mother trusted my father once and ended up pregnant and abandoned. She trusted him again and it didn't end well for me. Fool me once, shame on you—fool me twice, shame on me. I figured it was best never to be fooled at all. Which meant the only way forward was never to trust anyone. But I trusted *you*. Even two years ago on some level I trusted you, or I would never have slept with you. But even after the island it all seemed so hard—you were so distant. And I felt like I used to—that I didn't fit. Everywhere I went people compared me to Kaitlin and…'

'You should have told me.'

'I couldn't. After all, you said that Kaitlin was your ideal bride.'

'I'm an idiot.' He cupped her face in his hands. 'I swear to you that you are the only bride I could ever want. Not because of Amil. Not because of Lycander. But because you are you and I *love* you. You make me whole. And if anyone makes any comparisons you send them to me.'

'No need. I've worked out where I've gone wrong—in my assumption that Kaitlin is better than me. She isn't—she is just different. I need to be a princess *my* way. Need to be myself.'

'And I know that means being a model—I will support your career every way I can.'

'About that… I'd better 'fess up. I'm not enjoying it one bit. I miss you and Amil… I miss Lycander. So I will fulfil this contract, but after that I will put a fashion portfolio together and send it off. And I also want to work for Lycander. I want to make it a fashion mecca—maybe set up a fashion show. One day we could rival Paris and London… There are so many options. But, whatever I decide, as long as you are by my side I know it will be OK.'

'Ditto.'

As he pulled her into his arms he knew this was the best alliance he could have ever made—because the only thing on the table was love.

* * * * *

LET'S TALK

Romance

For exclusive extracts, competitions
and special offers, find us online:

 facebook.com/millsandboon

@MillsandBoon

@MillsandBoonUK

Get in touch on 01413 063232

For all the latest titles coming soon, visit
millsandboon.co.uk/nextmonth

COMING SOON!